MYSTERY CASE FILES:

Secrets of
SAN SABA

I0635508

JEFF PRESLEY AND SHELLEY PRESLEY

Mystery Case Files: Secrets of San Saba

Published by:
HAVAH Publishing
Ashland, OH
Havahpublishing.com

Address all inquiries to:
Jeff Presley and Shelley Presley
c/o HAVAH Publishing

ISBN: 978-1-64751-024-4

Editor and Interior Layout Design: Amy Sheesh
Cover Designer: Geremy Woods

Every attempt has been made to source properly all quotes.

Printed in the United States of America

First Edition

Contents

Foreword...5

Chapter 1: The Call..13

Chapter 2: Flashback: Knock…Knock............................33

Chapter 3: I'll Get to it When I Get to it...........................51

Chapter 4: That's Just Wrong.......................................71

Chapter 5: What Could it Hurt?....................................89

Chapter 6: Flashback: Mysterious Mystic.....................109

Chapter 7: Lowered Expectations...........................…...129

Chapter 8: Loyalty Only Goes So Far..........................143

Chapter 9: The Plot Thickens....................................159

Chapter 10: Values, Ethics, and Morals…OH MY!..........177

Chapter 11: Clues Are for Helping Each Other...............195

Chapter 12: Don't Celebrate Too Early.........................207

Chapter 13: Truth, Honor, Duty, & Integrity..................221

Chapter 14: Angels Amongst Us…Part 1.....................233

Chapter 15: Angels Amongst Us 2- What Are We Doing?...251

Chapter 16: Sphere of Activity…The Portal's Domain......265

Chapter 17: When We Don't Know What to Do Next........279

Chapter 18: Opportunity + Action = Auspicious Turning
           Points..297

Chapter 19: Denise's Candlelight Service......................315

Chapter 20: Our Shattered Looking Glass.....................325

Epilogue: Truth is Stranger than Fiction.......................335

Final Thoughts..351

Foreword

*"If I had an hour to solve a problem, I'd spend 55 minutes thinking about the problem, and 5 minutes thinking about solutions." - **Albert Einstein***

Before we share our experiences, it must be mentioned, this book was not written to seek fame or to make friends. We have nothing to gain from this, we have lost a piece of our family, and want to see justice on her behalf. The real story did not take place in San Saba, Texas. I would like to take a moment to thank the San Saba Sheriff's Department for sharing a handful of historical facts and details to help aide in the creation of this book. They were more than helpful and extremely friendly to my inquiries about this delightful and quiet town.

This real-life incident happened in Montgomery County, Texas. This county's government currently holds the title and reputation as the most corrupt county in Texas. The government corruption runs deep, and those affiliated or involved protect nefarious actions like a brotherhood. This story only adds another feather in their cap.

The intent of writing this story is to explain why a seemingly open-and-shut case remains unsolved. After using scientific methods and unconventional means to gather information, using deductive reasoning, studying vast works of behavioral scientists and psychological experts, it is difficult to unsee what we have been shown. This case began back in March of 2015, after the unexpected disappearance of Jeff's cousin. Our involvement picked up on the cold trail three years later, in February 2018. Four years after that, as of March 2022, our views on the case remain unwavering.

While you might automatically presume our evidence would be biased due to family relations, this was the exact opposite of Jeff's approach. After receiving a Bachelor's in Science- Kinesiology, the most important fundamental skill Jeff learned was how to analyze situations objectively and work from facts, rather than ideas, opinions, or even theories. Approaching this case objectively, he wanted to keep an open mind because if something hadn't been missed, his cousin would have already been found. To be fair, the evidence was initially sought to prove the husband was telling the truth. He claims his wife decided to randomly leave her life, her children, and have no contact with friends or family in (now) over 7 years.

Whether you believe everything or not, is solely at your discretion, and we invite you to form your own conclusions. Once answers began to surface, the means to how we got them become irrelevant.

After stepping back from this case, for various reasons, Jeff found the time to enroll as a full-time student at the Texas A&M School of Law in 2021. He is currently maintaining a 4.0 G.P.A. and after revisiting this case again in November of 2021, our conclusions remain the same. Even though law school is extremely demanding, we still managed to find time to compile the notes we have made along the way to write this book because of the serious implications behind it.

To say this was done alone would be an understatement. This was actually a great team effort, and we are very proud of the results. Shelley played a huge role in helping to bring all of this together, and it is also incredibly important to give special thanks to certain family members and friends who provided us with helpful insights into this case and book.

There are greater forces at work within this world. Few know how or why events and circumstances happen, but when a pattern presents, it must be examined. This case might seem as a localized or random occurrence, but in fact, it is an indication or reflection to the current free-for-all taking place within this country. This story is just one of many. How long must people wait before deciding to get involved and stand up for each other, when those who are sworn to protect your interests are instead protecting a menacing idealism or affiliation?

We are taught to fix and mend the branch of a tree while ignoring the root. If you plant seeds in poor soil, what fruits will they bear? Is the seed or fruit the issue or might it be the soil? We look at corruption, crime, and collusion as the issue, but it is merely a symptom to much bigger problems. Whenever there is an issue amongst leaders of a nation, the first indication to a problem is the rise in criminality. When you properly identify its root, it no longer remains a mystery. Why does this case remain unsolved? Is this a very illusive mastermind or simply the fruit of a system the people have neglected for far too long?

Is this a missing persons case, or is it a homicide? After seven years, we have diligently sought evidence to unveil the location of Jeff's cousin. Where she would have gone or at least some indication she left the area would surface, right? If she didn't leave the area as suggested, what are the next logical steps to take? If this is a homicide then where is the movement to solve it? A 32-year-old mother disappeared. Do her children ever get answers to hear that their mother didn't abandon them but has been denied the chance to be laid to rest? If she had been their daughter or family member, wouldn't more have been done to find answers? Why doesn't she deserve the same respect as they would show someone in their family?

"Nearly 2 in 3 female victims of violence were related to or knew their attacker."

-Ronet Bachman Ph.D.,
U.S. Department of Justice
Bureau of Justice Statistics

When it comes to spousal murders, a primarily psychological issue of prevalent family dysfunction or disorder becomes clear in the relationship, from on all sides. This dysfunction generates the foundation, or sets the stage, to the atrocities that can happen by the passions of family interaction between the wife and the husband.

You might be asking the same question we had: If she left seven years ago, why hasn't she been found or located? The mystery behind this case began to unravel, the deeper we dug. The events after her disappearance are more bizarre than the case itself. When the detectives publicly state they are investigating the case but when the witnesses, friends, and family were cross-examined, why do they tell a different story? To say the least, this case raised many red flags about the integrity of those who are meant to serve and protect.

While the suggestion might seem incredulous, it is our earnest effort to remain as accurate as possible with the facts and evidence for the purposes of sharing the truth. While names and places have been changed to protect the identity of those directly involved, you can rest assured the circumstances that took place are very real.

This story will take you on many twists and turns, it will all be tied together in the end. We want to personally thank you for your support, and we ask two things: First, please keep an open mind. The second request, please share with others what will be unveiled to you, with the same conviction and burden which was placed upon our shoulders, so justice can be served. The way to keep a case alive is to keep attention on it. Thank you!

Disclaimer: This book does not provide any legal, medical, or religious advice. We are merely providing information. It is up to you to research and educate yourself on these topics or seek professional advisement if you choose to get involved.

BASED ON TRUE EVENTS.

TO PROTECT THE IDENTITIES OF THOSE INVOLVED,

NAMES, DATES, AND LOCATIONS HAVE BEEN CHANGED.

Chapter 1

The Call

Sharon carefully opens the door to her large three-bedroom home, arms full of groceries, and exhausted after a long day of work. Her son, Cameron, is right behind her, talking away about the oddities he saw in school today. Sharon's dog, Mattie, is wildly barking and scurrying about because she knows it's almost dinner time. While trying to get through the door, Sharon's phone loudly rings. Stuffed somewhere deep in her purse but not wanting to miss the call, she quickly opens the door, tells the dog to get back, tosses the groceries on the kitchen counter, has Cameron close the door, and finally retrieves her phone. Almost out of breath from the all the excitement, she answers, "Hello?"

"Hi Sharon!" Confused momentarily to the identity of the man on the other end of the phone, Sharon realizes it's her cousin, John.

"Oh, hey John! What are you up to?" Not having seen or spoken to her cousin for some time, Sharon's mind begins to race. Why would John randomly call?

John continues, "Well, you know what I do for living right?"

"Yes," Sharon replies, as her son is chasing their noisy Beagle around the kitchen island.

"Well…" John begins but is immediately cut off by Sharon.

"Can you hold on one second?" Now taking the phone from her ear, and agitated by the noise, Sharon directs her attention towards her son. Sternly raising her voice over the dog and Cameron's excited chatter, Sharon asks, "Would you please take Mattie outside and be quiet? I'm on the phone!"

"Yes, mom," utters Cameron.

"Thank you!" she replies. Spinning around to the charcoal gray countertop where she dumped her groceries, she starts sifting through the bags to pull the frozen items out first. Putting the phone back to her ear, she quickly apologies for the interruption. "Sorry about that. I just walked in with groceries, and Cameron is chasing the dog around. I can barely hear anything over their racket."

"Not a problem," John laughs. "As I was saying, you remember what I do for a living, right?"

Pausing for a moment to think, Sharon says, "I guess...something like search and rescue, right?"

"Yes," John excitedly responds. "Currently, I'm with someone, and we're searching for his missing cousin. I can't say their names, and I don't want to give you any details, but they told me some kind of psychic helped to locate his missing cousin. I'm at the place right now, and we're not sure where to look. I told them I also know someone like that, who might be able to help, so I called you."

Sharon, taken aback by her cousin's sudden vote of confidence in a gift she rarely uses, goes along with the conversation..."Okay?"

John continues, "Well, without giving you any details or wanting to compromise what you pick up, are you getting anything about where this person's cousin might be?"

Drawing a sudden blank at first, Sharon pauses for a minute to clear her head. Then like a flash of lighting, the word 'water' begins quickly repeating itself over again in

Sharon's mind. Not fully understanding what this message means, Sharon blurts out, "Water?... Water! She's near water!"

John asks, "Do you mean like a river or stream?"

"No. Like a small body of water...like a pond! Are you on property? Like lots of acres or acreage?"

Without answering Sharon's questions, John quickly replies, "Hey, let me call you back," and he hangs up the phone. With a smile of victory, John has a gleaming sense of validation, and looks to Jason, who is standing a few feet from him.

"I told you she is good!" John exclaims.

"Wow! That is two people who have now said the same thing," Jason replies, surprised at Sharon's accuracy.

"Well, what do you want to do?"

Jason and John stand facing each other in the heavily wooded abandoned property in Brady, Texas. It has been three years since Jason's cousin, Denise, was last seen in this central Texas small town area. Roughly 130 miles Northwest of Austin, or 42 miles due West of San Saba, TX, her remains are yet to be discovered.

Flashback: Wild One

"Look out 'cause here I come!" Denise yells for all to hear.

"Denise, NOOO!" everyone shouts back.

It was pointless trying to reason with the loudmouthed and overly hyper seven-year-old. They all knew Denise was going to do whatever Denise wanted to do. Her loud laughter and stomping feet echoed all the way across Lake LBJ. Denise's grandparents own lakefront property about an hour's drive Northeast of Austin, TX, near Horseshoe Bay.

For as long as Jason can remember, each summer his parents would pack up the car and take him and his brother, Tyler, to their grandparents' home in Granite Shoals, TX. This family tradition was the highlight of their summer. From their adventures going to the Llano River Park, with its granite rock outcrops and shallow pools the locals refer to as 'The Slab' to exploring the massive dome-shaped pink granite mountain called Enchanted Rock, going water skiing with grandpa's old Johnson-powered boat, or even building forts, this is Jason's summer oasis.

Each day in this hot and dry hill country is an adventure awaiting to be explored. Jason's dad, Troy, comes from a large family of eight brothers and one sister. They would bring their families to their grandparents at the same time. Having plenty of cousins to play with, being an explorer and adventurer at heart, Jason can't wait for the fun to begin.

As Jason's cousin, Denise, tears off down the family's pier, she quickly builds up momentum with each step she takes. Slipping right past her mother's outreached arm, and unintentionally kicking over several half-full soda cans still sitting out, she races on. Undeterred by obstacles, Denise's feet fly faster as they flail wildly about from her eagerness to join her cousins already in the lake. Before reaching the waterfront's edge, Denise loses her footing, slams face first on the worn-out pier and falls off into the water.

"Oh my God, are you ok?" Aunt Lisa cries out as she rushes to her aide.

Jason and his older brother, Tyler, who are already in the water, erupt with laughter at the spectacle.

The brothers are still mad at Denise after this morning's fiasco with her. Denise snatched Jason's beloved Texas A&M hat and wouldn't give it back. The brothers both feel like this is karma seeking justice, after it took them the help of three other cousins to catch Denise and retrieve Jason's hat. Denise was rough, tough, and explosively fast. When Denise is around, the cousins know they must work together to have any chance at cornering her. Otherwise, you would have a better chance of hugging a greased pig on ice, than trying to catch her all by yourself.

"You guys are jerks," Tina, Denise's sister, condemns.

Tyler responds, still chuckling, "It serves her right. Your sister has been nothing but trouble since we got here."

Denise's scream is heard as she resurfaces from the quick dip in the green and brackish water of the lake. Bawling hysterically, most likely from a bruised ego, Denise is helped from the cool morning lake by her mother, Lisa.

"Yeah, but she's still your cousin. Besides, you shouldn't laugh when other people get hurt."

"Seriously?" Tyler fires back. "Do you know what she did to me yesterday, while you were in the kitchen? We were all sitting around watching tv, when she took grandpa's belt and smacked me with it. I ended up chasing her outside, all the way into the neighbor's yard, before I finally gave up."

"That's no excuse!"

"Look, you can still see where she hit me," Tyler contests as he raises his arm to prove his case.

"Grow up. You're three times her size and bigger than all of us. She's just a little girl." Tina sharply snaps back.

"GIRL?" Tyler acting surprised. "More like a *Tomboy*," he sneers as the two brothers begin to laugh again.

"That's not fair. You know her condition, and she takes medicine for it," Tina replies.

Tyler arguing back, "She's loud, takes what isn't hers, won't ever leave you alone, and finds a way to piss everybody off!"

Jason coming to the defense of his brother, "Yeah, what she really needs is a bear tranquilizer," laughing again. "Maybe if your sister wasn't such a pain in the butt, we wouldn't get in so much trouble all the time. We can't have fun when Denise is around because she ruins it for everyone."

"Like *you're* any better?" Tina reminding Jason of his behavior. "Don't be such jerks. She only does that because she likes you and nobody wants to play with her."

"YEAH...BECAUSE SHE'S ANNOYING!" both boys shout simultaneously.

"Kids!" Aunt Lisa calls from the pier. "We gotta go."

"Why?" Tina asks. "We just got here."

"Denise is hurt, and she needs to go lie down."

"Dang it," Jason says as he slaps the surface of the water. Now, directing his frustration towards Tina, "See? I told you. We can't ever have fun when she's around."

Tina growls with a threatening overtone, "If you don't get out of the water, then Denise won't be the only one crying around here."

"EEEEWWW," Jason mocks back. "I'm SOOO scared."

"Shut up," Tina says with glaring eyes.

"Kids, I said LET'S GO!" Aunt Lisa sternly hollers this time.

"Yes ma'am," the kids sulkily reply as they begin making their way towards the pier.

Not Going as Planned

March 2015

Jason directs his two children out of the kitchen to allow their mother, Samantha, the space to cook dinner. As he playfully herds the young kids towards the living room, past the dining room table in the four-bedroom Army housing duplex, Jason's phone rings. Without checking who's calling first, he opens his phone, "Hello?"

"Heyyyyyy!" an overly enthusiastic but familiar voice shouts back through the earpiece.

"Hey Denise," Jason, annoyed, replies. "What's up?"

"Oh, nothin'. Just wanted to see how the Army life's treatin' you."

"It's going well. No complaints," he grudgingly replies.

"That's good! That's good!... How do ya like the weather up there?"

"It's like living in Texas, but lots of trees."

"How are Samantha and the kiddos doing? Did those little cuties start school yet?"

"Yeah, they're doing good. Brittany started school last year and Brian starts school next year."

"That's good! That's good!"

Before Denise could ask any more generic conversational fillers, Jason interrupts. "Do you need anything Denise? I just got off work and trying to spend a few minutes with the kids."

Being born and raised in Texas, Jason decided to join the Army's 82nd Airborne. Now, in his early 30's, he is stationed at Fort Bragg, NC, living on post in military housing with his wife and two kids. Between his daily duties

20

as a soldier training for deployment, he is also physically preparing himself for Special Forces Selection. After being released from work each day, he spends a few hours in the gym or jogging before coming home. Tired and exhausted, Jason only has a short window to spend time with his family.

"Oh, I'm so sorry! I didn't mean to interrupt. I haven't seen you since we threw a going away party after you completed basic training, and I was wanting to come visit you."

"Here? By yourself or with the whole family?"

"Just me and my boys. I want to show 'em what real soldiers do! HAHAHA!"

"What about your husband?"

"No, he's workin'."

Hesitant, Jason asks, "When were you thinking of coming?"

"I could be there by this weekend!"

Surprised, "What? Denise, that's in three days!"

"I know! I'm excited just thinkin' about it!"

"You haven't changed a bit." Denise laughs with slight embarrassment to the little reminder of her ways. Still confused, Jason inquires, "That's a long drive from Texas and it's not cheap to drive this far. I thought you were working too."

"Oh...well...I had a job, but I don't work there anymore. Trust me...it's a long story." With much enthusiasm Denise asks, "So, can I come?"

"I remember the last time you wanted hang out...seven people got arrested."

Laughing, "Oh, come on! That was almost 16 years ago! You know things have changed, and we hung out after that."

"I know, I just can't be doing wild stuff like that anymore. We're not kids anymore. Hell, we got kids of our own."

"I know silly. We're all grown up now," Denise reminds Jason.

"Kids will do that to you."

"Tell me about it!"

From their history together, Jason knows Denise tends to call after she has gotten herself into some financial or relationship troubles. He felt sorry for her but over the years, he learned to keep his distance. Jason assumes she's this way because she is only trying to survive from the numerous bad decisions she has made along the way. Jason tries to flush out Denise's true reason for calling. "That's a long trip to stay just for the weekend. By the time you get here, you'd have to turn right back around and head home."

"No, you dork!" she replies. "I thought I could stay there for a few weeks."

"A few weeks? How could you afford to be gone that long? Your husband wouldn't care you'd be gone for so long?"

"You let me worry about the money and him. Won't this be fun, like when we were little? Maybe we can take the kids camping and you can show us all your Rambo training," laughing again.

Sensing something wrong in her voice, Jason changes the subject. "Is everything ok between you two?"

"Yeah, everything's great! I've been here my whole life and after you left, I decided I want to do some travelin' of my own. The kids are getting older, and now would be a good time for us to do it because I got a little money saved up. It's Springtime. ROAD TRIP!" Laughing once more.

"Denise, that's almost an 18 hour drive non-stop. It's not a good idea to do it all by yourself. What happens if you start getting tired or something? I don't want you falling asleep at the wheel," Jason says trying to change her mind.

"I'll have the kids with me, and they'll keep me awake. You know there's never a dull moment when they're around."

Jason, speaking now more like a responsible parent to a child, and feeling Denise isn't being forthcoming, tries digging a little deeper, "Denise, if you're not working, then how do intend to pay for the trip and almost a month's supply of food for all four of you?" Denise remains silent as Jason already knows the answer to his own question. Denise doesn't have the money and is most likely hoping he would generously shoulder the financial burden.

"Also, what about your kids? Aren't they still in school? Won't they get into trouble or be held back for missing too many days?"

"Jason, stop worrying so much! I'm a big girl now! I just need a break and change in scenery…see some new sights, you know? I'm tired of being couped up in this old town with nothing to do. I want to get out more and start seeing the world. Life's too short!"

"Look Denise, I love you and I appreciate you wanting to come here, but now's not a good time for us. Samantha just opened her new business and even if you did come, I won't be here for the next few weeks. They are dragging my unit out into the field for another training exercise, and I'll be gone for at least two weeks."

"Oh, I didn't know."

"Yeah, Samantha already has enough on her plate when I'm not at home. She turned our house into an on-post daycare to earn money, and with all the kids and guests, I'm not sure she would want the added stress right now. Especially if I'm not here."

"No, I get it. You guys are busy."

"Besides, why don't you wait until all the kids get out of school and get plane tickets instead? You'd be here in a few hours! It'll be safer, cheaper, and we wouldn't be pressed for time."

"Yeah, maybe your right. You always were the smart one, Mister college grad!" Denise playfully sasses, trying to mask her sudden disappointment. "I understand and I don't want to impose. I figured I would try, but I know your workin' hard to keep this country safe," Denise replies being uncharacteristically sad.

"Denise, are you sure everything's alright?"

"Yeah, I'm sorry. I just got a wild hair up my butt and wanted to come see y'all, but you're right. Maybe we can wait 'til summer when the kids are out of school."

"Me too."

"Get back to your family! I won't keep you. Give everybody a big hug and kiss for me, ok?"

"I will. You sure everything's alright?"

With forced sarcasm she replies, "You know I can take care of myself, thank you very much!"

Laughing, "Alright, I was just checking. Well, call me if you need anything else."

"Will do. Love you!"

"Love you too!"

"Bye!" Denise says as she hangs up the phone.

Hearts in Darkness

The next week, Jason is ransacking their small overflow room he uses as an office. Rummaging through his spare gear looking for his gas mask, due to a last-minute change by his platoon sergeant, he hears his phone ring from the living room.

"NOT NOW!" Jason exclaims as he hops up and dances around the mess he made to get out the door.

In his haste to find the needed equipment for the last-minute change before his unit leaves for the field, Jason mistakenly put his phone down in the other room. Missing a phone call from his unit during this time is punishable by an automatic field grade Article 15, which means a reduction in rank and pay. It's already stressful enough being on-call 24/7 but missing a phone call from his unit would be like committing career suicide. If this wasn't already stressful enough, Jason is barely able to pay the bills with the military's ridiculously low pay for enlisted soldiers. Considering how many hours they work, and the hazards they are prepared to face to keep this country safe, Jason thinks it's unfair how people working minimum wage jobs are better compensated for their time. Regardless, Jason can't afford another financial setback. Squeezing his way through the office door, he darts toward the living room coffee table, snatching his phone, and answering on the final ring before it goes to voicemail.

Slightly out of breath, Jason answers, "Hello?"

"Jason?" a troubled female voice asks. "I know you're busy, do you have a minute?"

"Mom? I'm in a hurry. Can this wait?"

"I have some bad news, Jason."

Jason recognizes his mother's tone and tries to mentally prepare himself for the news. "Is something wrong with Dad?"

"No, we're fine…. It's Denise."

"What about her?"

"She's missing."

"Missing? Like gone for good?"

Knowing how close Jason and Denise were growing up, his mother tries to be direct, but gentle.

"Yes. Law enforcement suspects foul play."

"What? I just spoke with her. I think just last week," Jason says quickly trying to recall when Denise last phoned him. "What happened? Do they know who did it?"

"She has been missing since Sunday and all we know right now is the evidence points to her husband."

Immediately Jason's heart sinks as he now realizes what his strange phone conversation with Denise was. What seemed like an innocent and random spur of the moment inclination, was rather a well disguised, subtle cry for help. As his mother continues, Jason slowly lowers his phone as the guilt creeps in.

The Day She Disappears...Part 1

March 2015

Driving up to her friend's home early one Saturday morning, in the small country town of San Saba, TX, Denise sees her friend already sitting outside on the porch having a cigarette. Excited to finally get out of the house, Denise honks the horn a few times as she arrives in her late 90's blue Ford Explorer. Her friend Trish, looking up from her phone, smiles and invitingly waves to Denise.

As she rounds the long curvy dirt driveway leading up to the house, Denise already has her head halfway out the window and shouts, "HEEEEY GIRRRRRRL!"

Trish jumps up from her chair and shouts back over her two black labs already barking, "Hey Denise!"

Being careful not to run over Trish's dogs circling her vehicle and after finding a safe place to park, Denise exits her midsize SUV. Getting her son out of the car seat in the second row and closing the door of her Explorer, in desperate need of a paint job, she wards off the excited and dirty dogs.

Before the women hug, Trish warns, "Denise, watch the baby around Rowdy," pointing out the oldest of the two dogs, who is easily identifiable with his white front paws and chest, "He's a jumper."

Heeding the warning and only slightly deterred, Denise goes in for a hug. "Oh my God, it's so good to see you!" she exclaims while holding her youngest son, Allen, in one arm and a shopping bag full of hair products in the other.

"You too! Hey boys," Trish speaking to Denise's two older boys hopping out from the passenger side, "the kids are around back playing football, if you want to join 'em."

Without saying a word, you can hear the gravel shift under the kids' feet. They dart off and disappear around the back of the house with the dogs hot on their heels.

"Oh, they are going to have so much fun," Trish says smiling at Denise.

"Good. They need it and thanks for letting me bring 'em. I only get to see them on the weekends now. Also, Aaron's been more than I can handle with the court date coming up this week."

"Huh? Court date? What's goin' on?"

"I didn't tell you?"

"No! Gurrrl...you better start talkin'.... What's goin' on?" Trish, concerned look on her face, asks as they make their way to the front porch.

"Aaron's trial is this week."

"What did he do this time? I haven't seen you in what...three months...and WHAT did you do to your hair? You chopped it all off!"

"I need a cigarette first, then I can catch you up."

"Sure, do ya want some water?"

"I'm good right now but you're gonna flip when you hear what I got to say!"

Running Late

Jason slaps the alarm for the third time before Samantha finally rolls over and nudges him, "Baby, you need to get up. You're going to be late for work."

Groaning and saying a few inaudible words under his breath, Jason tosses the covers off before sliding out of bed.

Worried, Samantha asks, "Are you ok to drive?"

"Yeah, I'm fine."

"Jason, I'm worried about you."

"Why?" he barks back.

"You almost drank the entire bottle of Jameson last night."

"I said I'm good. Besides, we live on post. I don't have to go through gate check points," he says stumbling to his feet.

"Do you even remember how you got into bed? You passed out on the back patio, and I had to ask Tim next door to help me get you upstairs."

"When?" he asks in disbelief.

"Last night."

"Oh, now your inviting guys over while I'm asleep. Did he help you with anything else or is there something else I should know about?" Jason sarcastically asks, questioning the integrity of their marriage after recalling their recent increase in arguments.

Still able to smell the alcohol on his breath, she softly replies, "Don't be ridiculous. It was 40 degrees outside, and I couldn't get you up. He's your friend, so I went next door to see if he could help me get you inside. Besides his wife, Ashley, is the one who brought the water up to you," pointing to the full glass of water on his nightstand, "while we were trying to get you into bed."

Angered by his embarrassing situation, "Why didn't you just call the whole neighborhood over to see if they could help too?"

"Jason, I really think you should go see someone about your headaches. Not only has your drinking increased since you hit your head on your last jump, but we can't afford to keep buying you a bottle every couple of days. It's getting expensive."

"Would you get off my back about it?" Jason says in a very sharp and hostile voice. "It's part of the job. What did you expect? You jump out of planes and smack your head. That's it. What else can I do?"

"Go to your PA and see what's wrong."

"If I go see Doc, he'll just put me on profile. Yeah, I'm sure the platoon sergeant would love that! He already rides me enough as it is, and if I hand him that, I will never hear the end of it."

"You've also been really mean to me and short with the kids."

"Geez, can't a guy catch a break? You want to know why I'm drinking so much lately? Ok, I'll tell you why! I bust my butt all day long, and I'm berated over every little thing at work, and then when I come home, do I get any peace and quiet? NO! As soon as I open the door, here you come, hammering down on me with all your stupid little problems."

"I'm sorry, I didn't know."

"I'm just worn out and I haven't had a vacation in three years. I didn't ask for all of this. This is what you wanted, remember?"

"*Shhh*! You're going to wake the kids."

"Then quit annoying me and let me go to work! You knew when I signed up for the military, it wasn't going to be easy. If anyone should understand, I thought it would be you, being a military brat."

"My dad was never home because he was always on deployment, but when he was, we would hide in our rooms and try to avoid him as much as possible."

"See?"

"I don't want the kids to be afraid like I was."

"I signed a four-year contract. It's not like I can just quit and go get another job. I'm stuck. Besides, it's not like we had many options anyway after we closed down my business in Texas."

"Our business. I helped too."

"Yeah, and who's fault is it we had to close the doors?"

"When are you going to stop blaming me for everything. I did the best I could. I've apologized I don't know how many times."

"A lot of good that does us now! Who's the one who had to sell off all their valuables to get us caught up on bills from the mess you made? ME! Who got to sit around for eight months while I'm out there busting my hump getting screamed at each day to get enough money to pay the bills you keep racking up? YOU!"

"I told you it's hard to find a job here, but the daycare is bringing money in now and you know how many inspectors I had to wait on to come here to inspect our home. I had no control over it."

"If it wasn't for you, we wouldn't even be in this mess in the first place, and I'm definitely not going to sit here and be chastised by you, telling me how to cope with all this stress."

"Are you ever going to forgive me?"

"Yeah, maybe when you stop making dumb decisions that put us deeper in debt, pull your head out of your butt, and start doing what's in the best interest of our family."

"I'm sorry," Samantha sighs as she rolls over and quietly says again, "you're going to be late for work."

Chapter 2

Flashback: Knock ... Knock

<u>Summer Of 1989</u>

Jason awakes to hear strange clunking footsteps in the hallway. Growing louder, someone approaches his room and then quickly passes by his door. *Clunk, clunk, clunk, clunk, clunk.* He hears a bedroom door open just down the hall. *Creak.* "Is anybody awake in here?" pierces through the walls, in the quiet early morning hours. Jason sighs because he realizes Denise is at it again.

"Get out of here Denise!" yells Uncle David. *Wham!* Slamming the door shut, the footsteps continue to the next room. *Clunk, clunk, clunk, clunk, clunk...*even louder creaky noise. "Is anybody awake?"

This time Jason hears his cousins, Mindy and Wendy, answer. "Shut up Denise," hollers Mindy who is quickly followed by Wendy "Go back to bed!"

Wham! Clunk, clunk, clunk, clunk, clunk. There was a moment's pause before Jason realizes Denise is now at his door. Jason waits for his turn to tell Denise to go back to bed. Her ruckus is worse than grandma's fire alarm going off each morning, as her breakfast bacon fills the house with a delicious aroma. In fact, Denise might have been better off marching up and down the hallway with marching drums or some crash cymbals.

Jason hears his door open. He sees, with a little help from the lamp in the hallway, Denise sporting a few band-aids, from her spill the morning before on the lake. Still wearing her dad's oversized t-shirt, he can barely make out what's causing his younger cousin's footsteps to sound like a T-Rex patrolling the hallway. Apparently, she found a pair of their uncle's shoes in the living room. Thinking it would be fun, Denise decided to stroll up and down the hallway on the cheaply made wooden floors of the double wide trailer to see who else was up. With wide and excited eyes, Denise pokes her head into Jason's room, in hopes to see if others are already awake. Before she can ask again, Jason angrily but quietly states, "Denise, I swear to God…"

"What?" she loudly replies.

"*SHHHH*! Would you be quiet? You're going to wake up the whole house," Jason tries to whisper.

"TOO LATE FOR THAT!" Uncle Jonathan booms from down the hallway, which was the only room Denise hasn't investigated yet.

The Day She Disappears...Part 2

As Denise sets Allen down to go play, she finds a wooden chair on Trish's patio to sit on. After banging the dusty grime from the worn-out seat cushion, Denise sits down and lights up a cigarette.

"Soooo...tell me what's been goin' on!" Trish eagerly requests. "Why can you only see your kids on the weekend? Do they not live with you anymore?"

"My ex-husband, the older boys' father, filed a CPS report on Aaron after he hurt the kids when I ran out to get a few groceries."

"Are you serious? Why would he do that?"

"He always treated them differently. It got worse once we had Allen, since my older boys aren't his."

"That's terrible!"

"He also makes me feel bad if he has to pay for anything they need."

"Why don't you get a job, so you don't have to ask him for any money?"

"I did! I just got a job at Dollar General around the corner. I had only been there a few weeks, working as a cashier, until I had to quit."

"Why?"

"He came in one day after he got off work. He was probably spying on me, and overheard the manager being nice and explaining how to give a discount to a customer. He'd already been drinking and by the time I got home, he was ready for a fight. As soon as I set my purse and keys down, he was already hollering at me and in my face. He accused me of cheating on him with the manager and was acting like he had lost his mind. You know how strong he is, right?"

"Yeah, Aaron is big! Isn't he like 350 pounds or something?"

"Bigger."

"Dang!"

"Anyway, so he's super angry, and goes to the fridge to get another beer. His hand missed the handle the first time, cause he's drunk, and it makes him even madder. When he grabs it again, he flings the door open so hard, it rips right off the hinges."

"What? Wow!"

"I know, right?"

"So here I am, tired from work, and he's screamin' at me for some stupid reason. Now, I'm mad he just broke the fridge, so I start yelling back at him. Smashing his beer on the table, he screams, 'You better shut your mouth.' So, I told him, 'MAKE ME!' Next thing I know, I'm pinned on the kitchen floor, and he's choppin' my hair off with one of the kid's toy scissors."

Trish gasps. "What did you do?"

"What could I do? I couldn't go to work with my hair all chopped up like that, so I called in the next day and quit. That's why I haven't been around. I've been too embarrassed to even walk out of the house."

"Denise, I'm so sorry. I had no idea. Why didn't you call me?"

"I appreciate it, but what could you have done?"

"I don't know...something? Call the cops maybe?"

Laughing sarcastically, "You don't think I haven't thought of that already? He knows just about everyone who works at the Sheriff's department, from either high school or his friend from around the corner. That's also why he didn't go to jail after CPS charges were filed against him, for leaving bruises all over my two other boys."

"Denise, that's terrible!"

"So anyway…I had to go to that wig store down on main street and buy a couple, just so I could go out in public."

Sitting in silence for a few moments, Denise takes a few drags from her cigarette to allow Trish to absorb her tiny confessional. As Trish searches for words, Denise's attention is drawn to the older brown horses, chewing grass behind the barbed-wire fence line 50 to 75 yards away. "Those are such pretty horses!"

The sight of the horses triggers a long-forgotten memory and Denise beings laughing hysterically. Barely able to catch her breath, she laughs even harder the more she thinks about it. Confused to the sudden change in demeanor, and unable to resist from chuckling as well, Trish laughs at Denise's ticklish and contagious joy. "What's so funny?"

Before she can stop laughing, Denise begins to explain, "Back in high school, I invited my cousin, Jason, out to a friend of mine's place. He didn't have a girlfriend, and she was single, so I tried to hook him up with my friend. Anyway," laughing harder, "he'd never ridden a horse before, so we thought we'd play a little joke on him. My friend, Jasmine, had a young mare who hated men, but we didn't tell him that before he got on. We saddled him up, walked the horse out into the pasture, and then Jasmine hands him the reigns. She said, 'just spur the horse a little with your heels to get started and trot around.' None of us expected that horse to take off so fast! Jason was hangin' on for dear life, doing everything he could to keep from falling off! We saw Jason and the horse disappear over the pasture hill, and moments later, he reappears like 200 yards down the way. Me and Jasmine were like 'oh man, how do we stop a runaway horse?'"

Trish bursts into laughter as she quickly relates to Jason's predicament, as she too had that happen once, trying to break-in one of her male stallions.

"Before we could do anything, the next thing we see is this horse dig its hoofs into the dirt and drop its head coming to a dead halt. It slung Jason right out of the saddle." Hysterically laughing. "All we saw was him somersaulting through the air, feet flying everywhere, and him screaming bloody murder!"

Gasp. "Oh my God, was he alright?"

Simmering down, Denise continues, "Yeah, he was ok. He looked like a cat falling from a tree, landed on his feet. He was so mad afterwards, and we were laughin' so hard, he left the horse right out there in the pasture. He stormed all the way back, walking right past us towards his truck. The best part is..." laughing even harder, "when he walked by us, we couldn't help but notice he had split his britches right down the seams! Jason was trying to be so tough, acting all macho but didn't notice his butt was hanging out of his shorts!"

Bursting into laughter, "Oh my God, Denise!"

"We tried to stop him but seeing his smiley face underwear flapping in the wind...I think we about peed ourselves laughing so hard."

Both in tears, Trish's asks, "So what happened after that?"

"He didn't talk to me for like three weeks! He was so mad. He blamed me for ruining his new Polo, khaki shorts. I said 'Hey, you should've known better than to wear shorts out to a farm.' I think he was more embarrassed than anything else, trying to look cool or something to impress my friend, Jasmine. He's one of those city boys, you know?"

Wiping the tears from their eyes from the good laugh, Trish is immediately drawn back to Denise's problems at home. "Denise, sorry to change subjects back, but what are you going to do? I had no idea Aaron was such a jerk if you don't mind me saying."

"No, go ahead! While I had my fair share of problems with my ex-husband, compared to Aaron, he looks like a knight in shining armor."

"Do you think things might get worse? Why don't you say something to him about his temper?"

"I don't know, but after I saw him pick his own dad up and throw him over a fence after their argument, what do you think he would do to me if I really made him mad? He already got himself fired from work because he was waiving his gun around at me in one of his work trucks."

"Shut up!" Trish says in disbelief.

"I'm telling the truth! We got into it, and he accidently shot out the windshield!"

Trish gasps again. "Were the kids in the truck?"

"No, thank God! Who knows what could've happened if they were in there! I couldn't hear straight for a few days because the idiot fired the gun in a closed cab."

"Denise, I'm really worried about you. Why don't you try going to your mom's to see if you guys need some time apart?"

"I already tried that. My mom told me she just got my sister and I out of the house and she is too old to have those kids running around there. She told me to get it figured out and doesn't want me coming home every time I have a problem with Aaron."

"Denise, this doesn't sound like you two are arguing over what's for dinner. I'm honestly scared for you."

"I can't say I'm surprised by my mom because I didn't get along with her when I lived there. We can only be around each other for so long before we are at it again."

"Do you want me to talk to Brian to see if he wouldn't mind if you stay with us until you sort things out?"

"I appreciate it Trish, but I don't want to put you guys out."

"You're not putting us out! I offered. If friends aren't there to help and support each other when times get tough, then what are friends for? I know you would do the same for me. Except Brian knows, if he ever lays a hand on me, he'd end up looking like one of those deer he's got hangin' out in the garage," Trish jokes trying to lighten the mood again.

"I tried going to my cousin's place in North Carolina. He's in the Army, but he said he would be leaving as soon as I got there. I figured a cross country drive might help me clear my head and see what's best for me to do. Do I stay or do I go?"

"Listen, after the bar-b-que tonight, why don't you just crash here for a few days? You can wear some of my clothes. That way, when Aaron leaves for work on Monday, you can go get a few of your things without him noticing or have any kind of confrontation."

Putting her cigarette out as her son Allen stumbles onto the porch, Denise fans the smoke away in the warm breeze. "What do you have there? Is that for momma?" Denise asks as Allen proudly hands her a few flowers, dirt, and grass, he found in the yard nearby. "Ahhh, you're such a sweet little man!" she says scooping him up to plant a kiss on his rosy cheeks. "Trish, if it's not a problem for you, staying here would be music to my ears," as a few tears stream down Denise's cheeks.

Allen seeing his mom getting upset, tries to cheer her up. He grabs the sides of her face and plants a big kiss in return. "Ahhh, thanks baby!" Denise says softly. Setting Allen back down, she sends him to find her more flowers. When he was far enough away, Denise continues, "I've never

40

been so scared in my entire life. I've been sleeping on the couch for the past month, I'm just trying to keep my head down. I'm counting the days until the trial, so I can get out of this situation, but I don't know if I can wait any longer. The closer we get, the crueler he becomes."

"What's going to happen at the trial?"

"What he did is a felony. I told him I wouldn't testify against him, but after what happened last week when he came home from work, it was the straw that broke the camel's back."

"What did he do?"

"It would be easier to say what hasn't he done, but as for last week…. He loves to keep the house at 65 degrees. The baby and I freeze to death! When he leaves for work, I usually turn the temperature up to 78 and switch it back a few hours before he gets home. Last week with everything going on, I forgot to switch it back."

"What did he do?"

"He was already mad from having a bad day at work, but when he saw that I changed the temperature, he started screaming at me in front of Allen. I tried explaining how cold we were, and he told me didn't care. When I told him I'm not arguing about it and I'm going to change it, to keep us from getting sick, he superglued the thermostat to 65. He said if I touch it again, things are going to get really ugly around there."

"That's just sick and cruel! Yep! Denise, you're staying here tonight!"

"So, after that, I was like…I'm done. Now, all I have is one more week, and then, I won't have to deal with him anymore."

"You're going to testify against him?"

"Are you kidding me? Hell yeah!"

"Good for you!"

"Screw him, I'm tired of feeling like a prisoner in my own home! He hurt me and my boys. At this point, I'd rather live under a bridge with my kids than keep going home to that. If I was stronger or big like he is, I would've already whooped him up and down the street."

"I'm so sorry Denise!"

"I wish Jason was here, because if he found out my hair got chopped off, Aaron would have to answer to him!"

"Has Jason met Aaron?"

"Once, when I was friends with him back in high school and this was before Jason got all big and buff in the Army. Do you know what Aaron said after meeting Jason for the first time?"

Intrigued, Trish asks, "What?"

"He said 'I hope I never run into your cousin in some dark, back alley.'"

"Why did he say that?"

"Jason's very protective of family."

"Well, does Aaron know you're here right now?"

"Yeah, he and some of his buddies have already talked about coming to your cookout tonight. I told him I was coming to help you set up, and you were going to put highlights in my hair. Even if I hadn't told him, he knows everywhere I go anyway and who I'm talking to."

"How?"

"He cloned my phone to his. He also put some tracking app which tells him exactly where I'm at. He can listen in to my phone calls, read my text messages, and even check my emails."

"Denise, that's a little much!"

"Yeah, I had to go buy one of those pre-paid phones just so I could have some privacy. He found the first one I bought and smashed it, so I had to go buy another. This time

I leave it under my seat in the Explorer, just in case of an emergency."

"Do you want Brian and some of his buddies to rough him up when he gets here tonight?"

"No, I don't want y'all to get involved. He will be gone in less than a week, but until then, I just want him to think everything is normal."

"So, do you think divorce is the answer?"

"At first, I held out as long as possible. Who wants to marry someone who's been divorced twice with kids from two dads? But, I can't take it anymore. I finally went to speak with a lawyer last week, after he superglued the thermostat."

"Good for you!"

"I would've left sooner, but he's so controlling. I knew he was from the beginning, but I ignored the warning signs. I was just trying to get away from my first husband, and I thought Aaron would lighten up. He's so insecure. The longer I am with him, the worse he treats me, and the more controlling he becomes. Even before my divorce with Barrett was finalized, he was already talking about us getting married. Now, he acts like he saved me or something. Doesn't matter what I do, it's never good enough and something he will never let go of."

Allen returns to the porch but forgot the mission his mother sent him on. He returns this time with a few rocks in his hand, instead of flowers. Searching the patio for the right place to hide his new treasures, something else catches his eye. "Whatcha got there, sweetheart? Is that for mommy?" Denise asks sweetly as her son ignores her questions. Allen drops the rocks and stomps his way towards Trish's yellow and white cat gliding about on the patio. Allen's unsteady approach makes the cat nervous. It quickly jumps onto the railing and then into the yard.

"Go get 'em," Denise encourages her son. As Allen goes in hot pursuit, scurrying off the front porch, Denise rolls her eyes. "He's not even three years old and already acts just like his daddy, chasin' tail."

"He's not cheatin' on you, is he?"

"He ain't goin' to the bar for beer, that's for sure! We got plenty of that at home."

"But do you think he has?"

Laughing, "I'm not worried about it. I'm sure he's trying, but he's probably getting shot down left and right. He loves those blondes though! Pointing at Trish's wavy, dirty blonde hair, "Would you take him home?"

Trish jumps back in her chair. "Ewww gross! No offense, but I don't think they make enough alcohol in this world for me to do that! I guess someone might think he's cute if they had the lights turned down really low."

"Or if they're really desperate," Denise says referring to her situation. "I still can't believe I even did it. Clearly, he caught me on a bad day," she says discouraged. "Seriously if they want him...they can have him...but no returns. SOLD AS IS!"

Giggling amongst themselves, the two mothers can hear their boys having fun out back. "I'm so glad our boys are around the same age. They need more friends. In our neighborhood, there's a handful of kids, but we don't see 'em very often."

"Same here. As big as the properties are out here, the boys would have to ride a four-wheeler for miles, to get to the nearest friend's house. Since they're not allowed to drive it on public roads, they must stay around here to play."

Reminiscing, Denise recalls "I don't have friends like I used to."

"Why is that?"

"Before I had Allen, Aaron would let me go out, but only with certain friends. After I had Allen, he doesn't want me to see any of them."

"Why?"

"I think he's afraid if I go out, I'll find someone better and leave him for somebody else."

"I don't get out as much as I used to, but if Brian didn't let me go blow off some steam every now and again, I'd lose my mind."

"I think, the only reason he allowed me to come over here alone is, he wants to search for the money he thinks I hid."

"What money?"

"Oh, I'll get to that in a minute, but Aaron thinks he's old fashioned. He thinks it's ok for him to go to bars or hang out with friends, leaving me at home, but I can't. He believes women belong in the kitchen and should wait on them hand and foot."

"I'm sorry, are we still in the 1920's?"

"I guess so."

"I don't care if this is some small country town. Times have changed and old fashioned simply means outdated. Brian helps with the kids, cooking, laundry, and cleaning."

"Wanna trade?"

"HELL NO! My man is good to me and treats me right. Do you want to know how to tell if you have a good man?"

"How?"

"It's the little things."

"Little things?"

"Brian doesn't drink coffee but makes me a fresh pot every morning. By the time I get out of bed, he has a cup waitin' for me with cream and sugar. He occasionally stops and buys me flowers, so I have something pretty to smell. He even still opens doors for me."

"Ahh, that's so sweet. I can't even get Aaron to pick his dirty laundry off the floor. He treats me like I'm his personal maid."

"That's not love, Denise. If someone really loves you, you're not their maid, slave, or property. Love has nothing to do with sex either. Love is treating you with kindness, thoughtfulness, appreciation, and respect, almost like you do with your kids or puppies. Love is to care for each other, grow and develop together. That's love!"

Looking around at the property, Denise questions, "This may sound stupid, but I have to ask. Is Brian selling drugs?"

"He'd better not be! If he was, we wouldn't be together. Why would you ask such a thing?"

"Don't take offense! I was curious how you can afford such a beautiful place, nice cars, and not have any debt, with Brian working as a mechanic? Did your grandparents leave you some money or something?"

"Huh?"

"Aaron makes more than Brian, except Aaron is also selling drugs on the side, just to make ends meet."

"He's selling drugs now?"

"He and Randy both are. They are trying some get rich quick scheme, but just like all the other hair-brained ideas they've had to make money, it never ends well."

"Denise, that's dangerous, and you don't need to be involved with that. I'm gonna give Randy a piece of my mind when he gets here tonight."

"No, don't do that! They'll know I told you."

"Then that's just another reason for you to leave him, but Randy and Aaron better not be bringin' none of that stuff around here."

46

"No, they got one of those small storage units where they keep their stash and guns."

"Brian and I have always treated money like we treat each other...with respect. We never spend more than we make, and we don't take loans out to buy things that don't make us money."

"Huh? How did you get your property and cars then?"

"You remember when we were stayin' in those crappy apartments for a few years right out of high school?"

"Yeah."

"We used that time to save our money. Then, we were able to get loans on a few homes in Austin and turned them into rental properties. After a few more years collecting rent money, we had enough to put down on this place. Instead of taking 30 years to pay off the mortgages, we paid a few hundred dollars extra each month to pay them off in 10. We saved almost $200,000 dollars in interest on one property alone. Once we paid them off, we sold a few and paid this place off."

"I think I did the exact opposite. As soon as I got out of school, I started maxing out credit cards to buy all kinds of stupid things. It didn't help with us buying cars and a house we could barely afford. When the kids came along, we couldn't even make the minimum payments on the bills, so everything went bad on my credit. After I got divorced, I couldn't get a loan to save my life."

"Now, as for Brian working as a mechanic, he's loved helping people fix things since he was little. He and his dad would spend hours fixing the neighbors' cars, and with his job now, he still feels like he's carrying on that tradition. To him, the pay is just a bonus. Since we aren't swamped in debt, he's able to take a job doing what he loves to do. Every car he fixes, he feels like he's helped someone get back out on the road and on with their life again. Brian comes home happy, and he's in a good mood each day because of it."

"That's definitely not Aaron. He hates his job and his boss. He comes home mad at the world. I told him to find another job, but he said he can't because this job pays well and helps us keep our heads above water."

"Brian and I weren't the party animals growing up, and we didn't waste our money going out to bars, concerts, and rodeos all the time. We kept a tight budget. It's not about how much money you make. It's about how much you keep. Life is learning how to manage yourself. Each day you're either doing things to improve your life or you're not. If you don't like how something is, then change what you're doing."

"You make it sound so simple."

"Trust me, nothing good ever comes without its challenges. Brian and I have had our fair share of arguments because everyone was out having fun and we're over here trying to be responsible. Had he not argued with me, I would have given into temptation like anyone else."

"I wish I would've known this 15 years ago! I've gotten myself in such a mess now, I don't know if I will ever get out or back on track."

"Says who?"

"Me! I just hope I can find the right guy who can take care of me and my kids."

"Denise don't think like that or you're no better than Aaron. You don't need someone to take care of you. You already have everything you need to take care of yourself. I won't lie. It's going to be difficult and you're going to have to make some sacrifices, but nothing is impossible. You're not alone and if you want, Brian and I can help get you going in the right direction. How's your credit?"

"Awful."

"Let's start there. Let's also see about finding you a job, set up a budget for you, and get your credit scores cleaned up. In the meantime, you can stay here with us. We've got plenty of room."

"Really? You'd do that for me?"

"That's what friends do. They help each other out. If you're serious about getting your life turned around, we will do what we can, but we don't run no charity!"

"Trish, that would be awesome," Denise says as her eyes begin to water. "Thank you! I've been too afraid to find another job because that's how the kids got hurt. Aaron didn't want me working and when I did, he took it out on my boys. He won't even let me have access to his bank account. He only transfers me enough money to get groceries, gas, and cigarettes. When we argue about me having my own money or me leavin', he says nobody's gonna love me or want me more than him. If he's right, I'd rather raise my boys on my own. So, do you know what I did to get away from him?"

"No. What?"

"While he was at work one day, I went to the bank and withdrew $10,000 dollars from the account. Then, I went to pay my lawyer."

"What did he say about the money?"

"Ooooh...he's still furious the bank allowed me to make the withdrawal," She laughs. "Now he's threatening to sue the bank, but I'm on the account."

"What an idiot. Serves him right!"

"Tell me about it! Now, he won't stop asking what I did with the money. I told him I hid it, and if he does anything else to me, I won't tell him where it is. He thinks I hid it somewhere around the house. He's probably tossing furniture right now looking for it. When he finds out I used his money to get a lawyer, I want to be as far away as possible."

"I know people have tempers, but Denise, I'm scared for you."

"What scares me the most is, he told me if I ever try taking Allen away from him, he'd kill me. Not once, but many times. He even said it in front of Randy."

"Randy was there? What did he say?"

"He's scared of Aaron, so when Aaron said it, Randy just laughed it off trying to calm the situation down. Just don't say anything to anyone tonight, promise?"

"Denise, you know me. I promise, not a word! You're safe now and there's nothing else to worry about. When Aaron gets here tonight, I will tell him I need you to stay here a few nights because I need help painting the boys' room."

"He would totally believe that!"

"If he gives you any trouble, then there's plenty of people here who wouldn't mind escorting him out."

"Trish, you're such an angel!"

"Anything for you, sweetheart! Sharing what you know to help others out is the best gift you could ever give anyone. Just promise me you will show your kids, when they are old enough, what we'll show you, so they don't fall into the same problems, ok? Now…let's get you inside, put that dye in your hair, and have some fun tonight!"

"I will! Trish…thank you...seriously."

Chapter 3

I'll Get to it When I Get to it

<u>June 2015</u>

Samantha, with a disappointed look on her face, opens the door to the small spare office bedroom. Jason uses this room to store his spare equipment and has recently turned it into his little man cave room. "Jason...Jason...JASON!"

Sighs. "What Samantha?" he rudely responds.

Samantha asks softly, "Can you please pause the game for a minute?"

"What now?" Jason says concentrating as his quarterback throws an interception. Annoyed, he pauses the game and tosses aside the controller onto the green suede sofa cushion beside him. "What is it this time? Can I just come home, relax, and play a few games without interruption?"

"Jason, you've been in here for over three hours."

"What?" Jason replies. "What time is it?"

"It's 9:30," she responds, opening the door a little further to see the game being displayed on the wall from the projector.

"I'm sorry...I lost track of time."

"The kids were disappointed because they have been waiting to play with you since you came home."

"Alright, where are they?

"I just gave them a bath and put them to bed."

Sighing again. "I'll make it up to them tomorrow, I promise." Jason grabs the controller, turns off the game console, and then the projector screen.

"I want to go see a marriage counselor, Jason."

"A marriage counselor? For what?"

"For us."

"Samantha, when do we ever fight or argue?"

"We don't. It's usually you yelling at me, and I just sit there quietly until you're done."

"What? We only argue once in a blue moon, and it's usually something you did putting our family in jeopardy. If anyone needs marriage counseling, it's Tim and his wife next door. When don't they argue? You can hear them screaming through the walls every other night? We have to turn the tv up just to drown them out."

"I'm not happy Jason."

"I know why you're not happy...you don't have any friends. Who would be?"

"I'm running my business, taking care of the kids, cooking, cleaning, or doing laundry. When do I have time for myself?"

"Why do you want to go see a counselor? You won't even talk to me?"

"I'm afraid to."

"What are you afraid of?"

"Whether you realize it or not, you're twice my size. Ever since you have been taking all those workout supplements, you've gotten huge and meaner. We even had to get you bigger uniforms because the others were too small. When you get angry, Jason...it scares me and the children."

"Samantha, why do you think I'm doing all of this...working out three times a day? Do you think I enjoy feeling exhausted and having to spend three to four hours in a gym each day? I'm trying to get ready for Special Forces."

"Aren't you supposed to be studying for the board?"

"Have you not been listening to me lately?"

"About what?"

"See? Even when I talk, you don't listen! Don't you think I would like to get promoted so we can have more money?"

"So why aren't you studying? Do you need me to make flash cards or something for you?"

"No. This is what I'm talking about. You want me to listen to you, but you never listen to me."

"I'm just trying to help."

"Samantha, something is wrong with me!"

"What do you mean?"

"I've told you I can't explain it. In college, I was taking anywhere from 17 to 20 hours a semester and made the Dean's List. I was like a sponge. Anything I studied, I retained. Now, when I wake up, it's like a clean slate with anything I read. I've also noticed my speech is different. I'm starting to slur my words and can't even find the right things to say. It's like the wheels are spinning in my head but nothing clicks. You're right…I've noticed I am starting to get more aggravated over every little stupid thing."

"Then don't take those supplements."

"It's not those! Do you hear the words coming out of my mouth?" Jason says frustrated. "Something is wrong! Not to mention, I get sharp stabbing pains in my head. It feels like a brain freeze you get after drinking a slushie too fast, but it does this several times a day."

"Maybe work is stressing you out. Why don't you put in a packet for a Warrant Officer?"

"Do you hear what I'm saying? We need money, but my brain feels broken. I can't use my head to get promoted or go be an officer. Now, I'm forced to use my body. Otherwise, I'm stuck here as an E-4, making half of what I made before joining the Army."

"You can't keep doing this each night, Jason! You come home, you don't talk to me or play with the kids anymore. You just go into your little man cave, drink, and play video games all night long."

"I'm beyond stressed, Samantha. I'm trying to figure out how to make ends meet here, and it would be a lot easier if you didn't screw my credit up before I joined. We wouldn't be in this mess right now."

"Drinking and playing video games isn't going to solve this problem, and how's this my fault?"

"Are you kidding me? Everything we had was under my name! The cars, the house, the business, the credit cards, the loans…. Everything! Then you defaulted on all of our bills for almost a year."

"I told you I thought I could handle the bills and before I knew it, we were behind on everything."

"Then how come when I asked, you told me they were paid on time?"

"I didn't want you to know I messed up."

"So, you let this go on for months without telling me. The only way I even found out was after I got mad at you and checked the mail myself. What did I find? Stacks of returned checks from the bank. I'm still amazed how you managed to turn my bank account into a basketball…because you bounced everything from here to the sun!"

"That's not all my fault! You told me to go buy stuff."

"BECAUSE YOU DIDN'T TELL ME WE WERE IN THE NEGATIVE! How can I fix something when I don't know there's a problem? Even when I tried to look at the books, you told me to get out of the office and it's all under control."

"As hard as you were working, I wanted to help, but I admit it, I didn't know what I was doing. We can't keep living in the past. What's done is done."

"That's easy for you to say. Your name wasn't on everything, and no, it's not in the past. I'm still trying to pay off those bad debts."

"It's going to be ok."

"HOW IS RACKING UP ALMOST $20,000 IN OVERDRAFT AND LATE FEES GOING TO…"

"SHHHH! Keep your voice down! The kids are asleep."

"You're the one who came in here starting a fight with me!"

"I'm not starting fight. Just please lower your voice."

Jason lowers his voice because he knows it's not healthy for his children to hear them argue. Quietly he says, "You throw TWENTY GRAND out the window, and then got our cars into repo status. I had to fire sale everything, including the business, all because you were keeping it a secret from me! Now that I'm trying to fix the mess you made, you have the nerve to come in here, telling me we need to go to a counselor because…YOU'RE UNHAPPY? So, please remind me again Samantha, how is that…HELPING ME?"

"I'm not doing this again tonight," Samantha turns and walks out the door.

"See? This is why we never talk. You come in here criticizing or guilt tripping me, but when I tell what's really on my mind, you don't want to hear it and just walk away."

Flashback: Sneaky, Sneaky

<u>*Summer Of 1989*</u>

Without opening his eyes, Jason can hear the voices of his three older cousins and brother whispering as their footsteps swish through the back of their grandparents' yard. "Denise," Jason says is a low but prompt tone. "Denise...wake up!"

Still groggy from the deep sleep she was in after a long day of being an energetic kid, she asks, "What?"

"Wake up!" Jason whispers. "I think they are trying to do something to our tent." Without another word, Denise springs from her sleeping bag and is already in an amateur looking karate stance.

Tonight, the aunts and uncles allowed the cousins to have a backyard campout. The group is too large for them to all huddle in one tent, so the big kids are sleeping in one, while the youngest of the cousins are sleeping in the other. Unfortunately for Jason, he is stuck with younger cousins Denise and Billy. Jason isn't old enough and has yet to earn his right to be promoted in their family ranks. Desperate for the approval of the older kids, he sees their prank attempts as an opportunity to earn their respect.

Rolling over, Jason sees his cousin, Billy, already sitting up and observing the shadows cast upon the tent. Billy whispers to Jason, "What are they doing?"

"I don't know, but grab something quick, so we can take 'em out."

Denise is already on top of it. "Here," she says handing Jason a boxing glove and Billy a red, oversized wiffleball bat.

As Jason grabs the glove, he smiles and thinks, *Brilliant! This is it!* The moment he's been waiting for! A chance to finally prove he's one of the big kids. His countermove must be creative, ingenious, and ruthless enough to gain notoriety. He must make them regret ever singling out the young cousins.

"Billy," Jason says quietly while pointing to the tent door. "You stand next to the door but off to one side. When one of them gets too close to the tent, I'm going to break their face," he says showing Billy the faded boxing glove. "When they rush in to beat us up, hit 'em hard from behind with the bat."

Jason sees Billy's excited but sinister expression of vengeance appear on his face. Billy wants revenge as much as Jason does. They are tired of being tortured, picked on, and left out of fun activities because they are 'too little' for the older kin. For the first time ever, the youth alliance finally has a worthy plan to foil their older counterpart's midnight sneak attack.

Jason quietly presses, "I will try to get as many as I can, but when they come in, you let 'em have it!"

"OK!" Billy joyfully whispers back as he jumps to his feet. Quickly, Jason and Billy get into position.

Grieved. Denise whispers, "What do I do?"

"Just stay out of the way so you don't get hurt. Here..." Jason says grabbing his favorite Ninja Turtles pillow and tossing it to Denise.

"Take this and help Billy whoop 'em when they rush in."

"Ok," Denise replies with disappointment in her voice. Jason can tell in her tone, being the precocious little one of the group, she wants a more active role in the plot.

Trying to convince Denise to not go rouge and give away their element of surprise, Jason implores, "Look, I need you to help me spot 'em as they pass by your side of the tent. When you see one get close, let me know so I can get 'em."

Now, feeling more of an important contributor rather than a hinderance, she enthusiastically replies, "Ok!"

With their eyes intently focusing on the tent perimeter wall, Jason rapidly scans back and forth at the hurried movements of the culprits outside. With Denise in his peripheral view, Jason sees what he has been desperately waiting for. One figure outside wanders too close to the tent wall. In a mad dash, Jason takes off with his gloved hand cocked in a solid striking position. Across the tent he flies to deliver a massive blow to an unsuspecting perpetrator. Now, within a few feet of initiating the greatest ninja style ambush in his mind, Denise suddenly appears between him and the target. Excited to point out another potential victim she sees, they unexpectedly startle each other in mid-stream. Denise's eyes get as large as beachballs as Jason delivers an accidental reflexive blow to her face. *Wham!* The force from the punch sends Denise careening backwards into the wall, like a boxer on the ropes, which brings down the entire tent. As the tent topples, so do their plans.

A sense of horror washes over Jason. First, for safety of his younger cousin, but second, he knows her tearful pleas for justice will definitely prompt a warranted whooping from his dad. Attempting to avoid getting parents involved, at all costs, as they usually do when things go wrong with their shenanigans, Jason leans over his fallen cousin, "Denise, are you ok?"

With her hands covering her face, Jason hears a large inhalation of breath, and he unmistakably knows what is coming next. Denise let's out a deep and loud cry that can be heard by the entire neighborhood. Laughter from the older cousins outside, quickly ceases. They too know what happens once the parents intervene and regulate the cousins' mischievous behavior.

"Denise be quiet!" Eric scoldingly calls out.

"What happened?" Jason hears his brother, Tyler, asking from outside the tent.

"*Shhh* Denise…are you ok? I'm so sorry…here…look…You can have my candy!" Jason says trying to hurriedly bribe and soothe Denise, but it's no use.

Like a knee jerk reaction, Denise yells back through her hysterical crying, "I'M TELLIN' ON YOU!"

Almost simultaneously and in unison, the cousins urgently join Jason's attempts to deter Denise. The sudden fear of belts snapping their behinds reach their minds as well. Their involvement in Denise's injuries would surely mean a ruined evening of fun with sore rears and hurt feelings for everyone. "Way to go Jason," Tyler and Eric scold as they stand there watching Denise disappear into the house.

"I told her to stand off to the side so she wouldn't get hurt, but she jumped right in front of me!" Jason contests.

"What were you doing?" Tyler asks.

Jason fires back, "What were you doing?"

"We were taking your stakes out of the ground so the tent would fall while you slept."

"Well, then this is your fault," Jason defends assigning guilt. "We were trying to protect our tent, and nothing would have happened if you guys would've left us alone!"

After a few more short, desperate exchanges of words, the backdoor wildly flings open to Jason and Tyler's mother standing in the doorway with fire in her eyes!

"ALL OF YOU…INSIDE…NOW!" their mother roars.

The Day She Disappears... Part 3

"Here you go Denise," Trish says as she spreads out a large comforter, covering Denise and Randy. Randy, who's not terribly social and one of Aaron's closest friends, is inside at the party while the other guests are outside playing cornhole and beer-pong.

"Thank you. I'm freezing," Denise tells Trish.

As the guests are preoccupied and enjoying the party, no one notices Aaron's one-ton Dodge dually truck arrive over the music still playing outside. With the guests out back, Aaron's undetected arrival allows him time to turn off his diesel motor and sneak his way to the front door. As he approaches, he sees Denise and Randy cozied up under the warm comforter Trish provided moments earlier. With his best friend sitting uncomfortably close to his wife, Aaron's jealous assumptions get the better of him. While the two are still engaged in friendly conversation, he takes a few snapshots with his phone through the windowpanes of the front door. Aaron hides as Trish passes through the living room and heads towards the kitchen. Through the door, he can hear her offering another round of refreshments to Denise and Randy. Denise shakes her head no while Randy raises his hand, accepting the offer for another drink.

As Trish returns with a beer for Randy, Denise mentions, "I can't thank you enough for letting me stay here."

"Not a problem," Trish acknowledges.

"Honestly, if I had to, I would live under a bridge with my kids just to get out of there," Denise states to them both.

The back door to the home abruptly opens, and a younger, heavier set boy eagerly enters. "Mom, can I have another Capri Sun?" Denise's hopeful son asks.

"No! You and your brothers have had enough sugar for one evening."

"AWWW MAN!" Denise's oldest son, Dewayne, exclaims.

"I don't want to hear it! We're going to bed soon and you still haven't taken a shower."

"Are we staying here tonight?" Dewayne excitedly asks his mother.

"Would you boys like to stay for a few nights?" Trish asks Dewayne.

"Yes ma'am!" he quickly responds. "Can we ride the four-wheeler tomorrow morning?"

"Sure, but only if your mother says it's ok," She playfully replies.

"Can we mom? Huh? Can we?"

"Only if you two round-up your little brother and go take a bath." Without responding, his sudden dart out the back door implies his will to expediently follow through with his mother's demands.

Chuckling at her son's haste, she turns to Trish and Randy, "I haven't seen that boy move that fast since Christmas, when I told him to go see what Santa brought him."

Laughing, "They're good boys, Denise. Considering the circumstances, I think they are taking everything quite well," Trish comments.

Randy, laughing as well, becomes curious at Trish's cryptic comment towards Denise, "What circumstances?"

"I'm not saying anything. If Denise wants to say something, then that's on her."

"Denise?" Randy directly asks her. "Something I should know about between you and Aaron?"

Pausing momentarily to consider her words, "Look, you can't say anything to Aaron, ok?"

"I won't. What's up? You guys having problems?" Randy says excitedly, loving being cut-in on local gossip.

With his ear close to the door, Aaron listens.

"Look, you're his best friend, so I won't go into all the details..."

The back door flings open again, and this time all of Denise's children emerge from outside. Dewayne is struggling to wrestle her youngest son, Allen, through the door. With Allen screaming and pawing at the door frame to avoid being dragged in, and the back door suddenly banging off the wall, Denise diverts her attention to them. "You guys keep the noise down, and Dewayne...be careful with him," Denise stiffly commands.

"Mom, he won't come in," Dewayne argues back. Getting up from the couch, Denise briskly approaches the boys as Allen gives up and sprawls out on the floor.

Scooping him up, she tells the other two, "I have him. Now, go get cleaned up and ready for bed."

"Mom, what are we gonna wear?" Dewayne asks.

"Don't worry, my boys have plenty of clothes you can borrow. Follow me..." Trish says as she uses her arm to signal for the boys to follow her.

Aaron hears a few guests walking towards the front outside and ducks into the shadows nearby. Denise sits back down on the couch with Allen calmed down. Randy is still waiting for her to pick back up where she left off.

Trying to coax Denise and reassure her, Randy conveys, "Look, don't worry about Aaron. If you need help like moving out or something, I've got you covered."

"Thank you, I know I can always count on you."

Leaning further back in the sofa recliner, Randy says, "I just don't want it getting back to him I'm helping you and he get the wrong idea about us. I care for you both like family, but I know how jealous Aaron can be. I don't want to see you struggling either. Worst case scenario, my door's always open. If you need to, you can always shack up with me at my place."

"I don't want him to suspect anything and think we are seeing each other. He thinks if I talk to anyone, I am cheating on him with them."

As a few unfamiliar faces hop into an old Chevy Sunfire parked out front, Aaron watches them leave before returning to the front door.

"Don't worry, I can keep a secret...trust me!" Aaron hears his friend Randy proudly boast.

"At this point, I don't care where I go, just as long as I have my boys. Without 'em, I don't know what I would do because..." Denise stops mid-sentence as a look of horror streaks across her face. With her jaw dropping wide open in disbelief, she now has her eyes locked on Aaron's, who can be seen outside. His shadowy figure becomes clear after Trish suddenly flicked on the hallway light, making her way back to the living room. "Oh my God..." Denise utters under her breath as she is frantically going over in her head the exact conversation she just had with Randy. *Did he hear?*

"What?" Randy says with a smile following Denise's frightened stare towards the front door. His curious grin quickly fades when he sees Aaron's angered expression through the front door glass. Trish, seeing shocked faces on Denise and Randy as she walks back into the room, instantly knows what they are staring at. As a giant knot suddenly forms in her stomach, she quickly looks to confirm her suspicions, and sees Aaron reaching for the door handle letting himself in.

Randy is the first to say anything as Aaron's unlaced work boots thud on the hardwood floor entering the home. "Hey buddy!" Randy calls out with a grin and a slight look of guilt in his eyes. "It's about time you showed up. You want a beer?"

Denise, promptly following Randy's lead, shoots up from the couch to greet Aaron. Before she gets halfway there, she can tell Aaron isn't buying their pleasantries. "Get the kids...and let's go," Aaron commands in a low, agitated tone.

Denise awkwardly laughs trying to maintain her innocence, "What are you talking about? You just got here!"

Trish also interjects, "Aaron, what's the matter?" Trying to quickly calm Aaron down and diffuse a potentially volatile situation, she says "Denise is going to stay the night with the kids and help me start painting the kids' rooms tomorrow."

Ignoring Trish's comment, Aaron repeats himself through clenched teeth, "I said...let's go." Aaron's disgruntled feelings are obvious and so are his efforts to conceal them. Trish feels like she is watching a tea kettle about to blow.

Denise, sensing the level of Aaron's anger, begins to slowly retreat a few steps backwards.

"Aaron, chill bro! It's just a party," Randy says half intoxicated. The tension in the room is so thick, it can be cut with a knife.

"Bro?" Aaron erupts as he can no longer contain his boiling emotions. "Bro?" Aaron repeats but this time with less volume restraint. "I knew Denise was a whore and a liar, but I could never prove it. Then, I come here, and guess what I see? My wife and best friend all cuddled up on the couch together having a good ol' time...like I wouldn't find out!"

"Yo!" Randy objects to Aaron's absurd implication as he promptly stumbles to his feet. "Dude, nothing's going on!

64

We…" but before he can finish, Aaron holds up his phone. The group sees the recent photos he took.

Offended, Denise replies, "Seriously?"

"Looks to me like something's going on," Aaron contests as an awkward silence suddenly fills the room. In a dark and threating voice, with his gaze piercing through Randy, Aaron continues, "You know what happens to people who cross friends in this business."

"Dude, nobody crossed you. You're my best friend!" Asserting his dominance over the two, Aaron rebukes, "You know all I have to do is show these to our friend," pointing to the phone with his other hand, "and you're through." Even though he's been wrongfully set up, Randy cowers and remains silent because of the unspoken grave consequences of such implications.

"Don't you be bringing that drug cartel nonsense into my house," Trish protectively chimes in.

Surprised by Trish's assertiveness, Aaron's eyes widen momentarily and then lock on Denise. Turning his attention to Trish, in attempts to inflict more intimidation, he asks, "Would you and your entire family care to join him?"

"What? You threatenin' me now as well?" Trish asks confrontationally.

In disbelief, Randy interjects, "Come on man! Aaron…bro! Not cool!"

With one hand on her hip and the other pointing outside, Trish yells, "Get out of my house! NOW!"

Ignoring Trish's command, Aaron looks back at his wife. "If I were you, Denise, I would get your things…right now…and get in the truck."

"No…" Trish begins before Denise stops her.

"Trish, it's ok. I appreciate everything. Do you mind if the boys stay the night? I can take Allen home with me now and I'll pick them up in the morning."

Just then, Denise's two oldest boys enter the room to see what the commotion is and stop cold in their tracks at the sight of Aaron. Seeing the boys frightened, Denise promptly flocks to them like a mother hen protecting her young.

"Mama's gonna go home and you two are going to stay here tonight, ok? I want you to go right to bed and be on your best behavior. I'll be back in the morning. Can you do that for me?" Sensing the hostile disturbance, the boys nod their head yes, but still have their eyes intently trained on their stepdad. "Look at me," Denise says while sharply snapping her fingers. Now, with the boys undivided attention, Denise leans over and looks deeply into their eyes, "Do you understand me?"

"Yes ma'am."

"Now, you two get to bed and I don't want to find you've been causing Mrs. Trish any trouble, do you hear me?"

"Yes ma'am," the boys reply again.

"I will see you in the morning, ok? I love you!" Denise says wholeheartedly. She pauses a moment to absorb their faces, almost as if she knows she might not ever see them again. Denise kisses them gently on their cheeks and steals one more hug from each of them.

The boys reply, "Love you too!"

Turning back down the hall now, with their chins tucked into their chests, the two boys retreat to the back of the house. They can sense something is wrong. Angered by the situation, Denise begins gathering her things. Trish and Randy silently watch as Denise angrily storms back and forth from the living room to the kitchen, cleaning up while collecting her personal effects.

Trish finally breaks the uncomfortable silence, "Denise, don't worry about it. I'll clean up!"

"No, it's ok! Aaron doesn't mind comin' in here accusing everybody of stuff they ain't doing... so he can stand there like the idiot he is until I'm through!"

"Keep it up Denise..." Aaron starts, but Denise's frustration emerges to cut him off.

"Or what...? You gonna throw me on the ground because I talked back? Chop my hair off again? Scream at me when no one else can hear?" Both Trish and Randy turn their heads to see Aaron amused by Denise's defiant attitude and subtle cries for help.

"That's fine. Keep talkin' that trash, tryin' to embarrass me in front of other people. Go ahead, I don't care at this point!"

"Oh, course you don't care, and why would you? I know about the other girls you talk to when you go to the bar before coming home."

Aaron struggles to mask his sudden surprise but it's too late. "Are you off your medications again?"

"Don't even go there, you jerk! I've known about your little side hussies for some time now," as she shoulders past Aaron and opens the front door.

Aaron, following her out, fires back, "Well if you didn't become a fat cow after having Allen, I wouldn't need to be looking around!"

Denise, obviously hurt by his comments, turns around and loudly retaliates, "You're going to bring up my weight? Why don't you take a real hard look in the mirror and step on a scale? That is, if you can even see the numbers around that gut of yours. If those girls want a fat, bald, and ugly man-baby, then go right on ahead!" Denise retaliates as she exits off the porch and heads for the truck.

Trish and Randy who are now in the doorway, burst into laughter and immediately try to refrain themselves. Embarrassed and angered, Aaron briskly walks to catch up with Denise. Without saying a word, he attempts to grab her arm to hurry her to the truck.

"GET YOUR HANDS OFF ME!" Denise shouts, violently yanking her arm away. Trying to gain attention from the other guests out back, she continues, "DON'T YOU TOUCH ME AGAIN!"

With a quick and uneasy look over his shoulder, Aaron angrily and inaudibly leans in close to give her a final warning.

"GET OUT OF MY FACE!" She hollers back. People from the backyard begin making their way to the front to see the commotion as Aaron heads for the driver side and quickly hops in, slamming his door.

Trish sees Denise stalling for a moment before calling out, "Are you sure you don't wanna stay?"

"If I don't go, he'll just sit here and keep causin' a scene!"

"Yer a good for nothing, sorry excuse for a wife! Get in the truck now," Trish hears Aaron yell from the driver side window. His angered words have escalated to a more rageful tone as a quick flurry of indistinguishable words soon follow. Denise, still standing there outside the truck, is listening to the apparent onslaught of verbal abuse and obscenities pouring out of the window.

"Is that how you talk to your wife?" Denise yells back making sure everyone can hear.

Aaron quickly opens his door to get out, but Denise knows better than to push this little victory any further. She opens the passenger door and gets in. As Aaron peels off onto the main road from the driveway, Trish, Randy, and several guests watch as his truck races away.

The Clock's Ticking

With lights still flashing from the emergency vehicles and several cop cars parked nearby, a man walks under the caution tape perimeter. Making his way through the small crowd of the search and rescue team, huddled volunteers, and police officers, their chattering comes to a halt.

"Alright people...listen up! Gather around," the slender built gray-haired man with a handlebar mustache calls out.

Standing on the porch stairs where everyone can see, he begins. "Can everyone hear me in the back?" a deputy from the San Saba Sheriff's Department calls out.

A few people in the back of the small crowd nod their heads yes.

"Here's what we know so far...the husband murdered her. There was some blood found in the kitchen, and we can't locate the body. We also know someone helped him. I know it's dark, and I want to be here about as much as you do, but we got a job to do. Let's get to work people!"

Chapter 4

That's Just Wrong!

September of 2017

Wiping the sweat from his brow, Jason is feverishly working to get the store ready for its grand opening. Now, being a disabled veteran, Jason struggled to find a decent paying job once he moved backed to Austin, Texas. Even though he has a college degree in business, is a prior business owner, and has a decade's worth of retail management expertise, he has yet to open a promising door. Never once has Jason had difficulty finding employment until now. Being a retired veteran doesn't have the perks he once thought it did.

"Sarah, I can't believe they expect the store to be opened so quickly," Jason says to his District Manager, over the store's loud Halloween themed music.

A short and curvy young woman, shaped like an hourglass in yoga pants, comes over to Jason with merchandise still in her hands. With a plain face caked with makeup, fake eyelashes, and fake blonde hair to match everything else about her, she sets down a few pairs of poorly printed pumpkin socks on some boxes nearby. Sarah puts her platinum bleach blonde hair into a ponytail and looks up at him still on a ladder, hanging a sign in the kid's section.

"You know last year, corporate gave us double the payroll, and we had a month to open the store. This year, we only have two weeks to get the job done with half the staff," Sarah informs Jason.

"Look, I went through Special Forces training in the military, and this job is breaking me off. How do they expect five people to build all these shelves, move 1,800 boxes of merchandise, and set the entire store up, with less than a week to go?"

"We are almost done. Don't quit on me now!"

"It's not a matter of quitting, it just bothers me that most of the workers here are women. If I'm struggling to keep up this tempo, I can't imagine what it's doing to y'all. Most of them are stay at home moms. Do you think it's fair for office nerds to barely give them minimum wage and slave drive them like this? I can't believe they expect you to open five stores in less than a month."

"I know. That's why I hired a big strong guy like you to help this year," Sarah says in a subtle, seductive tone.

"I guess what I'm saying is, do you think it's necessary to put this kind of workload on just a few people?"

"They keep costs down so they can open more stores."

"Exactly what I mean. Did you know that people who received a college degree in 1960, could land jobs for $40,000 a year? If you keep up with the average rate of inflation, guess how much you would be getting paid today?"

"You know I don't do numbers. That's why they make calculators!"

"A $40,000 job then would be the equivalent to starting out at $215,000 per year if corporations kept up with the average rate of inflation."

"What! That's outrageous!"

"Instead, retail store managers are still getting paid the same as when I was doing this over 15 years ago. Meanwhile, profits and the national GDP keep rising. Getting a 3% raise each year truly isn't a raise. That's just barely keeping up with inflation. Those companies who give only 1-2% raises are, in all actuality, cutting your pay. The push for

72

profits and corporate greed is destroying middle-class America. Now, you pretty much have the poor and super wealthy."

"Ok, maybe it's true, but if we don't get this done, then we won't get paid at all."

"I'm not saying we can fix it tomorrow, but our economy operates on people buying. If people don't have money to buy because a few are holding the majority of it, then corporations will eventually make people so poor, they will bankrupt themselves. If this trend continues, they will be bought out by bigger corporations until one corporation owns everything."

"What are you talking about?"

"You won't see this in the media, but most news and media stations are secretly owned by four to six large corporations. Each station appears to be different, but they pretty much have the same boss."

"Ok, how does this pertain to setting up a Halloween store?"

"I've already run the numbers, and this company could easily triple the staff on payroll, and still make a fortune. Do you know how much money these pop-up stores make in two to three months?"

"I know it's somewhere in the millions."

"Try, eight to nine billion dollars! Meanwhile, their greed for expansion and profits has 50-year-old Karla over there," Jason points, "working her tail off for pennies to the dollar. Yeah, we get paid more in America than sweatshops in Asia, but if you do the percentages, we're not much better off. It's not just this store, it's any corporation. What kind of quality of life is this for supposedly the 'greatest country in the world'? Yeah, great for who?" Jason rhetorically asks.

"I already spoke with the Regional Manager and corporate office about increasing payroll to get more workers in here. They told me all the other stores are meeting their expectations."

"Yeah, because their employees are working after hours and off the clock."

"Uh, that information stays between us, ok?"

"I know. I just think someone needs to remind them of the legal lawsuit liabilities and ethics violations they face by forcing others to meet their ridiculous goals."

"All I know is that if we don't hit our numbers with payroll and sales, then you nor I will get our bonuses at the end of the season. I don't have a regular job year-round and could really use the extra money. If we need to bend a few rules to achieve that, then we gotta do what we gotta do."

"I need the money too, and I'm not trying to cause wakes. I was just surprised that, as big as the company who owns Ghost and Ghouls Halloween Superstores is, they would slave drive women and their workers like this. I thought they only did that stuff overseas."

"I look at it this way, having two kids and not being able to exercise, I also get a gym membership out of this as well! This gives me an opportunity to work off some of this fat," Sarah suggests, but with her already firm and trim body, Jason can tell she's fishing for a compliment.

"You're not fat."

"Awww, that's so sweet," Sarah replies as she bats her fake eyelashes and begins to blush.

Turning away from Jason, she picks the socks up from the box, and purposefully drops a few. As she slowly bends over, she says, "And if you help me make our bonus this year, there might be an extra bonus in it for you!"

Picking up on her flirtatious tone, Jason asks, "What does that imply?"

"Well, I don't want to speak too soon, but maybe I might let you choose your own reward for all your hard work."

"Reward?" Jason curiously asks.

Quickly turning her head to see if she can catch Jason's eyes studying her backside, Sarah stands up disappointed he isn't sexualizing over her. Noticing her teasing and overtones are going unnoticed, she pushes a little more as she stands ups, "Let's just put it this way, if I get what I want, then…" leaning slightly forward to expose more cleavage from her loosely fit v-cut shirt, "you can have whatever you want."

There was a momentary silence before Sarah mischievously grins and slowly turns to walk away. As she carefully maneuvers around shipping boxes still stacked on the floor, Sarah makes sure each exaggerated step is getting noticed.

Disapprovingly shaking his head as she walks away, Jason realizes his boss would rather try to entice him, rather than standing up to her bosses to do what is right. That doubled the number of things he wasn't attracted to about her.

The Truth Hurts

Taking the steak out of the skillet and putting it on a plate, Jason quickly turns off the stove to grab his phone while it was still ringing. Without checking the caller ID, Jason answers, "Hello?"

"Hi daddy!" an excited and sweet voice replies.

"Hi baby! How are you?"

"Good," Brianna, his eight-year-old daughter, gently answers. "Are we going to stay with you this weekend?"

"No baby, I can't...Daddy's gotta work, but guess what?"

"What?" she asks sadly.

"I already spoke to your mom, and since my store is open, she's gonna bring you and your brother by on Saturday. I can help you pick out whatever costume you want!" Jason says trying to sound enthusiastic.

"Really?"

"Uh-huh, and I also have another surprise for you!"

"Really!" Now even more excited, "What is it?

"I can't tell you silly, or it wouldn't be a surprise."

"Daddy...?"

"Yes, honey?"

"Are you and mommy ever going to get back together?"

"Sweetheart, your mother left me almost two years ago when she filed for a divorce."

While Jason was undergoing treatment for multiple concussions from being a paratrooper, his then wife, Samantha, left without warning and moved backed to Texas with his kids. As if the invisible injuries weren't already hard enough on Jason, taking his children away devastated him.

"Well, you are here now."

"Yes, I am, and I'm so glad I can see you now on the weekends. It was hard having to wait six long months each time between visits, being in the Army."

"Why did it take you so long to come back home?"

"The Army wouldn't let me leave, sweetheart."

"Why not? Why couldn't you leave?"

"It's hard to explain, baby girl, but daddy got really hurt in the Army. I had to go through a very long process of being questioned, poked, and prodded before they believed I was hurt and needed medical care. I had to do this so when I left, they would give me good medical treatment and pay me for the injuries they caused."

"How come? When I go to the doctor, it only takes a few hours. Why did it take them more than a year?"

"Now you know why Daddy was so angry trying to get out of there."

"That's not fair Daddy. We missed you this whole time."

"I know baby, and I am truly sorry. They made Daddy jump through all their hoops so I could be able to pay for all your doctor visits each time you get sick. See, it's different if you come here from another country. When they come here, they automatically give them free doctor visits, money each month, a place to stay, food, and pay for their school. Soldiers, on the other hand, get treated much differently. They make you have to argue and fight long battles for those same things."

"That's not fair."

"I know. They treat the millions of brave soldiers, who keep this country safe from the bad guys like dirt. They also make soldiers who get hurt feel like poo-poo for trying to get the same things for their families. What they give freely to others, they made Daddy chase his tail for almost two years to get. They treated me like I was the bad guy for wanting to make sure my family was taken care of because I couldn't do the things I used to."

"That's so rude and wrong Daddy. They should treat you like kings for protecting us! You should be the first one to get everything and make those other people who come here jump through hoops to get that."

"Who taught you to be so smart?" Jason teases.

"You did, Daddy!" Brianna responds, a little angered from this news.

"I know, sweetie." To lighten the mood Jason continues, "They treat us like little poodles in a dog show." Brianna laughs. "Am I a poodle?" Jason teasingly asks.

"No!" Brianna giggles.

"Am I?"

"No, Daddy!" laughing even louder.

"Well, someone out there must think we are! To them, we are just a bunch of camouflage wearin' dancing, prancing, pouncing poodles with buckets on our heads, huh?"

Brianna burst out into a hard laugh. "No!"

"We just roll around in the dirt all day, and enjoy being yelled at, right?"

"No, but they don't even give you treats for being a good doggy."

"Hey now!" Jason laughs admiring Brianna's quick wittedness.

Going along with his daughter's humor Jason says, "What do you think we should do then? I know! Maybe…we should just go bite 'em for being bad to us and take our treats! How does that sound?"

"Yes!"

"Do they sound like very good owners to you?"

78

"No Daddy! Not at all! You should go bite 'em hard for keeping you away for so long when you could have come home much sooner."

"I think so too!"

"Daddy…"

"Yes honey…"

"If I were in charge, I would change all of that! I would make sure all soldiers get the best care. That way they won't have to wait and miss being home with their family too!"

"Maybe one day you will!"

"Daddy…?"

"Yes, baby."

"I love you!"

"I love you too, sweetheart!"

Coming Full Circle

Jason's parents arrive home from a long day at work and open their door to see their son laying on their couch in tears. Jason's dad, Troy, seeing his son's condition, grows very concerned, "Jason, how are you feeling? I know you are trying to help out at the store, but you can't overdo yourself with your condition."

"Dad, please not now."

"Can I get you anything? Want some medicine or water?" Troy asks trying to ease his son's pain.

"Jason, I've never seen you this bad before. Is it your hip or back this time?" His mother Ellie asks.

"Both," Jason responds while he winches to a new type of pain shooting down his leg and into his foot.

"I spoke with your Uncle Jim after you had to leave work, and he said the VA doctors in Austin are top notch. I can't keep seeing you like this. I told him if you won't go have surgery, he's coming down here to help me hog tie you up and drag you there ourselves."

Jason chuckles at his father's caring sarcasm. "Dad, it's not that I don't want to go...I have two little kids that want to play with their Daddy. If they fuse six vertebrae, like they want to, and do a hip replacement, then I'm done. The kids are too young to understand why daddy can't play with them anymore. It's hard enough on them I'm not there each day, and when I am, they want to have fun and play. It destroyed them when I had to explain over the phone, I wasn't coming home anymore. They didn't understand what a divorce meant or why daddy wasn't there to tuck them in each night. After Samantha did a snatch and grab and took the kids where I couldn't regularly see them, I lost two years of their life I will never get back. Now that I'm home, I'm sorry dad, but I'm not going to let them turn me into some Frankenstein. I just can't do it to my kids."

"Would you at least go talk to them about alternative treatments?"

"What do you think I was doing while I was waiting to be discharged? Every doctor literally told me they don't know what else to do, other than experimental surgeries. We tried everything, and I only got worse."

"But look at you now Jason!" His mom chimes in with tears welling up in her eyes. "You can't keep doing this to yourself."

"I just need some rest and I'll be fine. Ever since I worked for that Halloween store, my condition has gotten much worse."

"I'm sure the alcohol isn't helping either."

"It's the only thing to dull the nerve damage in my leg. Otherwise, I can't sleep through the night. It feels like I'm being hit with a cattle prod or tazer every five minutes," Jason winces again and finally a few tears escape his eyes.

His mom quickly sits down next to Jason to console him, "Honey...what's wrong?" Allowing him a few moments to calm his emotions, his mother could sense there was more going on than Jason's physical pain. "What else has got you so upset?"

After what felt like 10 years of pent-up distain came pouring out, Jason begins to regain his composure. Grimacing from the intense pain, Jason replies to his mother, "Here I was thinking I had life by the tail. I got married, had kids, opened my own business, and then little by little, it's all been taken away. I lost my business, so I joined the Army, then I lost my wife and kids, and now my health is gone. I can't find a job that isn't temporary, and even when I drove down here to help you guys, I can't even do that for more than a few days. Lately, it seems anywhere I go or anything I do turns south."

"No. You're just in a slump right now. You need to find something else to do."

"It's not so much that…I just haven't been happy in years."

"Well, you still have your children and us."

"Do you know what it feels like to not be able to do the things you love to do? For me, it's going to the gym, playing sports, and being physically active. I can't do that anymore. Then to top it off, I found out the kids had parent career day at school, and they were too embarrassed to let me know because I've been out of work."

"I'm sure they weren't trying to hurt your feelings. Did you want to go?"

"No, but that's not the point."

Chuckling. "Then what's the problem?"

"Did you know I've put in over 250 job applications, and I only got two phone calls back?"

"See, that's a start."

"The calls weren't jobs I applied for. They were recruiters seeing if I wanted to be either a car or insurance salesman. I don't want to be completely miserable, cold calling people all day trying to make a living."

"It's not so bad."

"Oh sure…" Jason plays out a mock scenario, "Ring...ring...ring...Uh yes, are you in the market to come buy this car we call 'American made' but everything's made in third world countries, using the cheapest materials possible, and the parts are sometimes made by children in sweat shops … if we can get away with it? 'Click'…Hello?"

"Jason…"

Pretending to dial another number. "Ring…ring…ring…Um, yes…is Mr. Williams home? Hi sir! How are you doing today?... Look, I know you're busy and you already have insurance for your home, cars, boat, stocks, pets, businesses, antiques, health, and life…but have you ever considered insurance…for your insurance? Let's be honest here Mr. Williams…they find every way to get out of giving you the money you've already invested to pay your claim…."

"Jason, you're so dramatic," his mother chuckles and waits for him to continue.

"…Well Mr. Williams, that's where we come in! When your insurance companies drop you for filing a claim, because we all know they aren't in the business to pay you back…then guess what…WE WILL TOO!" Jason's loud sinister laugh echoes down the hallway. "Wait, wait, wait! It gets even better!... Mr. Williams…hold on, it gets better…. Then we call you next week…to sign you up…for more insurance!" Hysterically laughing, "…Isn't that great…. Mr. Williams?... Hello?"

"Are you finished?"

"Sorry mom…but I think I'm gonna take a hard pass on those."

"Why don't you go back to school and become an accountant like your brother or do something in finance?"

"Why, so I can get paid to help wealthy people hide their money in offshore shell companies and evade taxes? Better yet, I can work in their corporate level Ponzi schemes, to help them control governments by making money using other peoples' money. Yeah, I mean, I guess I could, but are these my only options right now? Making a living from manipulating, controlling, and stealing from others, just so I can get a small piece of the pie?"

"You sure do have a unique way of looking at this world."

"It just seems our entire system is set up to see who can outsmart each other, so they can take their money. This is what we call being civilized or professional. Yeah, professional thieves who wear suits."

"What about politics and doing something in the legal field?"

"Even better! That way I can take legalized bribes and violate Article 2 Section 4 of the Constitution. Sorry mom, but I don't want to protect corporations who are destroying our country, economy, jobs, and self-sustainability by outsourcing production to China, Vietnam, or India. I'm not fond of making a living by helping corporations and the wealthy settle out of court and dance around the law," Jason replies.

"What do you mean?"

"Take General Motors as an example, back in 1999, they were ordered to pay out a $4.9 billion lawsuit settlement because they intentionally refused to spend $8.59 per vehicle to ensure customer safety. GM admitted they estimated they would only have to pay $2.40 per vehicle for fuel tank fire lawsuits. Profits are more important to corporations than human life," Jason concludes.

Ellie sighs and while rolling her eyes says, "Then why don't you go into law enforcement or become a teacher. I know you love protecting and helping others."

"You mean hired enforcers who toss regular people in jail and throw away the key for essentially doing the same things CEOs, elites, and politicians get a slap on the wrist for doing? Or better yet, I can use my authority to help cover up crimes the wealthy and corrupt people commit. You know, on second thought, teaching might not be so bad after all. Then, even with noble intentions, I will be forced to indoctrinate our youth to be excited to work for professional scam artists and train them to value money over people."

"Alright Jason, that's enough…."

"Being able to learn and apply the knowledge of life is a thing of the past. The ability to think to resolve problems in the real world are stricken from books. It's all about standardized testing now."

"If you're going to continue to be so negative, then I'll leave until you're in a better mood."

"Mom…I'm just frustrated, upset, and lost. It seems like you can't get ahead in this world by trying to do the right thing. Even if you are really good at something, it's almost like you have to sell your integrity to get ahead."

"What do you mean?"

"You don't get ahead in this world by what you know…it's who you know. Being qualified and capable comes second to those who have friends in high places."

"I'm sorry your dad and I aren't the social butterflies who have friends in the right places. We did our best to make a living, to raise you and your brother the best we knew how."

"I'm not blaming you. I give my best at everything I do, and just like in baseball, I had to sit the bench my senior year behind some kid who couldn't hit his way out of a wet paper bag because his daddy bought the school a new scoreboard. Then, when I started my business after college, how could I make a living with everyone wanting to charge me taxes on top of my taxes?"

"I know, we are dealing with the same thing with our company. We must pay taxes on the employees we hire even though the IRS will tax them anyway on their pay and then again when they buy something. There's too much double, triple, quadruple-dipping from the government when they can't even set a budget or maintain one. Then they continue to want more money from us!"

"Do you know why taxes keep increasing?"

"Why?"

"Why do you think this country fought for our freedom? Taxation from Britain. Then in the early 1900's we allowed them take over again and manage our banks. Today, they own much of our land and even our energy Power Grid. So, is this America or have they secretly regained control over us?"

"Hmm, that is interesting."

"I'm just upset because I've tried my best to be successful, but the laws and odds are stacked against us. We're heavily regulated but politicians, corporations, and the ultra-wealthy are not. Adding insult to injury, they use our money to make themselves richer. How's that fair?"

"Unfortunately, that's just how this world works," Ellie sadly replies.

"But it doesn't have to be this way."

"We've saved all our lives, counting pennies so we could pay for your sports, and barely had enough left over to open this business," Troy remarks.

"Yeah, kids of CEOs and politicians, get insider information on the stock market and know exactly when to buy in or sell. They put a little money into whatever stock their dad tells them to, and then virtually overnight, they're immediately worth millions or billions."

"That would take us several lifetimes to achieve," Jason's mom says softly.

"Please tell me how that's fair mom? Meanwhile, the rest of us work like dogs trying to make an honest living. We barely keep our heads above water, while these guys are out there manipulating markets to steal everyone's money. It's organized crime. From Vegas to Wall Street and then on to

Capitol Hill. Greed is like a virus, sickness, or plague because people can't control themselves to stop, and nothing is ever enough."

"I'm sorry we didn't go to college to get an education to know how to be more successful," Troy tells his son. "We did the best we could and tried to make enough money to put you and your brother through college, so you can give your kids a better life than we were able to provide for you. Unfortunately, we just don't have a circle of friends like that. In this household, we have always valued people, and how you treat others, not money."

"That apparently doesn't get you very far in this world."

"I know but at least your father and I can sleep at night. We can hold our heads high and not feel ashamed because we didn't screw someone over to get ahead," Ellie interjects.

"It would just be nice if people tried to improve the world rather than working to take from it and leaving it worse than they found it," Jason contests.

"I hear ya," Ellie says.

"Are you going to be ok?" Troy asks.

"Yes sir. When I'm feeling a little better, I'm going to head home."

"Are you sure?" Ellie asks. "You can always stay here for as long as you would like."

"I appreciate that and thank you. It means a lot. I've just got a few things in my head I need to sort out."

"Ok, just let us know if there's anything we can help you out with," Troy adds.

"Well, there is one thing…"

"Yeah…what's that?"

Feeling better now, Jason asks in a smooth tone, "Do you know of any single ladies looking for a good looking, out of work cripple, with a great sense of humor, and a fast car?"

"Geez..." Ellie utters as she rolls her eyes again and stands up. "Is that all you and your brother ever think about? You should be more focused on getting your life back together before getting involved with someone else."

Jason's dad now finds his turn to give fatherly advice, "Why don't you sell that car, get something you can afford, and use that college degree to start learning how to make money work for you?"

"I tried and look at where it got me. At least now, I can have some fun and a little excitement too. If I'm destined to be broke and poor, I might as well be happy, right?"

"You will find happiness once you find your way in this world and discover who you are," Ellie says offering some words of wisdom.

His mother triggered a memory in his mind. Jason asks, "Speaking of discovering people, whatever happened to Denise?"

Chapter 5

What Could it Hurt?

"Bye, Daddy, I love you!" Brianna calls out from the rear passenger window of her mother's car.

"I love you too, baby girl," Jason replies as he leans in to give her a final kiss goodbye. "Roll the window up so you don't let the heat out."

"Yes, sir."

"Bye, buddy! You did great this weekend. I'm very proud of you! I love you!"

"Bye, Daddy. I love you too," Jason's son Bradley replies, with an emotionless expression on his face.

"What's wrong with him?" Samantha asks Jason as Brianna rolls up her window.

Turning to face her standing beside him, Jason answers, "He did really good this weekend. I finally taught him how to ride a bike."

"That's good, but what's wrong with him?"

"He's upset, Samantha!"

"Why?"

"He doesn't want to leave. This bouncing back and forth between your apartment and mine is stressful on the kids. Brianna cried this morning because she wasn't ready to go home to you. They miss their dad, and don't want to leave."

"What do you want me to do about it?"

Playing coy, Jason replies, "Nothing. You asked a question, and I answered it."

"Did you find a job yet?"

"No. People with disabilities aren't in very high demand right now."

"Didn't your cousin go missing not too far from here?"

"Yeah, why?"

"They still haven't found her?"

"No. Why do you ask?"

"Isn't next month going to be three years since she disappeared?"

"I honestly haven't thought about it."

"They still haven't arrested her husband yet?"

"I don't know. Apparently not."

"Maybe, since you can't find a job, you can put that military training to good use and find out why."

"Like how?"

"You have ways of making people talk and were always good at figuring things out. Maybe the cops missed something, or you can find a clue that leads to Denise. Just a thought, but you know…"

Samantha's words fade as she continues speaking to Jason. His mind is now racing. *Why hasn't anyone been arrested?...* A million questions begin filling Jason's head. Samantha stops giving her two cents after seeing Jason's eyes glaze over.

"Are you listening?"

"What? Yeah, I heard you," Jason replies while trying to pretend he heard her.

"Anyway…you should check into it. It might give you something better to do than sitting around here filling out job applications."

"It's cold. You better get in before you catch a cold or something," Jason says as they walk around to the driver's side trying to sound caring, but he didn't care at all.

Each time he sees her now, he can't stop thinking of how badly she betrayed him over the years. First with the business, then bailing on him when he was hurt in the Army, and taking his kids and money, leaving him with nothing. What angers him the most is she made a vow...in sickness and in health...'till death do us part. Jason's concussions in the Army made him sick...very sick. Instead of being there to help him through his recovery, Samantha snatched his kids and left Jason when he needed them the most. In fact, he despises her for what she has done.

As Samantha gets into her car, Jason closes the door behind her, blows kisses to the kids and waves goodbye to them. As their car disappears around the corner, Jason reaches for his phone in his jacket pocket and makes a call.

"Hey Jason! How are you?"

"Hi mom! I'm good!"

"Are you feeling any better? How are the kids?"

"We're doing good. The kids just left."

"I'm glad to hear that! Any news on a job?"

"That's actually why I called. Did you realize it's going to be three years, next month, since Denise went missing?"

"Yes. I just talked to your Aunt Lisa yesterday."

"I thought you told me a couple years back, the evidence pointed to her husband."

"I did."

"Then, why isn't he in jail?"

"That's what the entire family and friends have been asking this whole time."

"What happened?"

"Has anyone filled you in?"

"The only thing I know, was what you told me when you called initially, and said the police were investigating it. Other than that, nothing."

"Can I call you tomorrow to discuss it? I'm right in the middle of cooking dinner, and I don't have my notes in front of me."

"Notes?"

"Yes. There are so many discrepancies with this entire case, I began writing everything down, and it'll take more than just a minute to go over."

"Ok...but I wanted to know if anyone has checked back with the Sheriff's department lately?"

"No, not since this Sheriff took over."

"What happened to the detective?"

"Jason, like I said..."

"That's fine, I was just asking a few questions because I want to start looking into her case to see if I can help. I'm thinking I might take a little drive tomorrow and go pay a visit to the Sheriff."

"What made you decide to do that?"

"Samantha just left, and she mentioned Denise's case."

"Are you two being cordial in front of the kids?"

"Yes, mom. I've always made it a point not to argue in front of them."

"That's good. Your father and I never did because there are topics children shouldn't hear, like money or relationship problems."

"I know."

"How's your leg and back been doing?"

"Much better, I'm finally back in the gym."

"Jason!"

"Don't worry mom! I'm taking it easy! I'm not lifting heavy weights. It's more like conditioning or a maintenance thing, ok?"

"Please don't get yourself hurt again."

"I won't. I promise."

"Why do you want to start looking into Denise's case? I didn't want to say anything to you because you've been through enough already. I didn't think you wanted another burden on your shoulders."

"I'm curious now why nothing's being done if it's clear there was foul play from Aaron."

"I don't know if that's such a good idea."

"Why not? I'd like to see if I can help or at least get some answers."

"Look, I'll call you tomorrow, alright? Just not a good time right now."

"Love you."

"Love you too."

"Bye."

"Goodbye."

Stirring The Pot

Jason's red Dodge Challenger SRT races through the modest and rustic looking town of San Saba, TX. He is pleasantly surprised to see the San Saba Court House currently under renovations. With its new structural face lift, the courthouse now looks more like an architectural work of art, deep in the heart of Texas country. With its four large pillars out front, it reminds Jason of buildings he had seen while visiting Washington D.C.

As Jason pulls into a half paved, half dirt, poor excuse for a modern parking lot, it wreaks havoc on his new ride. With windows down, Jason smiles as he hears his race exhaust reverberating off the dilapidated building. Revving his motor a few times, he backs his car into what one can only assume is a legal parking spot. Getting out and locking his doors, he observes the San Saba County Jail is in much need of repair. As he walks towards the front entrance, Jason figures this place is a few busted pipes away from being turned into a museum, rather than an active jailhouse.

The jail was originally built in 1884 and is now serving as the make-shift Sheriff's office, while their regular office in the courthouse is under repair. Entering the front door, Jason is immediately greeted by a young, and well-groomed deputy curiously approaching the entrance. Peering out the window behind Jason he asks, "Is that your Nascar parked out front?"

Chuckling. Jason turns around to admire his pride and joy with the deputy. "I just had the whole exhaust redone and a motor tune up."

Whistling, "She's a beaut!"

"Thanks."

"...buttttttt.... I am gonna have to write you a ticket." The deputy being more serious now.

"For what?"

"Maid service and dry cleanin'," he says pointing to the rather large water stains on his uniform. Jason stands there staring back at the straight-faced deputy with confusion. "Ya see..." the deputy continues as Jason notices the balled-up paper towels in the officer's hand, "I was just mindin' my own business in the restroom, when I hear a thunderstorm quickly rollin' in. Imagine my surprise to see it's still sunny outside. As I'm takin' a leak, the door hinges start rattlin' and shakin', and before I could finish my business...I guess someone thought it might be a good idea to scare the life out of me."

Jason tries hard not to laugh as he can already tell where this conversation is headed.

The deputy continues, "When you bumped yer motor a few times backin' in, I did everythin' in my power to keep from peeing all over myself, walls, and floor." Jason laughs, he can't hold it back any longer and the deputy finally breaks character to join in. "I'm just joshin'. I spilt my drink not too long ago and thought I'd have some fun with ya."

"Almost had me fooled," Jason jokes back.

"That's about the only action I get around here, but I guess I'll live to fight another day." *Chuckling.* "Now," The deputy changing subjects, "how can I help you?"

"Actually, I came here because I want to talk to the Sheriff, or whomever is in charge, about a missing persons case."

"Ok, do you have a case number?"

"Yes, I wrote it down," Jason states, handing the deputy a small piece of paper torn from his notebook.

Taking the note from Jason, the deputy enthusiastically instructs Jason, "Follow me."

As Jason follows the deputy heading down a short and narrow brick corridor, he notices the dusty and stale atmosphere from the old antique lighting fixtures. Trying to strike up friendly conversation Jason asks, "How long have you been working out of the jail?"

"Ah, just a few months," the deputy replies as they walk into a tiny office still packed with boxes from the move. "It's not too bad, but you can't see much with these lights. I get a headache if I stare at paperwork too long."

As the deputy signs into his computer, Jason begins to look around the deputy's office and spots a strange sight in an office across the hall. "Is that a bed?"

"Yep! Many years ago, the jailor would live and sleep down here. In fact, my grandpa was the Sheriff here over 50 years ago, and my grandparents used to sleep on that exact bed."

"Wow…" Jason exclaims from the bizarre little history lesson. "Is this place going to get renovated, like the courthouse, or is it close to being turned into a historical site?"

The deputy laughs. "We get people in here all the time, taking pictures and freely walking around. They don't realize this is still an actual jail. We struggle trying to keep this old place up to code. If we arrest somebody, and they can't post bail within 72 hours, we gotta send 'em somewhere else."

Amused. "Really?"

"Yes sir!"

"If you don't mind me asking, how many officers or deputies do you guys keep on staff?"

As the deputy slowly types in the case number given to him by Jason, he responds, "Shoot…It's just me and the

Sheriff, four other fulltime deputies, and one part timer." The deputy slides his tongue a little out of his mouth and off to one side, while using his index fingers to over-exaggerate pressing buttons on the keyboard, before finally hitting enter. "There…we gotta give it a few minutes to load. We don't have what you would call the latest and greatest," he states pointing to the early 2000's model desktop computer.

As Jason waits, he studies the interior of the office and thinks this would be a perfect set for some B rated Texas horror film. Now wishing he would have worn his cowboy boots and jeans this morning, instead of his designer clothes and shoes, he feels like an out of place city slicker in these parts. The computer continues to loudly hum, processing the request.

Finally, the deputy says, "Here we are! Let's see what we got…hmmm…Denise Sanders…" Jason can see the deputy's demeanor immediately change as he reads his cousin's name out load, and quickly trains his eyes on Jason. "What did you say your name was?"

"My name is Jason Prescot."

"Why are you askin' about this case?"

"Denise is my cousin."

"I've lived here for over 30 years. How come I've never seen you around here before?"

"I live in Austin. I just got out of the military about a year ago and moved close to the area. Next month is going to be three years since she went missing, so I came to speak with the Sheriff to see if I could help in any way."

Sitting back in his chair and crossing his arms, appearing to be more standoffish than helpful, he replies, "The Sheriff's gonna be out for a while. Ya just missed him!"

"Do you know when he'll get back?"

"Nope."

A long silence fills the room. Jason is taken back by the deputy's sudden passive hostility. "Ok, well I don't have anything else going on, so I guess I can wait until he gets back," Jason says expecting a response that never comes. Instead, he gets a cold stare in return. "Alright...I'll be out here waiting," Jason states while pointing to the little lobby area. "Is it possible to let him know I'm here?"

"I'll find out where he is."

Feeling odd and uncomfortable, Jason exits the office and heads back to the lobby a few feet down the hall. As he takes a seat, he can hear the deputy speaking with someone on the phone. "Hey...it's Deputy Randall...Yeah, I'm here at the jail and someone came in asking about the Denise Sanders case...He says he's her cousin...No...he said he's gonna wait in the lobby until you get here...uh huh...yeah...sure...I'll let him know."

Hearing a metal chair slide on the concrete floor, a few rustles of paperwork, and a desk drawer open and close coming from the deputy's office, before Jason hears the footsteps loudly approaching the lobby. As he comes into view, Jason's eyes are immediately drawn to the rather eloquent looking cowboys boots he is wearing. "Mr. Prescot..." Jason still seated in his chair, looks up to meet the deputy's cold and unfriendly stare. "I just got off the phone with the Sheriff, and he said he will be here in 15 minutes."

Realizing something is off with the deputy's demeanor, and not in a good way, Jason decides to stir the pot a little more. "Those are some pretty fancy boots you got on there."

The deputy, caught off guard by Jason's acute attention to detail, struggles to figure out what to say as his eyes wildly begin to dart around. He looks as if he wished he could now hide his feet somehow from Jason's view. Uneasily he shifts his weight.

Jason digs a little deeper. "Black alligator boots? Hmmm...considering y'all live this far out in the country, I can't imagine too many people could afford a pair, much less need something that extravagant around here." *Long pause.* "Alright," Jason breaks the silence, "let me take a guess then...are those Lucchese?"

What's Brewing?

<u>**February 2018**</u>

On the drive back to Austin, Jason's mother calls. "Hi, how you are?"

"Hey mom," Jason replies unenthusiastically.

"Look, I'm sorry about yesterday...I had my hands full cooking dinner, the laundry needed to be put away, and the dogs were hungry..."

Jason interrupts, "Mom, it's fine. I understand."

"Then why do you sound so glum? Is this a bad time? Are you driving?"

"How could you tell?"

"It's hard to hear you over that exhaust. You're going to need to speak up so I can hear you, but I wouldn't speed in that thing. The cops can hear you coming a mile away."

"I'm not."

"So, where are you headed?"

"Home."

"Well, I stayed up pretty late last night and got my notes together but I'm guessing you're not in the mood to talk right now..."

"No...it's fine."

"Well, I was trying to catch you before you went up to see that Sheriff."

"Too late."

"What? Why did you go up there before talking with me first?"

"Sometimes you call me back and sometimes you don't, so I went there to see what's up."

"...AND?" Ellie exaggeratedly asks.

"Mom, what is going on?"

100

"What do you mean?"

"With the Sheriff's office!"

"What did they say?"

"It got really weird, mom."

"Weird? Like how?"

"The deputy who helped me was nice at first, but his entire demeanor changed once he found out who I was looking for."

"I wonder why that is?"

"I don't know, but the Sheriff wasn't any better."

"That's why I wanted to talk to you before you left. We really liked the detective. He was very nice, respectful, and understanding. He kept us in the loop with the investigation and seemed to be making headway to find Denise. Then out of the blue, and only a few months into working the case, the Sheriff told us they had to close down a few departments and let some people go. One of the people let go was the detective and his department."

"Why would they fire their only detective?"

"That's what I wanted to know."

"After that, the Sheriff said he's taking over the case and was supposed to pick up where the detective left off, but Jason...he hasn't so much as called people for witness statements, searched any properties, and as far as I know, when we call asking for updates, he acts annoyed and gets an attitude with us."

"You don't find that peculiar?"

"Why do you think I started taking notes?"

"There's another strange thing I noticed about the deputy."

"What?"

"He was wearing a pair of Lucchese boots?"

"I don't know what those are."

"I didn't either until I saw a guy wearing a pair on tv."

"What's so unusual about them?"

"Oh, nothing if you don't mind throwing down five to ten grand for a pair."

"Good lord!"

"I know."

"What does a small-town deputy need with $10,000 boots?"

"I was thinking the same thing."

"What show were you watching when you saw them on tv?"

"It was a tv series with Mexican drug cartel enforcers, wearing almost the exact same boots. After the show, I was curious how much a pair of boots like those costs."

"Why? Are you looking to get into the drug smuggling business?"

"No mom, but from the shows and movies I've seen, those seem to be the types of people who wear them. Drug smugglers or members of the Cartel."

"So, what are you saying?"

"Nothing…I was telling you what stood out to me like a sore thumb."

"If anyone can find a needle in a haystack, it was always you."

"Also, when I asked the deputy about the boots by name, his eyes got about as big as saucers." Amused, "I think he was more shocked that someone like me even knew what they were."

"That is strange. So, you got a chance to talk with the Sheriff?"

"Yes, ma'am."

"What do you make of him?"

"He's a real piece of work that one."

"What do you mean?"

"He wasn't there at first but when he found out I was asking about Denise, he was there in 10-15 minutes. Then, when he came in, it wasn't like 'Hi! How are you? So sorry for your loss and we are working to get to the bottom of this.' Instead, he comes in, 'Are you the one asking about Denise? Why are you asking about her?'"

"He said that?"

"Yeah. Then I told him I was trying to find out more about what happened because maybe with my history with Denise, I might be able to help somehow."

"What was his response?"

"Well, at first he starts giving me a bunch of excuses about the budget cutbacks, and basically said they hadn't focused much on the case lately because it's a cold case."

"That's the first time I've heard that."

"Then I asked him, since he said it's only a missing persons case, if he didn't mind letting me look at the file. I asked to see if something might have been overlooked, and he started getting short with me and changed the story. First, he suggested to me Denise probably just skipped town without telling anyone."

"Denise would never just abandon her children. Those kids were her life."

"I told him the same thing. He said while it's not common, he has seen cases where a spouse has up and taken off. After a while, they turn up in another town or state, living a new life."

"What a load of crock. It's been three years! That's hot garbage!" Ellie angrily comments.

"I know. Then when asked about the file, he said they still have a few people of interest. What I want to know is…is this a missing persons case, or a possible homicide investigation?"

"This is what makes everything so strange because the detective was investigating this case like a homicide in the beginning."

"That's what I thought you told me from the beginning, but the Sheriff said Denise probably ran away, so naturally, I asked if he had recently run her social through their databases to confirm or deny that theory. He said no, but even if he had, he couldn't share anything with me on the case."

"What? That doesn't make any sense!"

"He also said they've thoroughly investigated every tip and interviewed everyone involved."

"The detective spoke with a handful of people involved in the case, but he was more interested in trying to find Denise. Then once this Sheriff took over, he hasn't called anyone, gone out to investigate...nothing!" Ellie says angrily, her voice elevating with every word.

"It's alright, mom. Calm down."

"That's why I haven't talked to you about the case much before because every time I do, it just makes my blood boil."

"After he told me they've thoroughly checked all leads and interviewed everyone, I called him out on it. I told him you must have not been that thorough. He said what do you mean? So, I said no one bothered calling me. He replied, why would we call you? Then, I told him how Denise called me just weeks before she disappeared, and she could have been in North Carolina for all they knew."

"Good point!"

"Mom, if this was a cartoon, he would've had sweat pouring from his face and adjusting his collar."

"Sounds like it."

"After that, he started raising his voice and getting confrontational with me!"

"Why would he get mad at you? It's them who had three years to find Denise and you're just asking questions as to why they haven't. What a jerk!"

"Then, I asked if they've at least checked her bank statements to see if she has accessed her account somehow, and he said no. So, I asked the next obvious question, what clues led them to believe she left the area, and again he said he couldn't say, but then flip flopped again saying they can't go out and actively investigate because it's still considered a missing persons case."

"What!"

"He said any information or witnesses must come to them voluntarily. So, then I switched it back on him. I said, well, if it's considered a cold missing persons case and they aren't actively investigating it, then what's the harm in me looking at the file?"

"What did he say to that?"

"This guy is lying through his teeth, and he did his best to get me out of there asap. When he kept being short and rude with me for asking questions, I told him, if they weren't going to investigate it then at least allow me the courtesy to see what I could come up with. He told me I need to just let the professionals do their job."

"Seriously? What an arrogant punk! What did you say to him?"

"You know me, I like to poke the bear…."

"Yes…I know."

"I told him, if the professionals had done their job, then I wouldn't be standing in his office three years later asking about my cousin, now would I?"

Ellie burst into laughter. "You're absolutely right! You're such a *smart-aleck* Jason, you know that, but you're not wrong for saying it. How did he react?"

"Basically, he politely told me to get out of his office, and they'll call if they find anything."

"Yeah, we heard that one before, but they never call! Do you want me to tell you what I found?"

"Mom, not yet. I'm still driving. This guy really aggravates me. Now, I want to do my own investigation. I'll be home in 30 minutes, but can I get Aunt Lisa or Uncle Clark's phone number? I lost theirs when I got a new phone."

"Why do you want to call Denise's parents?"

"Obviously the Sheriff's department hasn't investigated anything, so I want to start from square one and see what I can come up with. I want to go from where she left the party all the way back to her house. Just start looking. Who knows? Maybe I'll find a clue that explains why no one has found her yet."

"From the sounds of it, looks like you already did. You do know I've heard Aaron has buddies in the Sheriff's office, but I didn't think they would go as far as to smother an investigation. Now that's exactly what it's starting to look like. If I were you, I wouldn't waste time with the husband. From almost the moment Denise went missing, he won't speak to anyone about it. He immediately went out to get the best lawyer money can buy, which was the exact opposite of when Denise needed a lawyer to get custody of her children back. Basically, he got the bottom of the barrel attorney for her, but when his neck is on the line, he might as well of hired Johnnie Cochran. Not to mention, he put up no trespassing signs, and wouldn't even give any information to search teams because he said he was advised not to say anything."

"Seriously? Like that's not a red flag?" Jason says in disgust.

"Like I told you in the beginning, everything points to him, and don't go over to his place alone. He's got a bad temper, hangs around some shady friends, and I just don't

106

want you pushing back on his property. Denise is already missing, and I don't need you to end up the same."

"Mom, did you forget what I used to do for a living?"

"I just want you to be careful out there. That's God's country, and if something happens to you, there are plenty of places they could find to put you without anyone ever knowing and apparently no one willing to find out what happened to you."

"I'm not looking for trouble, I just want to find Denise. If he wants to start something, then," using his best Mr. T. impersonation, "I pity the fool who gets in my way!"

"Jason!" His mother trying to sound non-approving. "I don't think he's dumb enough to try something with you, but I wouldn't put it past him. I'm more concerned about guns. He's got plenty of them, and he would much rather shoot you than get into some brawl."

"Mom, stop worrying! I'm not going out there alone, and I'm not going to start anything with anyone, so relax. That's why I asked for their numbers, so Uncle Clark can go with me and show me around."

"Promise?"

"Yes, mom! Can have their number please?"

Chapter 6

Flashback: Mysterious Mystic

After waiting several hours, Jason is growing restless and impatient. Staring at the number on his ticket, he knows they should have been called long ago. Jason's ego is now getting the better of him. *Doctors don't even make you wait this long to see them.*

Just then, a couple walks in and are immediately called into the back. This is the 25th time Samantha and Jason have been skipped over being called to see the man Samantha's mother convinced them to go see. This being their first time to ever meet an Asian sage, they have no idea what to expect. All Jason can focus on is how long they've already waited. Leaning over in his chair towards Samantha, in a softly lit lobby, Jason rudely whispers to her, "You said this guy calls you back based on your number. We came early so we wouldn't have to wait so long. Why are we being skipped?"

"I don't know."

"Where did your mother find this guy?"

"A friend told her about him."

"Could this guy have found a worse part of town to set up shop? What's up with the all the bodyguards, security fences, cameras, and secrecy? You don't think it's a little overkill?"

"I don't know."

"Have you ever seen this guy before?"

109

"No."

"Then why did you drag me down here? You know I only get one day off a week, and this is how you convince me to spend it?"

"My mom said this guy is really good…and he knows things."

"Great!" Jason sarcastically says a little louder. "I know things too! Maybe I should start a business of charging people to sit around all day and wait to talk to me."

"Shhh!" Samantha warns. "He doesn't charge anything to talk with him."

"What? Who does that? What does he want in return?"

"You can give a donation if you want but he doesn't have a fee."

"Maybe he should start charging and find a better place in town. That's all he does? A good conversationalist?"

"No…Jason, mom said he's some spiritual mystic or something."

"Mystical like David Copperfield or Merlin the Wizard? Give me a break! None of that stuff is real. It's all an illusion!"

"Look…I'm sorry, I shouldn't have brought you here. I know you're tired from running the business. If you want to go, we can go, but my mom was insistent. She said he mentioned you by name the last time she was here."

"My name? How does he know me? I've never met this guy before."

"I know…like I said, he knows things. If you want to go, we can. Otherwise, they don't like it when you talk."

Offended, Jason's voice can now be heard throughout the lobby. "Oh! That's just rich! They're going to get upset with me for whispering, but don't mind having us wait here the entire morning!"

"*Shhhh*...I said keep your voice down!" Samantha warns again.

"No talking please!" one of the security guys instructs in Jason's direction.

"They ask everyone to be quiet out of respect," She reminds him again.

Rolling his eyes and sighing, Jason arrogantly leans back in his chair and starts looking around at the diverse group of people waiting in the lobby. A few were staring at Jason as if he had just broken a major rule, while others were lost in their own thoughts. Not sure why people would be willing to waste their day like this, Jason notices the desperation in their eyes. Observing the room for now the 100th time, he looks again at a hodge-podge of religious looking items everywhere. In the dimly lit building, Jason can see there are things from native American Indian decor, crosses, pictures of Jesus, the Pope, Chinese scrolls, meditating Buddhas, statues of dancing humanoid animals, incense burning, and some strange Asian styled elevator music playing in the background. Seeing all these strange items collected together in one place, gives Jason the creeps. He didn't want to touch anything in fear he might be cursed somehow or possibly become possessed.

Growing up in Southern Baptist and Methodist churches, Jason feels just being in this place was somehow a cardinal sin or possibly sacrilegious. "What religion is this guy anyway?"

"Mom said he's from Tibet, but he doesn't associate to organized religion."

"What? How's that possible?"

"I don't know. She said he knows all religions and even quotes Bible scriptures, but said true sages follow a path of their own...or something like that. I don't know. You can ask when it's our turn."

A few more minutes pass and it feels like an eternity. Jason keeps shifting his feet and body posture loudly, to let others know just how upset he is. Seeing a small group, come in hours after he got there, immediately called to the back, infuriates Jason. *That's it!* Jason thinks. *Who the hell does this guy think he is? We were one of the first ones here! Is he not calling us back because I'm white or something? What a RACIST! He's got me sitting out here on my only day off. I could be home already watching football BUT NOOOOOO! Samantha has to drag me here because her mom believes in supernatural hocus pocus stuff. I've got better things to do than sit around and listen to some old fart tell me what I already know....*"Forget this Samantha, let's go!"

Samantha grabs her purse and water bottle as an old man with long white hair enters the lobby from the back. Jason immediately knows it is the sage because everyone in the room comes to attention and immediately sits upright in their chairs. Bewildered by their behavior, Jason scans the room to see people either clapping, holding their hands together in reverence, giving praises in foreign languages or just saying thank you repeatedly. *What in the world?* Jason thinks. *These people are treating this guy like he's some kind of modern-day Jesus or something!*

Finally revealed, Jason gets to see the mysterious mystic, everyone has come here for. Looking at the thin long hairs of his beard resting on his chest, this guy appears no different than any other average looking, older stereotypical Asian man. Considering how long he has waited, Jason was expecting to see a guy wearing fancy robes, massive and exotic jewelry, a head piece or at least a staff of some kind. Instead, all he gets is a guy wearing regular street clothes without any shoes. This too infuriates Jason. He angrily thinks, *this is it??? I came all this way and sat here this long...for this joker? You gotta be kidding me...*

Before Jason could finish his train of thought, the older Asian sharply breaks the silence, "HEY!" staring at Jason and those nearby. "Please, let me explain something. This is how it works for those who are visiting for their first time. I don't go by the numbers. You are called back when I am told to call you."

This odd remark catches Jason's attention. He thinks to himself again, *if this guy is in charge, then who's telling him when to call people into the back?*

"God," the Asian says looking right at Jason, "tells me who to call back and when."

This makes Jason uneasy. *This is blasphemy! He's probably into some devil work or the devil himself...trying to trick everyone!*

"I'm not the devil," the old man says, but this time he's not looking at Jason. He is peering over the crowd of people still in the lobby but stops when he gets to Jason and intently stares. Jason wonders, *can this dude read my thoughts,* as the unusual man turns his head once more.

"Yes," the old man says but these replies confuse Jason because he's not looking at him but somehow keeps answering the questions in his mind....

NAH! Impossible! Must be coincidence.

"If this is your first time, please raise your hand."

Not wanting to participate in the roll call for new visitors or bring attention to himself, Jason doesn't raise his hand, but Samantha does. The mysterious man scans the room nonchalantly and suddenly stops when he gets back to Jason, who is still defiantly slouched in his chair.

Looking Jason over for a moment, this mystic asks, "Is this not your first time?"

Jason shifts to a more upright position to answer the question. "Yes," he replies.

"I already know," the mystic says as his smile gets even bigger.

In Jason's mind, he thinks, *PLEASE! I've seen it all. He knows I'm new because he's never seen me before. DUH! These guys always have some angle or say something vague to get you to believe anything they tell you. Well, he doesn't know who he's dealing with! The first opportunity I get, I am going to expose this fraud, so Samantha and all these people here won't be fooled into coming back. For making me wait this long, I'm going to...*

As Jason continues his mental rant, the older man looks at him, as his head slowly tilts side to side. His facial expressions seem to change with each new thought Jason has, as if he could hear his words out loud.

Right now, Jason's egotistical mind is a powder keg full of derogatoriness and his sudden thoughts become so disrespectful and so despicable, no one should ever utter them in the presence of others or even write them down. Before he could finish another mental tirade, the mystic interrupts his thoughts once again. He sternly demands, "That's enough!"

People are startled and silent. No one moves a muscle, not even the black cat licking itself in the corner. To make sure everyone can hear the sage, one of the security guards quickly moves to turn off the background music as the smile vanishes from his face.

Again, Jason's mind wanders. *No way! Can he hear me? Alright, if you can hear me, then ask me a question.* After a few moments of dead silence Jason becomes relieved the man hadn't heard what he was thinking. *Laughing in his head. Whew, for a moment there I thought...*

The mystic, somewhat perturbed, looks at him. "Is your name Jason?"

Jason's jaw drops as he realizes his worst fears are true. He feels terrible and embarrassed for how crazy he let his mind wander. He's heard about people who could read minds, but only in comics and superhero movies. *Is this dude legit?*

"How old are you?"

Before Jason can say anything, the mystic quickly answers for him and even says his birthday. "Is that correct?"

Beyond fascinated, Jason responds, "Yes."

"You also just got a speeding ticket."

"No, I didn't." Immediately Jason feels redeemed. *Haha! Got him! I knew he was a phony!*

"YES...you did," the old man insists.

"Nooo...I didn't," Jason defiantly replies.

"I'm not going to argue with you...but yes, you did," the mystic smiles again and says a few more comments before calling Jason and Samantha to join him in the back room of the building.

Whatever! Jason thinks to himself. The rest of the time visiting with this phony sage is pointless and becomes a blur. At this point, Jason goes on mental autopilot, because this mystery man has lost all credibility in his eyes.

Twenty minutes later, they are finally leaving the ghetto-fied, Fort Knox wanna-be building. Stepping over a few homeless people sleeping outside, Jason covers his nose after getting a whiff of rancid urine on the sidewalk.

"This place is nasty!" Jason says to Samantha, as they make their way to their car. "I can't wait to get home and take a shower." As they head towards the car, Jason continues his rant, "I can't believe you brought me here and wasted my day, Samantha! I should go back in and charge him for my taking up my time!"

"What's the problem? He was really nice!"

"Nice, but he's a phony!"

"What?"

"Samantha...I hate to break this to you, but your Asian buddy is quack!"

"How?"

"Seriously? Do I have to remind you?"

"What?"

"THE SPEEDING TICKET???"

Jason couldn't stop thinking about the old man's insistence on a speeding ticket he never received. "Look, I told you this dude was a joke even before we got here! I know these kinds of people. Like everyone else, they're pretending to be some mystic, sage, spiritualist, fortuneteller, or psychic."

"How did he know your brother's and parents' names?"

"That stuff is public information!" Jason argues.

Sarcastically, Samantha retorts, "Right! Like he knew you would be here exactly today and had a file on you in case you suddenly decide to take a trip from Austin and visit him in downtown San Antonio. We didn't make an appointment Jason, so how would he know we would be there ahead of time?"

"Who knows? With his level of security, I'm sure he knows people who can get him anything he wants."

"Jason...if anything...he gave some really helpful advice."

"If I want advice, I'll go see a counselor or shrink!"

"Ok, then explain how he knew our exact birthdays and that your grandparents are deceased?"

"A lucky guess and again, PUBLIC INFORMATION!"

Sighing, Samantha lowers her head in attempts to conceal her smile, but it catches Jason's attention.

"What so funny?"

116

"Nothing."

"What?"

"I'll tell you when you're not so argumentative."

"Samantha!" Jason says using his tone to suggest it's not a good time to toy with him.

Now about 10 yards from their car, Samantha says, "Remember two weeks ago, when you were running late for work...."

"Ok?"

"You told me, you passed a dump truck doing 100 mph, but the officer gave you a ticket for going 80."

Jason comes to a sudden stop with his mouth gaping wide open as he now recalls getting pulled over. *Holy smokes! How could I have forgotten?* Jason thinks in disbelief.

Seeing Jason's bewildered face, Samantha playfully replies, "I told you he was legit!"

"No seriously...Samantha!"

Spinning around almost in a dance of victory, "Yessss?"

"He argued with me about it...."

"Maybe next time you'll believe me," she joyfully teases.

Still in somewhat of a shock and slightly infatuated, Jason shoots a final glance over his shoulder at the shabby industrial building he just left...*Who is this guy?*

The Best Place to Hide
Something Is...

Jason sifts through some papers he printed out a few days ago as Uncle Clark's four door Chevy Silverado hits a large pothole on the country road. The abrupt bump causes Jason's energy drink to splash out onto the center console.

"Whoaa!" Uncle Clarks calls out as he apparently didn't have his eyes fixed on the road.

"Crap!" Jason says to himself as he sees his drink beginning to quickly streak down the sides. "Uncle Clark, do you have any napkins?"

"Yeah...in the glovebox," he replies, noticing the mess. As Jason snatches a few fast-food napkins from underneath the dash, Uncle Clark states, "You shouldn't drink that stuff. It's bad for you!"

"Sorry about that," Jason says trying to wipe up the spill.

"Ah, don't worry about, it happens. Hey, look over here off to the left! This is Denise's neighborhood," he says while quickly doing another double take at the homes as he continues driving on down the main road.

Scanning the neighborhood and surrounding area, Jason compares it to the map he brought and marks the area for reference. "Ok, are you taking me by the friend's home she was at, the night she disappeared?"

"Yeah, she lives down the road quite a way. I also want to show you a few properties we searched and the one place...where the hunter lives...said he smelled a rotting carcass a few days after Denise disappeared. He knew it wasn't an animal coming from the property next door to him."

"Did he go investigate?"

"No, he's a 70-year-old man and said he didn't know of Denise's disappearance until weeks later, and by then, the smell was gone. Do you know who owns that property where the smell was coming from?"

"No." Jason answers.

"You know Aaron's best friend, Randy? His daddy owns it and happens to be a deputy in that county."

"Why isn't the county where she was last seen investigating anything?"

"Denise and Aaron live in San Saba which is a different county than where her friend Trish lives. When we finally gave Aaron an ultimatum to call in Denise's disappearance or we would, San Saba County opened the case."

"Ultimatum?"

"Oh yeah! Your mom didn't tell you?"

"Not that part."

"Your Aunt Lisa gets a call from Aaron, early Monday morning, saying Denise didn't come home and wasn't answering her phone. But Jason, Denise didn't take any clothes, make-up, prescription pills, cigarettes, purse, car keys, or pictures. She left her Explorer at the friend's house after she and Aaron rode home together with their boy, Allen. Aaron said Denise just vanished, but I don't believe it, not for one minute. After Lisa got the call, we called Denise but her phone's off. Then called all her friends and no one had seen her. We knew something must be up, so we called Tina. Tina and I took off work and headed over there. It couldn't have been two hours before her sister and I showed up. The first thing we asked was to see Allen, but Aaron said his mom already drove up and took him home with her."

"I didn't know that."

"Aaron called us around 7 am on Monday to tell us Denise was missing but when we got there around 9 am, grandma already got Allen and was heading back to Louisiana!"

"Hmm." Jason mumbles.

"That's the funny part, just like everything else Aaron was saying. He called us early Monday, but his mother, who lives several hours away in Louisiana, had to have left before midnight on Sunday, to get there before we did. He only told his friend around 6 pm Sunday night Denise left, and the grandma drives straight through the night to pick Allen up?"

"Has Denise ever allowed her kids to do that before?"

"Never. She won't even let the kids stay with us for the weekend, and we live 20 minutes down the road from her."

"That's doesn't seem suspicious at all," Jason sarcastically replies.

"Here's the best part, without even hanging out or sticking around to see if she can help, the mom grabs Allen and makes a 12-hour non-stop round trip. You tell me something fishy isn't going on here! Some people believe Aaron loaded Denise up in his mom's vehicle to take her back as well, but I don't believe it because if she got stopped on the way back, then she gets arrested, and they take Allen away. It's too risky."

"I agree."

"...and when we got there, Jason...boy, Aaron was sweatin' bullets...He was acting all weird and kept fidgeting. When we asked why he hadn't reported Denise missing already, he said he wasn't ready to. That's when Tina climbed down his throat. She said Denise wouldn't take off without at least telling somebody. Tina said, he'd better call it in, or we would. Jason, when he made the phone call, his entire

120

demeanor changed. It looked like he knew he was going to jail. But apparently, everyone knows everybody around here. He has good buddies in the Sheriff's department."

"Sounds like it," Jason replies.

"So, why now?"

"Huh?"

"It's been three years. What made you decide to start looking into this after all this time?"

"Honestly, I've felt guilty that I wasn't able to help out with the initial searches. I was stuck in North Carolina when she went missing and couldn't get back here until now."

"Don't feel guilty, we all understand."

"After having no luck with finding a job and the job market slowing down, I figured I have the perfect opportunity to look into it myself."

"Your mom said you've been struggling to even get a call back."

"Uncle Clark, I've never had a problem getting hired anywhere. Sometimes I would get hired on the spot. Now, they see the military on my resume and won't touch me with a ten-foot pole."

"Is that right?"

"I guess they assume everyone who gets out must have PTSD or be some ticking time bomb. Even the most desperate companies looking for people won't return my calls," Jason says discouragingly.

"You even have a college degree!"

"I know. It's not like I'm applying for some over the top positions either. Just retail management jobs I could do with my eyes closed."

"That's a shame! When we get back, I'll put the word out and see if we can't find you some work."

"I appreciate it! In the meantime, I wanted to see if I could help somehow."

"Well, you need to understand how this area works. Even though there's not too many people living out here, San Saba is no different than big cities."

"How so?"

"The rich and wealthy live by their own rules. Like Aaron, many of them have good friends in the right places. People don't get wealthy by following the rules and abiding by laws. They cheat, steal, and lie to get it. If they get caught, then their buddies get them off the hook. This town's corruption is as crooked as they come, and it's a bunch of snakes keeping Denise's case from moving forward, I just know it!"

"Have you ever thought about getting outsiders to come in and investigate the case, like the F.B.I. or Texas Rangers?"

"I talked to your mother about it, but she said the Sheriff's office has to invite them in to investigate. Even if they were invited, they can't just come in and take over, they can only assist."

"What better way to keep your dealings in-house and away from any checks and balances outside their little network."

"The whole system is screwed up."

Just then, Uncle Clark slows the truck down, "There's Trish's house," he says gravely as he points through the windshield to show Jason. "That's the last place anyone else saw Denise alive, other than Aaron."

Jason knows just being here must be extremely difficult on Uncle Clark. He remains respectively quiet as Uncle Clark shows him several properties near Trish's home already searched. "We searched everywhere..." Uncle Clark begins as his voice cracks a few times.

The painful memory of losing a daughter suddenly reemerges after being successfully suppressed deep within. Regaining his composure, he tries to fight back the tears, "We searched over 26 properties and walked countless acres trying to find any signs of Denise. I can't tell you how many people called us with clues, and we checked out every last one..." Uncle Clark clears his throat as a few tears escape, landing on his black Harley Davidson shirt.

"I know it must be tough, Uncle Clark. That's why I'm here. I want to help you, Aunt Lisa, and Tina finally have some closure."

"I wouldn't wish this pain on my worst enemy, and I hope to God you never have to go through what we have. I know Aaron did it...not a doubt in my mind. The stress of not knowing where she is has destroyed me so bad, I had to retire from my job. Aunt Lisa doesn't sleep anymore, and she is driving herself crazy spending countless hours talking to people online, seeing if anyone knows anything, just looking for any clues."

Jason can see the despair and desperation in his uncle's eyes. He struggles to find the right words to console his uncle's anguish. Having a daughter as well, Jason can't imagine the pain he must be feeling... knowing your daughter must be out there...somewhere...even close by...without a trace or clue how to find her."

"I'm very sorry, Uncle Clark, to hear all of this, and I'm going to do what I can."

"Yeah, we've heard that too. I can't tell you how many people have come in to help and after a while they give up and still no sign of Denise. I must be honest with you, Jason, me being out here again just lights me up. It's been so hard. I was just getting to a place of finding some peace with all this, and then you come in now...stirring all this back up again…it's like ripping off a giant band-aid on a broken heart," his uncle says while angrily cutting his eyes at Jason. As they come to a stop at a four-way intersection to go home, Jason remains quiet. His uncle continues, "I'll help where I can, but I don't know how long my body can hold out doing any more searches like this, physically or mentally. All I know is, I don't want to die never knowing what happened to my little girl."

As they sit in silence for a few moments, listening to the diesel engine churning, and uncomfortably staring at each other, a gust of wind reveals a bright light that shines in Jason's eyes. From the tree line over his uncle's shoulder, Jason notices something metallic in the nearby wood lines. "Is that a building or barn behind those trees? I see something."

Turning to look out his driver window, Uncle Clark takes a quick glance and says, "Nah, that's all woods and brush line back there."

"Did you guys search that property?"

"Nah. There's no way to get in there. It's all fenced up and so thick Aaron wouldn't be able to squeeze through those tightly packed trees."

"I don't know, Uncle Clark, something shiny flashed in the trees when that gust of wind just blew. Can we turn in and take a closer look since we're already out here? I want to leave no stone unturned."

"Alright," he replies steering the truck left, rather than right to head back home. "I'm telling you, there ain't no way, even if you wanted to, no one could get in there. There's no driveway, no gate or anything. Just straight barbed wire all the way around."

As they drive a few hundred yards down the road, Jason could see what his uncle explained. "I guess you're right, I just wanted to check. Uncle Clark, it's getting late, why don't we just head back."

"Ok, but I don't think there is a turnaround or driveway on this road for some while."

"What's that?" Jason asks in almost disbelief.

Without needing to be asked, Uncle Clark turns into a well concealed entrance to the wooded property. Curious, Uncle Clark steers his one-ton pick-up onto the hidden pathway and follows it into the wood line. "What in the hell?" Uncle Clark shockingly exclaims. While he gazes at piles of trash lying about, he comes to a stop in front of a gate at the second fence.

"Man! You could hide a million bodies in here and no one would ever know! I can't tell you how many times we have passed by this place, and I've never seen this entrance before. We even wrote this place off as uncleared land."

"Do you see that?" Jason points to a silver sheet metal reflection seeping through the trees. I told you I saw something."

"YOU'RE RIGHT!"

Suddenly Jason has a thought, as his uncle is already discussing what they need to do to put together another search. Knowing his uncle's condition, Jason could only think of one thing. "Uncle Clark, to not waste any more valuable time and walking every square inch of this countryside, I might know someone who could help."

"You do? Who? Do they have special equipment or something?"

"Well, sort of…I know this might not be what you are used to, but I know someone that if anyone could find Denise, it would be this guy."

"We don't have money to pay anyone to come out here. We drained our savings looking for Denise."

"No…it's not like that. This guy knows things."

"Knows things?"

"Yeah, you're going to have to trust me on this, but he doesn't charge anything. I think we need his help, he could pinpoint and tell us exactly where she. I honestly feel stupid I didn't think of it sooner. If I'm wrong, no one's out anything, but…if I'm right…that would save us a lot of time and resources."

"Well…Yeah! Let's call him!"

"I don't have his number, but I know where to find him."

"Huh? Is he psychic or something? We had a few of those contact us before but nothing really came of it."

"Not exactly. It's hard to explain, and I don't want to go into details right now, but if anyone would know where Denise is, then it's this guy."

"Sure, I'm in!"

"Good, let's head back. I can probably get in contact with him this evening."

"Alright, but before we go, I want to take a quick look around," Uncle Clark says shaking his head in disbelief. "I want to see if I can spot anything recognizable beyond the second fence line."

Not wanting to trespass, they find a sign with a number on it. "Looks like this property is for sale," Jason tells his uncle.

"Would you just look at all this junk piled along here. It must have taken years to get like this."

"You ready to go? It's getting dark, and I'm not sure I want to be near this place when the sun goes down," Jason suggests.

As well hidden and eerie as this place is, Jason feels uneasy being out here. Hopping back into the truck, Uncle Clark manages to get turned around to head back. "It still blows my mind we never saw this place before."

"There are no coincidences," Jason recites.

126

Ironically and true to his words, the two men can hear multiple fast approaching vehicles abruptly stop on the other side of the tree line. As they round the turn and the main road becomes visible again, Uncle Clark skids to a stop.

"What in God's name is all this about?" As Jason and Clark look at each other with confusion, they slowly look back to see four cop cars blocking the property entrance to the main road.

"Like I was saying Uncle Clark…No coincidences."

"You got that right…"

Chapter 7

Lowered Expectations

<u>March 2018</u>

"Jason, relax! At least, give them a chance," Jason's mother says trying to calm him down.

"This is unbelievable! We're the ones who told them about this place, and they won't even let us join the search! Did they make y'all sit out when you searched the other properties?"

"No, we were just using local volunteers, friends, and family to search. These people are the real deal."

"Real deal?" Jason mockingly replies. "I was expecting ground penetrating radar, cadaver dogs, or some C.S.I. kind of stuff. Instead, we get a rag-tag team of kids, wearing safety vests, walking around with poker rods. With as much debris as there is on the property, there would be no way of knowing if they've found anything or not."

"Cool your jets! We have to take what we can get, and besides, there is a cadaver dog inbound. I just spoke to the handler when you were talking with the Sheriff. He said he would be here in less than 30 minutes. What did the Sheriff have to say?"

Pointing to the two San Saba deputies and the Sheriff down the road, closer to the property's entrance, Jason asks, "Did they come out on other searches or is this their first time as well?"

"Since this is considered an official search, they must be present in case something is found, and they need to preserve the scene."

"I seriously doubt that."

"Jason, what did he say to you?"

"As soon as he got here, he pulls me off to the side and says, 'If they find Denise, it doesn't automatically imply Aaron is guilty.'"

"Why would he say that to you?"

"No clue, but I was expecting him to say more along the lines of, 'I hope we find her, and if she is found, we will do all we can to get to the bottom of this.' Instead, he thinks it's appropriate to put out a disclaimer to immediately protect Aaron."

"No kidding."

"I don't trust that guy, mom!"

Just then, a short brunette with highlights makes her way towards Jason and Ellie. The woman's light complexion suggests she doesn't go outside much, and her frail figure implies she must not be from this area. Also, from the woman's style of clothing, Jason presumes she must be in her mid to late 30's. "HEYYYY Lydia! Long time no see!" Ellie says to the woman over the noise of few local onlookers slowly driving by.

"Ellie! Oh my God!" the woman hollers back over the noisy cars and trucks on the main road. "It's so good to see you again! It sucks we have to keep meeting under these circumstances!"

"I know. Hey, I don't think you two have met, but this is my son, Jason!"

"Hi, Jason! It's so good to finally meet you! I heard so many stories about you from the family, Denise, and Tina. It's good to finally put a face to a name."

"You too," Jason says slightly annoyed by Lydia's fake morning enthusiasm. *No one's ever this happy this early in the morning,* he sarcastically thinks to himself.

"Jason…" Ellie explains, "Lydia is a long-time friend of both Tina and Denise. She's the one keeping all the records, organizing the searches, and even helped to create Facebook pages for Denise after she went missing."

Jason nods to suggest he approves but looks back down the road at the San Saba deputies and Sheriff glaring back at him. He notices how incredibly close they are huddled to each other in quiet conversation, and then slowly turn their backs to Jason.

"Oh…don't mind him," his mother says, referring to Jason's rude manners and lack of interest in Lydia's arrival. "He's a little grumpy this morning. The Sheriff informed us they won't let friends or family of Denise participate in the search."

"I didn't know that either," Lydia replies.

"Well, we can all hope and pray, today is the day! It's been three long years, and her kids need to know what happened to their mother."

"Oh, don't get me started on that!" Uncle Clark says loudly after overhearing their conversation from the cab of his truck. With the tailgate down and facing the road, all three turn their attention to Clark, as he hops out. Happy to see his uncle join the conversation, Clark proclaims, "Aaron's been tellin' them kids their mom is nothing but a whore and ran off with another man. I sure hope we find Denise today because I can't wait to see the look on his face when they lock him up and throw away the key."

"According to the Sheriff, he made it abundantly clear, if we find Denise, it doesn't immediately make Aaron a suspect," Ellie informs him.

"I heard that too! What do we gotta do to get people to do their job around here? They're not out searching, and it was Jason and I who found this property. For him to say that...I just want to call some news stations here and have them camp out. Maybe it will put the pressure on their department to actually do something."

"Local stations would probably do a better job of that. National new stations read scripts rather than report news," Jason edges in.

"It wouldn't surprise me if they had them paid off as well. Man, this whole area is crooked and if you would've told me this before Denise disappeared, I would've thought you're some whack-a-do, but after what I've seen, this is insane," Clark says discouragingly.

"It's people like them who give law enforcement a bad name," Ellie adds.

"Sad part is not everyone is rotten, but I know how the game works. I don't care if it's law enforcement, government, or even the news, everyone has dirt on each other. They wait for the golden opportunity and then exploit whoever, to get what they want. People trying to do good in this world and provide for their families are forced to do things they don't want to. They fear they'll lose their job or ruin their career if someone leaked private information about them to the public," Jason conveys.

Angered, Clark raises his voice, "People can't make an honest living anymore and live comfortably. You got local law enforcement and officials taking bribes to make things unfair for the rest of us. Things have gotten so unfair, and the rewards are so high for not playing by the rules, it's rubbin' off on others. If they are allowed to get away with it, why would anyone else want to play by the rules? It just keeps 'em poor or barely able to make ends meet. If politicians actually worked for the people to make our country fair so we can all get rich, like they're supposed to, people wouldn't be desperate enough to commit crimes."

"It's not that they don't work for us, it's the ones at the top of the pyramid in the political arena. They've been in the game for decades and making pacts with other politicians to write laws the way they want. Then they block those who are trying to make a difference."

"TERM LIMITS!" Ellie hollers out, pretending she is giving an answer on a game show. "I've been sayin' it for years. If the president has term limits, then politicians need the same."

"Agreed," Jason comments.

"Because they don't, they're out there becoming millionaires and even billionaires, living like playboys, off taxpayers' money while the rest of us are struggling," Ellie finishes.

Laughing, Jason suggests, "The Wild West never ended. In this country, it's a free for all. People are still just doing whatever they can get away with because the rewards severely outweigh the penalties for being honest. It's just like the Iran-Contra Affair, but it doesn't stop there. Now we have a war on drugs but who do you think is supplying and flooding our streets with 'em?"

"The same ones writing the laws!" Clarks responds. "That's why they say Aaron and his buddies are involved in selling drugs. From what I understand, I think Denise was going to rat him out to get her kids back. CPS wouldn't allow her to get her kids back if Aaron was still there. With him out of the way, she had a fighting chance, but look what happened to her."

Lydia interjects, "You know, people are just a reflection of the leadership in this country, and it shows."

Angered again, Clark retorts, "Well, the government harasses the little guy over small amounts of money while the wealthy and corporations go unchecked or barely monitored."

"That's not true. They tax corporations and the wealthy just like everybody else," Ellie contests.

"No, mom, Uncle Clark is right. Corporations hide or conceal their true value and net worth. They only report 20-30% of their true value to avoid taxation and other legal constraints."

"What?" Lydia exclaims. "Then can we start only reporting 20% of our income to the IRS?"

"No! Like I said, the government and IRS would be all over you like white on rice, on a paper plate, in a snowstorm, for trying to hide a few thousand dollars, and then charge you with a felony. They pay no mind to the millionaires and billionaires who keep moving money around like a shell game."

"That's really unfair!" Lydia remarks. "They can play hide and seek, but we can't, huh?" She sarcastically replies.

"People are tired of officials telling us to do as they say but not as they do," Jason comments.

"People are tired of laws protecting big businesses and the wealthy, while exploiting those living paycheck to paycheck."

"Don't let anyone fool you, corporations, insurance companies, and banks make the rules in this country, not the politicians," Clark replies.

Jason backs Clark's statement, "Did you know over 50 of the largest economies in this world are run by corporations...not the government?"

Clark resumes, "With the rise in corporate level crime, the rich and wealthy live by a different set of rules. They lie, cheat, and steal from the system and are grandly rewarded for it. Meanwhile, those who pay their taxes and obey the law, are following a system designed for only a small few to ever reach the top."

"Then why doesn't someone do something about it?" Ellie chimes back.

Jason responds, "The low and middle working class ignore politics, and when something happens that they don't like, they sit back expecting the same ones who created the problem to correct themselves. Then, they keep voting in people who are secretly working against our economic and social interest. They're only interested in what they say and not watching what they're doing."

"How so?"

Clark is quick on the draw, "We are supposedly a land that despises socialism and communism, yet our biggest international trade partners are China and Vietnam! They send our factories, corporations, and our good paying jobs over there, so they can make more profits. WE FUND AND SLEEP WITH THE ENEMY!" Clark excitedly exclaims. "That's like going into business with Al-Qaeda because they make cheap products. Then give all their buddies the good jobs and benefits, while selling the American public a delusional dream, that anyone can get rich too if they work hard. It's all a hypocritical scam! They live in luxury while the rest of us are rotting away in substandard living."

Moved by Clark's passion and enthusiasm, Lydia immediate shouts, "AMEN!"

"Then, they send our children to fight wars for corporate interests, who are secretly funding both sides to fight. Then use law enforcement and the legal system to protect their interests stateside from us," Jason adds.

"I swear! When you two get together," Ellie starts in before Clark interrupts.

"If rules, laws, and taxes were fair, people were happy, and living comfortably, then there would be less of a need for those like Aaron and his buddies, wanting to be mixed up in dangerous get rich quick schemes."

Jumping in, Jason says, "The government used to raise money through tariffs and import duties, but now the individual person pays 40% of their total income in taxes to the IRS, while businesses only pay a measly 10% collectively."

"We've been lied to and sold out. Everyone is too busy following rules, but few have stopped and asked, to whom do these laws apply to? The IRS only has authority to tax income on people who live in the Virgin Islands, Guam, Puerto Rico, Washington D.C., and American Samoa. You are not allowed as Citizens of Several States or those who live in the 50 states, to file a 1040 ever!" Clark elaborates.

"No way!" Ellie objects. "Now you are just being ridiculous!"

"Oh yeah," Clark argues back, while opening his phone. "Look for yourself!" Clark opens a page that reads **26 U.S. Code § 7851 - Applicability of revenue laws.** "Right here, it even tells you Chapter 1, 2, 3, 6, 7, 9 11, 12, 13, 15, 25, and most importantly the ones that apply to you Chapter 26, 27, 28, and so on, of the Internal Revenue Code of 1939. They have been repealed or revoked, yet they are still locking people up, taking their homes, garnishing wages, and collecting money you give them. They claim it as a gift from you to them, so they can do whatever they would like to without having to follow strict guidelines."

Jason comments, "This makes sense because the people are now conditioned to feel this is their civic duty to support the government from their own pocket, rather than business and imports carrying this burden. We work as individuals in this country, rather than cohesive communities because of it."

"Yeah, they've placed the responsibility for federal, state, and local taxes wrongfully on the American people and it has created competition amongst each other and everyone working for themselves. It's people trying to figure out how to get rich on their own, rather than working together to make progress."

"Isn't that the American Dream?" Ellie reminds Clark.

"Mom, you wouldn't expect everyone to be good farmers now, would you? Not without first telling them how to do it or making sure they have the equipment and training they need to do so, right? How would they know how to make a living? It's no different when it comes to making money. You either know what you are doing or not," Jason responds.

"I will give you that," Ellie agrees.

"Otherwise, people don't know what they are doing," Clark finishes.

Jason replies, "I came across a good read the other day, and it highlights in every good society throughout the ages, they assign people to roles they are good at and then trade fairly amongst each other. No one is valued as more important than another because they are all needed to produce a successful society."

"So much for wise words these days," Lydia comments.

"Now we got these morons in charge exploiting others out of their homes, businesses, and livelihoods, to horde it for themselves."

"They're not morons, Uncle Clark. They know exactly what they're doing."

"I seriously doubt that!" he contests.

"Well, someone's fired up this morning!" Ellie teases Clark.

Playing devil's advocate, Jason argues, "We can't pin all the unfairness and financial inequality solely on the politicians' shoulders. It's not like we're helping ourselves to close the gap."

"How can you if the system is rigged?" Clark disbelievingly asks.

"Maybe we can't, but we can't sit around waiting for things to be fair either before taking action. Most people borrow money to get into debt or blow their paychecks on entertainment and excitement, while the rich use loans to invest into businesses, real estate, and assets that gain value," Jason divulges.

"How can you invest if you don't have any money in the first place?" Lydia curiously asks.

"They use other people's money to get rich, and they don't buy a bunch of crap they don't need. They would rather have money than a bunch of stuff."

"Our country worships money," Ellie sadly remarks.

"It's the new religion, Ellie," Clark condemns.

"Don't say that! Not everyone is obsessed with money," Ellie argues.

"I didn't say obsessed. Money has been placed before consideration of others."

Throwing in another historical fact, Jason says, "Philosophers used to call that being humane. Who wants to follow rules or laws if you're being cheated and taken advantage of by your own leaders and then want to grill you about ethics and values?"

"Speaking of unscrupulous behavior," Clark says while looking at Lydia, "did anyone tell you what happened the last time we were out here?"

Concerned, Lydia inquires, "No! What happened?"

"Jason and I just pulled into the property's entrance way over there," Clark points in the direction where volunteer searchers are now disappearing into the wood lines. "We weren't here even five minutes before four cop cars came screeching up on us and blocked us in!"

Gasping, "NO WAY! Four?" she responds.

Clark shouts, "Jason, tell her what you told the officer after they took our ID cards!"

Jason turns his head towards Lydia. "Like Uncle Clark said, we were here for maybe a few minutes, and we got swarmed by the cops like they were doing a drug raid. They told us to get out of the truck and checked our IDs. I asked them how they even knew we were out here because we were in the wood lines. They said an anonymous person tipped them off to illegal dumping on this property."

"Lydia, there's trash everywhere out here!" Clark booms.

"So, I looked at the cop and said, 'Was that call from 1992 because from the looks of it, you boys are about two decades too late.'"

The group laughs. Ellie shaking her head in disproval at her son, "Good thing they can't arrest people for their mouth, because you would already have 20 lifetime sentences!"

"Then I asked if it was a slow day, and he asked why. I told him, even if we were dumping trash, why does it take their entire police force to come check it out?"

Clark laughing and speaking loudly, "YOU SHOULD HAVE SEEN THE LOOK ON THAT DUDE'S FACE!" hysterically laughing now.

"You've never been shy to call it like it is," Ellie remarks smiling at Jason.

"Ellie…" Clark says with overexuberance to finish the story, "When Jason said that they were all fiddlin' around like they had ants in their pants! After we explained the situation and he showed them his military ID, they couldn't hightail it out of here fast enough!" Hysterically laughing again. "Bunch of morons!"

They all share a much-needed laugh as they begin to reminisce memories with Denise while waiting for the handler to arrive with his dog. About 30 minutes later, an old Nissan Pathfinder arrives with a chocolate lab in the back.

"I think this is our guy," Ellie says, hopping down from Clark's tailgate. "They say this dog is really good. The handler is from this area and drove all the way here from a case he was working in Mississippi, just to help us out. You guys sit tight, and I'll go fill him in on the situation."

Jason watches his mother cross the street and make her way down the road to the newly arrived vehicle. A tiny older man gets out of the SUV. Jason watches his mom greet him and strike up a friendly conversation. This goes on for a few minutes until Ellie points to the San Saba Sheriff, who is waving the handler over to them. After the older, sloppily dressed man reaches the group of law enforcement officials, Jason intently watches the Sheriff lean over and whisper into the man's ear. Snapping backwards suddenly, the olive complexion of the man's skin soon turns pale. A few quick exchanges of heated words send the man hastily retreating to his vehicle. Without stopping to explain to Ellie, the man walks right past his mother and beelines straight for his vehicle. With a look of confusion, Ellie approaches the handler's Pathfinder, already started and in gear. Rolling his window down to speak momentarily to her, he then speeds off down the road.

The commotion gets Clark's attention, "What the hell's goin' on? Where's he going?"

Alarmed, Jason replies, "I don't know, but it doesn't look good," as his mother is angrily speed walking back.

"Where's he going, Ellie?" Clarks shouts.

Not wanting to shout back, Ellie waits until she rejoins the group before answering. "I don't know what's going on, but as soon as I said the Sheriff wanted to talk to him, his entire attitude changed. When he saw him, it was almost like he was surprised and scared at the same time. When he came back, he walked right past me without saying a word and got in his vehicle. He rolled his window down and got short with me. There must be some bad blood between those two because he asked why no one bothered to tell him the Sheriff would be out here. I told him I didn't know there was a problem, and he said the only reason he agreed to come here was the property is outside of San Saba's jurisdiction."

"So much for a thorough search and investigation," Jason disappointedly states. Perplexed, Jason looks in the direction of the San Saba Sheriff, only to see the Sheriff staring directly back at him with a subtle smile.

Chapter 8

Loyalty Only Goes So Far

April 2018

"Are you Randy?" Jason calls out to a heavier set guy sitting at a picnic table.

Just outside of a truck stop, near Lometa, TX, 20 miles east of San Saba, a man in his early 30's and lost in contemplation looks up at Jason. Randy is wearing a long-sleeved plaid button-down shirt, a faded tan cowboy hat, and boots.

"Yep, that's me!" Randy says, trying to suddenly cheer up.

Jason sits down across the table from Randy and takes out a black voice recorder. "You don't mind if I use this do you?"

"Go right ahead! You're going to need it with what I have to say."

"Thanks for agreeing to meet with me," Jason says to Randy, who drove 60 miles from Brady, TX, a town West of San Saba, in McCullough County, where Denise was last seen.

"No problem, and I appreciate you trying to be discreet about me meeting up with you," Randy replies.

"It's the least I could do."

"You were in the service, huh?" Randy quickly asks, figuring his knowledge of Jason's career might somehow impress him.

"How'd you know that?" Jason inquires.

Gloating, Randy replies, "I was friends with Denise and…word travels fast in small towns. People get curious when a man of your size goes around asking questions. It's hard to miss someone like you in a town that's never seen the inside of a gym before!"

Jason laughs at Randy's attempts of flattery.

"But bear in mind," Randy says, "it also seems you've created quite a few wakes for yourself."

"How so?"

"Just keep a close watch on who is around you is all I'm saying. This might be a small town, but this is more than just Denise's disappearance. She got caught up right in the crossfire of a bad situation."

"Well, I truly appreciate you talking to me, and knowing Aaron is your best friend, I have to admit, I'm kind of surprised you're willing to talk. Now, it's no mystery people have accused Aaron of foul play, but I'm here to find Denise."

"Accused? Look, I've known that kid since we were in diapers…I know he did it!"

"What?" Jason replies, shocked at Randy's boldness to tell on his best friend. Curious as to what else he might say, Jason asks, "How do you know? Did you talk with the Sheriff's office?"

"Ha! I'm not trying to get myself into trouble, but the Sheriff's department in Aaron's town ain't gonna do nothing to solve Denise's case."

"What do you mean?"

"Look, I'm not one to be a rat, but after Aaron told us Denise left him and was gone for good, I knew he was lying!"

"How?

"I'll put it this way, when the cops confiscated our phones, I just knew…with what was on them…we were both going to jail."

"What happened? What was on them?" Jason probes.

"Stuff I don't care to share man, but the cops didn't do a thing! No one even bothered to call me to come pick up my phone. I had to go to them three months later, and when I did, they told me both our phones got destroyed in the process. What are the odds of that happening especially on the same case?"

"How did they get destroyed?"

"When the police take your phone, they do one of those cellphone dumps at the station, to pull the information out. By some mysterious circumstance, the person in charge of extracting information somehow damaged both our phones."

"Really?"

"Man, I don't think you understand…Aaron knows the right people. I've been his best friend all these years, but now we don't hang out or talk."

"Why not?"

"Truth is…I'm scared to."

"If you guys are such good friends, what are you afraid of?"

"After Denise went missing…he changed. He ain't the Aaron I knew. Yeah, we're a different breed than what you might call normal, but I don't recognize him anymore."

Pulling a map from his back pocket, Jason points to the location where Denise is suspected to be, "Do you know anything about this property?"

"Oh, yeah!" Randy laughs. "We all know that place! That's where the locals throw their trash or use as a place to sleep off a late night of drinking at the bar. You drive in and no one knows you're there." Silence takes over as Randy is suddenly trying to piece together a forgotten memory. "Come to think of it…well, before I tell you that, I need to explain something else first."

145

"Ok."

"Growing up, me and Aaron were what you might call...morbid children." A look of confusion spreads over Jason's face. "See, Aaron and I loved to watch all those crime shows and horror movies growing up. We loved them so much, we started our own little game of who could come up with the best place and way to dispose of a dead body."

"Most kids enjoy playing sports or collecting things."

"Yeah, like I said...we were morbid children. I needed to tell you that first, so you can understand this...one of Aaron's places to hide a body was this property. He kept bragging he found the perfect spot there. He said there is one big tree which is different from the others. Aaron told me, he could easily take a back-hoe right up to it and dig deep enough to dump the body underneath the roots. He said no one would ever know."

"Did he say anything else about this tree?"

"Let me think..."

"Take your time."

After a long pause, "No. Nothing specific comes to mind...just remember him saying it was different. We have lots of pecan trees out here so maybe the one he's talkin' about could be a mesquite or oak tree or something like that."

"Has Aaron tried to contact you recently?"

"Like I said, we keep our distance."

"What can you tell me about the friend who was throwing the party on the night of Denise's disappearance?"

"Trish? That's another weird thing...weeks after Denise vanished, she up and left to somewhere in Oklahoma."

"Left?"

"As soon as things started to hit the fan, she sold everything off and bolted. If you want, I can give you her number and you can ask her for yourself."

146

"Thanks," Jason replies as Randy uses Jason's pen to write her number down on a nearby napkin. "She was next on my list to get in touch with."

"I'm curious though, why were you asking about this specific property? Did you find something?"

Jason, not fully trusting Randy, and not wanting to give too many details away, replies, "We have a few clues leading us there."

"They've already searched that place, ya know?"

"Who did?"

"The San Saba Sheriff's office," Randy answers.

"When?"

"Right after Denise went missing."

"They did? I was told no one stepped foot on it until we did."

Sneering, "Who told you that?"

"Denise's parents."

"No, man, that was the first place they started looking. Here's another mystery for you. The lead detective was hot on the trail to finding Denise and was searching this exact property. The detective did a cellphone trace on Aaron's phone the night she supposedly disappeared and said his cell phone pinged right in front of the property for a long time, right after they left the party."

"How do you know this?"

"Man, like I said, it's a small town and people talk."

"Oh, so just word of mouth then?"

"I'm sure, by now, you know my dad's a cop in our town, right?"

"Yeah, no offense, but I did a little homework on you before coming here."

"None taken. Well, you might also have noticed I have a criminal record."

"Yeah, I saw that too."

"And you probably seen some of those records are sealed, right?"

"Yeah."

"Well let's just say, it's good to have family in law enforcement. It was a bogus allegation anyways. I didn't do it."

"Well, how does this explain how you know about the search?" Jason inquires.

"The detective had to first call my dad's office to get approval to search in our county. When my dad found out my friend was under investigation, he told me what they already had on Aaron and said, when they find the body, it's a done deal. My dad would beat me with a rubber hose if he knew I was talking to you like this."

"Why?"

"Him being a cop, I'm sure he called in a favor at the San Saba Sheriff's office, and had those phones taken care of. I don't know this as fact, but I do know how it works around here. They cover for each other, especially if friends or family are involved."

"So, the detective did a search?"

"Yeah, he came out with a few guys the first time but it's a big property. It's like 50 acres or something, so he went back to recruit more help. I heard he was putting together a big search team. Anyway, before he was able to get back out here, he was let go."

"Do you remember anything else unusual with Aaron around the time before or after Denise went missing?"

"Man, there ain't enough hours in the day to explain how odd this kid was acting."

"Could you explain?"

"Sure. For starters, Aaron was trying to provide some alibi for Sunday morning. The morning after Denise and him drove home angry together, Aaron was up early and already back over here wanting me and another friend from that party, to go hang out at a bar."

"I didn't know bars were open that early on a Sunday," Jason replies, not fully buying Randy's story.

"It wasn't. A friend of his owns the joint and was already there to unlock it. We went in and literally just sat around for hours."

"It's strange but how does that prove anything?"

"Did I mention, before we got there, Aaron had already taken their youngest boy to his real dad's house?" Randy adds.

"No."

"He did, and then came to meet up with us. First off, that must have been like 7 am when he dropped that kid off, on a Sunday."

"That is a little weird. Has he ever done anything like this before?"

Flustered, "Those kids never left Denise's side, and she definitely wouldn't let Aaron take her child, by himself to his alcoholic dad's house, after Aaron beat the crap out of her other two."

"I figured, but I had to ask."

"Secondly, Aaron has two dads. He has his real dad and Jack Dimes. He doesn't talk to birth daddy because he's a complete drunk, and I can't remember seeing him sober."

"What do you know about Jack Dimes?"

"Well, he isn't someone who I would call a model citizen but he kinda unofficially adopted Aaron when he was a little boy. He helped to raise Aaron by taking him under his wing. Even though Jack is a former police officer, there are several stories going around about him, about people coming up missing, if you catch my drift."

"So, Aaron dropped Allen off at 7 in the morning to his real dad's place, after Denise was last seen?"

"Yeah, but the funny part is, for Aaron to drop the kid off and be at Trish's by eight, meant he would have had to leave his house around 6-6:30 in the morning."

"I thought country folk get up bright and early," Jason mocks.

"Not Aaron. He'd be late to his own funeral! Have you ever tried getting up early when you're smashed or hungover?"

"I might know a thing or two about it," Jason smirks, hinting to his time in service.

"Then you know what it's like, but if you ain't gettin' paid to get up at the crack of dawn, you're sleeping in!"

"You were at the party, right?"

"Yes, sir!"

"Did you stay the night or drive home?"

"I crashed at Trish's, but guess who's calling my phone and showed up at 8 am to wake me and our cripple friend up? Aaron did. He took us to a bar while I was trying to sleep it off...but in this town, when a friend calls, you go."

"If the bar was closed, wouldn't that be suspicious?"

"Aaron said if anybody asks what we were doing there, he wanted us to say we were there to move furniture and chairs. There ain't but a few chairs in the place, and I knew no one would believe it took all three of us to get the job done without looking suspicious. Especially since one of us is a cripple. How the hell was he gonna help? Do you see what I'm getting at?"

"Yeah. What did you guys do then while you were at the bar?"

"We played some pool and darts but mostly just sat around. I asked why we were really there, and he wouldn't say."

Suspicious, Jason redirects, "He's your best friend. Why wouldn't he tell you?"

"That's what I'm getting at. We tell each other everything! From the girls we date, our dark secrets, deepest fears…I mean everything, but this time, he wouldn't say a word. The oddest part was he kept asking us to tell him when it was 3:15." Randy impersonates Aaron "'Is it 3:15 yet? Is it 3:15? How about now?' All morning we had to listen to him asking about 3:15, and when it arrived, all he said was, 'ok.' He wouldn't tell me what was so important about the time. Do you know anything about it?"

"No, but I'll see if anything pops up from the other people I talk to. I have to ask…seeing that you were around Denise a lot more than I was…was she using drugs?"

Chuckling, "No. We used to make fun of her just because she almost never drank. If she did, it must have been a blue moon or what not. With her being a momma, she also tried several times to quit smoking." As Randy was about to say more, he notices a car pulling into the gas station and quickly lowers his head until he was certain it wasn't someone he recognized.

Jason waits a few moments until Randy feels safe before asking, "What about you and Aaron? Are you guys using or selling drugs?"

"I won't answer that on tape. Let's just say I'm finally getting cleaned up and my life back together after Denise went missing."

"Was there anything else that stood out to you about Denise missing?"

"I could go on all day, man…it was just one thing after another. For instance, after we left the bar and Aaron drove us back to Trish's house, she came outside worried about Denise. She had called her several times to come pick her two boys up, but Denise wasn't answering her phone. When I called her, it was going straight to voicemail, but I know her. Her phone is either in her hand or on a charger."

"Wasn't her vehicle still there since Denise and Aaron drove home together, after he showed up?"

"Yeah," Randy confirms.

"Why wouldn't she just take her own ride home?"

"I can't tell you what I don't know. What I do know is, she decided to ride home with him and left her ride at Trish's."

"What time did you get back to Trish's house that Sunday afternoon?"

"Late. We didn't get back until almost five."

"So, Denise's kids were there all day, her phone's off, and her vehicle is there as well…then what happened?"

"Aaron said he would go home and bring her back. He leaves and less than 45 minutes later, he's back there, but in a friend's vehicle with someone else."

"Isn't it at least a 30-minute drive, one way, from Denise's house to Trish's?"

"You see! Aaron left around 5 was back around 5:45 with another friend, and in a different vehicle. Trish asked where Denise was, and he said…and I quote…'You don't have to ever worry about seeing her again. Denise is gone for good.' Then he said, 'she's a flake, so you don't have to worry about her calling either.' Immediately, we were all thinking the same thing you're probably thinking…"

"Like how he had enough time to make it home, look around, and know for certain she left permanently, and then drive to a friend's, swap vehicles, and make it back to her house in 45 minutes?"

"EXACTLY!" Randy exclaims.

"Before coming here, I heard about this friend and did a MapQuest for drive times to the location of his friend's place. It's slightly out of the way, but unless he was doing over 100 mph in 45 mph speed limits and running every stop sign from here to there, he still wouldn't have had time to

152

make it back so quickly. That doesn't include time to park, look around for Denise, and then drive to the friend's house. Yeah, his story doesn't compute."

Intrigued, "You are pretty good! I did what you are doing now, when Aaron said she disappeared, but I didn't think to map out the drive."

"I'm just retracing every detail carefully because something was missed. Otherwise, Denise would have been found already."

"True. Even if she left like Aaron said, how could she leave without a ride? Even if she planned on leaving, she wouldn't have skipped out without Allen. Knowing her, she'd be over here instead, chewing Aaron out for leaving her kid over there with his dad. Denise rarely dislikes people, but she hated Aaron's dad."

Jason, having already picked up on a few inconsistencies with Randy's story, probes a little more, "Answer me this…if you didn't know what Aaron was up to, then why would you say you would have gotten in trouble if Aaron isn't guilty?"

Laughing, "Man, you and Denise got to be cousins."

"Why is that?"

Randy proclaims, "That girl was a human lie detector test! She knew when people were trying to pull a fast one on her and wasn't afraid to say something either. You couldn't get anything past Denise, even if you tried. You're just like her or the other way around."

"…and the phones?" Jason persists.

"Look all I can say is…and I've probably said too much already…but if you saw what was on those phone messages…we wouldn't be having this conversation right here and now. We'd be talking on phones through plexiglass, with me wearing an orange jumpsuit. That's all I'm saying."

A long pause arises between the two. "Look man, I hope you find her, and I just wanted to let you know, I loved Denise like a sister. It's wrong what happened to her, but...you're not wrong for thinking foul play or the Sheriff is covering it up. I know that you know more than you let on, and that's ok. All I'm saying is everyone who's come to talk to the Sheriff or questions why Denise hasn't been found, are told a few details to make them believe they're working on it. They just tell them what they want to hear to get rid of them."

"They did the same to me," Jason confirms.

"I'm telling you all this because I'm too close to the chest to do anything, and the only reason I'm talking to you is maybe you can do something about it, being in your position. Nobody else will come here asking the tough questions like you've been doing and wanting results, not excuses. I like you. I want Denise found, and Aaron needs to go to jail for what he's done, but do me favor though..."

"Yeah, what's that?"

"Just be careful. You don't know these people like I do, and there's plenty of trees to hide people under if you catch my drift."

"I'll keep that in mind."

"I know it's a shame what happened to your cousin, but it's part of the game."

"What game?'

"If you live in this town and need money, it's not like you have options. If you're lucky, you go to school and can get a decent job to get out of here. Otherwise, the rest of us are fighting over minimum wage jobs. Doing what I do, you can make in one weekend what it takes months working a job around here to make. Nobody wants to pay enough for people to work. They don't provide healthcare, and good luck trying to get promoted. The only way positions open up is if somebody dies or moves away." Laughing, "You do the math. We all got bills and families too, tryin' to make ends meet."

"I can understand that, but what happens when families like mine get affected by what families like yours do?"

"Hey! I already told you I didn't kill Denise!" Randy sternly defends himself. "Look, I want to help anyway I can."

"Would you be willing to testify in court?"

"If you need me to, I will, but until that time comes, please don't tell people I spoke to you. I don't want it getting back to my dad or Aaron's family, I'm telling you this, alright?"

"Anything else I should know?'

"Yeah, one last little mystery. Like I said before, the detective was onto Aaron, and he lawyered up real fast. He got the best lawyer money could buy, and that's when he stopped cooperating. The detective had to get a warrant to search their place and truck, but before they came to serve him, he was tipped off the night before. When they came to officially search Aaron's place and impound his truck, someone from the Sheriff's Department already let him know. So, he cleaned his truck and cleared stuff out, he didn't want them to find in his house. I've never seen his truck so clean as long as I've known him. He used it as a work truck, and it was more like his own personal trashcan on wheels. If you rode with him, you'd have to shovel a way in to find a seat, and when you opened the doors, trash would come spillin' out. Just filthy man, but when they took his truck, it was spotless. He even used Armor All, inside and out."

"From what I've found out already, it doesn't surprise me."

"You also need to talk with his neighbor."

"Why is that?"

"Again, right before the cops showed up, he took a bunch of guns wrapped in blankets over to his neighbor's place, along with several other things he didn't want to get caught with. I don't know all the details, but his neighbor might have a few things to say about the case. Apparently, Aaron left a message on the neighbor's phone about secretly putting guns in his flowerbed or something."

"I'll look into it. Thanks for taking the time to meet."

"No problem but Jason…just do what I was never able to do."

"What's that?"

Frustrated, Randy says, "Just bring Denise home."

Randy gets up and the two men part ways. As he's leaving, Randy checks again to seeing if anyone notices him before hurrying to his small SUV parked behind the building. As he drives off, Jason picks up his phone and calls his mother.

"How did it go? Did he talk?" Ellie eagerly asks her son.

"Do you remember the 'Street Sweeper?'" Jason cryptically asks over the phone. He is referring to a specialized tactical shotgun he gave his mother and told her to hold on to in case of emergencies. Immediately, his mother knows something is up.

"Yeah, what about it? Jason, are you in trouble?"

"No, but from the looks of it, I just want to make sure I can keep it that way."

Being suspicious of the San Saba Sheriff's Department or others in authority abusing their powers to tap his phones illegally, Jason begins using coded phrases over the phone. Only his mother knew how to decipher what he meant, and she also knew better than to ask why.

"Yeah, right where you left it."

After Randy confirmed his suspicions of being tracked and monitored, along with all the other unusual irregularities from the people involved in Denise's disappearance, Jason already established a secretive communication system with his mom…just in case.

"Good, I have to pick up a few things first, and then I'll head down there tomorrow." Which was code for: Jason is heading her way tonight and to switch the conversation over to their prepaid burner phones to ensure privacy.

Chapter 9

The Plot Thickens

Jason is exhausted after the long day of driving to meet with Randy but quickly stops by his aunt's house to pick up some papers. Once obtained, Jason drives to his parents' beach house in Rockport, TX, three hours south of Austin. After parking his car and locking his doors, he breathes deep, taking in the salt in the air from the warm ocean bay breeze, as he climbs the stairs to their home on stilts. He reaches the second floor, and his parents' dogs let his presence be known. Smiling, he watches his mother through the large bay window overlooking the bay canal, scowling, and scurrying about trying to silence her three dogs making a fuss. Turning to Jason, she signals for him to come in. Pointing to the cigarette still lit in his hand, he gestures a few more moments to finish.

Inhaling another puff, Jason spins around looking over the balcony at their parents' boat tied to their pier. The homes in his parents' neighborhood subtly remind him of Venice, Italy, from pictures he has seen over the years. Residents here can drive their boats right up to their backyards and dock, like in Italy, using the small street like water channel ways. Looking at the neighbors' mansions, Jason remembers he has yet to bump into the famous country singer, George Strait, who has a beach house just a few blocks away. Soaking in the beautiful palm tree tropical setting and the romantic glow coming from the backyard landscape lighting, he compares his view to a resort he stayed at, near Cancun, in Playa Del Carmen, Mexico. His thoughts are interrupted as his mother opens the door to the balcony.

Overexaggerated, *cough cough.* "You need to cut that out."

"Yeah…I'll get right on that," Jason sarcastically replies, rolling his eyes as he takes another drag.

"Seriously, you know with my allergies, I can't be around smoke."

"Mom, you came out here," Jason reminds his mother. "I'll be done in a minute."

"I've been waiting to see the phone records," she says walking over to him, "Are those it?" she asks pointing to the yellow envelope in his other hand.

"Yes, ma'am," Jason replies as he hands the package to her.

"Good. Go ahead and finish. I want to see whose numbers are on here," she says quickly walking back to the door.

"You and me both. I can't believe Aunt Lisa lied to me about having Denise's phone records this entire time and didn't bother letting me know!"

"We have them, so that's all that matters now."

"MOM!" Jason raising his voice to vent his frustration. "She's known for two months that I've been requesting those. I asked her if she knew how I could obtain a copy for myself, and she played dumb. Then, I find out she's had them this entire time! Then you had to climb down on her…just to give me a copy of them!"

"I don't know what to tell you, but I'm thankful we have them now. *Coughing,* "I can't take the smoke anymore. Come inside," his mother directs, closing the door behind her.

"Yes, ma'am."

160

Jason watches his mom walk to her desk near the living room, flick on a small lamp and take a seat. Pulling documents from the folder, Jason studies her facial expressions to get an indication if she recognizes anyone on the list, near the time of Denise's disappearance. A look of perplexity on Ellie's face spurs Jason to quickly gather another glance at the charming midnight glow, take a final puff, and head inside. Plopping down on the leather sofa, Jason sees his mother flipping back and forth between two sets of stapled papers.

"Do you recognize any of the numbers?" he asks.

"Did you do anything to these before bringing them down here?"

"Huh?" Jason responds to the unusual question. "What do you mean?"

"Did you look at these before driving them here?"

"No. I haven't had to chance to review them. As soon as Aunt Lisa handed them to me, I drove straight here. Why?"

"Come look at this," Ellie says as she extends the documents in Jason's direction. Curious, Jason works to escape the clutches of the comfy brown leather sofa to retrieve the paperwork, before returning to his seat.

Comparing the two sets of papers, his mom adds, "Do you see anything odd about those?"

Immediately picking up on his mother's discovery, he replies, "Yes, these have two different formats."

"That's what I saw. One looks to be a copy of her official phone records, and the other looks to me like a hand typed Excel spreadsheet, made to look like phone records."

"What the hell!" Jason exclaims in disgust.

"Also, look at the dates."

"Yeah, this one," Jason says holding up the official record, "is dated March 2014! What good does this do us? It's a year before she disappeared." Tossing the copy angrily aside, he holds the other one up to show his mom, "The unofficial one is dated March of 2015, the month Denise disappeared."

"I know. It looks like someone did a sleight of hand on her phone records and made something up to appear as official paperwork."

"Didn't you tell me the real reason the detective was let go was not because of budget cuts...but he got fired for giving Aunt Lisa a copy of Denise's phone records?"

"Yes."

"Mom, first off...these records wouldn't even be admissible in court. This copy," Jason holds up the official phone records from 2014, "is a year prior to her disappearance. It has no relevance to the time of her disappearance." Plopping the document back on the sofa, Jason grabs the other stack of papers. "This document dated March 2015, isn't even an official copy, so it wouldn't be allowed in as evidence. Secondly, if this was a missing persons case, as the Sheriff claims it to be, and they are trying to find her, then why would the detective get fired for giving Denise's mom her phone records? Unless this is considered a homicide or criminal investigation from the beginning and now the Sheriff is covering it up and he deescalated the case."

"That's why I asked if you did anything to them."

"When would I have had time?" Jason scornfully replies. "Check your phone from the time I called you to the time I got here. I left as soon as I got them. Plus, I don't have a mobile office to type, print, and staple documents while I drive, just to fool you."

"Don't get short with me! I believe you! I just asked because I'm ruling out any possibilities."

"Mom, as I've been telling you since I started looking at this case...from the beginning, nothing adds up. From the

Sheriff lying about interviewing people, collecting evidence, and checking reports, to even him changing the story about how they are investigating the case. He even told me, after saying they were looking into it and investigating everything, it's a missing persons case so evidence and witness statements must be brought to them voluntarily. When I grilled him, the Sheriff finally told me himself, he knows Aaron did it!"

"Then why hasn't he brought Aaron in for questioning, or better yet…arrested him?"

"I asked him the same question. He told me he couldn't talk with Aaron because of the lawyer he retained, and she advised Aaron not to talk. I also asked why Aaron's phone records haven't been checked or requested, and he cut me off, telling me I needed to leave so he can get back to work on the case."

Disapproval showing, his mom shook her head, "Unbelievable!"

"I wouldn't believe half the bizarre crap I've discovered surrounding this case had I not been the one discovering it myself."

"Did you know Aaron even got his lawyer to represent his son, so the detective couldn't speak with him either?"

"But Aaron's innocent, right? The Sheriff also said they checked everything out and Aaron is no longer considered a suspect. That's why it's still a missing persons case."

Shocked, "When did he say that?" Ellie asks.

"I've been so busy, I also forgot to tell you I went back a second time to confront him on every lie he told me. I took note of who he said he interviewed, the properties he checked out and so on. Come to find out, not one person could confirm the Sheriff told the truth."

"I still can't wrap my head around it. You only see this stuff in movies or murder mysteries, not in real life like this."

"Mom, as soon as I walked in the second time, the look on his face...he knew I found out he was lying to me. He figured I might have left it alone and gone away, but to his surprise, you can't make me go away that easy. Not when it comes to family still missing. I guess he wasn't expecting me to cross check and verify his statements, because I blasted him right there in the lobby."

Gasp, "You hit him?" his mother shockingly asks.

"NO, mom! I verbally let him have it, but he could sense I wanted to sock 'em because he had one of his deputies come stand behind him, just in case I tried."

"Jason, you know better than to go start trouble with those people out there. You're lucky he didn't arrest you!"

"Oh no...he threatened to!"

"He did?"

"Yeah, after puffing his chest and getting loud with me, he said he could have me arrested for causing a disturbance in their office."

"What? You can't arrest someone for getting loud and demanding answers! Did you say anything else, or did you leave?"

"I told him to stick it where the sun doesn't shine, and I didn't appreciate him giving me the run around. He backed off after I said, 'I find it odd that he's so quick to suggest arresting me but hasn't even so much as bothered to try to put Aaron behind bars once.'"

"He needs to be removed from his office and put in a cozy cell with Aaron. Well, now that you're here, I want to open the packet we requested from the Sheriff's office."

"The Freedom of Information Act request we sent them?"

"Yes, it came in the mail today."

Jason's eyes widen, "Where is it?"

"Right here," his mother gloomily says, handing up a very thin letter envelope.

"What's this? That's it? That's all they sent? I've seen Denise's file, it's about three to four inches thick. Since it's not an active investigation or an ongoing criminal investigation, they are supposed to send everything they have."

"I don't know what it is, Jason. Maybe, it's a response letter or something."

Taking a letter opener from the desk, Jason's breaks the seal and pulls out two sheets of paper. Dropping the papers on the desk, Jason turns and starts walking to the door without saying a word.

Confused, "Jason, where are you going?"

"To have another smoke."

"Why?"

"Can anybody else try to prevent and hinder us from finding out what really happened to Denise?"

"Well, before you go outside, can you first tell me what you're seeing here," Ellie says inspecting the two pieces of paper for herself. "This looks like the initial call out report when Denise was reported missing."

"Look at the name on the report!" Jason calls out, scooping up a handful of his favorite M&M candy Ellie leaves out in a bowl each time he visits.

Gasp, Ellie realizes her son's discovery. "This isn't the original Incident Report, because the Sheriff didn't get involved until three months into it, after this was written up. Aunt Lisa said the deputy who came out was a young guy and if anything, the detective's name should be on here, not the Sheriff's."

Chewing on a few handfuls of candy, waiting as his mom reviews the pages thoroughly, Ellie finally asks,

"Would you stop eating those and come see if there is anything useful on these."

"I'm hungry," Jason tries to say through his chewing. "I didn't stop to eat on the way down here. I thought we would be researching numbers and names, but so much for that!"

"Quit talking with your mouth full and come here please," Ellie politely asks, knowing her son is exhausted and agitated.

After momentarily glancing at the pages, Jason immediately hands the papers back. "I thought you said it was only Aaron, Tina, and Uncle Clark who were present when law enforcement filed the report?"

"I did."

"Look at the witnesses on this report. Tina's on there, but who are these other people? Do you recognize any of these names?"

After looking at the report, Ellie replies, "No."

"So, why are these people listed, but not her dad?"

"Jason, this is my first time seeing this, with you."

"Look at their addresses…it's not even the same zip code as their neighborhood. So, I guess random people just decided to show up to be witnesses to the report?"

"That is strange…but that's why I wanted you to look at it, you catch things like this," Ellie states, trying to justify calling Jason away from the bowl of candy. "Jason…what is going on?"

"Welcome to my world, mom! Nothing makes sense or adds up…. Nothing!"

"You know I can't be there to help you investigate, but yes, if I didn't know you and your intentions, I would think you have a very vivid imagination because of how ridiculous everything you've found is. It just sounds so far-fetched."

"I have neither the time, energy, nor creativity to come up with this utter nonsense. I feel like I'm in a puppet show, looking for answers, and everyone's pulling my strings. Besides, why bother trying to make anything up? The real world is stranger than fiction."

"From what we've seen with this case already, I would have to agree!"

"Hold that thought, mom," Jason says. He was already on his phone.

"Hang up! Who are you calling at this hour?"

"Tina."

"Jason, it's too late to be calling anyone."

"She stays up pretty late, and I want to get to the bottom of this."

After the call to Denise's sister, Jason and Ellie sit in silence trying to process all the disinformation they keep receiving. Without saying a word, Jason looks back at the police report and opens an app on his phone.

"What are you doing now?" Ellie inquires.

"I want to see where some of these people live, because I would like to chat with them tomorrow. Also, I'm going to track down the detective to verify questions I have for him."

"Like what?"

"First, if this incident report has been changed or altered in anyway, then this is possibly tampering with government documents. Secondly, I want to find out what evidence they found to get a warrant when he was on the case, and how he obtained these phones records. I'm curious if he's aware he got fired for giving Aunt Lisa unofficial documents, or if there is something else going on we should know about. Maybe he will let me know what he was investigating or working on right before he got canned."

"That's a long shot but…you never know."

"Well, if he's disgruntled, he might tell me everything, or he could definitely point me in the right direction."

A few moments after searching on his phone, Jason passes it to his mom seated on the sofa next to him.

"Why are you showing me a rundown motel?"

"That's the address listed for one of the witnesses on the report."

"Jason...I don't see how this could get any stranger."

"From now on, mom...do not talk to anyone about what I'm working on or who I'm talking to. Not even to Aunt Lisa. I don't know who I can trust."

"Jason, you don't trust your Aunt Lisa?"

"I'm not suggesting she helped in anyway, but what were the reasons you suspected Aaron of foul play?"

"Well..." Ellie angrily charges up, "each property we searched, Aaron wouldn't help. If anything, he just sat there cracking jokes with his buddies. Then, he and one of his buddies hitched a ride back from one of the searches...maybe he didn't realize a few of the volunteers in the car with him were actually a few of Denise's friends...but when one asked if Denise might randomly show up, he chimes back, 'She better never show back up!'...I mean...who says that? He claims they were supposed to be in love and tried to play it off as a joke but joking or not...that's just sick! He knows exactly where she is because he doesn't seem to have a care in the world of her whereabouts, he's not cooperating with the investigation, or giving anything useful to help find her."

"You see? You said he's guilty because he was crackin' jokes, won't help search, and doesn't seem to be helping to find her."

"How does this have anything to do with your Aunt Lisa?"

168

"You said she has been out there on every search, being involved, right?"

"Yes."

"Mom, the property I found, we've already had three searches on it, and what has she done? She won't step foot on it."

"She told me she doesn't believe Denise is there."

"How does she know with certainty? So, she was convinced Denise was on the other properties before you searched them? She apparently didn't mind rolling her sleeves up and getting dirty for all the other searches, but won't even give this one a chance?"

"Maybe she subconsciously knows she's there and isn't ready to find her or come to grips with the possibility Denise is gone. Who knows?"

"That's one theory, but the times she's gone out to this property, she sat off to the side crackin' jokes, and having a good time. Did you know she even took a swing at Uncle Clark?"

"What?" His mother exclaims.

"Oh yeah, I left that little detail out, didn't I?"

"When did this happen?"

"The last time we were out there, Uncle Clark told me Aunt Lisa had vehemently refused to go. She even threatened to divorce him if he made her go there."

"I thought she was there the last time."

"She was, but when they were at their house, Uncle Clark had to force her to come out. He finally told her, 'You better get in that truck, or I'll drag you there myself,' so she took a swing at him!"

"This is news to me!"

"Let's also not forget how many months now it's taken her to give us these falsified phone records, but only after you ripped her a new one for sending me on a wild

169

goose chase, trying to retrieve them. She insisted Lydia had them and Lydia said 'no, I gave everything back to Lisa.' Back and forth, back and forth, for weeks, until I had you get involved and have her tell me where those phone records were."

"Yeah, I don't know what's going on with her lately."

"Maybe someone's holding something over her head, but since you're a mom, if you had found credible evidence she could be somewhere on a property, would you be taking swings at dad, or would you be the first one out the door?"

"I hope I never have to find out."

"It just looks even more suspicious when she intentionally arranged for me to go out to this property alone with a supposed psychic private investigator, who turned out to be more like a psycho meth-head criminal informant. Not knowing who she was, because I was new to the investigation, I agreed to go. I was headed out to the property when you happened to call me and found out who I was going there with. You immediately hung up the phone with me, called Aunt Lisa, then told her to get Uncle Clark out there ASAP!"

"I don't know why she did that."

"Guess what she said when I later confronted her about sending me out there with this shady woman?"

"What?"

"After I pointed out the track marks on her arms, constant sniffling, thin as a rail from rapid weight loss, looking like she hadn't bathed in weeks, removed potential evidence from the property, not using gloves, possibly destroying a crime scene, put her prints on everything, and took no photos...Aunt Lisa blew it off and said, 'Well, I never trusted that woman anyway!' If you're investigating the murder of your daughter, why would you recommend sending them with me to the property? Also, why would you

170

allow someone, who you don't trust, to have access to potential crime scene evidence?"

"I know Jason. Your Aunt Lisa and I got into a big argument over this. That woman she sent you out there with already has a police record of her own."

"Really? Do they even research anyone they speak with? If this lady has a record, then there's no way the state would allow her to become a private investigator. If that's true, then it means she is lying about being a private investigator," Jason informs.

"I don't think they checked or verified her credentials, but I can't say for sure. I haven't told you this until now, but Aunt Lisa told me the real reason she sent you out there with that lady. She told me she didn't trust you, didn't believe Denise was on the property, and was sending you on a wild goose chase to keep you preoccupied."

Offended, Jason asks, "Not trusting me? I've done more for this case in two months than the Sheriff has done in the last three years!"

"I know, that's what I told her."

"What did I do to her? I'm family. Why else would I be helping? Everyone's been jerking me around since I started asking questions, and no one is giving me straight answers."

"I was no different. The Sheriff told me he was working on it. While I had my doubts, I couldn't bring myself to believe he was doing the exact opposite."

"This wasn't the first time she had set me up with questionable people."

"Jason, she and I both thought you might have lost your marbles telling us everything you discovered because you had multiple concussions in the Army."

"I can understand that, but after I found out the Sheriff wasn't doing any investigating, and found credible evidence, you would have thought she would be more willing to give me a chance."

"In her defense, she didn't ask you to get involved. You did that on your own."

"She apparently doesn't mind allowing people she doesn't know look at her information, but not the one who's piecing it all together."

"Trust me, I've got a bone to pick with her! I've been driving out there to help out when I can and spent time looking up information while you were driving around."

"I saw the container of files she has on Denise's case, and when I asked if I could look at them, she declined and told me she didn't want the paperwork leaving the house or getting lost."

"Maybe she's afraid you'll give up or something."

"Mom, who else is still working the case besides you and me? Besides, let's not forget that co-worker friend of hers, who tried getting me drunk before driving me to Aaron's place. She was trying to get me pumped up for a fight, and when I went to the front door, she secretly drove off."

"I still can't believe she did that either."

"I'm not making this up!"

"No, I'm agreeing with you and just meant the nerve of her feeding you beers, getting you ready to fight, and leaving you out there without telling anyone. She knows what those people are capable of, and she was setting you up!"

"Tell me something I don't already know! To her surprise, she was mighty shocked when I called her 30 minutes later asking where she went. She was already halfway home. The excuse she told me was that she was afraid something happened to me, panicked, and drove off. I asked if she called anyone to let them know I was there. Well, guess what? She hadn't called anyone, not even the police!

172

Now, if you drove someone to the house of a suspected murderer and thought something bad happened to them, would you just drive off and not bother to let anyone know? Would a rational or logical person do this? Sorry mom, I'm not buying it!"

"Me either. She wanted you to start a fight on their property, and they could have easily shot you, and claimed self-defense. You were trespassing, drinking and she was hoping you would act confrontational."

"How long did it take you to believe me about that, hmmm?" Jason asks sarcastically.

"After I overheard your conversation with her, about her so-called friend in the Sheriff's department, told her Aaron's plan to move to Dallas and start a new life with his son."

"That's right! Do you remember how belligerent she became when I told her great job on her tip?"

"Yes. I still don't understand why she flipped her lid when you were trying to congratulate her."

"That's just it. After my sources verified her statement, I was letting her know her source was credible because the information checked out. Afterwards, she lost it and completely denied having ever said it to me. Then, when I reminded her, I wasn't working with anyone else, she immediately said, she is washing her hands of the case and no longer wants to be involved." Jason says matter-of-factly.

"I know. I heard her say that when I was there to see the kids. It's so weird because she was the one who also helped to raise the reward money for Crime Stoppers. There must have been someone else listening in to your phone call or standing right next to her. Why else would she become so argumentative to the good news, unless she was going to get in trouble if they found out she told you?"

"Now, for my final observation, and remember, try looking at this from an outsider's perspective rather than being a relative of Denise…in three years, what has Aunt Lisa done to find her? You made the comment yourself, she has sat back while everyone else coordinated events, searches, made websites, and even talked to the Sheriff to get updates on the case. Since I've arrived, she has just been completely hands off. As a mother, Aunt Lisa was always the loudest, most challenging, and in your face person, like Denise could be. I found it extremely odd, after I put this information on Denise's Facebook page, Aaron's friends and family were basically savagely degrading Denise, and not a word comes from Aunt Lisa to defend her child's honor? When has she EVER let someone get away with badmouthing and disrespecting our family? She's the most confrontational and explosive woman I've ever known, but when people were slamming Denise…crickets! Not a peep came from her."

"This is making my head hurt," Ellie says as she leans back in her chair.

"Again, just pretend you were an investigator with no personal vested interest in this case. Her behavior is throwing up some serious red flags."

"I honestly hadn't put two and two together until tonight. It's absurd to even think about it."

"Now, doesn't it seem a little odd or suspicious that since I've started my own investigation, she has been constantly calling you wanting to know everything we discover but keeps us in the dark with what she knows or has? Which begs the question, does she really want Denise found or is she only appearing to care?"

"I'm still not convinced, but I can definitely see where you are coming from."

"Something is off when it comes to Aunt Lisa. I can't put my thumb on it, but for her to be this disengaged as soon as I started searching this property is uncanny."

"I need a break. This is just a lot for me to take in all at once."

"Admit it!" Jason says holding up the phone records and the envelope from the Sheriff's office, "What I've been saying doesn't sound so far-fetched anymore, does it?"

"I'm honestly amazed how you've been able to pinpoint what's stopping the case from moving forward, and it's not because there's a lack of evidence. It's like everyone is working to keep Denise hidden. It's not that I don't believe you, Jason, I try to explain away the abnormalities, especially when it's going against the crowd."

Jason rests his case to his mother. He feels validated and satisfied she's finally on board.

"So, what do I say when Lisa calls wanting an update?" Ellie questions.

"Just say I haven't found any new leads, and I'm just going over what I got. Can you do that?"

"Ok."

"It's been a long day, I'm ready for bed."

"Ok, the guest bedroom is set up."

"We can talk some more in the morning if you would like."

Ellie stops him, as she fetches a note from her desk, "There is actually one more thing I needed to share with you about Aunt Lisa. She called when you were driving down here to ask if I could give you information on a new lead she received online. They left a phone number."

"Why didn't she call me directly then?"

"She knows you're not happy with her right now and asked if I wouldn't mind passing the information along to you."

"Did she talk to them?"

"No, she wants you to call and find out what they want."

"Do you see how this looks to me? If my child was missing and someone contacted me trying to share information on the case, I wouldn't be asking someone else to contact them at their convenience. I would have immediately been on the phone finding out what they know."

"I can't speak for her or what she does, I'm just relaying to you what she asked from me. Do you want to contact them, or should I tell her you're busy?"

Hesitant, Jason takes the note from his mom. "Who's John?"

"I don't know, but she wants you to find out."

Chapter 10

Values, Ethics, and Morals... OH MY!

<u>*April 2018*</u>

Pulling up to a respectable looking bar-b-que establishment in Llano, TX, just 30 miles south of San Saba, a wonderful aroma of woodfire mesquite begins pouring into Jason's car. Skipping breakfast to make the drive from his parents' place, his stomach growls, as he smells the sweet brisket cooking in the smoker. Backing his car into the parking spot, as most military veterans do, he scans the lot looking for suspicious persons and activity. Satisfied, he enjoys a few more puffs on his Marlboro cigarette, before slowly making his way into the restaurant.

Once inside the old timey themed bar-b-que joint, Jason immediately sees who he came for. A medium built man wearing oversized sunglasses, sitting, nervously waiting at a long table, in the far-left corner. The lone man quickly notices Jason hopping in the self-serve line to get lunch. Playing it cool, Jason gets his meal and nonchalantly makes his way over to him. "Anyone sitting here?" Jason casually asks.

"No! No! Sit where ya like," the man says uneasily, playing along with Jason's lead. After permission is granted, Jason guides his tray onto the polished wood tabletop and takes a seat. After a few moments of silence, the man starts in with conversational filler. "What is with this weather? I sure hope it turns out to be a nice day," but Jason is unresponsive to the man's meaningless engagement.

Jason's level of cynicism and distrust of people involved with Denise's case, is at an all-time high. The only reason he even agreed to meet with this unknown man at a restaurant, out in the boondocks, is to fulfill his Aunt Lisa's request. After the unknown man sent a Facebook message claiming he had vital information on Denise's disappearance, Jason was able to get in touch late last night for an in person meeting today. Already being leery of anyone new, and for good reason, Jason wants to get right down to business. Having to skip breakfast, which is Jason's favorite meal of the day, he isn't in the mood for pleasantries. Having to wake up early to drive four hours, to find out what this man's sense of urgency is, only makes him warier to his intentions.

Before the peculiar man can ask another mind-numbing question, Jason rudely requests, "Would you take those ridiculous shades off? Between your bright yellow palm tree Tommy Bahama shirt, wearing sunglasses indoors on a cloudy day, and baseball cap, I wouldn't call your attempts at being discreet...inconspicuous."

Embarrassed, the man, in his late 50's, removes his Houston Astros ball cap and aviator glasses. Shocked at Jason's boldness, he says apologetically, "I'm sorry. It's not like I do this often. I feel like I'm in *Mission Impossible* or some spy movie, trying to share my information with you."

"I hate to break this to you, but the only movie that comes to mind from your choice of wardrobe is *Weekend at Bernie's*."

Laughing, the man replies, "Touché!"

"So, you must be John."

"Yes," the middle-aged man quietly replies.

Jason takes note of the man's skinny arms and mediocre build under his flamboyant shirt. "Are you going to tell me why you needed to urgently drag me up here on a Saturday afternoon to talk?" Jason asks before sinking his teeth into a savory piece of brisket.

Fidgeting and slightly hesitant, John begins, "I could lose my job if someone finds out I'm here talking to you."

While Jason is mentally rolling his eyes to John's apparent over-exaggeration of the situation, he boosts him for more, "Oh yeah? How's that?"

Keeping his voice low, John continues, "I was there from the beginning."

"The beginning of what?" Jason asks, talking with a mouth full of food.

"A few days after Denise was reported missing, I was one of the first people called out for the official search to find her."

Momentarily pausing his rate of chewing, Jason goes back to enjoying his meal. So far, from his experience, everyone he's met had good tips to share, but he's discovered their true intentions were to gain his trust, for the purpose to extract information from him.

"Well, what do you know about the case so far? Maybe I can fill you in on a few more details," John uneasily inquires.

Eyeing John with skepticism, and not wanting to get burned again, Jason responds, "Look, you can either spill what you got, or I'm going to finish enjoying this delicious meal, get in my car, drive off, and never think twice about this little rendezvous ever again. I've had more than my fair share of dealing with the clowns from your neck of the woods, jerking me around trying to find out what I know. So, you can either talk, or we're done here. If you do have

179

something to say, and it checks out, then I might do the same in return."

Mentally regrouping from Jason's abrupt bitterness, resentment, agitation, and hostility, John takes a few moments to choose his next words carefully. "I work directly with the San Saba Sheriff department's marine division. As I was saying, I was called out for the first official search to find Denise. My boss is a deputy there, and he called us into a huddle. He told us from the get-go, Aaron did it. He said, *'There's blood in the kitchen. Aaron killed her and he had help. Let's get to work.'* After we worked hard and collected what we could, which was more than enough to put Aaron away, there were no arrests. Months pass, and I inquired a few times because this case really touched my heart. Denise is a mother of three boys who still do not know what happened to their mom. My boss initially told me the detective was diligently working on the case. Then, almost seven months after our search, I messaged him for an update, and he replied not to worry about Denise's case anymore. He said it's a cold case and I should focus my attention elsewhere."

Nonreactive to the statement, Jason narrows his eyes, "Do you have proof to back this up?"

"Yes!" John excitedly remembers, opening his phone. "As a matter of fact, I do!" Scrolling for a few seconds, John locates the alleged conversation. "Here it is…give me a sec, I have to scroll back…it's been almost three years since he sent those messages to me," he says, rapidly pressing buttons on his phone.

Not getting his hopes up, Jason continues scarfing down his food, military style. Jason had things to do and doesn't feel John can be much use to him. Already preparing himself for another disappointing outing or expecting to hear some excuse John might give after discovering the messages have been conveniently deleted, Jason waits.

"Here it is!" John says sharply, while spinning the phone around where Jason can see.

Setting his fork down, Jason asks "Do you mind if I take a look?" Many people have already tried to fool Jason, and he knows better than take people's word around here.

Excited, John replies, "Sure! Please, be my guest!" handing the phone to Jason.

After wiping his hands on his napkin, Jason carefully examines the text message, and verifies the dates from the timestamps on the screen. Jason's opinion of the importance of this meeting begins to change as he reads, verbatim, John's recollection of this discussion. Jason has been relentlessly searching for months for the slightest shred of evidence to explain why this case hasn't moved forward or to explain why Denise still hasn't been found. Here it is...John is telling the truth.

"Wow," Jason replies, now softening his attitude towards John, but still suspicious of his intentions. "You've known this for three years? Why did you wait until now to say something? Why didn't you go to internal affairs or at least make an anonymous report?"

Cynically laughing. "You're joking, right? I can't go tattle on anyone in this town! Everybody knows everybody. As soon as I say something, it's a matter of hours before the whole town knows it was me sharing confidential information. Secondly, those anonymous hotlines and emails aren't as anonymous as they claim to be."

"How so?"

"With today's technology, emails, phone calls, and messages, have traceable codes where the right people can easily trace who's leaking or sharing info. Everything is monitored and being recorded by someone. If I had the clearance, I could find out what you searched online, from 10 years ago. The same is with internal affairs and HR departments…they can easily find out who's trying to be anonymous. Considering what I know about San Saba, people look the other direction, if the price is right."

"If you know this, why don't you go work somewhere else?"

"You think it's just our department? You see, this almost everywhere you go. Currently, finding people who consistently uphold integrity is rare. As for law enforcement, even with the F.B.I., this whole 'Serve and Protect' motto takes on a completely new meaning. I think they leave that part vague for a reason. I'm sure if the public knew who they are truly protecting and serving, we would all be out of a job because it's sure not the people. There's too much politics involved, and people like me, who genuinely want to do our job, struggle to do our basic duties and responsibilities because of it."

"Why don't you get out then? I wanted to go into law enforcement after the military, but after dealing with the Sheriff and deputies in San Saba, I've reconsidered," Jason grudgingly responds.

"It's a shame because the force needs people like you. It's a popularity contest to hold positions rather than who is the most qualified."

"I know, I saw the same in the military and why good people don't want to re-enlist. If you're smart, you get out because it's a lot of *brown nosing* and stroking peoples' egos. I wasn't there to make friends. I joined to serve my country and keep it safe."

John states, "It's difficult to find good help in my line of work because of the politics, but it's not just law enforcement. It's in the legal system, politicians, government, and corporations. We've become a culture of accepting and promoting unqualified people who also lack strong ethical foundations or morals. As long as there's people like them, no one will say anything."

"It's a buddy system, and you protect the ones who got you there," Jason adds.

"Don't get me wrong, there are more good cops than bad, but rarely do corrupt motives only involve one or two people within an organization. Those who go into law enforcement do so with noble intentions, but over time, they start hiring and promoting the wrong people. They keep their nose clean and work their way up in the system undetected. Once in authority, they start hiring and promoting people like them and firing those who might be a hinderance to their agendas and VOILA! Let the corruption games begin!"

"You also have those who didn't intend to grow up being professionalized crooks. They possibly lack strong ethical or moral foundations from childhood which becomes their morality. All it takes is for people like this to feel cheated in life. Then they feel entitled to compensation for their struggles. When an opportunity presents itself to cheat or steal to get ahead, they do."

"In my field, you would be amazed at those who will sell their soul for a slice of the pie. Sometimes, it's the church-going pillars of the community and seemingly good wholesome people who you'd never suspect, are the ones running these crime waves."

"People are innately good, but when times become so unfair by government and political officials or CEO's, their values, ethics, and morals are the first to go. In our country, when people are trying to survive, they will even double cross their own family members. Do you know why?" Jason asks.

"Our customs and traditions have lost the significance in values. Common values of a society lead to ethical behavior. Without values, societies act unethically, and eventually crumble because they have no foundation, integrity, or structure."

Impressed, Jason inquires, "Did you study ethics in school, or philosophy?"

"Why do you ask?"

Jason replies, "You don't see many hardcore religious people these days. Religion has served as the primary vehicle for societies to receive moral education, but with the mass exodus of people leaving the church, those teachings are being lost. Otherwise, people who come from small towns, talking like you, are typically throwing in Jesus and God at the beginning and ending of every sentence."

John laughs, "I've had many struggles in my life, and it wasn't until I started reading European and Asian philosophy that I finally found the answers I was seeking. People take the stories in the Bible at face value and overlook the message of the story. Plus, it's written in a language which is outdated to the times. In philosophy, it removes religious lore, and gets right to the meaning behind what you need to know."

"Who did you study? Aristotle, Socrates, Confucius, Lao-Tzu?"

Smiling, John replies, "Close! Many Greek and European philosophers were students of ancient Asian teachers. 'The Middle East,' where most of the stories in the Bible take place, used to be known as West Asia, until the late 1800's."

"Hmm. Interesting."

John explains, "After reading Plato, Socrates, Voltaire, Immanuel Kant, Friedrich Nietzsche, and Thomas Aquinas, I went back to the little-known origins of their sources. I found, after studying Asian philosophy, it was much easier and simpler than Western thought. I've read *The Art of War*, *The Tao Te Ching*, the *I-Ching*, studied *Zen* Buddhism *or*

Bodhidharma, and discovered it doesn't take a rocket scientist to understand these great philosophical minds. Asian philosophy is actually so easy to get, it's taught in many of their schools, to kids at a young age."

Jason adds, "Yes, what we call education here, only teaches kids how to work at a job. It doesn't teach them how to function in life."

"Exactly. I take it you've studied similar works."

"Yes," Jason answers. "I've read works like the *Lotus Sutra*, but Buddhism is widely misunderstood. It's not a religion like Westerners have been taught. The truth is, if you collectively took the core messages from Confucianism, Buddhism, and Taoism, and implemented these simple values into a society, you would almost have a Utopian culture and way of life."

"I'm impressed. You have done your homework, but why those three?"

"Confucius teaches how to treat others and behave in society. Buddhism teaches how a person should manage and treat themselves on personal levels, while the Tao is more geared towards how a person should behave within the environment they live. Each section is also a cool and mysterious work of art. Each time you read it, you gain deeper insights, like peeling back layers of an onion."

"Yes! Great analysis. It took me years of digging to eventually stumble upon the works of one man, who I can almost assure, you've never heard of before."

"Oh yeah? Who's that?"

"Mencius."

"You're right. I don't know who that is. Was he Greek or Latin?"

"Neither. Western authorities love to change Asian names, titles, and teachings, but his original name was

Mengzi, and was later changed to Mencius, which is European."

"What's so special about him?"

"That's just it! Few know of his works! What Mencius wrote is so impactful, imperative, and powerful. If they required CEOs, government, and political officials to know the *Works of Mencius* front to back, before taking high office or high-ranking positions, our country would be headed towards abundance and prosperity for all Americans. His works have the answers to help alleviate 80-90% of the corruption in this country. Instead, we have a few insanely wealthy people while the remainder of us are fighting for leftovers," John concludes.

"Interesting. I will have to check him out then."

Excited, John informs, "Please do! If you want my recommendation, read *Mencius* by Irene Bloom. In fact, every school in our country should, at minimum, be teaching his works. Since Mencius and other similar works aren't taught in our schools here, that could directly explain why we have upstanding people and agents being targeted by those who don't want their dirty little secrets being exposed. Just like what happened to the detective on Denise's case. This case was moving right along, and just as soon as he started, he was let go. Don't be fooled into thinking it was because of department funding issues."

"You're not the first person to tell me that," Jason retorts as he is absorbing the new insights. "I have to be honest, I thought small towns like yours would be more like Mayberry, and the Sheriff would be more like Andy Griffith."

"Ha. I wish!"

"Why don't you talk to the media or reporters, and tell them what you told me?" Jason asks to test John's determination to come clean.

"Reporters?" *Sneers.* "Investigative reporters are a dying breed. We used to have trusted news anchors, but this new generation of reporters and journalists only care about looking good in the spotlight. Real reporters, back in the day, used to be the voice of the people against scandal, corruption, and crime in business, government, and politics. Nowadays, they're so desperate to become famous, they've sold their integrity to the highest bidder. Now they cover up the news they once investigated and reported on. They took a once well-respected profession and turned it into a bunch of parrots reciting scripts from executives, rather than reporting the actual news. The news today is so diluted, altered, and biased. Only two percent of the information is real. The rest is sugarcoated and manipulated to condition how people think."

Skeptical, Jason asks, "Brainwashing? That's stretching it a bit, don't you think?"

"No. Not at all! We used to have laws protecting the people against the use of propaganda, but now they legally use taxpayers' money to air or print what they want you to see."

"Are you referring to the 2017 National Defense Authorization Act, where they snuck in the Countering Disinformation and Propaganda Act?"

Delighted, John responds, "Yes, and I see you're also keeping up with politics. Good for you! Most people couldn't care less what officials are doing in office, and then complain when they feel the effects of their corrupt ways. What this act did, was legally allow news stations to use government funded propaganda, to bring us back to the Cold War Era. In short, we are now paying them to lie to us."

Jason elaborates, "Real news, back in the day, used to present what happened to you, and let the viewers form their own opinions about the story. Now, their stories incite

187

emotional extremes from the viewer. It's chock-full of opinionated commentary judging and condemning other political parties and government leaders. Opinions don't belong in the news. They belong on talk shows."

"Exactly! Does that answer your question?"

"I guess."

"What I'm getting at is if I call them," John begins, "they'll swoop in with lights, cameras, ask a few obvious questions, and then call it a wrap. If it looks good to editors for a ratings boost, they'll air it. If not, they move on to something else. They don't use their training to help solve cases anymore. So, where does that leave me? High and dry. Knowing how dangerous the people are here in San Saba and the people they are associated with, no thanks!"

"Alright, but doesn't that actor Tommy Lee Jones have a home in San Saba? Why not recruit his help? He might have some connections or friends in high places."

"He has a home here, but this place is more like a getaway for him. He tries to steer clear from the public and paparazzi, rather than drawing attention to himself at social hour with the local hometown folk."

"Makes sense, but what can we do then?" Jason, discouraged, asks.

"That's why I reached out to your aunt. You're making headway around here, and if anyone has a chance to break this thing wide open, it's you."

"I'm glad you think so highly of me, but if you haven't noticed, I'm fighting an uphill battle."

"That's my point, when we get the information out, and with the right people backing you, what couldn't you do?" Jason waiting to see what John will say next, leaves both men speechless for a moment.

"There is one last thing…that has bothered me for years," John says sheepishly as his words trail off.

"Yeah, what's that?"

"I don't know how to say this, and I definitely don't talk about it to other people, but since you're a little more worldly than most residents of this small town, I have something else to share."

Curious, Jason leans in a little closer, "I'm pretty open minded at this point."

As if John couldn't contain himself to finally get a secret off his chest, he hurriedly digs in his pocket. Pulling out a tightly folded yellow piece of paper, something else catches Jason's eye. "I hope you can appreciate what I'm about to say without thinking I'm crazy. I have Native American blood in my family. I'm not the only one, but certain people in our family have unique gifts."

Somewhat doubtful Jason responds, "Gifts?"

"Things happen to us. Whether we see or unexpectedly pick up on activity, it has run in our family for generations."

"Unexpected activity?"

"With each person in my family, we have different abilities. Some hear things, some see things, some have visions when they dream, and some just know information others don't."

Curious, Jason asks, "Which one are you then?"

"I have random visions when I sleep. I awake with vivid images burned into my mind. I keep a notebook on my nightstand, so I can write down and draw what happened in the vision." Waiting to see Jason's reaction leads to two men uncomfortably studying each other once again, but their silence is broken as Jason begins to chuckle.

Confused, John asks, "What's so funny?"

"You're good! I'll give you that."

"I don't follow."

"You almost had me fooled with your ridiculous over the top outfit and trying to appear concerned about your safety."

"I don't know what you're talking about. Can I at least show you what I brought, allow me to explain?"

"It seems I'm all outta food, and you just ran outta time. The ethical and political piece was interesting, but I have a long drive home, and I have to take a leak," Jason casually declares as he collects his silverware and trash. Before getting up, Jason quickly scans the restaurant's freshly painted red walls with gray sheet metal siding, looking for the restroom sign. After locating his next pitstop, he returns his gaze back to John's expressionless face and blank stare.

As Jason moves to get up, John desperately asks, "You're not going to let me finish and at least tell me what you think?"

Pausing slightly as John takes the bait, Jason slowly slides back down into his seat and smiles. Jason starts, "You wanna know what I think? I think I don't like being lied to or played."

Offended, John contests, "I'm not playing or lying to you."

"You can cut the act, John, assuming that's your real name?"

"Yes," John replies as he quickly retrieves his driver's license from his wallet as proof. "See? Now you know where I live. Do you believe me now?"

Jason doesn't bother to closely look at the ID card because he had his sights set on a much bigger prize. "Why don't you really tell me how you ended up in such a small town like San Saba?"

"I moved here about 10 years ago."

"Yeah, but from where?"

"I was a teacher on the east coast."

Bursting in laughter. "Is that what they call you guys these days?"

"Call who?"

"I know you're not going to tell me if I ask, so I'll just go ahead and tell you what I gather. Yeah, you worked on the east coast, but not in some school setting. No…you don't develop peripheral vision like that writing on chalkboards," Jason flippantly responds. Pulling his hand away from the butter knife, he watches John slightly relax after he's been slowly edging the blade from John's line of sight, in case he tried something funny. "Easy John! Your secrets are safe with me," Jason taunts.

Sitting more upright at the table, John clears his throat trying to remain in character.

"Here's the thing, since we've been intermingling," Jason mocks, "I can tell you've been casing this joint. I bet you can tell me exactly how many people are in here, the color shirts they're wearing, and where the exits are."

Chuckling, "I think you've watched to many spy movies as a kid," John jabs back.

Unfazed by the comment, Jason continues, "From what I know, and if I had to put money on it, you got that shirt in South Beach. That was your hub as a contractor working overseas. There you worked with Special Forces, SAS, or whatever high-speed unit was in that country. I bet before you were helping to find dead bodies in San Saba, you left a path of your own deceased, doing covert jobs in other places." John couldn't help but to crack an amusing smile.
"Before that," Jason resumes, "you retired as either a sniper or medic in the military…or possibly both." John is fully grinning now. "Tell me I'm wrong, John." John remains silent because he wants to see how sharp Jason truly is. "Alright, then explain to me why a regular old man is wearing a belt with concealable daggers? I noticed them as you retrieved the

191

note from your pocket. Are the daggers hidden behind the buckle or on the hip?"

Still smiling, John quickly looks around to see if anyone was paying attention. Sliding a dagger from behind his belt buckle, he sets it on the table. Jason's hostility subsides as he scoops up the tiny blade, closes his fist around it, leaving the tip's triangular blade protruding an inch or so from his fist. Jason, still being circumspect, already knows if John wanted him dead, he wouldn't have agreed to meet.

"The weapon of American mercenaries!" Jason proclaims. "The only guys I know in civilian clothes who carry these. See, if they ever get backed into a corner," Jason begins explaining how the daggers are used, "or have to fight their way out of a dangerous situation, they secretly slip these out and punch targeted pressure points to quickly debilitate the threat."

John admires Jason's well-rounded knowledge, and figures it is pointless to continue to insult his intelligence. John confirms his analysis. "I must say, you're sharper than you lead on. For obvious reasons, I can't just come out and let everyone know my background. You understand…for safety precautions. I've done things in the past, and people will be looking for me until the day I die. Call it karma or conscience, but I don't want that life anymore. Thus, why I moved here. What I told you about your cousin is true, and I can't let this go. It's terrible what they've done to Denise, your family, and her kids. I can't turn a blind eye any longer to this happening on our own soil. What they send us to fight overseas, has somehow set up shop in our own backyard. Do you believe what I'm saying now?"

In a way Jason did, but he still has his reservations about John. Jason can't help to think, *why now? It's been three years. What's John's angle on this? People don't just do things anymore because it's the right thing to do. They always have some hidden motive for helping.* Either way, Jason's guardedness remains firm.

"Just take a look at this and tell me if this means anything to you," John says as he opens the piece of paper and slides it to Jason. Spinning the paper 180 degrees, Jason sees an oddly shaped tree next to a pond. He stops and looks up at John.

Desperate for an answer, John asks, "Well?"

Adding some humor to his sarcasm, Jason answers, "It's a tree next to water."

John playfully engages back, "You don't say! That's the image I saw when I was visited by Denise in my dream. I don't know what it means and can't make any sense of it. I was hoping you might have a clue that will finally put my mind at ease."

As Jason remains silent, John snatches the paper back. "I knew it was a stupid idea to mention it. You probably think I'm some kinda nut job, but I just want to say I am genuinely sorry about what's happened to her. I hope I didn't completely waste your time," John announces defeatedly as he crams the paper back into his pocket. Looking up, he sees Jason smiling again. "You know what this means?" John asks, pulling the paper back out of his pocket. "Is it a message?"

"No…it's an actual tree."

"Are you serious?" John replies like a kid, losing all sense of professionalism. Feeling dumb for thinking Jason could solve his own personal riddle, he becomes uncomfortable.

Allowing John to mentally squirm, Jason eventually says, "Would you like to see it?"

Hesitant, John replies, "You know where this is? It's an actual place?"

"Yes," Jason confirms.

"You can take me there? It's close by?"

Jason nods his head yes. "I don't know what your schedule looks like but…"

"I will make time. You tell me when and where and I'll be there."

"I can take you there now, if you don't have any plans."

With a sense of a long overdue personal validation, John says, "I'm ready to go whenever you are!"

Chapter 11

Clues Are for Helping
Each Other

<u>*April 2018*</u>

An hour and a half later, John is standing in a clearing on the abandoned property with Jason. Noticing the property's collection of old boats, car parts, motor homes, sheet metal, broken tractors, and piles of trash strewn about, John sees the land as a graveyard of many things.

"Do you recognize this place?" Jason inquisitively asks.

"I only know of it from passing by here a few times."

"I thought you said you were on the local search team for Denise?"

"I did, but we never searched here. We were told to get ready for a big search a few months after Denise went missing, but it was called off after the detective was fired. What's so special about this place?"

"This is where the detective was going to search."

John spins around like a veil was just whisked away from his eyes. "This is it?" he energetically asks while carefully absorbing the scenery with wide eyes.

"Yeah, do you wanna see the tree?"

"Yes!"

Being that both men are prior service members, Jason is hesitant to open up to John, even though there is supposed to be a code of brotherhood to watch each other's back, both on and off the battlefield. For the moment, Jason is still unclear if John honors this unspoken duty.

Taking the lead, Jason guides John down a winding nature trail on the property. Using his military training and instincts, Jason relies on his ears, instead of his eyes, to keep tabs on John, following a few meters behind him. Not fully trusting John yet, Jason is on high alert. As they walk, he is listening intently for any sudden movements. Instead, as they round a bend, Jason hears a gasp from John. "Look! There's the pond," John exclaims immediately recognizing the scene.

Jason hears John's pace increase as they get closer to the pond. Just an arm's length away, John is dangerously and uncomfortably close. Ready for a struggle as John moves closer, Jason's hand hovers over his Glock 19, easily concealed underneath his baggy hoodie. As John trudges past, he relaxes and watches the gray-haired man reach the pond's edge first.

"This is amazing!" John exclaims. "I've been relentlessly looking for this place...I thought I was either going crazy or this was some place in another state...*Gasping*, "It's been right here the entire time!"

Awestruck and analyzing the surrounding vegetation overgrowth nearby, John temporarily forgets Jason is with him. Remembering the picture in his pocket, he pulls it out for comparison. Quickly walking left and then right along the water's edge, John tries to identify the exact vantage point from his dream. The tightly grouped trees and brush nearby, makes it difficult to see farther than 50 meters. Trying to solve his own mental puzzle, John becomes impatient. "Where's the spot?" he quietly says to himself still wandering.

Jason, who walked in the other direction on the water's embankment, stands motionless. He patiently watches John working like a mad scientist trying to solve a difficult equation. John frantically looks for the spot.

Stopping and looking around, John notices Jason's calm stillness. "Did you find it?" John desperately calls out from around the small pond.

Without saying a word, Jason turns his head away from John's view to gaze across the pond to the tree in his picture. From Jason's mannerisms, John knows the long-awaited answer to his perplexing riddle has finally arrived. Immediately, John dashes in his direction. With heavy thudded footsteps echoing off the surrounding trees, he diverts his attention back to John, to see him comically hopping over debris and trying to maintain balance on the uneven and slippery terrain. Almost as a flashback, had they been on a covert mission downrange, John's excitement would have assuredly given away their position. From the keys and coins loudly jingling in his pockets, to not missing a single twig to snap, Jason, amused, watches John lose all sense of tactical bearing. Hurrying his way around the pond, John's heavy panting almost drowns out his flopping footsteps, as he finally reaches Jason's spot.

Stepping back a few feet, he allows John to behold the real-life version of his vison, with no obstruction. He could sense a heavy burden has been released from John's shoulders. With his jaw dropped, flabbergasted, he rapidly compares the isolated tree across the pond, against the crumpled picture he had drawn, unable to dismiss what he perceives. John looks at Jason and lets out a burst of relieved laughter. "This is it! This is this spot! Look, even the unusual shape of the tree is identical to what I drew!"

Apparently a little more comfortable than Jason, John steps in and gives an unexpected hug. "Thank you!" John sincerely says, no longer trying to hold back the emotions. Sniffling and wiping his eyes, he relinquishes his bear hug, to see a surprised look on Jason's face. "I'm so sorry, I just can't begin to explain to you how much this means to me!"

Jason remains silent to allow John to feel comfortable enough to expand his emotional vulnerability. Peering back out over the pond with his hands triumphantly on his waist, John looks just like a mountain climber who endured a treacherous journey, finally reaching the summit of Mt. Everest. For all Jason knows, maybe this is John's Everest...in his own mind. After getting his fill, John snaps back to reality with a sense of urgency.

"Ok, now we know the location, we need to get a search team in here!" John directs.

"Not to rain on your parade," Jason interrupting his flow of thoughts, "we've already conducted three searches out here."

Surprised he responds, "You have?"

"Yeah, but with no luck," Jason acknowledges.

"But did you have dogs out here searching as well?"

"We had one come out but before he could search, the Sheriff ran him off...it's a long story."

Ecstatic, John follows, "Well, we're in luck. I know how we can get one. My friend has a cadaver dog used by the San Saba Sheriff's Department and the Texas Rangers. Are you interested?"

"If you could get him out here, yeah I'm interested!" Jason loudly replies.

"Good...if we do this, I need you to know this won't be considered an official search."

"Truthfully, I would like concrete evidence we are in the right location. If we find something, then we can go from there."

"If Denise is here," John says scanning the property, "this dog will find her."

"Perfect!"

"Ok, I can shoot him a message. The handler loves conducting unofficial exercises to keep the dog sharp, plus he owes me favor."

"Awesome! Sounds good to me."

John queries curiously, "If you don't mind me asking, how did you find this place?"

"Someone I know helped me find it."

"Like a psychic or something?" John inquires again.

"Well…not exactly."

John explains, "The reason I ask is, I also want to see what you think about bringing a psychic out here to see if they pick up on anything."

Recollecting, Jason replies, "I've been out of work for several months, and I don't get paid for another few weeks from the VA. I don't have money to pay anyone."

"No, she's not a practicing psychic and doesn't charge anything. It's actually my cousin. She's kind of like me. Instead, when prompted, she randomly picks up on unusual activity. If that type of stuff makes you uncomfortable, I won't mention it again. If my hunch is right, she can possibly help to pinpoint where Denise is or give us some vital clues."

"I'm game. Like I said before, I'm a little more open minded than most."

"Great," John happily replies. Patting his pockets for a few seconds, he looks up at Jason, "I left my phone in my truck. If we head back now, I can start making calls to get this organized."

As they return to their vehicles, parked in a clearing in the middle of the 42-acre property, John impatiently unlocks his vehicle and snatches his phone. Looking at Jason he asks, "May I call my cousin?"

Interested, Jason agrees, "Go ahead."

"Ok, I haven't spoke to her in a few months, and she lives on the south side of Austin. I'm going to put her on speaker phone so you can listen in on the conversation. She's good, but I want to test her abilities."

"Ok."

"I'm not going to give her any clues about where I'm at to see if she can pick up anything on her own. Are you ok with that?"

"Sure," Jason says skeptically.

Dialing a number, Jason hears the phone ringing. A woman picks up on the other line, apparently catching her breath.

"Hello?" the woman answers.

"Hi Sharon!" John enthusiastically replies.

"Oh, hey John! What are you up to?" the woman replies but sounds confused to the nature of the call.

John continues, "Well, you know what I do for living, right?"

"Yes," Sharon replies, over the commotion of a dog's relentless barking and the laughter of a hyper young boy.

"Well…" John begins but is immediately cut off by Sharon.

"Can you hold on one second?" Jason hears Sharon's voice trail away, "Would you please take Mattie outside and be quiet? I'm on the phone!"

Being a father, Jason smiles as he relates with the antics of his own two young children. To him, it sounds like Sharon just arrived home, and the dog and kid are excited too. Moments later, after John ends the call to Sharon, he focuses his full attention on Jason.

Boasting, John states, "I told you she was good. Well, what do you want to do?"

As Jason and John stand facing each other on the abandoned property in Brady, Texas, Jason finally replies, "If you want to coordinate getting the search dog and bringing your cousin out here, set up a date, and let me know."

"If I do this, only we can know the dog is out here. I don't want the handler getting into any trouble with local law enforcement."

"The only one I would say anything to is my mom, but that's it. Most likely, she will want to be here as well."

"That's alright by me, but we don't want a large gathering. The less people the better. We want to allow the dog to do its job without distraction or disruption."

"Works for me."

"After I check their schedules and mine, can I call you when I've worked out the details?"

"That's fine."

"I can also try to set a few other dates to ensure everyone's schedule is agreeable, and you can choose what works best for you. Is that alright?"

"Yes. I just hope this dog and cousin of yours are as good as you say they are…for Denise's sake."

"Me too."

Flashback: Her Last Stand

Peeling off down the dark country road, Aaron reengages in argument after leaving Trish's party. "I swear to God, woman, just wait until we get home!" Aaron screams over the motor racing full throttle.

"Why, so you can smack me around some more?" Denise sarcastically fires back.

"OHHHHH! You just don't know when to shut your mouth, do ya woman?"

"Don't call me woman…. MAN!"

"SHUT THE HELL UP DENISE!!!" Aaron screams at the top of his lungs, unable to contain his raging emotions any longer.

"Don't scream at me in front of our son, you're scaring him." Allen starts to wail from his car seat.

"Now look what you made me do!"

"Lower your tone!" Denise commands.

"Tell me what to do one more time, and I'm gonna backhand you into next week. You think you're gonna sit there, after embarrassing me like that in front of everyone, and get away with it?"

"I wasn't the one acting like a psycho! Taking pictures of me through a window, really? Who does that?" Denise petitions. "You're also the one who came in there accusing me of trying to hook up with your best friend," Denise finishes while trying to console Allen.

"I just knew you was trouble from the moment I met you!" Aaron argues.

"I'm not the one selling drugs and has friends who are junkies! You're such an idiot! You seriously think all your little get rich quick schemes are gonna finally pay off."

Aaron slows his truck to a halt at a four-way intersection just outside Trish's neighborhood. Aaron strains to see the face of his wife, scorned one too many times, on this dark country road. Denise knows what awaits her when she gets home alone with Aaron, but this time she is going to recoup the lost dignity he has taken from her over the years. With nothing to lose, and possibly not having another opportunity, Denise lets Aaron know her true feelings about him. Appearing to be patiently listening to Denise's two-minute rant, Aaron sits there letting Denise stand up to him. This is new territory for the couple, and Aaron is trying to mentally process how he can regain control of the situation. His go-to has always been intimidating her back into submission.

Denise's years of pent-up resentment, anger, and hostility towards Aaron, begins pouring out uncontrollably, right there in the truck. With each passing insult Denise can muster, she feels a tiny shimmer of who she was reawakening.

As a child, Denise was a fearless fighter. Whenever she felt wronged, she became a relentless pit bull, who would stop at nothing to right the wrong. She was this way until she started to date boys. From the troubles she had at home with her family, Denise seemed to gravitate towards psychologically and physically abusive relationships. An over eagerness to feel loved, appreciated, and respected, provided an insecurity where she would settle for whoever was willing to give her attention, rather than waiting for the right one to come along. Her haste to escape problems at home, rather than resolving them, produced a lifetime collection of bad choices. The consequences of these poor habits forced her to make even worse decisions, trying to get her out of the fix she was already in.

In desperation to start a life of her own, Denise slowly began to lose her identity. After she had her first child, Denise tried to settle down and conform to the role as a compliant housewife. This was not who Denise was. She was a free spirit, an adventurer, a daredevil, and a dreamer. Her notions to be a stay-at-home mom stemmed from the psychological conditioning society had placed on her. Thinking this is who she was, rather than who she truly wanted to be, Denise sacrificed her hopes and dreams to fulfill a role in life, in hopes of receiving approval.

Trying to escape a terrible marriage, Aaron gave Denise and her two sons refuge. In her haste to be rid of one bad circumstance, she unknowingly stepped right into an even worse situation. Not having any other place to go, she quickly felt trapped and afraid. From Aaron's sheer size and strength, she compared his rampages to the Incredible Hulk. For years now, Denise placed her pride and dignity aside in attempts to show gratitude for Aaron's generosity. Little by little, Denise's light and warrior like spirit began to fade. In attempts to become Aaron's Stepford housewife, she cooked, cleaned, and cared for the children. Denise took his verbal and physical abuse quietly, but not this time. This was her final straw, and the window to get the troubles off her chest was closing fast.

"Who do you think you are talking to me like that? You must have gone and lost your mind! One more WORD out of you, woman, and it's going to be twice as bad when we get home."

After a few seconds pass, Denise leans in and loudly shouts, "WORD!"

His knee jerk reaction, Aaron backhands Denise hard across her face as she flies into the passenger window hitting her head. "I told you to shut your mouth!" Aaron angrily responds. Arrogantly, he says, "You never did learn your place." While waiting for Denise's reaction, Aaron decides to fan the flame, "See what happens when you get out of line?" Watching Denise pull down the passenger visor to inspect her bloody lip, Aaron laughs. Antagonizing her more, he continues "You gotta be the dumbest person I know. I took you in, fed you and your two little brats, paid all your bills, and this is the thanks I get?" Denise closes the lighted mirror and slams the visor back up into the headliner of the truck. "Oh…now you're gonna break my stuff too?" Aaron booms still reaching for words to ignite Denise's anger. Denise slowly turns her head to Aaron with a quiet and fierce look in her eyes. "What? Are you gonna hit me?" *Huff*, "I'd love to see you try!" Aaron instigates as he peers out the windshield to see if anyone was out driving by this late at night. "You know…if you weren't so stupid, I'd…" before he can say another word, the dark night is filled with dancing stars.

Aaron, still in a daze and ears ringing loudly, realizes Denise unexpectedly socked him in the face…hard. Over their terrified son's screaming, Aaron can barely hear Denise yell, "I'm calling the cops!" as she quickly unlocks and exits the cab of the truck.

As a last stand, she calls out even louder, "We'll see how big a man you are when they take turns raping you in jail! When the cops find out you're dealing drugs and just hit me…you're done, you coward!" Denise angrily hollers in the desolate darkness. Aaron watches Denise dart toward the back of the truck. She quickly opens her phone and starts dialing. Aaron is dumbfounded his wife had the nerve to stand up to him, but she crossed the line.

Hearing him put the truck in park and hop out, Denise frighteningly peers over her shoulder as she escapes to the ditch nearby. With poor cellphone reception, her call doesn't go through. While she is frantically trying to redial, Aaron removes a wooden stick, from the bed of his truck.

"Hang up the phone, Denise," Aaron warns as he quickly closes the distance between them.

Still unable to get cellular service, Denise panics as Aaron is not far behind her now. Ignoring his warning, Denise tries to hurry away in the ditch a few more steps in hopes her delays might somehow connect her call.

"I told you not to..." Denise hears as she steps into a small hole trying to redial. Unfortunately, the only connection made is Aaron's wooden stick striking her on the back of the neck, as she stumbles.

POP. Denise's spine gives way to the blow. Aaron watches in horror as her body goes limp and lands lying face down in the grass.

"Oh man! Oh man...Denise? Denise! GET UP!" Aaron says loudly, but there's no response from his wife.

A million thoughts flash before his eyes as his mind wanders off the deep end. The future outcome from this mishap incessantly stirs in his head as he plays out every worst-case scenario. Unsure of what to do next, the cry of their son abruptly interrupts Aaron's thoughts. Still strapped in his car seat, Allen is screaming for his mom.

"Oh, Jesus! Oh God! WHAT DID I DO?"

Chapter 12

Don't Celebrate Too Early

May 2018

Jason, Ellie, and John guide the handler into a safe parking spot, underneath a canopy of trees, near the property's pond. As the man opens the door to his tan four-door Ford F-150, Jason sees two dog kennels in the back seat of the truck.

John, quick to make the introductions, says "Hi, Bobby! This is Jason and his mother, Ellie."

"Good to meet you," Bobby, smiling, says, extending his hand.

"I want to first say thank you! We appreciate you taking the time to come out here!" Jason says with deep sincerity.

"My condolences to you and your family. I know this must be hard, but don't thank me yet. We haven't found anything," Bobby replies.

"Don't say that," Ellie refutes. "You came all the way out here, on your own, to help us search. Whether you find anything or not, we are entirely grateful for it!"

"I say it because people get their hopes up, and sometimes there just isn't a body to be found. At any rate, here's the moment you've all been waiting for…" Bobby says opening the rear passenger door of his pickup. Swelling with pride, Bobby introduces the dogs to the group. "This one needs no introduction! This here is…Sirius!" He booms like a professional Master of Ceremonies. "Best cadaver dog

East…and West of the Mississippi!" With a great sense of joy on Bobby's face, he allows Sirius to sniff around and become better acquainted with his new surroundings. Bobby continues, "Now, I know Sirius' reputation proceeds him, but I hope you don't mind…. I also brought another dog still in training…Luna." Careful with his words, Bobby wants to ensure his plans don't disappoint his new acquaintances, "Sirius is about four years old now, and Luna, just over a year old. One day, she is gonna replace him when he is old and retired. Do you mind having two dogs out here?"

"Not at all!" Jason replies. "I've never had the chance to see these dogs in action before."

John adds, "We lucked out! Bobby and the dogs are about to start another case in a few days in East Texas. When I called him, our schedules worked out perfectly!"

"John, thank you so much for putting this together on such short notice," Ellie says graciously.

"No problem, it's the least I could do," John says with a hint of personal guilt. "Had I known, when Denise first went missing, how this case was going to be handled, I would have been more proactive, and gone outside my chain of command. Then again, I didn't even know this property existed until a few days ago. I guess I don't know if it would've made a difference."

Ellie, sensing John struggling with moral dilemma, tries to give reassurance to their gratitude. "Everything happens for a reason. We can't change the past. We are all doing the best we can with what we know now. The only thing that matters is to take what we learn and try to be the best we can moving forward."

"Hallelujah!" Bobby hollers back.

"We're just glad everyone could make it out here. If nothing turns up, then we'll just keep continuing the search for Denise…until we find her." Jason advises.

As Bobby begins to suit up in protective gear, overhearing the conversation while sitting on his tailgate, he loudly interrupts the three, "If your cousin is on this property, there's no doubt Sirius will find her."

As the group makes their way closer to Bobby, Jason asks, "I've read a few articles in the news about the amazing finds Sirius has made. With the weather being hot like this, does that help or hinder these dogs' capabilities?"

"The hotter the better," Bobby replies. "Just like in science when air warms up, it expands and moves, so does the ground. It allows the scent of decomposition to escape the ground. That's what these dogs are trained to pick up on. When it's frigid and cold, the air in the ground condenses, making it harder for them to smell. Being in the low 90's today, the hot ground will be releasing smells like a chimney. I'll be honest though, the only challenge I see on a big property like this, is the undergrowth. It makes it extremely difficult to navigate or even allow the breeze through, to carry the scent to the dogs. In conditions like this, the dogs must be in a closer proximity to detect the body. In the cooler fall and early winter, much of the undergrowth is gone and you can navigate much easier."

Knowing all too well what Bobby is referring to, Jason remembers his Special Forces land navigation courses at Fort Bragg. There, Jason saw even some of the best soldiers become victims to its unforgiving terrain and swamp like conditions. Soldiers who make the mistake of going to the Army's Selection course during late spring or summer time have the odds stacked against them. From the heat, humidity, and some of the thickest brush he had ever seen, the Land Nav Star Course at this time of year is almost guaranteed to knock out even the best of Special Forces hopefuls. Knowing this ahead of time, Jason is already wearing a pair of ratty looking ACUs he had worn going through Selection.

Bobby, almost reading Jason's mind and taking a quick glance at his attire, comments, "From the looks of it, you know exactly what we're about to get into out here."

Humbly replying, "Yes, sir! I've unfortunately had my fair share of playing around in terrain like this. I put on my old uniform because the material is less prone to snagging on the thorns and vines."

Wincing, "They'll eat you alive out here," Bobby recalls. Pointing to his shiny black and healthy-looking lab, Sirius, patiently awaiting command, adds, "This poor fellow got all tore up on the last run we did. His ears were ripped to shreds and bleeding everywhere. He was a hot mess and still managed to find the body. I mended his wounds, but I wish they made some type of protective shield for dogs who do this. Could you imagine walking through here with no clothes on? If you did...you might enter these woods a man, but God help ya, your momma's gonna have herself a new daughter when you come out!" The thought of Bobby's imagery now makes Jason wince.

"On that note, was John able to catch you up to how Denise ended up out here, or the locals out here?" Jason asks Bobby.

"Yeah, I brought this just in case," he replies, removing a matte black handgun from his holster and handing it to Jason.

After a quick inspection, Jason turns to his mother showing her the gun. "This is a Sig Sauer P226 DAK. A prime choice for law enforcement agents and, not to mention, the Navy Seals." Ejecting the magazine, Jason again displays for his mother, "This one is outfitted to shoot the .40 caliber Smith and Wesson rounds. Packs a punch for sure."

"Neat," Ellie replies trying to appear knowledgeable about whatever Jason just described.

Approving, "You know your hardware," Bobby commends. "Being out in thick wooded areas like this, I usually carry my Beretta, but this baby," receiving the handgun back from Jason, "can punch a hole right through a fridge."

"With all the junk out here, you may just have to. That's why I brought this," Jason says nudging the AK-47 slung across his chest. If we run into trouble, then good luck hiding behind concealment. This beast easily blasts through cylinder blocks, unlike AR-15s."

"The only thing an AR-15 is good for out here, is target practice and ricocheting off trees."

Laughing, Jason replies, "I know what you mean."

Bobby looks at John as he hops down from the tailgate, "I thought you said another person was going to be here...your cousin?"

"Yes, she had to drop her son off before coming. She should be here any minute now."

Almost on cue, John's phone rings and he quickly answers, "Are your ears burning?" Laughing, "We were just talking about you!... Yeah, we're all here about to get started. Where are you?... OK, I will see if Jason can come meet up with you and guide you to where we are."

Ending the phone call, John looks to Jason, "Would you mind heading back to where we parked in the clearing to meet Sharon, and walk her to us?"

"I'm on it," Jason responds already heading in that direction.

As Jason comes to the clearing where they parked, instead of standing in the open, he decides to conceal himself in the brush nearby. Not knowing if he and his mother were still being played, Jason didn't want to take any chances by making himself any easy target. Moments later, he sees a gray Dodge Ram dully making its way across the property. He observes a single passenger scanning the scenery and eventually parking next to the vehicles already beside each other.

Wasting no time, the lone woman immediately turns off the truck and opens her door. Jason, who knows better than to observe targets in vehicles, directly in front or from behind, makes sure to position himself in the driver's blind spot just in case devious plans were previously made. If there is trouble, from this position, Jason is well situated for a clean shot.

As the door to the truck swings open, a petite red-haired beauty hops out of the driver seat. As her small feet strike the ground, Jason's jaw slightly ajar, he almost chokes on his stick of gum. Her soft flowing hair, adjusting to the sudden movement, looks like angelic flames in the sun. About to make his presence known, Jason sees Sharon quickly conduct a 360-degree scan of her surroundings. Curious as to what she might do next, Jason waits. Feeling confident no one is looking, Sharon slightly hikes up the front of her shirt, and undoes the button on her pants. Suddenly feeling like a '*Peeping Tom*,' Jason prepares to look away to give her some privacy. Instead, she opens the rear passenger door of the truck, and rapidly removes a 9mm Beretta. Quickly scanning again to make sure the coast is clear, Sharon drops the handgun down the back of her waistline, before buttoning herself back up. Clueless as to her intent, Jason waits until her back is turned before quietly exiting his hiding spot and making his way to her undetected. Moving expediently, just like he was trained, Jason gets within a few feet of Sharon before loudly saying, "Hello!"

Startled, Sharon swings around to the sudden surprise. As their eyes lock, Jason senses something unfamiliar, but familiar at the same time, almost like they had met before…but not in this lifetime.

Uncomfortably laughing, "You scared me," Sharon says, catching her sudden loss of breath.

Even more tantalizing up close, Jason can't help but to lower his instinctual prowess in the presence of her smile. Even if she is there for dubious reasons, and if Jason could choose, he would much rather it happen at the hands of this cute Southern Belle.

Sharon asks a short series of questions to get caught up on the day's activities, but the only thing Jason can hear is soft and euphoric music in his ears. As his mind goes on temporary vacation from her enchantment, Sharon notices his stupor. "You ok there, big fella?" she asks, as Jason's sense of admiration makes her gently blush.

Having to return from this little moment of bliss, Jason regains his professionalism. "We are huddled down by the pond around the bend," Jason firmly says as he points a pathway off to the right.

"For full disclosure, and I hope you don't mind…I'm carrying," Sharon says showing Jason the gun she concealed. "Yeah, that's fine. Who knows what we might run into out here? Obviously, I'm packing too," Jason says as he slightly lifts his weapon and turns his head to look at the pathway. A sucker for a man in uniform, Sharon seizes the opportunity to discreetly scan Jason's muscular body.

"What's so funny?' Jason inquires to her sudden smirk.

"Oh nothing," Sharon replies as she quickly closes her door. Gently brushing past Jason, Sharon smirks while looking over her shoulder. "My cousin failed to mention I would be in good hands while I'm out here."

From her sweet voice, charm, and gorgeous natural beauty, whatever the reasons might be, Jason only knows he is glad she is there. Meeting back up with the small group, Jason sees Bobby ready to get started.

As introductions happen once more for the newly arrived Sharon, John eagerly says, "Come look at this," as he suddenly tugs on Sharon's arm and quickly escorts her to the pond's edge.

Even being half a football length away, Bobby, Jason, and Ellie easily hear their conversation. Jason has noticed each time on this property, he doesn't hear crickets, grasshoppers, birds chirping, or tiny critters generally scurrying about. The feel of this property seems to be devoid of God's own creatures other than snakes, poisonous vines, or a few turtles poking their heads above the water to get a fresh breath of air.

The group hears John say, "See?" giving Sharon a chance to observe the picture versus the real-life version.

"Even the tree branches are shaped the same!" she exclaims.

"I know…spooky right?"

"You know it takes a lot more than pictures and trees to get me shaking in my boots," Sharon jeers back.

"I'm not as comfortable with paranormal stuff, like you are. I try to ignore most of what I get because it freaks me out."

"I know, but you should open up more and just embrace who you are."

"Maybe later, but right now, I just want to find Denise. What I can't figure out is, do you think this is a clue? Does this mean she might be underneath our feet, by that tree, or a sign to let us know we are on the right property? That's why I wanted you out here. I want to see if you can help make sense of this."

Quiet for a moment, Sharon replies, "I'm not picking up on anything now, but I do sense a few entities in the area. One is a woman with brown hair, an older man, and something else. I'm not sure exactly what it is. It might be good, malevolent, or just curious to what we are doing out here."

"If you had to go with your gut, where do you think Denise is?"

"She's here alright. Although, I am being strongly drawn to the tree from your picture."

As Sharon and John conclude their mini-investigation and head back over towards the group, Bobby asks Jason, "You ready to get started?"

"Yes, sir! Since we didn't have access to a good aerial view of this area, I took the liberty of making a map of the property on my own," Jason tells Bobby as he hands him his work.

"Wow! You did this? Did you walk the entire property or is this a 'guess-ti-mation' from what you have already seen?"

"No, I walked every square acre, carefully annotating landmarks, and points of reference. I figure with this grid on the map, we can actually keep track of what's been searched."

"Impressive. You're following me, right?" Bobby asks Jason.

"I am?"

Overhearing the conversation while approaching, John quickly interjects to inform Jason on the standard search and rescue procedures when using a cadaver dog. "Bobby is going to let Sirius patrol the area, while following behind 25 meters or so. This gives the dog a clear path for detecting scents. You are to follow five to ten meters behind Bobby in case he steps in a hole, or if something happens to him, you'll know exactly where he is, and how to get help to him."

"Gotcha!" Jason responds.

"Where do you want us to start?" Bobby asks.

Jason responds first, "I'm glad we have at least identified the property, but as big as this place is, your guess is as good as mine. If Denise was by the pond, would the dogs already be picking something up?"

"It all depends on the soil, the weather, and breeze. Considering it's not a large pond, if she was in the area, it's possible the dogs would be chasing the scent," Bobby informs.

"I'm picking up on something in the direction of the tree, maybe we start there and work our way back to the property line," Sharon suggests.

Almost a prelude to their future relationship as husband and wife, Jason counters with, "I agree with Sharon in the direction, but I don't think Aaron would be so negligent to put her in an easily accessible spot, like right next to the pond. Why don't we start with the property line first and work our way back here, just to be sure?"

Agreeing. Bobby comments, "Since the dogs aren't picking anything up at the moment, I'd have to agree with you, Jason."

After conferring with the group, and all in agreement, they follow a small side trail Jason mapped out that takes them to the south side perimeter and begin to get to work. Five hours later, through the heat and torn up from the harsh brush, Jason deflatingly returns with Bobby, back on the same side trail they first left on. Taking a moment to collect his thoughts and breath, Jason is quietly furious.

Ellie, sensing Jason's frustration, tries to calm him down, "Honey, you did good. We are all proud of the work you have done. No one has pieced this all together like you have."

Angrily he blurts back, "What good does it do if we can't find her?"

Trying to raise his spirits, she says, "We'll just keep looking and searching. Eventually something is bound to turn up. Maybe she just isn't here."

Mad, Jason flings the gloves he's holding, hard against a tree nearby, and uses his arm to brace himself, as he peers over the pond's water surface for answers. Bobby remains quiet as he tries to silently load the dogs into their kennels.

"What about the tree, Jason?" Ellie asks. "Do you want to see if Bobby wouldn't mind taking the dogs over there, just to be sure?"

"Mom, we already wasted enough of this man's time. We've been out here half the day, and I'm sure he and the dogs are exhausted."

Still, not wanting to get involved, Bobby overhears the conversation, but continues packing up.

John and Sharon can see Jason is about a hair away from exploding and can't begin to imagine what it must feel like being in his shoes. After closing the doors with the air conditioning already blowing for the dogs, Bobby patiently waits to say his goodbyes. Noticing everyone is at a standstill until he comes to his senses, Jason scoops his gloves from the ground. He hurries over to let Bobby know how thankful he is for searching this rough and uncleared wasteland. "Thank you, Bobby," Jason says shaking his hand. "I'm sorry for losing my cool…. I'm just mentally and physically exhausted…I was seriously hoping this was our day."

"You don't have to make any apologies to me! Remember we only searched half the property. I am more than willing to come back again to search the rest. I don't know when that might be, 'cause we pack up tomorrow to head out of town. I can assure you, my first opportunity, I'll be right back here. If that doesn't pan out, then we'll just keep coming back until we find her."

217

A sense of relief washes over Jason as he fears he might never get access to expertise like this again. In his mind, this is his one chance to prove his efforts weren't in vain. As Ellie, John, and Sharon say their goodbyes, something else comes over Jason. Pausing before getting into the truck, Bobby sees Jason lost in slippery contemplation. "What's the matter, Jason? Keep your head up, brother! These things take time! We're on the right path! Is something else on your mind?"

Regaining his awareness to the situation, Jason replies, "I know you've loaded up the dogs and are ready to head out…" Jason hesitates.

Without Jason needing to finish his statement, Bobby cuts in "You want me to run the dogs around the pond?"

"Do you mind? Something is pestering me now to make a close inspection of the pond's embankment."

Seeing the pain and sheer frustration in Jason's eyes, Bobby enthusiastically replies, "Not at all! I'd be happy to do it!" Without saying another word, Sirius is already out of the truck, ready to get back to work.

"Come on boy," Bobby commands patting his leg as he guides the dog a few hundred yards down the pond edge's.

As the pair disappear behind a tall wall of overgrown grass near the water, Jason knows this is probably just wasting more time. In his mind, he doesn't want the question looming as to why he didn't check the pond thoroughly, if he never got the chance again.

With Bobby out of view, Sharon and John slowly walk behind them and stop near the grass wall. Trying not to make a scene, Jason walks in the other direction to release his pent-up frustration. With nothing to throw, Jason ejects his rifle's magazine and launches it into the nearby woods. Squatting to the ground and ready to pull his hair out, he begs the universe, God, Denise, or anyone who could hear him for help. Quietly talking to himself, "PLEASE!!! What am I missing? Denise…where are you?.... ANSWER ME! I don't know what else to do! I've done everything I can! I've spent the past three months, day in and day out, driving thousands of miles, and spending much more than that trying to find you. I've interviewed. I've questioned. We've searched…what else do you want from me?" Of course, no reply. "If you're not going to help me, then at least let me get on with my life! I have kids to feed, bills to pay, and I've reached a dead end…Denise…if you're here…give me a sign…something…anything!"

Sirius wildly begins barking. "JASONNN!!!" John excitedly booms from the distance…. "WE GOTTA HIT!!!"

Not wanting to get his hopes up, Jason slowly collects his thoughts and rises to his feet. Retrieving his magazine resting in the tall soft grass nearby, he hears excited barking traveling along the south bank until the dog appears from behind the brush, next to the tree, and sits. "JASON!!!" John yells again.

Momentarily staring at his mother with her face still in shock, Jason looks to find John and Sharon. John is jumping up and down, waving like a mad man, while Sharon on the other hand, is giving Jason a look. A look he will soon know all too well. A forgiving and compassionate smile, as to kindly say, 'I told you so.'

Chapter 13

Truth, Honor, Duty, &
Integrity...?

April 2018

Walking up the stairs to the two-story building in Waco, Texas, Jason and Ellie are nervous about their meeting. Never has a civilian gained the audience and had a one-on-one meeting with this high-level official within the Texas Rangers law enforcement organization. Traditionally, to gain access to such a meeting, people must be a government or law enforcement agent. This was a long shot, but Jason has done his due diligence and brought proof to support his claims.

Upon entering the dated lobby on the second floor, a secretary comes out from behind the magnetically sealed door to get their names. "Mr. Prescot, thank you for coming. If you'll have a seat, I'll let Ranger Warren know you've arrived," the elderly woman says.

"Thank you!" Jason replies and finds a place to sit a few moments later.

"Are you sure you're ready for this?" Ellie asks her son.

"Yes, mom, but please remember to keep your emotions in check. I know this is upsetting and that's why we're here. We can't present this case to Ranger Warren as disgruntled family members. We must stick to the facts," Jason states. "If you throw in speculation, thoughts, or opinions, we'll quickly lose all credibility."

"I want you to do all the talking, and if you leave something out, I'm here to back you up. You did a great job putting the pieces together and found her."

"Mom, I couldn't have done this without you! We worked well together. Now, I hope they'll at least allow us to objectively present what we found, and not laugh us out the door."

"Me too. I'm floored Ranger…whatever her name is, agreed to meet with us."

"Me too."

The lobby door unlocks and opens again as the secretary reemerges, "She will see you now."

As Jason and Ellie enter the main area of the second floor, Jason is surprised the high-ranking Ranger Warren's department offered such little real estate. In his mind, he figured the building would have many floors and plenty of agents running around, like the F.B.I. regional office building in San Antonio, TX. Instead, Ranger Warren's location is a tiny, two-story brick building previously constructed for the Baylor college campus. With the college's recent expanding student body, this building no longer served its needs, and the Ranger's organization took over the second floor. Wearing her cowboy hat indoors, Jason recognizes Ranger Warren from a picture on their website.

Smiling, "Mr. and Mrs. Prescot?" the average looking Ranger politely confirms.

"Yes," Jason replies.

"Nice to meet you and glad you could make it. My office is at the end of the hall."

Taking the lead, as directed by the Ranger's hand gesture, Jason is the first to enter the office. With his mother and Ranger Warren behind him, Jason immediately spots an irregularity in the room. Out of the corner of his eye, he sees his hopes for a fair evaluation quickly diminish. A man who's also wearing a Ranger uniform, stands creepily in the shadows of the dimly lit office. Jason stops his movements and looks him square in the eyes.

"Please have seat," Ranger Warren says as she makes her way behind her country styled wooden desk.

Warren's office appears more like a novelty gift shop for a Cracker Barrel restaurant, rather than a preferred prestigious law enforcement agent, Jason doesn't move. Instead, he continues to give the man the infamous 1,000-yard stare.

"I believe you know, Ranger Lewis," the uniformed woman pleasantly says, in attempts to distract their attention from her failure to uphold her promise to Jason.

Without taking his eyes off Ranger Lewis, Jason coldly replies, "Yeah, we know who he is. As a matter of fact, Ranger Warren, he's the reason we came all the way here to have this conversation. You assured me, when we last spoke, he wouldn't be here," Jason reminds as his eyes now meet the uncomfortable gaze of Ranger Warren.

"I don't recall ever saying that" she contests, but her body language suggests otherwise.

Unbeknownst to her, Jason can detect when people are telling the truth or if they are lying to his face. Right now, Ranger Warren is anything but truthful.

"I was listening into the conversation, and I heard you tell my son the same thing," retorts Ellie, coming to Jason's defense.

"My apologies for any confusion or misunderstanding, but considering San Saba County is his jurisdiction, I felt Ranger Lewis needed to be here to clear up any potential discrepancies. Just pretend he isn't here. I agreed to hear what you have to say, as I take such allegations seriously. If I find what you have to be credible, then I will instruct Ranger Lewis to provide me the necessary answers I require. If you've had a problem with his involvement, here's your chance to tell me your grievances. If I find his actions are not consistent to regulations or find any other agency guilty of misconduct, then I will handle it within my vested powers."

Jason's already heard this same scripted response from the San Saba Sheriff and Ranger Lewis. He knows why Ranger Lewis is here, and it isn't because he cares to solve this case. From the sinister grin on his face, and from their previous encounters, he knows Ranger Lewis' true intentions.

At this moment, Jason remembers the previous conversation he had with John. Maybe he's right about law enforcement's not so anonymous "whistleblowing." Here is a classic case. Having to air out grievances about Ranger Lewis while he's present in the meeting is as uncomfortable as having the victim of a crime, giving a statement with the known perpetrator standing right beside them.

Jason doesn't intimidate very easily, and he isn't about to put his tail in between his legs now. At this point, this case is not only about Denise, but this has also become something much bigger. From the people Jason spoke with, it seems this area distrusts those who swore an oath to protect them. In fact, the law enforcement agents are only doing what is convenient for their interest. Disturbing as it is, Jason discovered several key officials in the county are also abusing their authority because who's going to stop them? This meeting is also for all the citizens of San Saba who feel their town is under siege from corrupt leaders and law enforcement agents.

Jason was rather impressed to read of Ranger Warren's career success, being one of only two women to ever reach this high rank within the Texas Rangers' organization. His respect for her was immediately tarnished after he explicitly requested to remain anonymous. Jason's sure not every Ranger lacks truth, honor, duty, and integrity, but if their boss, such as Ranger Warren, doesn't uphold these values, then the lower ranks won't either.

"Ranger Lewis caught me up on Denise's case and her disappearance. He also briefed me on the leads they've checked out, but Mr. Prescot, you stated there is other compelling information I would be interested in hearing. If you care to share, I will let you decide what you feel most comfortable with."

Jason faces Ellie, "Mom, do you want to leave?"

"Why?"

"They're not going to listen. Once again, we share what we found, they might act interested, and make us think they're going to check it out..."

"Excuse me, Mr. Prescot! I said I would hear what you have to say!" Ranger Warren objects.

Ignoring her statement, Jason proceeds, "I figure we save our breath, go get something to eat, and enjoy the rest of our afternoon, before making the drive back home."

"Jason, Mrs. Warren said she's ready to listen. Give her a chance."

"For God's sake, mom! This man's girlfriend works in the evidence department," Jason exclaims while pointing at Ranger Lewis, "which conveniently had not one, but two cell phones destroyed doing a routine information extraction for Denise's case. Not to mention he's been good friends with the Sheriff for over 15 years and their offices are two doors down from each other! How is this not a conflict of interest? And again, the one person I specifically requested not to be here, so we would remain anonymous, she invited here!"

"Mr. Prescot, I have my reasons for Ranger Lewis being here. Now, do you want to continue this meeting or is this where we part ways?" sasses Ranger Warren at Jason.

Quickly whipping his head around to the Ranger seated at her desk, "Excuse me?" Jason angrily sasses back. "You got a lot of nerve getting an attitude after pulling a bait-n-switch on us, and it's not your cousin who's missing…it's mine!"

Humbling her demeanor, she replies back, "You're right. I do apologize…. Look, I think we got off on the wrong foot here, and I genuinely want to help. I can't do anything if I don't know what the problem is."

It takes Jason a while to respond. If this were a court proceeding, Jason would want his objection annotated, to appeal to a higher court for a fair and unbiased hearing. Unfortunately for Jason, this isn't an option. After letting his objection be known, and secretly recording the conversation, Jason begins. Jason spends the next hour verbally walking Ranger Warren from start to finish. He shows her a four-inch stack of key witness statements yet to be questioned by the Sheriff's office, and identified relevant evidence not being collected. He also lets her know the Sheriff said, 'When you find Denise, then come and get me.' Aside from all of this, he let her know there was blood found in the kitchen. Going through this entire walkthrough, Jason saves the best for last.

As he suspects, when he finishes sharing a sample of the mounting evidence pointing to foul play, law enforcement corruption, and collusion, Ranger Warren replies, "I appreciate you bringing this to my attention, but without a body or hard evidence, your claims are nothing more than good theories."

"Then explain to me why, when I went to see the Sheriff on my second visit, he informed me that he too believes Aaron killed Denise, but said they were backing off hoping he would make a mistake?"

"I don't have the case file in front of me, so I am not at liberty to say," she replies.

"Then explain when I asked why he won't escalate this to a homicide…if he even believes there was foul play…he said he couldn't because the DA is the one who has to do that."

"Yes, that's correct," Ranger Warren says defending the Sheriff's statement.

"I asked, what would it take for the DA to escalate it from a missing persons case to a homicide investigation? He replied they must take evidence to them, and they decide."

"Yes, that too is correct."

"My question is, how can the DA escalate a case if everything being brought to the Sheriff is being dismissed as uncredible evidence? Everything I presented, he automatically said wouldn't hold up in court. Is this not outside his scope of authority? Isn't his job to collect whatever he can, and let the DA decide what's credible and what's not?"

Ranger Warren is silent.

"Then, I had to remind him, cases aren't won on one piece of evidence alone. It's a collection of evidence to show motive. There are three so far. The first is the felony CPS case the same week which got dismissed after Denise disappeared. The second motive is they left the party in a heated argument where he accused her of cheating and is the last one to see her alive. The third motive has to do with large sums of money being transferred from his bank account in the days surrounding her disappearance. Most court cases have trouble establishing just one motive. What else do you need? Most importantly, how can you expect a DA to prove any of these motives in court if the Sheriff is not actively gathering evidence?"

Ranger Warren remains silent for a few moments trying to find the right professional words to let Jason know she's not interested. "Mr. Prescot, at this time, there's nothing we can do. It's your word against his."

In a last-ditch effort, Jason pleads further, "I even talked with the detective, and he also said he believes Aaron killed Denise. Let me make this clear Ranger Warren, I have admission from both the detective and the Sheriff, yet three years later, no one questions why this case continues to be classified as a missing persons case. The husband isn't even considered a suspect! Does this not sound contradicting to you or to this case?"

"Mr. Prescot, I appreciate your concern…" Ranger Warren says, trying to blow him off as expected.
Without skipping a beat, Jason cuts her off, "I wasn't finished." Ranger Warren is deeply confused, as Jason is grinning from ear to ear.

"It just so happens, before coming here, we were able to use cadaver dogs on the property we've been searching."

Without even allowing Jason to finish, Ranger Warren already fires back a knee-jerk response, "Oh dogs? We don't believe in using cadaver dogs because of the inconstancy with trainers. It provides poor results for those volunteer search teams. We only use professional dogs on our searches. There's only one dog we use in this region, and he is hands down the best around…tried and true. There is no comparison, and Mr. Prescot, we are splitting hairs at this point. If you don't have anything else for me, I will keep the statements you provided on file if something else comes up."

"It's funny you should mention that. We too only used one dog and handler…yours!"

Jason watches her sudden look of surprise as her face goes pale. "Um, what do you mean ours?" she stammers.

"I believe you know him as Sirius. If my memory serves me correct, how did Bobby describe him, ahh yes, '*the*

228

best dog both East…and West of the Mississippi,'" Jason says impersonating Bobby's thick Texas accent.

Speechless, Ranger Warren finally grabs her pen, and starts frantically scribbling messages on her scratch pad for Ranger Lewis to read. Jason didn't want to use this trump card, and possibly get the handler in trouble for the favor he had done, but Ranger Warren's deaf ears to their pleas, left him no alternative. Besides, while Jason is entirely grateful Bobby volunteered his time to help them, he is appalled the handler hadn't already come forward with his findings on the property. If an off-duty law enforcement agent stumbled upon a dead body in the woods while jogging, whether they anticipated finding anything or not, are they not obligated to report it? Do they carry on pretending they didn't witness anything? How's this any different from Bobby doing an unofficial training exercise with Sirius, and received two confirmed hits from both of his dogs, yet mentioned nothing about it? It has been weeks since the confirmed hits, and Bobby has yet to come forward. Considering his position, working directly with law enforcement agencies, it's his duty and responsibility to sound the alarm. By not doing so, Jason sees this as a cowardly move and Bobby too, has lost Jason's respect.

As Jason waits for Rangers Warren and Lewis to stop passing notes back and forth between each other like two elementary school children in love, he doesn't believe he's asking for anything astronomical, like reinvestigating the case. The fact remains, an investigation has yet to be conducted. A blind monkey could see this, and that is all Jason is asking for. For law enforcement to do their job!

When the Rangers refocus their attention back to Jason, he continues, "Now Mrs. Warren, we not only had a confirmed hit with Sirius, but the handler also brought another dog in training named Luna, who confirmed the exact location on a separate and lone pass. Let me tell you something, I've never had the opportunity to walk with a cadaver dog before, but I spent five hours watching Sirius and Luna, patrol the property. For five hours, these dogs had not a care in the world. Frankly, they seemed a little lethargic after hour three, from being out there for so long. As soon as Sirius came within 50 yards of the spot on the south side of the pond, I heard this dog go into full blown excitement. Barking, sniffing, spinning, and hopping around like it found its favorite toy. This is also exactly how Bobby explained their behavior to me…it's a game to them. From puppies, their toys are tainted with decomposing human remains and then hidden. When the dogs find their toy, they are grandly rewarded. Imagine their excitement when they find their favorite toy, just like a young puppy does when it finds a raw hide bone. Now, you might be able to get an idea to these dogs' behavior on this property. It was actually Bobby's professional opinion, after Sirius had a confirmed hit, he didn't need the other dog. Just to be certain Sirius had a positive identification to a dead body, I asked if he wouldn't mind bringing Luna to the south side of the pond, but from the other direction than Sirius walked. Standing back in the wood lines, as to not impede her smell, she picked up the scent quicker than Sirius had done. Being a younger dog, Luna was much more animated in her behavior. Darting back and forth in the area, to even launching herself into the pond not once…but three times. Sniffing and licking the water, but eventually ended up in the exact same spot as Sirius had sat. I asked him how far he would estimate the body could be from the confirmed hit location. He said, from his professional experience working with Sirius, the body can be within a few meters, but in the worst-case scenario, no further than 150 meters away."

Ranger Warren and Ranger Lewis could do nothing but listen in astonishment at this point.

Jason finishes, "To be completely objective and fair, I have no way to confirm the dead body on this property is Denise, but what I can definitively say is, someone was recently buried out there. After informing the current landowner of our finding, and to their knowledge, no one has been buried out there. Thus, leading us to the conclusion, there's an unofficial gravesite at this location. Since you have as much faith in Sirius as we do, there should be no reason for your team of Rangers to not immediately head out there and excavate the body. I would be misleading you to say I'm not hoping the body is Denise's, but either way, we stumbled upon a crime scene. We have not mentioned our find to the San Saba Sheriff's Department, or Ranger Lewis, because of the apparent conflicts of interest we've encountered in dealing with them. Their lack of interest to investigate this case, and inability to properly preserve evidence, is why I've brought this information to you directly. I didn't want to take another chance of this being, yet again, swept under the rug."

To Jason's surprise, Ranger Warren's attitude towards him changes. "Mr. Prescot, in light of this new evidence, I can assure you, my best men will be on this case immediately."

Before leaving the Ranger's office, Jason ensures they have provided everyone's contact information. Leaving the office feeling vindicated, his eagerness to know whose body is on the property grows by the minute. Finally, Denise or whoever is on that property will finally be discovered, bringing peace to their family, and be given a proper burial.

Chapter 14

Angels Amongst Us… Part 1

July 2019

In a demeaning tone over the phone, Ellie asks her son, "That's it? You just give up?"

"Who said I ever gave up?"

"No sooner than Ranger Warren decided to take the case, you up and disappeared. You started focusing on a relationship with Sharon and dropped the case entirely in my lap."

"God, mom, you're so dramatic! NO… I… DID… NOT! I told you, after Ranger Lewis found out I was the anonymous person reporting the tip, we've been followed everywhere we've gone. I told you, when we tried handing off the kids at our meeting point with their mom, of the lady who followed her into the gas station parking lot. Remember?"

"No."

"You don't remember the lady who was following Samantha, who wasn't even trying to be discreet?"

"The dark haired one?" Ellie asks.

"Yes. Samantha, Sharon, and I saw the woman. It only caught my eye, when I had gone inside to get a drink, and she was sitting in her truck staring at Samantha and the kids across the parking lot. She looked out of place. She wasn't getting gas, wasn't waiting on anyone in the store, or even attempting to go inside. She was just staring at our vehicles until she noticed me coming back out of the store. As I walked out, I got her plate number and when I ran it through the database, guess what? BINGO, the plates came back to one of Aaron's acquaintances and a known member of the Gypsy Mafia."

"Maybe she was traveling and became interested in what you were doing."

"If it were a one-time only random occurrence or coincidence, then I'd have to agree with you. Regrettably, this was not the first time, or the only member from that group, who I've caught lingering around my neck of the woods. Mom, I live over an hour and a half away from the San Saba area. What are the chances they just happen to be at the same gas station near our house, and also happen to be eyeballing my wife, kids, and Samantha? The more recent time was after I left the San Saba area after conducting interviews, and I was followed all the way back to Austin by that gray Jeep Compass."

"Was this the time you pretended to quickly get off the road and dine in at Dairy Queen and they were stupid enough to follow you inside?"

"Yes, I got their faces on camera, and after running their plates, it came back as a 1986 Datsun registered to who? Another friend or acquaintance of Aaron."

"I'm curious, how did you pick up they were following you?"

"It's not like they were hard to spot. When I sped up, so did they. Then, when I slowed down, they did the same. They wouldn't pass me after driving 55 mph on the freeway, and when I punched it over 120 mph for a few minutes, guess who was doing everything they could to keep up? When they caught back up, they again matched my speed. Each time I changed lanes, so did they."

"Amateurs." Ellie replies.

"I also figured out why everyone involved in Denise's case conveniently has a bald head. Like Aaron, Randy, the Sheriff, and Ranger Lewis. There happens to be a large following of a Neo-Nazi white supremist Brotherhood in the area, and do you know what they do? They use law enforcement to help them recruit members in prison and provide protection for them on the outside."

Curious, Ellie asks, "Use them for what?"

"To help them maintain their drug operation. I won't even get into the sex trafficking throughout that area."

"Sex trafficking? In that small town?"

"It was hard to wrap my head around this being bigger than some small-time operation, but their network extends internationally. Where do you think the drugs come from?"

"I don't think they're smart enough to pull off an operation like that."

"It's the perfect setup. I was impressed myself. No one suspects small towns of big-time crime, but it's the perfect hub. Who's going to bother you out there? Farmer Fred and his brother Jimmy? Even if they do, they can either buy them off or make them disappear." Jason elaborates, "Do you think this is only happening in this small town? No. For the past hundred years or so, our own government has been helping to target minorities, both foreign and domestic. Even over in Ukraine, people don't realize a Neo-Nazi styled regime took over when their government fell in 2014. Hate groups worked their way into authority much like what has happened on many levels in our own country."

"Yeah, we are far from treating minorities fairly in this country and abroad, but it doesn't make sense to me why. It just makes me sick when I read stories about how our own government funded and supported the Tuskegee experiment, but what really bothers me is, Denise is still missing. Then you quit working the case like you did and ran off to get married. You go start a new life like nothing ever happened."

Sighing heavily, Jason responds, "If it hadn't been for Sharon's comment to check near the tree, we might have missed the opportunity to finally know where Denise is. We have no more speculation to where she is. We got two confirmed hits because of her involvement, and no, I didn't run off to get married. You were there!"

"You know what I mean!" Ellie contests.

"Mom, it took them over eight months after our meeting with Ranger Warren to say they went and searched the property because she turned the case back over to Ranger Lewis. In fact, they never even called to let us know they were going out there or the result of their search. We only found out through the grapevine. Why wouldn't they have us come point out where we discovered the hits or to help streamline their search? Why did it take them six months before they even made a single phone call? Lastly, why wasn't Aunt Lisa hounding them daily to see if the body was Denise or not? She didn't call them, they had to call her, and how did she respond? She called you all pissed off because she received a random call from the Rangers while at work. Mom, why did six months pass, and she showed no interest?"

"I don't know what to say, Jason. If I had reason to believe a child of mine was detected, I'd be out there the same day with shovels, hopping fences, or blowing the Ranger's phone up daily asking why they haven't been out there. Not waiting six months later, but again, I can only speak for what I would do."

"That's my point! Ranger Warren told us the Rangers were going to immediately investigate the case, but as soon as we left, she put Lewis back in charge. Six months passed before he even called anyone, and who did he call?"

"He only called your Aunt Lisa."

"We never received one call back. He also didn't follow up with even one witness we provided to them. We gave them names, phone numbers, and their statements. How do I know this? I've kept in touch with those I spoke to, seeing how long it would take them to be contacted by the Rangers, and not one person received a phone call. It's been over a year now and still nothing has happened."

"Yeah, I can't believe it either, Jason. Lord knows, if they wanted to move the body, they had plenty of time to do it."

"Also, when did they claim to have finally searched the property?" Jason questions.

"Please, that's actually giving them credit they even went out to search. I don't believe anything they say anymore. I don't listen to their words, I watch their actions, and from where I'm sitting, those two are polar opposites from each other."

"True, but how cold was it when they claimed to go out there?"

"It couldn't have been above 55 degrees," Ellie recalls.

"And what did Bobby say about searching for bodies in the cold? It makes it extremely difficult for the dogs."

"Did I tell you what John told me?"

"You still talk to him?"

"Yes. He's also mad you quit searching."

"I didn't quit, mom."

"Anyway, after you outed Bobby, the Rangers went ahead and put him on their payroll."

"Doesn't surprise me. How else do you keep people quiet? You also thought I was crazy for the longest time because you couldn't believe all the inconsistencies I discovered."

"I do now!" Ellie argues.

"Let's not forget the biggest sham of it all, when I did a follow up with Aunt Lisa's co-worker."

"I can't believe what that woman did to you. If I ever see her again, I'm going to punch her lights out!"

"Take it easy, champ!" Jason teases. "If anything, we now know her co-worker's 'anonymous source' was at the San Saba Sheriff's department."

"Yeah, it was the Sheriff the entire time."

"Not a day after I called her pretending to vent, I also gave her false intel. I told her I was going to have my people start following and keeping close tabs on the Sheriff. Then, what happened the next day? You received a blocked call of someone impersonating Ranger Lewis, wanting me to come in alone."

"I remember, Jason. You stood right behind me listening to the conversation."

"This is why I backed off. I have yet to find a person who is trustworthy from the San Saba area. Until our country can provide unaffiliated agencies who are policing the police, this behavior will continue to get worse. Any power given, and left unchecked for too long, eventually leads to wide scale corruption."

"I agree. Where are you right now?" Ellie inquires.

"You know I won't disclose my whereabouts on this line. Look, just because I'm not out walking the property each day doesn't mean I'm done. There's nothing more I can legally do at the moment. We hit a brick wall. I'm having to think outside the box to see if there's something we missed or a different direction to take this. As a matter of fact, that's what I'm doing right now."

Hopeful, Ellie asks, "Really?"

"Yes, Mom, I've never stopped looking or searching. Instead, I've stopped dealing with Aunt Lisa because of her reaction when we informed her we found a body on the property. What were the first words out of her mouth? I honestly expected her to come flying out of her chair. After three years of searching, we found her, and she seemed annoyed by us being there. I was expecting, 'OH MY GOD! HALLEJULAH! PRAISE THE GOOD LORD! OUR PRAYERS ARE FINALLY ANSWERED!' What did she say instead? Almost like she didn't care, she replied, '*So, what are you going to do now?*'"

"Yeah, I was a little put off by her reaction to the good news."

"Just the whole thing stinks to high heaven!"

"I know" Ellie replies in disgust.

Jason replies reassuringly, "Now, you can understand why I took a leave of absence from the scene. I'm doing things on my own and currently I'm trying different avenues to see if we get different results."

"What can I do to help?" Ellie asks.

Sharon sitting in the passenger seat of Jason's car, nudges him and points to the time on her watch. "Hey mom, I need to let you go. Sharon and I are here where we need to be. I'll call you later, ok?"

"Ok, Jason. Please be careful. I love you!"

"Always. I love you too!" Hanging up the phone with his mom, Jason looks at his wife, Sharon, patiently waiting in the passenger seat.

"Sorry about that."

"Do you think she's still upset?" Sharon asks.

"Not at us. Her anger is with the Rangers for breaking their promise and dropping the ball with the case. She wants answers as much as we do. I told her I'm working on it. It's making her upset because it's not the way she expects to see me doing things."

"I think we're all upset over this."

"…and I guess this brings us here," Jason says looking at the historic buildings surrounding his car.

Sitting in Jason's Challenger, the couple observe the early morning sun before exiting the vehicle. Tired from their three-hour drive from Austin, they arrived at the business of Sharon's old friends, in the historic downtown district of Corpus Christi.

"They just opened, so we need to hurry."

"Relax, I thought we had all day."

"We do, but I wanted to catch up with Mark and Karen. I also want to make sure we have ample time to use the portal before they get busy. I didn't tell them we were coming, but I'm sure Karen already knows we're here unless the angels want it to be a surprise for her."

"About that…" Jason begins to say as he slips a $10 dollar bill into a parking meter in the car lot behind Mark and Karen's business.

Jason suspects his bank card transactions are somehow being monitored and is careful to not use his debit card. After his visit with Ranger Warren, each time he uses it, strange vehicles and people suddenly arrive at his location. Then they appear to be conducting surveillance and following him around.

Trying to forget about having to look over his shoulder, Jason wants to enjoy the day with his wife. As they start walking from the back parking lot towards the busy street already full of people, Jason begins to sweat from the Texas summer heat. He's glad he decided to wear his Punisher tank top, board shorts, and flip flops. Anything else and he might literally melt.

"What's this place again?"

"I know you're 'Mr. Science Guy,' but this is a different type of science. It's a spiritual shop."

"What's that?"

"It's really cool! They sell books, crystals, jewelry, music, and other neat things to help people connect with energy. It usually freaks people out because they don't understand how energy works. Church tells them 'You're the devil if you go in there' type stuff, but since I was a child, I could receive or transfer energy to help people feel better. I can't explain it, and neither can science or Church."

"Sounds super exciting," Jason teases. "I'm so glad you dragged me all the way down here on a Saturday morning to stare at some rocks! WEEEEEE!" Jason playfully mocks awaiting Sharon's reaction.

"Come on! It'll be fun!" she pleas.

"Don't they say the same thing in every scary movie? Yet it never turns out as fun, and the people usually end up dead anyway. Oh boy, I just can't wait!"

Laughing, "Stop it! Wait until you see how this portal machine works. You might think twice about the world we can't see around us. It's where science meets the energetic realm."

"Sounds totally safe! What is this device powered by? Ouija boards and ancient sacrificial relics?"

Smacking Jason playfully on his rear, "You'd better be nice while we're in here, and don't give Mark and Karen a hard time. They're really nice people."

"I'm sure they are," Jason sarcastically replies.

"Mark is actually a lot like you. He too was skeptical of spiritual or universal energy. In science, you guys call it quantum physics, but I think our way of saying it has a better ring to it. Don't you think?"

Rolling his eyes. "Sure!"

"Anyway, after they moved their business into this old building, which once served as a hospital during the Civil War, and Mark being a technical guru, he started building equipment to catch whoever kept moving his tools around the shop. It only seemed to happen when no one was there."

"Tools moving around?"

"Yes. He was able to capture his tools floating off his peg boards, doors opening and closing, and items in the shop moving on their own in the middle of the night. He's also captured strange floating orbs on camera moving about…"

"It's dust!"

"Ha-ha, no! You can see it for yourself. He keeps all his findings neatly filed, and loves showing people when they come in. It helps establish credibility for non-believers such as yourself!"

"I too can set up cameras and make things move at night using fishing line and ropes!"

Sharon suddenly stops on the sidewalk near a novelty shop with a machine blowing bubbles, and Jason turns around to see what the problem is. With her head tilted to one side and a hand on her kicked-out hip, she lets Jason know, enough of the jokes and to get serious.

Now standing only a few yards away from the entrance to the business, Sharon says, "If you don't want to go in, we don't have to. I thought after meeting Mark and seeing what he does, it would really interest you. Mark is the technician on the paranormal investigation team I was on before meeting you. On the last investigation I was on, we investigated a haunted hotel not too far from here."

"I feel like I'm on a man play date, so you and Karen can reminisce about what ghost and goblins say or what goes bump in the night."

"For your information, Karen doesn't speak with ghosts. She only hears angels. Look, this was your idea to come here, but if you've changed your mind, let's go home."

"Noooooo," Jason teases as he starts quickly walking towards the shop entrance door, "I can't wait to find out what the bling-bling palace in the clouds looks like in the afterlife."

"Jaaason!" Sharon warns following close behind him.

"I hope it has waterslides!"

"You won't be alive at that point anyway, so what does it matter? If you keep this up, you won't need to ask Karen about heaven because you'll find out soon enough," Sharon says, trying to sound intimidating.

"Ohhh…. Please don't hurt me!" Jason teases back.

Sharon rolls her eyes and sighs. "Please remind me why I married you?"

"Because of my charming looks and handsome smile!" Jason jokes.

"Let's keep it that way, ok?" she says, as Jason opens the door for her and gently kisses Sharon on the forehead.

Upon entering the small shop, they are immediately greeted by the natural blond-haired Karen. After short introductions, laughs, and hugs, Sharon grabs Jason's arm and yanks him around the store. She can't wait to show him her shared obsession with Karen. Crystals, crystals, and more crystals!

Some people are into collecting baseball cards, coins, stamps, model toy trains, dolls, and antiques, but not Sharon. She loves rocks! Already collecting goodies as they go, Sharon hands Jason a basket to put items in that she wants to buy. Not fully understanding her passion, and Sharon seeing Jason's uninterest, she stops near a collection of large purple amethyst geodes, which are split, exposing the crystals inside.

Looking at the price tag, Jason blurts out, "$2,000 for a stupid rock! It's neat I guess, but it's a rock! Who would seriously pay that much money for this dumb thing?"

Smiling, Sharon becomes a little more patient with Jason, trying to explain the significance of the stones in the store.

"So, you say you can feel energy flowing from these things, huh?" Jason asks doubtfully.

"Yes."

"I know we are married, but I'm sorry honey, you sound like a whack-a-do! I still love you, but do they also sell straight-jackets in this joint?"

"Ha, ha, very funny!" Smiling, Sharon scoops up a small, polished stone from a basket collection nearby and places it in Jason left hand.

"What's this for?" he asks.

"Just wait," she replies. "I need you to clear your mind, relax, and take a deep breath."

"What are we doing here?"

"I want you to close your eyes and focus solely on the stone in your hand," Sharon instructs.

After a few seconds pass, Jason impatiently asks, "Now what?"

"Just wait."

"Wait for what? I don't know what you are trying to show me…"

Before being able to answer Jason, he jumps when he feels a hard thump in his hand. "Woah! What was that?"

Sharon laughs, "Jason, welcome to the world of crystals!"

Quickly opening his eyes and spinning the stone around several times in his hand to closely inspect it, Jason asks, "Is this rock like one of those Mexican jumping beans?"

Chuckling, "No," she replies. "Each rock has a life force energy, and they all have their own unique qualities. Some crystals absorb negative energy, like a sponge, while others repel it. Some are even used to amplify, transfer, or store qualities about you."

Still in disbelief, Jason quickly places the rock back into the basket and reaches for a larger blueish and black stone on the shelf. "That one is called labradorite," she informs him.

"What does it do?"

Before Sharon can answer, Jason closes his eyes trying to repeat the experiment. Seconds later, Jason feels a soft zap pass into his hand, and travels halfway up his forearm.

Excited, "This one just shocked me!" Jason says incredulously.

"Uh-huh. Like I said, they all behave differently. Labradorite helps to relieve stress and amplifies mental acuity."

Instincts taking over, Jason places the stone in their shopping basket, instead of back on the shelf, and reaches for another one.

"Oh…now you want to buy one? I thought you said I was crazy," Sharon jokes.

Ignoring her chides, Jason is in scientist mode, and ready to conduct more experiments on his newly found discovery. With each rock he grabs and tests, his preconceived notions slowly begin to crumble from the science he thought he knew. Several experiments later, Sharon sees Karen making her way over to the couple.

"What do you think, Jason?" Karen gently asks.

"This is bizarre and incredible at the same time…seriously! All this time I've looked at stones like inanimate and lifeless objects. I'm honestly dumbfounded, shocked, and humbled at the same time."

Giggling, she exclaims, "Mark was the same way!"

"I'm already wondering how science could detect or even measure this type of activity. I have a million questions right now stirring in my head. I'm wondering why this isn't taught in schools."

"It's natural energy connections we are all born with. Unless it has twinkling lights or fancy names, mainstream science dismisses it as pseudo."

"If I'm just learning about this now, it makes me wonder what else I haven't been taught. I know this might sound corny, but everything I thought I knew just 10 minutes ago, has quickly been dismantled by some tiny little rock."

Softly smiling, Karen reassures Jason, "I think we were all like you at one point in our life, to some degree, but there is nothing new about energy. I didn't become aware of it until about 20 years ago, after I became very ill and was barely able to walk. It was through this experience which helped to open my mind, heart, ears, and eyes to what's going on around us." Karen playfully whispers, "Did Sharon tell you what I'm known for?"

"Yes ma'am," Jason politely replies to the woman in her early 50's wearing a long fashionable purple and yellow dress. "Sharon said you can hear and talk with angels."

"Well, I call them angelic beings, but yes."

After meeting the mysterious Asian man, who knew things only God could know, Jason was anxious to speak with Karen. Having his degree in science, Jason enjoys discovering how things work and operate. Karen was also much more accessible to speak with about supernatural phenomena. She isn't shy about explaining how she accidently developed her keen sense of hearing while sitting outside listening to the sounds of nature when she was sick. Only when her condition took a serious turn for the worse, did she begin to hear their voices.

"When I first heard angelic creatures, it sounded like music, windchimes, tiny little bells, or ringing in my ears. The more I strained to hear the sounds, the louder they became. I realized these weren't just random noises. I was being spoken to. I felt silly for a few days, before this realization, as I kept searching my yard and the neighbors' for bells and chimes. I swear Mark was a week away from having me committed to some institution, or something like that, before I could understand these were actual words. It was the angelic creatures who told me, it was my diet and the medications I was taking that were making me sick. It wasn't some illness. A year later, after slowly detoxing my body from the medications I was on, I regained my health. Now, I can hear them just like I hear you speaking with me."

"What causes disease or illness?"

Taking a moment, Karen appears to be listening for the right words to say to Jason. "Disease to your health is a manifestation of your ignorance."

"I don't understand."

"The ignorance is your neglect to the needs of the body. Self-healing is the ability to demonstrate and apply your knowledge of your own body, to recover or save yourself."

"I can see how this is true."

Karen adds, "We show our faith through our work. There used to be a time when true doctors didn't charge to heal others. Now the practice of medicine has become focused on making money, rather than healing patients. They didn't like praise or notoriety. It was an honor and a privilege to practice such healings. If you look at doctors today, they have put themselves on pedestals for not healing, but making patients become dependent on pharmaceuticals or false medications."

"False medications?"

"Medicine might make you better but unless you correct your behavior, you will continue to get sick. Education is the true medicine."

"Do they communicate to you once in a while or do you hear them all the time?"

"Both. It does get annoying at times when I'm talking to people. They often interrupt, telling me something about the person I should know or give me messages I need to share. If they are being a 'Chatty Kathy,' I'm over here going...'Huh? I can't hear you! You're going to have to speak up!' Ha-ha, sometimes when I'm in quiet settings alone with Mark, and angels, as you call them, are just chatting away, I startle him by breaking the silence. I end up hollering so I can hear myself speak."

The group laughs. Curious, Jason asks, "How can you tell they are angelic?"

"They sound different."

"Compared to what?" Jason probes.

Lowering her tone and volume, "The deceased and other entities."

"Other entities?"

Lowering her voice again, as not wanting to spook the nearby customers walking into her shop, Karen continues, "You might call them demons, but they have a metallic sounding voice when they speak. It's not harmonious and euphoric like Angelic beings. It sounds like metallic discord or unsynchronized dissonance. Almost like they are on different frequencies when they communicate. To me, it sounds like nails on a chalkboard. Just very harsh and jarring to listen to."

"How do the deceased sound to you?"

"Umm, they sound the same as you, rather coming from a distance, or behind layers of a thin wall. Rarely have I heard demonic beings. I don't know if it's some subconscious selective hearing I have, or maybe I was allowed to hear the various types for reference. Who knows? What I do know is, the only things coming through now are Angelic voices."

"Do they wake you while you sleep?"

"No. We have a system. When I'm ready for bed, they quiet down. When I wake up, they're sharing begins. If I'm being lazy and don't want to get out of bed, I will instantly smell fresh coffee, and they will say 'It's time to get up.' Using pillows to cover my ears so I can't hear them is pointless. It's weird. I've tried earplugs, covered with headphones, and put my hands over my ears, but their voices still come through crystal clear."

Giddy, Sharon answers, "Jason wanted to come visit down here because he wants to ask the portal a few questions."

Looking like someone is speaking in her ear, Karen is slow to respond, "You have questions about your missing cousin?"

Surprised, Jason looks at Sharon. "I told you…she talks with angels."

"We'll talk later. Don't let me keep you from your shopping. Looks like I have a few customers anyway who are ready to be helped out. When you are finished, come meet me over by the register, so I can give you a good discount," Karen says. Looking directly at Jason, she finishes. "They must really like you."

"Who?" Jason replies.

"The angels. As soon as you walked in, they quickly gravitated to you. Seems you also brought a few of your own. They are very protective of you."

"Huh?" Jason responds confused. "I don't understand."

"We will talk later."

"Thank you," Sharon replies as Karen intriguingly looks Jason over before walking away to the counter in the back of the shop.

"I told you she's really sweet." Sharon quietly whispers to Jason.

"It would be neat if I could get more time to ask her more detailed questions."

"It's the weekend, so she might be too busy, but maybe when Mark's done, he can show you a few of his gadgets or some of the videos he's recorded."

Chapter 15

Angels Amongst Us 2 – What Are We Doing?

July 2019

Browsing another 30 minutes in the spiritual shop, Jason sees items ranging from various dream catchers, energetic cleaners like Palo Santo, beautiful statues of Jesus, angels, and a variety of products from India and Asia. He also comes across technological metaphysical crystal applications like orgonite or orgone energy pyramids. Watching Jason inspecting the unique samples on display, Mark uses this as an excuse to offer good selling points. "A little fun fact for ya," Mark calls out approaching Jason, "if you throw one of those orgonite pyramids into the ocean, it attracts dolphins."

Amused, Jason inquires, "What is orgonite?"

"It's a combination of different crystals and metal in resin," Mark boasts. "Sharon told me you're into science and got a degree in this field. Is that true?"

"Yes, sir."

"I did too! You might appreciate this little tid-bit of information then…those pyramids are based on the scientific research of Wilhelm Reich. Using torsion field, zero-point energy, and sacred geometry, you now have the foundation or building blocks for these babies," Mark says as he picks up a pyramid on display. "To make these orgonite pyramids, you combine a few different crystals, metal shavings, resin, and some copper wire inside of these clear pyramid shaped pieces of plexiglass."

"That's interesting."

"Do you want to hear something even stranger?"

"What's that?"

"Reich's technology is still banned in several states."

"Why?"

"The science we learn in public education today was changed back in the 1920's, and good luck trying to find a science book referring to geology before then."

Somewhat offended by Mark's comment, Jason asks, "How so?"

"Take for example, gravity. Before the 1930's, gravity wasn't based on the earth's magnetic core or on Isaac Newton's theory of gravity like they teach today. Back then, you were taught regardless of being on land or in the water, the Principles of Archimedes' Specific Gravity."

"I'm not familiar with that."

"To put it simply, it's the science of hydrostatic buoyancy and equilibrium but it's not specific to water alone. Have you ever put a magnet in water?"

"Yes."

"What happened?"

Jason doesn't respond.

"Nothing! Water is not magnetic! So, how then does magnetic force keep water pinned to the ocean floor on a ball planet, while we spin at 1,000 miles per hour? Does this seem logical or sensible?"

"That actually makes sense. I'm curious, how did you find out about this?"

"My grandmother was the one who told me about it first but then I found hydrostatic equilibrium on NASA's website. As for my grandma, she was born in 1917. I remembered her saying as a child in elementary school, they were taught the earth was flat, not a sphere. She said it changed sometime during grade school and remembers when images of the globe started popping up everywhere. I know what you're thinking, another '*Flat Earther,*' right?"

Jason chuckles.

"I thought my grandma was senile in her older years until after she passed away a few years back."

"My condolences."

"Thank you. Well, we were going through her things in her attic, and in an old dusty box, there it was! I found an old elementary school science book of hers. Sure enough, after reading it for myself, she was telling the truth."

"What did you do with the book?"

"I still keep it on my bookshelf at the house. Maybe one day, you and Sharon can swing by so I can show it to you. You wouldn't believe the stuff they were teaching kids back then compared to today."

"I would be curious to check it out."

"You guys are welcome to come over anytime."

"I would like to know more about it."

"It's simple and logical. Now, whether you believe the earth is flat or round is entirely up to you, but the science before the 1930's works without exceptions. Today, if something doesn't fit into the mold of a theory, it's immediately discredited and brushed aside."

"I can't argue with you there."

"As I was saying, the science today doesn't give students the entire picture of how forces of this world operate. It makes science and this world is a big mystery. It might introduce you to land, rocks, water, electricity, and stars, but they won't teach you how to work with them."

Puzzled, Jason asks, "Work with them?"

Mark explains, "You're taught to see trees and plants, for example, as lifeless or inanimate objects, but everything has a life of its own, which influences human behavior. Real sciences like this, have been banned from schools here in the West. It's the Science of You!"

Jason argues, "I took those classes. Health, physiology, kinesiology, biology, psychology…"

Placing his hand on Jason's shoulder, "That's kids play compared to what the human body is capable of."
Mark allows Jason a few moments to process this new information, then continues, "Please don't take offense, I'm merely sharing what I've discovered. Considering we share similar interests, I think you might find this new information compelling like I did. Remember, true scientists and historians explore the unknown to better understand what we think we know." Keeping an open mind, Jason lets Mark present the material he unearthed. "Let's look at modern science."

"Ok," Jason responds.

"When we think of a cure today, we visualize it as some magical miracle or potion, right? In truth, a cure is a solution to your problem. Take the human body for example. Each person's body is different. What cures or fixes a deficiency in one person, might be an overage to another. We place our trust in doctors and pharmaceutical companies, but they treat everyone the same. Illnesses aren't onset by age, it's a culmination from years of nutrient deficiencies in our diet, and improper exercise to stay fit and mobile."

"Then how do you explain relatively healthy people, who exercise regularly, and still develop disease or illness?" Jason defends.

"Simple. Let's take optometrists or eye doctors as an example. These doctors would be out of a job if people knew natural sunlight and healthy liver functionality maintains your vision. Instead, they make money from you buying their prescription eyeglasses, contacts, and surgery to manipulate your vision. Wearing sunglasses, reading in low light, eating bad foods, and drinking alcohol, destroys your eye vision. If you correct these habits and do the appropriate eye exercises, then you naturally regain your eyesight."

"Drinking really does give you beer goggles then," Jason jokes.

"More than you know!"

"How can I find these exercises? My vision isn't what it used to be."

"We actually have a book right here which walks you through the process. I was blind as a bat, but after I did them," Mark handing Jason a copy from a nearby shelf, "I have 20/20 vision."

Lowering his defensiveness, Jason replies, "Great! Thank you!"

"It's really fascinating stuff."

"Sounds like it."

"There is an entire world of information out there our society doesn't want us to find out about. Life is simple."

"Yeah, it's called cause and effect. Problems have a cause and there are effects from those, but if you know what caused something, you can use common sense to easily identify the proper solutions."

"Exactly," Mark responds. "Have you been reading up on our beaches here in Texas?"

Almost afraid to ask, Jason probes, "What's wrong with the beach?"

"You should look up 'heavy water' or 'heavy hydrogen' in saltwater. Did we really think detonating atomic bombs in our oceans wouldn't have lasting effects? Now, the deuterium oxide isotope toxicity in our oceans and beach water is scary. After doing some homework, tell me you still want to go to the beach on a regular basis."

"I haven't heard of this before."

"Most haven't either, but mysteriously, this extremely dangerous compound is also in our drinkable water. We aren't drinking H20, it's HDO or 'semi-heavy water'. Hydrogen Deuterium and Oxygen. You would be amazed how this one agent limits your life span, accelerates cell decay to induce sickness, causes cancer, depression, and anxiety. It also depletes energy levels and inhibits the body's natural ability to recover from exercise and injuries. These are common side effects, and by ingesting or absorbing this stuff regularly, we are only functioning at 50% of what the body can do. Fluoride is child's play compared to this stuff."

"Thanks for the heads up."

"If that doesn't keep you out of the water, then maybe you might like to hear our beach water is not only filled with pharmaceutical and manufactured wastewater, but also an excessive amount of feces…literally."

Jason uncomfortably laughs, "Geez! That's gross! We were just thinking about taking the kids to beach in a few weeks."

"You would be better off having them splashing around in a dirty toilet than go swimming at the beach."

"Gross!" Sharon chimes, overhearing the conversation.

"Tell me about it! The health inspectors and officials come out once a month to test the water along the coastline. More times than not, it's over what they call tolerable. The fact any of it is tolerated is a problem in itself. It's unsanitary! Our coastlines here aren't brown because of 'dredging' as they claim."

"Ok stop," Sharon protests. "You're gonna make me throw up!"

Laughing, Mark adds, "Now you know why I won't go to the beach anymore."

"I thought they treat sewage?" Jason comments.

"Ok, I'm going over here," Sharon says, pointing to a section away from the conversation. "I'll let you two talk amongst yourselves."

"We're damaging and polluting on mass levels. Our coastline conditions are just the result from what happens from over-industrialization and greed for money. This is what we call *Progress*!" Mark sarcastically states. Karen, trying to be a buffer, comes to the rescue.

Butting into the conversation, she sternly comments, "Would you leave Mr. Jason alone?"

"No, it's fine," Jason contests to Karen trying to save him from awkward conversation.

"Believe it or not, I prefer having people tell me the truth, rather than comforting lies."

Giggling, "Ok, but don't say I didn't warn you!" she replies heading over to greet new customers entering the store.

Jason states, "You should check out the allowable levels of arsenic and fluoride they put into our drinking water. The newest problem is Teflon. Researchers have found more than 600 drinking sources, in over 43 states, now contain Teflon. This is no coincidence, and Dupont is responsible for developing it. Now millions who drink tap and bottled water in residential areas, businesses, military bases, and airports, have been exposed to chemicals that create birth defects, cancer, thyroid disease, infertility, immune system complications, and neurological disorders."

"Dang, and here I thought petroleum-based products in kid's foods, candy, soaps, shampoos, and hand sanitizers was bad enough," Mark shares, "It's like we're all slowly being poisoned to death."

"90% of the problem with health-related issues are from the foods we consume."

Laughing, Mark states, "You should write a book on this. It would help so many people."

"Once I changed my diet away from canned or preserved foods, my mind was much cleaner and clearer feeling. I just felt better."

"That my friend…IS SCIENCE!" Mark broadcasts.

Jason compliments, "I like how you think!"

"The wisest answers or solutions in life are often the simplest. We just tend to overcomplicate and confuse everything."

"Agreed!"

Karen, having too often to reel Mark back in from his tangents, walks back up to Jason and places a motherly hand over his shoulder. Speaking closely to Jason's ear but audible enough for others to hear, "Don't mind him. I apologize because I usually keep him locked in the back. I only let him out today because of good behavior, but if he keeps it up, straight to the back with you, MISTER!" Karen teases pointing to Mark.

The group laughs. Mark shrugs his shoulders, "Sharon said Jason likes science, and we are talking about a few scientific things."

"A few?" she sarcastically replies.

Sharon laughs, "Jason is the same way!"

"Hey, don't bring me into this!" Jason jokes.

Smiling, Karen counsels, "What's the point of studying anything if you're not going to use it to help improve your life and others you know? If you're not applying what you learn, then why read it? Cramming useless information into your head without the intention of using it, is senseless and a waste of valuable time. People who don't know what they want from life, do this to keep themselves occupied, distracted, and entertained. Mark, is your conversation with Jason, any different than preachers sharing the gospel, who aren't practicing what they preach? Why don't you do something more productive, like show Jason and Sharon your latest finds on your videos?"

Hearing the suggestion, Sharon becomes even more excited. "I wanna see!" she exclaims.

"That's right!" Mark remembers. "Since Sharon stopped helping with investigations, I haven't been able to show her all the weird stuff I caught on film.... I'll be right back," Mark says as he hurries off to a little office in the back of the store.

"I swear, boys and their toys," Karen says, rolling her eyes, making Jason smile.

Finding their way to the register, Karen takes the items to ring up. The collection Sharon and Jason want to take home is more than the cash he brought with him. Figuring he was far enough away from anyone wanting to keep tabs on him, he goes ahead and pays using his debit card.

A few hours pass, as Jason and Sharon enjoy their conversation with Mark and Karen. Jason is pleasantly surprised to find his cynicism of Mark and Karen was unfounded. Jason expected to see dancing hippies, chimes, or some crazy lady with feathers in her hair. To Jason's dismay, he was expecting to see the beating of little drums while telling people their fortunes. As it turns out, Mark and Karen are just like Sharon described. They are two normal, rational, highly intellectual, funny, and down to earth people. Time flies as they continue their conversation in between guests, until Karen's face changes, as if hearing something important.

259

As Karen relays the message, Jason listens intently. Oddly enough, she also says verbatim, the same comments as the mystical Asian. Being analytical, Jason wants to know more about the angels. Karen carefully explains their duties and hierarchy as angels. She also explains the offices held by ethereal beings and how people can gain such positions from the work they do here. Eventually her explanations cease as her curiosity of Jason peaks. "You know, I can usually read people like an open book...but not you. It's almost like I'm being blocked from knowing too much about who you are," Karen says, slightly embarrassed, feeling like her gifts are being purposefully inhibited. "It either has something to do with a past life of yours or something you might do in this lifetime. Either way, you are heavily guarded and protected."

Confused, Jason asks, "Protected? Like how?"

Gently smiling, Karen elaborates, "Angelic beings have roles, as messengers, protectors, warriors, or healers, to assist certain people throughout their life who devote themselves to bringing benefit to humanity and earth. Then, there's you."

Chuckling, "Me? What about me?"

"From my experience, I can sense or pick up on the strength or intensity of each Angelic being around me. They've explained these variances have to do with their rank and authority. There is one Angelic being, who is closely watching and very protective of you. It's the first time I've felt a presence so strong."

Growing up in a traditional church setting, Jason hearing Karen's explanation of Angelic beings is beyond captivating. He especially likes how she describes the sounds she hears as they move about.

"The best analogy I can use to explain how I hear them move is to compare it to the sounds of free-flowing metal netted body armor jingling. As they move, it sets the sounds into motion, but sudden, fast movements, produce different sounds which are accompanied by large and powerful, feathery wing thrusts." Laughing, "I know this might sound odd, but to me, fast movements sound more like winged light sabers." Karen chuckles at herself again and at her inability to appropriately convey to Jason her experiences. She continues, "All I can say is, whoever you are or were, it would be unwise for someone to speak poorly about you or try to hurt or harm you in any way."

Perplexed at even the thought, Jason uncomfortably asks, "Why is that?"

"While someone speaking bad about you might not get you upset...this doesn't mean they don't."

"Who...the angels?"

Karen gently nods her head up and down a few times to answer Jason's question.

"I thought angels only did good things."

"Perspective, my dear!" Karen refutes. "Perspective."

"It makes sense, I guess."

"The importance of what they want me to convey to you is, be mindful of how you speak and treat others. You never know who's watching over them. Angelic beings often accelerate the lessons we need to learn. Take for example, if you are refusing to grow, learn, and develop, they might influence the circumstances in your life to make it uncomfortable and miserable to get your attention. When you pay attention to what you are doing or not doing properly, it gets you back on track and learning. Angelic beings only intervene when higher authority deems it necessary or if you ask for assistance. Otherwise, they act like silent friends or parental figures who might give the occasional clue and hint, to help us figure out our own little mysteries in life." Karen's soft face suddenly changes again as she carefully listens again and quickly turns her head to Mark.

"Honey, I think it's time you show Jason the portal."

"Yeah, I'll go grab it from the back," Mark says as he darts to the back again.

"Take Sharon and Jason into the room I do my readings in. It will give you more privacy," Karen elevates her voice, so Mark can hear as he rushes off to the back office again.

"Jason," Karen says turning her attention back to him, "it's been a pleasure to meet you!"

"You as well!" Jason politely replies.

Turning her attention now to Sharon, and leaning over the counter, Karen uses her hand to playfully shield her mouth from Jason's view. "You found a good one! He's definitely a keeper!" Karen loudly whispers so Jason can hear as well, while giving him a friendly wink.

As the women giggle, Mark comes back with a strange black handheld box and a laptop computer. "If you two want to follow me, Karen wants us to use her room," he says walking briskly past them.

Jason looks back at Karen, "Do I owe you anything for your time?"

"Not a dime, my dear! I just want you to take special care of our Sharon, and congratulations on getting married!"

"Thank you and I will!" Jason assures her.

Knowing time is always money, and having good manners instilled from his mother, Jason pulls his wallet out and places $60 dollars in a jar, already halfway full of other contributions.

"Thank you...how very thoughtful!"

"You're welcome! It's the least I can do."

"Here...wait!" Karen blurts out as Jason turns to follow Sharon and Mark, already heading towards Karen's reading room. "Take this for protection," she states, reaching into a glass showcase at the counter. Pulling out an antique necklace with a charm in the shape of an angel, she hands it to Jason.

"Thank you," Jason graciously replies.

"No, thank you!"

"Come on Jason," Sharon excitedly calls out from across the little shop.

"One last thing…I am to remind you of writing a book. It's important because it opens the door to changing the way we think. That's all I'm allowed to say," Karen smiles, relaying a subtle clue to Jason.

As Jason slowly turns and heads in Sharon's direction, this was now the third time he's heard someone like Karen and the Asian sage, telling him the same clue about a book. *What book?* he thinks. As he heads over to where Sharon is, he now understands why she told him Karen and Mark have always felt more like loving parents, than friends. As he reflects on his morning with her longtime friends, Jason's previously held stereotypes, are left at the door as he enters the room.

Chapter 16

Sphere of Activity...
The Portal's Domain

July 2019

As Jason joins Mark and Sharon in Karen's reading room, he familiarizes himself with the small and quiet setting. Away from the noisy customers shopping, and Karen sharing stories of her inspiration, Mark opens his laptop and powers up the box. Impressed with Mark's technological ingenuity, Jason finds the portal, or 'spirit box,' extremely alluring.

"Go ahead and get comfy," Mark tells Jason and Sharon.

Anxious, Sharon says, "Isn't this cool?"

"How does this thing work?" Jason asks, while carefully analyzing the electronic parts and lights wired together.

Mark, proud of his creation, replies, "It was relatively easy to build. You just need a few parts from the hardware and music store and a soldering gun."

"Music store?" Jason confusingly asks.

"Sure! See that is a modified Vox mini guitar amplifier. You can buy one at a music shop or from a store on-line. I found the blueprints to the *Wonder Box* and built a better, more powerful version."

"Why do they call it a portal?" Jason inquires.

Mark explains, "When you ask questions, this box can receive voices from spirits or entities around you, similar to

265

how a radio picks up music floating in the air. Even this concept of communicating with what you can't see scares most closed-minded people. Especially when you tell them there's more going on around them than what they can detect with their eyes and ears."

Jason nervously laughs.

Mark continues, "The energetic or spirit realm, as some call it, operates and communicates on different frequencies than the physical realm does. People are naturally open or receptive to quantum energy as children, but as they get older, they lose this ability. Many are too young to even realize what they experience and forget what they saw as kids. That's why you hear about children who can see or hear ghosts when they're little but seem to grow out of it as they get older. Now, what isn't taught in schools is if you have poor dietary food selections, like fried foods, junk food, or basically the American diet, your body can't process all these preservatives. It clogs or closes your natural energetic channel ways within the body. There is hope! A person can retrain their body to open them back up again, but it takes time to detox from medications and the pre-packaged food we regularly consume. If you're lazy like me, instead of spending years detoxing and training your body to tune in, you can just build a contraption like this," Marks says, gently patting the box with his hand. "It achieves similar results."

"What's with the tiny blue lights across the front of the portal? Do those help to draw in sound and amplify it?"

"Nope! Just decoration and gives it some flare. Looks neat when you turn off the lights. They're LED graphic equalizers powered by converters I installed, so they flicker as sounds are heard."

Jason chuckles, "Got it. Is this a product you can buy or special order online?" Jason probes further.

"Yes. You can buy the original versions, like this one, for $1,000 dollars or more online, but if you're like me, you can easily build this in a day or so for around $200. I prefer to save the money doing it myself."

"What's with the copper wiring wrapped around the crystals?"

"That's my little secret addition. Before, you could hear voices through the portal, although the sound seemed distant and distorted. After installing copper wiring around one of the crystals, it became a more powerful antenna. When I added a few more of those babies in, the voices came in stronger and clearer than before. When this app is done loading, I'll show you."

"Sounds good," Jason replies.

As Jason waits with Sharon to have his first experience with the highly peculiar piece of equipment, he peers around the room. He spots, in one corner, an old wicker rocking chair, and a large Tibetan singing bowl in the other. On a shelf above the bowl sat a medium sized, low watt oriental themed lamp, along with a few artificial plants. Above the lamp was a highly detailed bamboo and papyrus scroll with a painting of a watchful and colorful samurai hanging on the wall. Behind Jason was a three-foot-tall statue of an Angel with its head bowed, and a rather large cross hanging on the pastel blue wall behind it. He also notices the freshly installed Berber carpet on the floor, and a small homey *Welcome All* sign hanging above the door.

With three random chairs positioned around Mark's tiny desk, Jason doesn't know what to expect. To break the silence in the room and pass the short wait time, Jason jokes, "Don't we need to light some candles to do some kind of spiritual ritual or seance to get this box to work?"

Mark laughs, "No. Just turn it on and start asking questions. Sometimes we can pick up one or two voices during a session. I record it on my computer. That way I can go back over it and clear up any distortion or interference. Do you have anything specific in mind you want to ask or to whom? If we don't initially get anything, sometimes using specific names may get a response, but I offer no guarantees. I can't force entities or energy to communicate in ways we want to perceive it. It's still a mystery to me how it all works. If we do get more than one talking over each other, we may have to ask them to speak one at a time. It's no different than we do with people. The cool part is you can hear their accents. I've picked up a few German, French, and Spanish spirits talking on here. I don't speak those languages, so I don't have any way to interpret what they said."

Skeptical to the box's capabilities, Jason remains silent, as Mark's programs are almost finished loading. Before Mark is ready, a barrage of several voices boom through the portal speaker. *"Jason, Jason, JASON… Jason… JASON, Jason, JASON…Jason, Jason, JASON! Jason…"* numerous male and female voices exclaim, clamoring for recognition.

Surprised by the sudden results and clear voice distinction of the words, Jason looks from the box's twinkling blue lights to Mark and Sharon for confirmation to the sudden activity. Looking back at him like he had a squirrel suddenly perch on his head, Mark and Sharon are staring at Jason with wide eyes and mouths open in disbelief.

"Somebody must really want to talk to you!" Mark exclaims.

Noticing their sudden surprise, and based on their experience with the equipment, Jason questions, "Has this ever happened before?"

"NEVER!" Mark replies, still stunned and staring at Jason.

Sharon, realizing Mark has temporarily become a fascinated spectator rather than professional paranormal investigator, interrupts, "Mark, did you press record?"

"AGH!" Mark huffs as he hurries to click a few buttons while the voices continue to pour in... '*Jason!*'

Not knowing what to do next, Jason awaits further instructions from either Mark or Sharon. Looking back at him, Mark says, "The floor is all yours!"

Jason looks back at the soft blue flickering glow of the portal and asks, "What do I say?"

Sharon, sensing Jason's hesitation and trying to comfort him, softly replies, "We came here because you wanted to see if you could find more information on Denise's case. Ask questions about the case or see if Denise will come through."

After Jason takes a few seconds to collect his thoughts, he requests, "Denise, are you here with us?"

A few unrecognizable voices begin talking over each other on the portal and Sharon steps in to control the situation.

"If you are not here to help Jason with Denise's case, please remain quiet," Sharon politely asks, and the commotion subsides. "There Jason, ask again."

The level of responsiveness from the unseen voices impresses Jason and he becomes less dismissive of this purposeful means. "*Jason!*" is heard again, but this time he recognizes the voice. It's Denise! "*Jason,*" Denise says again.

"Denise?"

"*Hey!!!*" she calls out loudly. "*Now you can hear me!*"

Looking at Sharon in amazement of the clear distinctive voice, Jason tries to explain to Mark, who has never heard her speak before, "That's my cousin, Denise! You can even hear her country twang!"

Mark and Sharon laugh at Jason's excitement.

"What's up?" another male voice comes through. After hearing the male's multiple obscenities, Jason knows exactly who it is!

Excitedly, Jason looks to Sharon again, "That's my other cousin, Billy!"

Billy died three months after Denise disappeared, while Jason was still stationed in North Carolina. As close as they all were growing up, losing these two cousins, was the same to Jason as losing a brother and sister.

"What's up man?" Jason responds, but only a long unintelligible reply comes through.

Jason feels guilty he was unable to attend Billy's funeral, and has yet to even visit his gravesite, since he took his own life on Father's Day, back in June of 2015. Billy was involved in a bad motorcycle accident in 2012. It resulted in him losing one of his arms and leaving him with severe neurological pain. No amount of prescription pills and alcohol could offer any relief. Billy was diagnosed with Complex Regional Pain Syndrome (CRPS) and said the pain he continually felt was similar to being lit on fire, but nothing worked to extinguish the flames. Having a less severe experience with such neurological pain, Jason didn't condone Billy's actions, but he understood what would drive him to such measures. The insurance company forced Billy to remove the only device which numbed the pain, because they said it was experimental treatment and it wouldn't be covered by his policy. After that, Billy couldn't take the years of mental and physical pain any longer. One thing Jason learned from his cousin's actions was suicide doesn't end pain. It just passes it along to family and friends. After the accident, Billy lost his arm, his job, his wife, his kids, and his sanity. He was desperately seeking a means to subdue his anguish from the accident because it was destroying his life. Losing the medical pain suppressive treatment was the final straw which pushed Billy over the edge. The constant reminder of Jason's avoidance to visit his cousin's grave is fueled by the guilt of not being able to successfully solve Denise's case. He figures when both his cousins are placed respectfully and at peace, then Jason can rest too, by officially paying his respects to their graves.

Mark, not knowing the previous circumstances in Jason's life, Jason quickly catches him up to speed.

"Denise, how do we solve this case," Jason begins, but doesn't receive a response back.

Readjusting his line of questioning, he asks another question, "Who is involved in your disappearance or helping to cover it up?"

"*Peter Holmes*," Denise booms back over the portal.

Mark and Sharon both look at Jason and simultaneously ask, "Who's that?"

Not surprised, Jason replies, "That's the name of the San Saba Sheriff now in charge of Denise's case."

Waiting a short pause for more information to come through, Jason finally asks, "Who else is involved?"

"*The husband*," Billy replies.

"Anyone else?" Jason asks before interference distorts Denise and Billy's response to the question.

Sharon looks at Mark fidgeting with the equalizer controls on his laptop. "*… he killed her (inaudible)…had help covering it up (heavy distortion) … Peter Holmes (inaudible) the body with (static reverb) … the kids (echoing feedback) … property…*" the two voices seem to urgently convey.

"Man, there is a lot of energy in this room," Mark says adjusting the levels. "It's causing disturbances in the sound quality, and it's hard to filter it out."

As Sharon and Mark try to figure out how to make the voices sound clearer, Jason swears he hears Denise say, "*It's time to go. Leave now!*"

Looking at Sharon and Mark to see if they too heard the message, he hears the worry and urgency in Denise's voice, "*Get up! Go down the street. Leave…Go now!*"

Getting Sharon's attention as Mark still works, "I think we are being told to leave…like right now."

"No, it's ok, Mark almost has it figured out."

Somewhat annoyed by the two, Denise booms, "*GET THE HELL OUT. NOW!*"

"Ok, that was clear," Jason responds looking at the worry suddenly appearing on Sharon's face.

Mark, who is listening in, stops immediately. "I don't know what's going on, but I heard that clear as day! I think you two are being given a warning of some kind, and you might want to listen."

Jason can see the disappointment in Sharon's expression as they are being advised to abruptly leave. Casually, Sharon tells Mark, "We will try to come down again when we can get another chance. I was hoping we could stay longer."

"*Jason,*" Billy interrupts, "*They're here!*"

Springing from his chair, Jason hears Mark ask, "Who's here?"

Jason replies, "I'm not sure, but it's probably the same people who've been following us around for some time now."

"*Holmes and his (inaudible)…here. Get out! Leave now,*" Denise interjects.

Looking at Mark, Sharon says, "It sounds like she's saying the Sheriff is here, and he brought some goons with him."

"Come on Sharon, let's go! We can call them later," Jason tells her. Looking at Mark, he says, "Our apologizes for having to jet, but when we get more time, we can explain a little better what this is all about."

"Hey, I understand," Mark replies as he stands up and gives Sharon a hug. "Be careful."

"Let me go say bye really quick to Karen," Sharon states as they hurry from the room.

As Sharon reengages conversation with Karen and Mark, not heeding the warnings, Jason is standing by the front entrance, and gets Sharon's attention. He mouths the words while waiving his arm towards the door, "LET'S GO!"

As she strolls to the door, they wave their final goodbyes, and Jason quickly opens the storefront door for Sharon. Before making it completely out the door, Sharon almost runs smack dab into a tall, large, and younger bald-headed man. Caught by surprise and their rapid exit from the store, the man, in his mid-20's, retracts his outstretched arm reaching for the door. Startled, the man wearing a blue long-sleeved checkered button-down shirt, cowboy pants, a large belt buckle of a bucking bull, and tan snakeskin boots, diverts his direction and starts walking away down the street.

Noticing the man's unusual behavior and his completely out of place attire for this hot ocean front environment, the pair watch as the man crosses the street without looking back in their direction. Continuing, the younger man appears as if he's trying to play off getting caught in the act. Sharon states the obvious, "That's no coincidence. How did they know we are here?"

Thinking rapidly, Jason remembers, "I used my card, but how did they get here so quickly?"

"That's right," Sharon says. "Honey, we've been here for almost four hours," she replies checking the time on her watch.

"I think we need to go this way," Jason instructs pointing in the opposite direction the man went.

"Good idea."

Before leaving the main street to head to where their car is parked, Jason checks one last time over his shoulder, to see if he catches any staring eyes. Feeling the coast is temporarily clear, they hurry to their vehicle.

Jason's turn to state the obvious, "Who wears a country kicker outfit to the beach in the middle of the summer...in the middle of the afternoon? God, it has to be close to 100 degrees out right now!"

"That's what guys wear to country dance halls or saloons," Sharon informs, "but yes, it's usually at nighttime and much cooler outside."

"He sure was in an awful hurry to get out of our line of sight." Jason remarks, referring to the man's expedient exit from the scene.

Ending the conversation, Jason opens the passenger door to let Sharon in and scans the area before getting in himself.

"Hurry, Jason," Sharon urges as he climbs in the car.

"Oh...NOW someone's in a rush! You didn't mind taking your sweet time leaving the store, but you feel inclined to light a fire under me?" Jason sarcastically teases.

"Seriously, Jason, I don't like this," Sharon pleas, looking out the window at the other cars in the parking lot.

"I'm going to take the back roads to get out of here."

"Whatever! Just go!"

Smiling, Jason watches the fear and suspense building in Sharon's body. Cool as a cucumber in stressful situations, Jason starts the car, and allows the throaty V-8 to come to life. The lope of his new racing cam slightly jostles the car, back and forth. He slips his manual transmission into reverse and heads towards the exit. Before leaving the lot, Jason inspects the other vehicles parked along the street. As he is about to pull off, he recognizes the Sheriff with a blond-haired woman sitting in a newer gray Toyota 4-Runnner gawking at him.

Pretending he doesn't notice the infernal onlookers, Jason slowly turns onto the street, and casually drives off. The 4-Runner pulls out of its parking space, keeping a safe distance behind him. Looking in his rearview a few blocks later, Jason sees the Sheriff didn't come alone. Now tailing with him, is a Blue F-250 and a White Chevy Tahoe. Jason makes a series of four right-hand turns to drive in a circle, to see if they were, in fact, tailing him. After the fourth turn, all three vehicles are still following. Not sure of their intentions, Jason has a plan. As he makes his way over to an industrial area nearby in town, the vehicles continue to match his speed. Jason looks over to Sharon, and playfully smiles.

"This isn't funny Jason! What are we going to do?"

Without giving a reply, he looks back out the windshield, and analyzes the layout of the buildings close by. When he sees what he is looking for, Jason slowly drops his car into second gear. Then, without warning, he dumps the clutch and punches it. With Sharon pinned to the back of her seat, and sharply steering his hotrod, they drift around the first corner. Loving the smell of burnt rubber, he peers again into the rearview mirror, as he slams into the next gear. Shortly afterwards, the Sheriff's mini convoy following in pursuit, exits the plume of white smoke he's left behind. Watching them make the turn almost on two wheels and desperately trying keep up, Jason smirks. They are no match against the responsiveness and agility of his car.

Quickly reaching speeds over 100 mph, Jason calmly says, "Hang on!" as he throws the emergency brake and cuts the wheel again. Screaming for her life as they slide around the next turn, he intently concentrates beyond Sharon's ear piercing shrill of 'GOOD GOD!' and the roasting of his new Pirelli widebody tires on the pavement. The beast on wheels barely loses speed in the turn, as the high-performance Scat Pack suspension, easily absorbs the G-force from the hard lateral cornering. As the car straightens out, they are rocketed forward, like two astronauts in flight. As the couple zip along the industrial complex, Jason spots an exit a few hundred yards away. As the sticky tires of his Challenger strike the hot asphalt of the access road, he is glad to hear the whine of his tuned supercharger, pumping out more horsepower than a Dodge Hellcat. Having a clear shot for the next 10 miles and nothing to lose, he leaves the gas pedal on the floor.

Comfortably watching the speedometer in his car go from 181 to 182, then 183 mph, Jason sees why this desolate stretch of road is the town's favorite local hotspot, to host their late-night weekend drag races. Unable to conceal his grin from the raw power of American muscle under his feet and without a car in sight, Jason pushes his modified Challenger even faster. "I'm glad to see the few extra thousand I spent for the upgrades is finally paying off," he mentions as Sharon is still unsure to be relieved or terrified from the breakneck speed.

"Are you sure the car can handle this speed?"

"Oh yeah, she'll easily break 200!"

"How fast are you going," she asks looking at the speedometer. "190!" she screams. "SLOW DOWN!" Slightly disappointed, Jason brings the car back under 175.

"Let's not make their job easier by getting us killed," Sharon advises.

"There's no one on the road," he contests.

"I know but I don't see them either," Sharon points out checking the side mirror of the car.

With the villainous tails long gone from view, Jason cruises along for a few more moments, until he spots an old train station yard just ahead. Rapidly slowing the vehicle to turn in, he has just enough time to conceal the bright red Dodge, behind a few rail cars and an abandoned building close by. Moments later, the pair watch as the three vehicles chasing them zoom past.

Less than a mile down the road, they catch the vehicles' brake lights flash simultaneously, as they come screeching to a halt. "Quick. Give me your phone!" Jason commands, as he powers his phone down and removes the battery.

"What are you doing?"

"They must be somehow tracking our phones. Hurry!"

Seeing the vehicles turning around to double back, Sharon retrieves her phone and hands it to Jason. After doing the same to Sharon's phone, Jason hops out and rushes to toss the phones into a nearby dumpster.

"RUN JASON! They're coming!"

Slipping back into the driver seat, Jason jokes, "See! Whoever said marriage is supposed to be dull and boring?"

"Jason! When we get home..." Sharon begins shouting. She is immediately cut off when she gets pinned back in her seat again, as Jason launches the car and tightly steers onto a narrow lane undetected.

Slowly driving down a few parkways, side streets, and alleyways, the couple somehow manages to slip past the Sheriff and his goons. Knowing there might be more lookouts staged elsewhere, Jason finds a backway out of town, and heads to his parents nearby home in Rockport.

Chapter 17

When We Don't Know What to Do Next

<u>*April 2021*</u>

Sipping on his drink, Jason sits comfortably on a leather sectional, listening to his brother angrily reminiscing over the good old days. Full of resentment, Tyler reconfigures how things might have been. He feels like his opportunity for fame or glory is long gone. "I mean, my life turned out pretty good so far, I guess, but who doesn't miss being in the spotlight?"

"I know what you mean!" Jason replies understanding his brother's worldly distain for not becoming famous and collecting a fortune. Jason passed on two opportunities to play major league baseball for reasons he attributes to immaturity and lack of wisdom. The first time he passed on his dreams was for a girl he thought he was madly in love with, and the second time, he thought getting his college degree was more important to attain than mixing it up in the big leagues. Either way, passing on both opportunities always left him wondering, what if he had the chance to do it all over again? Would his new choices be the answers to his lost happiness and fulfillment?

Four years had passed after the mystical Asian man told Jason about the book, since then, he's been diving deep into obscure books about religion, culture, philosophy, law, finance, relationships, kids, politics, quantum physics, health, medicine, astrology, metaphysics, history, and secret sciences, trying to become as worldly and knowledgeable as possible. His confidence in achieving such a mission began slowly diminishing with each new book he reads. The more he reads, the more he realizes he doesn't know. When Jason met Karen, the Angel lady, his ambitions and mission were reignited, but once again his drive has been fading over the past year. The brothers both sit frustrated as they watch their kids take turns on the indoor golf simulator Tyler built for his only son in the upstairs game room. Jason, taking another sip of his drink, shares his similar frustrations with his brother.

"I've spent the past four or five years reading and studying everything I could get my hands on, to figure out this impossible mission I'm supposed to complete."

"I remember you telling me about that. How's it going by the way?" Tyler asks his brother already knowing Jason's response.

"Dude, I've learned more, in this past year alone, than I ever had in all my years in school and college."

"Like what?"

"Around the world, there are these secret societies who teach their own little niche of information. Apparently, they're on every continent, and there's some ongoing struggle for these secret factions to control the world."

Skeptical, Tyler asks, "What do they teach?"

"I know you don't get into oddball material..." Jason starts before Tyler cuts him off.

"No, that's not true. I thought you were nuts, at first, until I started checking out the material you mentioned for myself. As it turns out, you weren't crazy. You're just ahead of the curve."

"Well, the more I've studied, the more disappointed I've become."

"Why?"

"People need to know this stuff growing up, and they don't teach it in public schools. They might tell you a little bit about it, but not how it pertains to you," Jason answers.

"I'm not sure I understand."

"Take for example, we all learn geography, the continents, and land features, like mountains and hills, right?"

"Yeah."

"What they won't teach is how the land you live on affects your health, prosperity, family, and livelihood." Tyler stares at Jason with honest confusion. Jason further explains, "It's rather compelling. In Europe, and even Asia, they know how to determine if the land has an underground stream or fault lines, without advanced and sophisticated technology. A farmer can tell exactly where to build a barn to keep pests and rodents out, or where to build a home to make his wife extremely fertile."

"That is pretty cool!"

"It has taken me years to attain this knowledge, but now I ask myself, what do I do with all this information?"

"I don't know. Why don't you go on *Jeopardy* and make some bank? It would at least give you a little nest egg to fall back on."

"Yeah, sure…I can see me now…. Hey Alec, I'll take the Secret Meaning of Ancient Symbolism and Advanced Meditative Postures for $400, please!"

Laughs. Tyler asks, "I'm heading downstairs to grab a refill," holding up his empty glass. "Do you want one?"

"Actually, I'll go with you. I need a cigarette."

☙❧

Leaving the kids playing and their wives talking amongst themselves, Jason and Tyler head downstairs.

281

Grabbing refills and heading outside through the garage, Jason walks past Tyler's early 80's Porsche restoration project, before lighting up a smoke.

"What else do you have left to complete on this thing before you're finished?" Jason jests at his older brother, while pointing to the cherry red car propped up on jack stands.

Disgruntled, Tyler replies, "What started as a weekend fixer-upper has turned into a year-round overhaul. With each new part I replace, I find something else that's either worn out or needs to be fixed soon. Hopefully, when it's all said and done, I won't need to work on it for another 10-15 years."

"What happened to the old 70's truck you were trying to restore?"

"Ah, I sold it because it was even worse than this one," Tyler responds, joining Jason outside of the garage. "Ever since I took the accounting position at my new job, I barely have any time to myself. So, what's going on with you? What are you going to do now?"

"I figure if I keep plugging away, my efforts will someday pay off somewhere down the line, but it's been four years. I'm no different than when I began. What started, as a project of my own, to find Denise has sent me on a quest to discover the mysteries of this world. At this point, I have no clue what to do!" Jason answers.

"Welcome to the fabulous life of being a responsible adult. You must work, day in and day out, and what do you have to show for it? Someone else getting filthy rich off your hard work, while you struggle to make ends meet! Is there any meaning to the hamster wheel of life, other than keeping you busy, working and paying bills?"

"That's just it. I don't want that life anymore."

Trying to be helpful, Tyler suggests, "Why don't you take all that knowledge you've learned and put it down in a book? This country is so screwed up nowadays. We have presidents who are supposed to be overseeing the military, but are instead, writing and influencing legislative policies. Isn't that supposed to be Congress' responsibility? This overstepping and muddying of their legal authority have helped to turn this country right on its head!"

"Even if I wrote a book, who's going to listen to someone like me? In this country, you could be the wisest person alive, but if you don't have a master's degree or Ph.D., no one will listen to you or take you seriously."

"Our country is like this because we don't have core values and want change without changing ourselves. We try to be so politically correct. We are allowing people to bring their communist, socialist, or totalitarian beliefs here, trying to get us to change to be like them. Since we allowed this, America has become the Heinz 57 of the world because our leaders have no spine to reinforce Constitutional values."

"We don't know what we value or believe in. Did you know there are still some places you can go to in Japan that follow a different set of rules for society?"

"Like jobs or money?" Tyler asks.

"Kind of…but check this out! We all saw what happened during Hurricane Katrina. Rapes, killing, looting, and crime levels soaring."

"I know, it was terrible!"

"Well, a tsunami hit Japan in 2011 and their area looked much like what happened in Louisiana but something different happened. There was money and jewelry strewn everywhere but even the homeless were turning it in to the authorities. Even though this could have easily changed their lives, their society doesn't believe in taking what's not theirs. They also didn't have food and water for days, but when help finally arrived, no one was fighting or arguing. Instead, they helped each other, and allowed the children and women to eat first," Jason informs.

"Yeah, meanwhile in our country, we have men beating up women and the elderly, then posting it online for everyone to see. Could you imagine if someone from here went to a country like China and start demanding free speech or freedom of the press? If you did, you wouldn't be around long enough to tell the tale. You would either disappear or be silenced. So why don't we do the same to people coming here trying to change our country to communist and socialist views?" Tyler questions.

"If we don't stand for anything or uphold any core values as a country, then who are we?"

"I agree. Well, why don't you get back into the medical field and be a doctor or something like that? I know you like helping people."

"I wanted to until I began researching alternative medical systems and homeopathic treatments. They call them secondary or experimental, when in fact, it's a commonsense approach."

Tyler replies, "What do you mean?"

"Let me put it to you this way. There are cultures who have local doctors. If they didn't do their job to educate the people how to remain healthy, they were deemed false doctors and exiled from their communities."

"Medicine and science have come a long way," Tyler argues.

"Has it?" Jason asks. "They produce more medicine and fancier machines, but still use the same approach towards the human body. For instance, when I used to check blood pressure on a patient, I only used the left arm to determine their blood flow. Imagine my surprise to find out, other medical systems check the pulse of the patient in both arms and legs. You might have good flow in your left arm but poor circulation in your right leg. Checking one pulse site or location, would give no indication of problems elsewhere."

"See? That's newsworthy stuff right there!"

"A guy I talked to turned me onto an entirely different medical system which easily identifies a commonality in illnesses, diseases, and why people get sick with things like cancer."

"What is it?"

"It's simple really. Stagnation or congestion."

"Stagnation of what?"

"Wherever there is stagnation, congestion, or lack of circulation in the body, it creates a buildup in the body caused by improper diet and exercise. This creates stress on the body and if a person ignores this over a few years, it creates 'dis-ease,' or their body is considerably overstressed."

"Hmm."

"Who is ultimately responsible to take care of your body? The government? Doctors? Your neighbors, or is it you?"

"Me of course," Tyler answers.

"Exactly. Like all things in life, you must continually educate yourself…on you. You, your body, your life, and the ability to properly manage and maintain them. Everything is a mystery in your life until you learn how to solve your own problems. When you figure it out, then you work on other mysteries in your life. People are currently so confused because they are too distracted by social media and the news to focus on how to get their life together. They're too involved with wanting to know the latest gossip on celebrities and what other people are doing right now."

"You're right. Between reality tv shows and social media apps, people can't get off their TVs or cellphones."

"Just look at our country. Look at how many overweight, sick, ill, diseased, and depressed people there are! Look at how many people are dying before reaching the age of 60. This is literally half the life span of what the human body is designed to live. If we had leaders trying to make this country prosperous, they would be taking serious measures to educate our people on health and self-care. Instead, it's become a racket and an exploitation from our lack of education. The US spends more than four trillion dollars each year on healthcare. Our entire medical system and the way we practice medicine is so perverse, I just couldn't rejoin that field and be able to sleep at night. The ones who haven't done their homework are its biggest cheerleaders. The ones who know enough about it, openly speak out against it."

"I can't say I'm any different. I guess I've trusted the government and the medical industry to have my best interests in mind."

Jason laughs, "I felt the same way until modern medicine failed me, and I rapidly healed using '*alternative*' treatments."

"I thought what you were doing was strange at first, until you got better. Now I see you running around with your kids again. Not to change subjects, but what about Denise and her kids? Are you done with that whole thing?" Tyler probes.

Shrugging his shoulders, Jason replies, "It just bothers me, had Denise known what I know now, she would have never ended up the way she did."

"Maybe, but did you consider the number of women like her, in similar situations? I'm sure they could use your help and advice to find the right guy. Maybe you could help them to avoid the same circumstances."

"Tyler, I wish I would have known earlier how to pick a good partner, rather than rolling the dice and praying I made a good decision. Do you know how much time and money I would have saved knowing what I know now?"

"Like what?"

"For example, if you want to know how a relationship ends, then look at how it begins. That means, if your partner is controlling, jealous, or abusive when you first start dating, this will continue until you separate."

"Good point. People rarely change."

"If people ask the right questions in the beginning, it will potentially weed out many bad decisions."

"Like how?"

"If you ask yourself, will this person make a good spouse and be a good parent? Do they hold similar values and ethics, and manage their life responsibly? If they have kids from another relationship, do they pay child support or are they involved in their lives? Do they take care of themselves physically, mentally, and emotionally? Do they value you and your time? Do they smoke, use drugs, or alcohol?"

"Now, that's a good list," Tyler commends.

"Last point to consider, where do many people try to pick up dates or partners?"

"At a bar or nightclub."

"Yes, and these are the worst possible places to find a decent or suitable lifelong partner."

"How so?"

"Smoking, drugs, and alcohol are harmful habits people do to themselves. These are high indications they are holding on to unresolved issues they are suppressing or ignoring. Later, these coping mechanisms fester into larger problems because they develop the habit of ignoring themselves and others around them. This also correlates to health complications these people will later develop."

"Well, I guess we're screwed then," the brothers laugh as Tyler takes a sip of his drink, while Jason lights up another cigarette.

"Yeah, everybody seems to be coping with some mental or physical pain," Jason sarcastically replies. "I started doing it to fit in or thought it was cool, but did you know these two items are responsible for killing more people globally each year, than war, heart attacks, and accidents combined?"

"Dang," Tyler responds.

"If the government was truly concerned for our safety and welfare, then alcohol and cigarettes would be the most illegal products on the planet!"

"Then it really makes you wonder why they are pushing so hard for vaccines right now during this pandemic."

"I know. Let's see," Jason recollects, "So far, they paid celebrities and actors, censored information on social media and in the news, offered people money, prizes, sporting event tickets, concerts, put groups together to go door to door, sent out reminders in the mail, tried passing legislation forcing people to take it, fired people for not wanting to take it...all for your health and safety."

"It is odd. So, are you a Republican or Democrat?" Tyler asks.

"I'm neither."

"How come?"

Discouraged, Jason responds, "You lose either way you choose. Did you see the choices from the last election? Are these the two very best options our country can choose from to run for president? No offense but we can't find some young and intelligent person to run for office?"

"Voting for politicians is a double-edged sword and having to vote for the lesser of two evils."

"That's my point. Our politicians spent the last four years focusing on removing Trump rather than working on the people's social and economic problems. How do we look as a nation, or to the rest of the world, that we openly bash our leader?" Jason questions.

"Right now, we are the laughingstock of the world. Even foreign news stations blast our media networks to how biased they are when reporting on Republican versus Democrat foul ups. If the media doesn't like you, they turn you into public enemy number #1. One thing still bothers me though. How does a guy make a handful of appearances on a campaign trail but get more votes than even Obama? Then, this guy was also caught several times on camera making racist comments, but is still allowed to run for president as a Democrat?"

"The Democratic party talks a good game, but a large percentage of the cities where their supporters live, are starting to look like third world countries."

"I would talk trash about the Democratic party because they want their supporters dependent upon government programs, but I can't say Republicans are doing any better helping to improve peoples' lives. Republicans are too focused on corporations and big business kickbacks," Tyler suggests.

"Our problems aren't a cultural or political division. Our attention is being distracted away from the growing division in the socio-economic class or economic positions in society. As this divisional gap continues to grow, then so will crime and corruption."

"You nailed it!" Tyler acknowledges.

"Regardless of political affiliation, do you think it's wise to allow legislators to pass a bill officials aren't afforded time to read and able to verify the beneficiaries have no conflicts of interest before voting on it?"

"No."

"If our government was run like a corporation, it would prevent legislators and officials from having an opportunity to steal from the people."

Tyler comments, "Being in my line of work, taxing businesses are one thing but to tax the people who work for them is a European feudalism concept. We exiled this practice a couple hundred years ago, but it has somehow managed to work its way back into our society."

"Did you know, not once in history has bringing taxation on the people ever brought prosperity to the country or its citizens? It just helped to create larger wealth disparity," Jason advises.

"Politicians are using legislation to pickpocket and drain us like ticks or leeches."

"Even when the public has stood up against them, they have yet to concede authority or power."

Angered, Tyler touts, "They plunder us as cash cows. Then turn around and make you feel guilty for even objecting to this legalized thievery. The truth is, there is enough money in this country for everyone to live abundantly. In fact, we should all be living debt free and in mansions. Yet, they've taken away many financial obligations from corporations and placed them onto the backs of the working class."

Jason replies, "Each time money moves or exchanges hands, the IRS found a way to tax it."

"Let's not forget about the insurance premiums we are forced to pay each year," Tyler adds.

"No kidding! After everything is all said and done, between the tax dollars and insurance premiums, they get your money coming and going. It's safe to say, people in the lower to middle tax brackets, close to 80-90% of their annual income, is spent on taxes and insurance each year. What is left for you to save?"

"It's no wonder people are broke and in debt."

Jason discouragingly responds, "All those people are institutionalized to call this capitalism but are promoting expansion of corporations and big government. They don't realize, corporations and government don't promote success on a personal level. They drastically inhibit wealth and prosperity amongst the masses because they monopolize markets and become money syphons to the people."

Tyler reminds, "This is why we have quickly become the joke of the world. The people are too distracted and too trusting of our government officials and CEOs. They aren't playing by the rules, nor do they have our best interest at heart."

"How bad has our government become when not only much of the world hates us, but Americans despise our own government as well?" Jason asks.

"No kidding! Our system is broken."

"The system isn't broken," Jason argues. "The people are supposed to be the referees to government, but many don't know the rules or how to legally put them in their place. They expect lawyers to do this but it's not their job, it's the peoples' responsibility."

"Like how?"

"Take for example, in this prior election, they used an emergency to by-pass legislation to implement mail-in-ballots. We could continue to go shopping but apparently, we needed emergency mail-in-ballots to vote in the newest president. Was this an act of irony? Not a chance. If you allow officials to change laws in states of emergencies, then they will continue to create more emergencies, to unconstitutionally change laws they don't like. The Supreme Court already ruled in 1934, *Home Building & Loan Assn. v. Blaisdell*, an emergency does not increase constitutional power, nor diminish constitutional restrictions."

"Yet, we saw politicians changing our election procedures during a state of an emergency."

"Yep. What laws do they change in states of emergencies? The ones which regulate and restrict their power."

Tyler smirks at how smart and worldly his brother has become over the years.

"Before you pop a blood vessel from information overload, let's head back inside. I'm getting eaten up by mosquitos."

"Yeah, me too," Tyler says, as he swats one that's biting his neck.

❧❧

Heading upstairs, the two brothers return to their seats as the kids are in heated competition.

"Daddy," Jason's daughter calls out, "we need your help! It's me and Bradley versus Jackson."

"Yeah dad!" Bradley hops in. "We don't stand a chance against Jackson. Can you help? PLEASE!"

Tyler smirks, "You can try, but that boy has been out driving me on the golf course for over a year now."

Looking back to the desperate faces and sad puppy dog eyes from his children, Jason replies "Alright."

"Yay!" the kids erupt.

Jason walks back to his seat in defeat, 20 minutes later, after being royally shown up by his nephew on the golf simulator.

Tyler chuckles. "I told you, he's gotten good."

"Yeah, no kidding! I almost came out of my shoes swinging, trying to keep up with his drives. I'm impressed!"

As Jason gets comfortable, Tyler gives him a few minutes to get situated.

"Hey, I still wanna talk about what we were talking about in the garage," Tyler begins.

"You mean…what am I going to do with my life?"

"Well yeah…If you don't want to talk about it, I understand. It's not like we get the chance to see each other as much as we did when we were younger. I just think if you find what you love to do, you'd really excel at it."

"Possibly. I just don't know what that is exactly. Not too long ago, people were crafters and masters of trade who found satisfaction in their work. Now mankind has become operators of machines who steal this satisfaction from the people. It's no wonder people are miserable and hate their corporate cookie cutter jobs. They can't express themselves. They have to look, act, and work just like everyone else does."

"Good point. If you don't want to go back into medicine, then why don't you become a financial advisor. You would make a good therapist or something like that," Tyler offers.

"Why, so I can listen to people complain and instead of helping them to discover the true root of their problems, just give them pills to keep them quiet about it?"

Tyler laughs.

"Instead of giving people the proper education to know how to do it themselves, we are conditioned to pay others for our lack of knowledge, which creates a form of dependency."

"You're not lying," Tyler admits. "What about a career in financing?"

"There is also a reason Albert Einstein said, *'Compound interest is the 8th wonder of the world,'* and why it should be banned everywhere. It's the primary reason, almost every country in this world, is in massive debt to banks."

Tyler shakes his head. "True."

"Money is a powerful tool and can be used for good things. It provides opportunities to those who use it wisely."

"Yeah, but most of us struggle to put any money aside. The average American doesn't even have $400 dollars stashed away in case of an emergency," Tyler argues.

"This is the dilemma of our society," Jason begins. "Do we spend the few dollars we have at convenience stores, on clearance sales, or are we to be more mindful with our money? Millionaires don't become millionaires from having bags of money dropped into their laps. They start small like the rest of us, but they focus on the steps to get them to their objectives. They don't waste their time thinking about winning the lottery or dreaming about what it would be like to be rich. Each one will tell you, the best investment you can ever make is into yourself."

"I've got too many things on my plate, as it is, to focus on anything else," Tyler offers an excuse.

"It's those who pay attention to the little things and details who receive the biggest dividends. Plus, they don't bite off more than they can chew."

"This is true. While these are great words of wisdom, how does this relate to Denise?" Tyler asks.

"If Denise had known much of this before getting involved in relationships, she wouldn't have picked a partner based on if they could support her or not. Instead, she could have found someone based on love, rather than money. Public schools teach you how to manage a company, but rarely are you taught how to manage your own life. School is about how to make the rich people richer."

Tyler suggests, "At this point, people are fed up with our current leadership helping themselves to our money and taking care of themselves first."

"As a country, we are only as strong as our weakest links. Right now, if our leaders truly wanted to see this country thrive, they would be taking extraordinary means to teach our children ethics and how to become highly skilled problem solvers in all areas of life. Otherwise, people like Aaron will continue to resort to a life involving crime. Tyler, could you imagine what our country would look like if we started pumping out generations of highly trained and intelligent kids, or give people like me, who had a rough start in life, a second chance to redeem themselves?"

"It would be way better than what we are dealing with today. We're all stuck in financial tarpits we created for ourselves."

The brothers sit in a long silence watching the kids still whacking away on the golf simulator. Tyler tries again, "Have you ever thought about going to law school?"

"And do what exactly?"

"Many people who have law degrees aren't stuck in courtrooms arguing cases each day. Some go into politics, corporations, government jobs, and considering what you know, maybe you can help make a difference in this country."

"Everything is so backwards now, and many actions our leaders are taking are either illegal or unconstitutional."

"Seriously man, give it some consideration."

"I know, but you have to pay to play in that world. So, unless you have some buddies who have deep pockets and connections…" Jason trails off.

"Well, don't think too long or too hard about it. Time is money."

"Speaking of time," Jason says, looking at his phone, "we really should be getting home."

After saying their goodbyes, Tyler stops Jason as he walks out the door. "Hey man, think about what I said. I think you'd make a great lawyer and could do a lot to help people. Besides, you still have those VA benefits which would pay for your schooling. Just get accepted and it's a free degree…. Just think about it!"

Realizing Tyler is serious but knowing his chances to get admitted into a respectable law school would be a long shot, Jason says, "Alright man. I'll at least look into it. Thanks for having us over! Love you and call me when you want to hang out again."

"Love you too! I will! Drive safe!" Tyler replies as Jason gets everyone loaded into his car and drives off into the night.

Chapter 18

Opportunity + Action = Auspicious Turning Points

June 2021

Over the next few weeks, his brother's words keep replaying in Jason's mind. It had been almost 20 years since he stepped foot on a college campus, as Jason starts looking at the requirements for law schools. Looking at the lowest ranked schools first, he's not excited over his choices.

After hours of searching, Jason recalls his childhood dream of always wanting to go to Texas A&M. For entertainment purposes, he checks to see how far off he is from being accepted into his favorite school. Comparing his transcripts against their requirements, Jason triple checks the results. The only thing missing are a current GMAT or LSAT score to get in. Otherwise, everything else Jason has meets their requirements.

Not saying a word to Tyler or his parents, Jason takes the test, and puts together his admission packet a few months later. Even though he thinks it's a long shot, he works hard on the essay and puts the packet together like a professional business plan. Arriving at the post office, Jason thinks to himself, *Here goes nothing!*

Two days later, Jason's phone rings. Upon answering it, he hears an upbeat and very friendly administrator from Texas A&M. "Hi, is this Mr. Prescot?" *Oh no,* Jason thinks to himself. He was sure he had gone over his paperwork several times to catch any grammatical and punctuation errors. He even made sure all forms were together before sending it.

Replying Jason says, "Yes, ma'am, that's me."

"Great, I was calling to see if you've had a chance to check your email? I sent you one this morning."

"No, I apologize. I was busy and hadn't gotten around to it today."

"Not a problem. If you can open it really quick, there's some information I sent and need to go over with you concerning your admissions packet. Is this a good time?"

"Yes, ma'am. If you can give me a moment to get to my computer, I can read it easier from there while talking to you."

"Sure, I can wait." Still racking his brain as to what he left out, Jason can't believe his stupidity and starts berating himself for messing up his only chance at getting in. Any errors would show his lack of attention to detail.

"Here it is," Jason says, as he sees the email.

"Great, if you don't mind, can you read through it and just let me know how you want handle this?"

"Yes, ma'am," Jason responds as the email takes a few seconds to load. Sitting in silence, Jason almost drops the phone as he reads the first few lines of the email.

Howdy, Jason!

Congratulations and **welcome** ***to Texas A&M University School of Law! It is with great pleasure that I write to offer you admission into the Master of Jurisprudence Degree Program for the Fall term.***

Stupefied, Jason's voice cracks, "Are you kidding me? Is this real?"

Delighted, the young woman replies "Uh-huh!"

"Oh my God…Sharon!" Jason hollers from across the house. "Hurry, come quick and look at this!"

Sharon hustles into Jason's office to see what the commotion is all about. Concerned, Sharon asks, "What's going on?"

Fighting back tears of joy for a long overdue win, Jason points to the email and allows Sharon to read it for herself.

"Oh my God! This is great! You did it! I'm so proud of you honey!" Sharon calls out.

Laughing, the administrator cuts in, "I'm sorry, I couldn't wait to speak with you any longer. I was the one who received your packet, and as soon as I opened it, I knew right away you are Aggie material! I was excited to read your exceptional essay, review your impressive resume, and after seeing your references, I didn't want to present it to the board. Instead, I took it straight to our Dean of Admissions! After he saw what I did, he wasted no time in approving your packet as well…. Soooo…" Jason hears the excitement in her voice, "Do you accept our offer?"

Trying to remain calm, poised, and professional, Jason can't contain his excitement and blurts out, "YES MA'AM!!!!!" as he tightly embraces his wife.

When Life Hands You Lemons...

"Hey mom!" Jason says as she answers her phone.

"Hi Jason! How are you?" Ellie replies.

"I want to share something with you. Do you have a couple of minutes?"

"Yes, but I don't have long. I need to get to the grocery store before traffic hits. What's going on? How's your first semester in law school going?"

"That's what I wanted to speak with you about."

"Ok, what's up?"

"I wanted to read you some feedback I got from one of my professors this semester."

"Make it quick, I don't have a lot of time."

"I can call you later."

"No, go ahead. I want to hear what they had to say. Just give the Cliff's Notes version."

"Ok, this won't take long, but this is what my professor had to say:

'Jason, I really like your original thinking, creative ideas here - on how to curb corporate misdeeds and fraudulent behavior. Really intuitive, fascinating analysis, really unique insights at opting for greater adoption of the common good approach by all members in our community - some of whom seem to have lost their values, ethics and virtues as you describe it, rather than respect and contribute to the community, many are extracting from the community for personal gain above societal welfare as expressed in your analysis....

thank you for sharing - a very meaningful analysis to the state of our country...."

"That was very nice of them!" Ellie cheers.
"Here's another one," Jason continues.

"'Jason - really a very inspirational post - thank you for sharing --and I see how you weave ethics into your discussion - as you know, ethics are the standard of behavior for the benefit or welfare of others - and as you point out, disputes often happen because of implicit bias-- new people seen as a threat by others.

...and totally agree regarding large groups and one autocratic leader - never reduces bias, never results in great outcomes, and never really generates consensus of buy in.....

fascinating discussion as well about racial bias in law firms - same for accounting firms...succession of like-minded thinkers - they look alike, have identical backgrounds, culture and biases...and shut out those who don't.'"

As Jason finishes, Ellie congratulates him again, "See, I always told you, you are smart! Every duck just needs to find their pond! Do you like your professors this semester?"

"I'll be honest, I didn't know what to think because I was concerned professors would push extreme political views or agendas, but as it turns out, they are wonderful! The professor who wrote these comments is very intelligent, very insightful, extremely knowledgeable, and thinks along the same lines as I do. He was telling me, for example, currently our country, in times of crisis, doesn't have a risk management team in the presidential cabinet in D.C. This means, whenever something bad happens, people are running around like chickens with their heads chopped off, rather than having proper plans in place to know exactly what to do. That is to say, if we aren't being fed fabricated and planned stories to create chaotic crisis through the media. If so, this would keep people in fear, and forced to comply with their new rules."

"Wouldn't surprise me."

"You know, mom, not in one ancient society until now, has a good leader ever forced its people to comply. What does that say for our country's situation now?"

"Don't even get me started on what I think about our current politicians!" Ellie angrily objects.

"I know."

"Well, how did you do in your classes?"

"In one class, I got 100!"

"A 100? Wow! That's great! What about the other classes?"

"It gets better! One class gave 5 points extra credit, so I ended up with 103!"

"103? Jason, way to go!"

"The other two class grades were a 97 and a 94."

"What's up with a 94? I guess somebody was slacking," Ellie sarcastically teases.

Jason laughs, "Sorry, I'll put more effort in next semester."

"What's that equate to? A 4.0 GPA for your first semester in law school?"

"Yes ma'am."

"I knew you had it in you!"

"Thanks mom, but I wanted to share those comments first, before I read another response I received."

"Ok good. I thought you were just calling to brag!"

"Maybe later, but this professor really got me thinking."

"About what?"

"He gave us an assignment in which Denise's case applied perfectly, so I shared information regarding it, and this was his response…

'Jason – Wow - I have been in publishing, both consumer and professional - what an incredible and sad story. What an incredible amount of investigation - this is not only a book but a screenplay. The deceit, deception, and dishonesty of elected officials is unconscionable. So, what is the ethical issue you have observed here now? A coverup, deception, criminality, and collusion --are the core Aggie values not in play here? Aggies do not lie, cheat, steal, or allow others to do so.

Have you considered writing a book or would you consider talking to a few ghostwriters I know, who can take your story and turn it into one? I keep in touch with many anonymous writers, and they would love to speak with you - please let me know how you would want to proceed on your book or when you are finished, I can make the introductions. I would also be honored to read the book and provide some constructive feedback - during my publishing days, I probably published hundreds of titles and wrote a few myself. I did boring book reviews on legal, tax, and business type books – but this story is in a category on its own.

Happy Holiday Season...and please stay in touch. Wish you the best of success and let me know how or when I can assist.'"

Ellie is silent.
"Mom?"
"Yeah, I'm here," Ellie replies, a little choked up.
"What's the matter?"
Clearing her throat. "I just want this nightmare to be over with. I want Denise found, the people who are

responsible locked away, and for her kids to know what really happened to their mother."

"Me too," Jason softly responds. "Like I said before, everything happens for a reason, and there are no coincidences. Maybe things were supposed to happen this way. I've been wondering why I spent countless hours reading and studying over the years. I figured somehow, the answers to our prayers were buried deep inside one of those books. I studied trying to find answers for this case, but instead, it helped me discover solutions to many modern-day problems we're all facing. Denise's story needs to be told because of the message we can all learn from this."

"What about her body still at the property? John offered to rent a backhoe and dig her up," Ellie asks.

"If he does, then you are disturbing a potential crime scene. The evidence could get easily thrown out in court, and not to mention it looks like they've been trying to pin her murder on us. Mom, we've tried everything we could legally do, and they played their hand, like a move in a chess match. The only exception is, I've been extremely patient looking for a way to counter their move."

"What does your studying and Denise have to do with this?"

"Here's a golden opportunity to not only help Denise, but so many others like her."

"How can one book make a difference?"

"It's the same as one professor's encouraging words, helping to inspire me to make a difference. One person, one book, or one generous act can really make a change. Had he not said anything to me, I'd still be trying to figure out what to do with all I know. It just amazes me how far one person's inspiring words or influences can be felt. His words helped me to realize the importance of how we treat each other as human beings. You never know who else you might be helping or harming by how you treat someone. If you hurt one person, you're not just hurting them. You hurt their family, relatives, friends, and their community. It's a chain reaction. I guess the moral in this is: if you help, encourage, or inspire someone to light their candle, it too becomes a chain reaction. Essentially, if you can light one candle, then you can light or change the world."

"So now what? Are you going to write a book or screenplay now?" Ellie asks doubtfully.

Jason laughs, "What do I know about either one? I've never written a book or screenplay before."

"So, what are you going to do then?" Ellie questions.

"If we are going to share her story, I want to do it right. We may only get one chance to get the right eyes on this. This could also get this information outside their little network to those who have the authority to do something about it. Plus, my professor knows people who could take this story and run with it. With the right exposure, we can get advocates demanding and hounding the Sheriff's department and the Texas Rangers to clean up their staff. Maybe this might be what the F.B.I. needs to see to step in and remove those who have abused their authority and badges."

"What if the book is a success, what will you do with the money?"

"I want to take the money to open schools or facilities in Denise's memory. I want to open places that offer the right education. I never started down this path looking for fame, fortune, or even notoriety. I stayed the course because of the principles and the values I hold dear. Put yourself in my shoes. Can you imagine what it's like to search for years for an answer you don't know the question to? Now, I know!" Jason answers.

"If you think this is the best way, then I support you. I do have one question."

"What's that?'

"How will you remember all the details?"

"Easy. We took plenty of notes, but I wanted to speak with you first."

Sobbing and searching for a ray of hope, Ellie asks, "Do you think this will finally bring her home?"

"I don't know, mom, but this would definitely put the spotlight on what they have done, or better yet, what they failed to do. I think with plenty of local and national pressure, it's only a matter of time before someone takes a plea deal to save their own skin. Whoever is the first to talk…walks. Otherwise, they will be charged as accessories to homicide and will be sharing cells together. Early bird gets the worm, as they say."

"At this point, I don't care who comes clean, I just want Denise given a proper burial."

"We can't do that at the moment because law enforcement won't cooperate in solving this case or go arrest the obvious suspect," Jason reminds his mother. "In March, we mark the seven-year anniversary Denise has been declared missing. Did you know, in the state of Texas, after seven years, we can request law enforcement search all their known databases for Denise. If they can't find her, then they must officially declare her legally dead. At which time, this would completely disprove their theory of her running away. Then they will have to answer for not acting sooner. Either way, this should get interesting. Do you want to know what else I found out?"

"What now?" Ellie replies with a stuffy nose.

"Guess who's back from the dead?"

Excited, "JFK Jr.?"

Laughing, "Not political, mom. Think about the people involved with Denise's case."

Without missing a beat, Ellie answers, "Jack Dimes!"

"Yep! Aaron's second dad."

"How do you know for sure?" Ellie interrogates.

"A little birdie told me!"

Even more curious, Ellie insists, "One of your friends I take it?"

"Yes, ma'am. Since the Sheriff's department won't voluntarily run Denise's information through their databases and fail to report their findings, I asked if one of my friends could do it. They told me there hasn't been any sign or use of her social security number, driver's license, or anything. Except in 2020, Aaron used her name for a phone that traces back to him."

"WHAT? Why's he still using her name?"

"That was the same response we had."

"Did you get the number?"

"Yes, ma'am."

"After I found out, I was curious about Jack Dimes' mysterious death. Don't you remember it wasn't a few months after I started putting heat on this case publicly in 2018, he fakes his own death? After my friend went through all known databases, there was no death certificate, or anything to indicate he is deceased. Which means he's still alive and kicking."

"I knew there was something off about all of that."

"Well, his family made sure to post his death all over Facebook, but Sharon and I kept searching the obituaries, and funeral homes. To no surprise, he was a no-show."

Ellie responds, "Why am I not surprised?"

"Anyway, Jack's ex-girlfriend came clean to me on how Jack used Denise's name in an unusual sale of a black F-150, a few days before she was declared missing."

"Why did she tell you all of this?"

"After Jack attacked her and was charged with aggravated assault, she had a few things she wanted to get off her chest. No surprise, the case got dismissed."

"Scorned women leave no stone left unturned. I can tell you that!"

"Yes, ma'am. She told me Jack was previously arrested for a DUI and needed a breathalyzer device installed in his truck. To avoid this, Jack went to their county tax office, where Aaron's real dad has a girlfriend, who has a sister working in that office. Jack slipped her some money, and she falsified DMV records to put the truck in Denise's name."

"It still chews me up when the detective went to Jack's house, asking if he knew Denise, and he said he'd never seen her before. Denise held her baby shower for Allen at his home!"

"I know, mom. Jack's ex-girlfriend also secretly recorded the Sheriff and Jack having a conversation. I guess their problems had gone on for a while, and she was looking for dirt to burn Jack. Anyway, turns out the Sheriff and Jack are best buds too! She didn't know this until she asked the Sheriff *'Isn't it against the law when Jack lied to the detective, denying he ever knew Denise?'* The Sheriff said on the recording, *'It's nothing to get worried about. I'll take care of it.'* Then, you can hear Jack and the Sheriff continue their conversation and shooting a few rounds off with their guns on Jack's property."

"Those lying scumbags!"

"Anyway, back to the F-150. Jack's ex informed me that he slipped that same woman more money to put the vehicle back in his name two days before she died," Jason clarifies.

"Um, that makes me wonder if Aaron wasn't already considering or premediating her murder."

"Well, if Denise went missing before the title was transferred out of her name, then law enforcement would be looking for the truck, thinking Denise would be with it. Then, his whole story, lying about not knowing Denise, would be exposed and raise a bunch of other questions. Either way, when this information found its way onto social media, Jack mysteriously dies. Guess what else?"

Growing agitated, Ellie considers, "You never did tell me the entire conversation you had with the investigator?"

"Troy? Yeah, there's a gem!" Jason answers. "Did you know he has the same name as Dad?"

"Yes. That's the only way I could remember his name. Did he share anything else useful?"

"He pins the tail on the donkey! If only news journalists or outside investigators spoke to him instead. They would realize why this case remains unsolved."

"How did you track him down?"

"Aaron's not the only one with friends."

Laughing, Ellie comments, "You never cease to amaze me."

"He's a very nice guy. In fact, when I told him what I was doing, he was forth coming. He confirmed they found blood in the home, triangulated Aaron's phone in front of the abandoned property the night Denise went missing and tried speaking to Aaron in the beginning. Aaron told Troy he wasn't allowed to answer questions because his lawyer advised him not to. Troy also shared, there was a flurry of cell phone activity between 1 am to 3:12 am on Aaron's phone. He said there were a bunch of text messages and phone calls, the night Denise was last seen alive."

"Did you ask him his thoughts on being pulled from the case?"

"Get this…he wasn't shy about letting me know, this is direct law enforcement obstruction of justice. He was on the same path I was. He spoke to Jack Dimes, and even identified the property. Troy was pushing to escalate this case into a criminal homicide investigation. Then he got submarined by either Aunt Lisa or Lydia, telling his boss he gave them Denise's phone records."

"Yeah, you told me that part already."

"Here's the best part...the current Sheriff, Ranger Lewis, and cold case investigators are claiming they've searched the woods, properties, drained ponds, and investigated all leads or suspects, but that was Troy's work. Since the Sheriff took over three months into the case, they've been using Troy's efforts to deter reporters, and people like me, who question what they've done recently. When asked, they simply say, 'Oh we're looking into new leads.' Troy laughed and said 'They haven't followed up on anything! They are doing everything in their power to keep this case hush, hush, because of who's involved and who it would expose.' He said, it's not just the Sheriff's office, but he also mentioned the DA and local judge are somehow in on it too. That's the reason her case hasn't gone anywhere since he was let go. Denise's disappearance has nothing to do with lack of evidence. Troy is just as upset about it as we are. He shared this with me, in hopes I can help expose the corruption."

"Why won't he come forward then?"

"I asked him if he would testify in court and he said, 'Absolutely!'"

"Why wait until then?"

"He said this is not a few bad apples or bad barrel of apples. He said this is a bad orchard! Let's just say he's got a huge bone to pick with these guys for screwing him over for doing his job. Troy said not everyone is corrupt, referring to the new guys, but the ones with any authority were hand-picked because they would go along with their little system."

Irate, Ellie starts, "Maybe you should do the book! This is just beyond belief, Jason!"

"Mom."

Ignoring her son, "I can't believe law enforcement is letting Aaron and Jack get away with this! What's the point of having law enforcement if they won't enforce the law?"

"Mom," Jason says a little louder this time.

"I'm just so mad! It's inconceivable!"

"Mom!"

Taking a deep breath, Ellie calms down. "This is so wrong on so many levels. Is there no one who can help? You might be too young to remember him, but this was exactly how Marvin Zindler from KTRK-TV news station in Houston made a name for himself. It was before you were born, but he's the one who rattled cages back in 1973 to expose the Chicken Ranch brothel scandal. Ever heard of the movie, *The Best Little Whore House in Texas,* with Burt Reynolds, Dolly Parton, and Dom DeLuise?"

"Nope! Didn't see it, but I do remember Marvin Zindler. He was that flamboyant 'Slime in the Ice Machine' guy, right?"

Chuckles, "Yes. Same guy. Well, the movie is based on Marvin's investigative reporting of the Chicken Ranch. He was good. Marvin was asked by the Attorney General to investigate illegal prostitution in two different counties. The Chicken Ranch is what they made the movie about, but Marvin didn't care who he got in trouble. He blasted them on air to expose law enforcement and politicians turning a blind eye to illegal activity. This story is what put him on the map! Since then, other reporters have tried to copy his 'in your face' style, to get stories out in the open."

"Can you imagine, then, whose career would be launched after exposing Denise's case for what it truly is?"

"Oh Jason, his story made national headlines! Denise's story has the same elements as the Chicken Ranch, but this isn't just a sex scandal, this is a full-blown concealment of murder, involving law enforcement and elected officials. That is to say…if there's still good people out there doing investigative reporting."

"I have faith there's good people still left in this world, and I believe in my heart, when they see what's happening here, this whole area will get cleaned up. The F.B.I. would have a field day with these guys, and since news ratings are in the toilet, what kind of frenzy do you think will happen when they start reporting real news like this?"

"Let's hope so."

Cracking up, Jason states, "Now, I understand!"

"Understand what?"

"I get what John was talking about and his whole little 'Cloak and Dagger' routine. He was telling me about the area's widespread corruption and how these small, tight-knit counties operate."

"It's the 'Good Ole Boy' system," Ellie chimes back.

"But moving forward," Jason begins, "if I go through with this, I do have one request."

"For me to calm down?"

"Ha-ha, that too, but if I do this, I want to ask something from you."

"Like what?"

"Do you remember when Aunt Lisa asked you to write something for Denise's candlelight service?"

"Yes," Ellie's voice crackles. "Are you trying to peg all my emotions in one sitting?"

"No."

"I haven't thought about that for a long time. What about it?"

Sincerely, Jason recalls, "If I go forward with this, I want it to be my contingency for approving whoever writes the book or movie. If it's not included in either one, then it's a no-go. I want Denise's memory preserved the way we all remember her, and you did a great job capturing who Denise truly was."

"Thank you," Ellie's voice quivers.

"Do I have your permission to share it?"

"I would be honored…I'm sending it to you now."

"Thank you."

"Jason, I'm so very proud of you, and thank you for all that you've done to help!"

"It's family mom."

"Well, if anything ever happened to me or if I ever went missing, you'd be my first pick for someone to come find me. I know you wouldn't rest until I was found!"

"I love you, mom."

"I love you too!"

Chapter 19

Denise's Candlelight Service

October 2015

As Ellie looks over the crowd of more than 100 people huddled in the late 1920's church in San Saba, TX, she struggles to see the faces in the audience waiting for to her to speak. Holding electronic candles, Ellie strains to see what she wrote. Standing at an old wooden podium in front of the congregation, Ellie does her best to share Denise's message. After a quick introduction, Ellie holds the candle closer to her script from the dimly lit sanctuary, offering little illumination.

"On behalf of the family of Denise Michelle Sanders, we want to thank each and every one of you for being here tonight. Thank you for your support and sharing Denise's story on Facebook, word of mouth, posters, flyers, stickers, and magnets. It is much appreciated. Denise has been missing now for seven and a half long and heart-breaking months. There have been so many people and their spouses who have generously stepped forward and volunteered their time, services, and financial assistance. It has all been so overwhelming, but there is no way Denise's story would have been in local papers, social media, radio, local news, or even national news, if it weren't for your tireless help and determination. We are forever grateful!" Ellie shares, making sure to take occasional pauses to make eye contact to connect with the audience.

"When Lisa asked me to say a few words about Denise, I was deeply honored. I've known Clark and Lisa for over 40 years now. We met when I was in high school when Lisa's little brother, Troy, brought me home to meet his family. As awkward as this might have been, they made me feel right at home. It was easy to remember Lisa because she was the only girl with eight brothers. I consider Lisa my sister and best friend. We've had a lot of similarities throughout the years, but the most significant ones were our children. She and Clark had Tina and Denise, while Troy and I had Tyler and Jason. Lisa's older brother Chad and his wife, Heather, had C.J. and Billy. The kids were all around the same ages and grades in school. Tragically, we lost Denise on March 22, 2015, and her cousin, Billy, this Father's Day on June 21, 2015. It has been quite a blow to the family, but it has not diminished our will for getting answers to find Denise, bring her home, and lay her to rest. We won't stop looking for her, ever!" Ellie says, making sure to take another pause.

Seeing aunts, uncles, cousins, friends, and family begin wiping their saddened tears discreetly, Ellie struggles to continue, "Denise was a devoted daughter and had a very loving relationship with her parents. She always kept her mom in the loop about what was going on in her life and she definitely was daddy's little girl. As a toddler, if Denise saw Clark and Lisa hugging, she would race up to push and pull them apart, trying to squeeze between them. I think she thought they were wrestling or something and didn't want to be left out." The congregation laughs. "When Denise was a teen, she knew how to push people's buttons. One time, when she and Lisa got into a heated argument, Denise stopped and said 'You gotta love me mom! I'm the baby!'" Congregation softly chuckles.

"When it came to Denise's heart," Ellie fighting back the tears, "it didn't matter if something was inconvenient to her. If she could somehow help those she loved, she was the first to volunteer. When her parents would take little vacations, Denise would drive half an hour to let their dogs out each day until they returned home, and never once complained. She was just happy to help. When Clark was in the hospital, she was there to cheer him up and just be supportive for her mother. Whatever they needed, Denise was always there. I know if she could, she would also be comforting them right now. She'd be the first one to start a search, check on the kids, and would do so without ever having to be asked. She'd be leading the charge!" Ellie takes a few seconds to turn the page.

"Denise and her sister, Tina, shared a special bond. They enjoyed each other's company, looked out after one another, and would even take vacations together. Looking at Denise's pictures, you can see the love in her eyes, especially when they are all bunched together. My favorite picture of her, is the one when she was in a tiny camper, just spending time with loved ones," Ellie comments, while sharing a framed picture of Denise to the audience.

"She was an amazing aunt to her nephew and niece. Denise became like an older sister to them and a confidant. Someone who they could trust to share their best kept secrets with. They had a special love, loyalty, and kinship, with each other. Not to mention, they had many fun sleepovers during summer vacations and school breaks." The audience chuckles again.

"Denise never was a stranger to those around her. She was outgoing and easily made friends wherever she went. There wasn't anything she wouldn't do to help a friend in need. She loved her time spent with them, doing make-up, hair, nails, and going shopping together. She was full of life, and when someone else was down and blue, she would do her best to lift them up. Denise might not have been perfect, and Lord knows we've all made mistakes, but she saw the good in people even when they couldn't see it themselves. She was everyone's biggest cheerleader," Ellie taking a few moments as a few tears land on her speech.

Struggling to maintain composure, Ellie quickly dries the few fallen drops from the paper before continuing, "Denise had an indelible personality. If you met her, you wouldn't forget her. How could you? She was beautiful inside and out. Her sweet and loving spirit expounded her generous and compassionate heart. One day, when she was little, on the way to the bus stop, Denise noticed their little dog, Ginger, had followed her there. When the bus arrived shortly after, Denise couldn't bear the thought of leaving poor Ginger there, all alone on the corner because she might get hurt. Not wanting to miss the school bus, she picked the dog up, put it in her backpack, and hopped on the bus. Upon arriving at school, she placed her bag in the classroom closet, but apparently Ginger ate her way out. When Denise went to check on the dog, Ginger came scampering out." Everyone laughs. "Needless to say, Lisa received a peculiar phone call from the principle, needing her to pick both of them up from school because dogs were not allowed." Audience laughter continues.

"Oh, my goodness, how Denise enjoyed a good laugh. Her uproars were so loud and infectious, you couldn't help but laugh with her. Also, Denise was the type of person you could hear well before you could see her. She found joy in the simple things in life and would be the first to laugh at her own mistakes. What she really enjoyed, was including others in her joy. Like the time she was so proud of herself, attempting to make banana pudding, but there was only one problem. She forgot to add the bananas." The audience laughs. "Or the time when she was little, and borrowed Tina's 'hair mousse', she found in the bathroom cabinet. After fixing her hair, she came out and stood next to her mom, so proud of her new stylish hairdo. Lisa and Tina, noticing an unusual smell coming from her hair, knew something was wrong. Tina didn't have mousse. They discovered Denise had put Nair in her hair and quickly rushed her to the tub, frantically trying to rinse it out. By that time, it was already too late. Denise's hair was coming out in clumps," Ellie smiles looking back out to the audience.

Flipping another page, and before Ellie could resume, she is interrupted as the sanctuary doors open and a young woman enters the building. It's Denise! Ellie looking down at her papers and quickly looking up again, Denise's tall, slender, and muscular build, is unmistakable. With her blonde highlights, jeans, tank top, and hat, Ellie watches as Denise slowly makes her way down the center aisle. Like a punch to Ellie's stomach and taking her breath away, she can't believe her eyes! A rush of relief, confusion, and anger washes over her, but finally, all this stupidity can end. Speechless and feeling sick to her stomach, Ellie is the only one who recognizes Denise slowly approaching the congregation. Waiting for Denise to announce herself and to tell everyone to quit worrying about her because she's fine, doesn't happen. Bewildered, Ellie watches instead, as she slides into one of the wooden church pews in the back, and intently returns her stare. As the young woman lights her candle and offers a better visual of her face, Ellie's heart sinks. It's not Denise. The young woman is Denise's older cousin, Molly, arriving late to the service.

This 30 seconds to a minute leaves Ellie temporary discombobulated. Feeling as though she's been zapped in and out from an episode of *The Twilight Zone*, she takes a moment to collect her thoughts and mentally pick up the pieces from her shattered hopes.

With a shaky voice, Ellie resumes, "Denise loved life and lived every moment to its fullest. Whether it was going down a water slide, riding a jet ski, trudging through the mud on four-wheelers, unloading rounds at the shooting range, or just going for a ride on the back of her dad's motorcycle, it didn't matter what she was doing. What mattered to her was who she was with. She just wanted to be around the ones she loved and have a good time."

Looking back at Molly a few more times, Ellie struggles to brush off her uncanny resemblance to Denise. While secretly wishing the woman to be her, Ellie must proceed on with the commencement.

"Speaking of loved ones, Denise's pride and joys are her three children, Dewayne, Eric, and Allen. According to her, they are her greatest achievements. Denise lived for her kids and couldn't get enough of them. They were her strength, as she was theirs. She enjoyed going to their ballgames, reading stories, roughhousing, playing games, or just giving them hugs from momma. One of Denise's greatest qualities was how she treated other children like her own. She loved kids! She loved being around them, caring for them, playing with them, and sometimes just being a kid herself. If the situation demanded it, Denise became a fierce momma bear to protect the children and couldn't stand to see any child hurt or crying. She was also the first one on the scene to check on and comfort them," Ellie recalls, pausing to make uncomfortable eye contact with the people in attendance.

"Denise had the most loving heart and was the most generous person I'd ever known. When my son, Tyler, and his wife, Megan, were expecting my first grandchild, Megan had a high-risk pregnancy. She was placed on bed rest in her last few months of pregnancy. What did Denise do? She would make the long trip from her home to Megan's house, in Austin, and do her hair and make-up each day. Denise said, 'Pregnant girls should look pretty too!' When Megan was no longer able to reach her toes, Denise was there to paint them for her. When Megan wanted to color her hair, Denise went out and got all organic products because she knew they couldn't use chemicals. Meticulously, Denise colored Megan's hair to perfection. When their son Jackson arrived six weeks early, Denise was the one who drove Megan to the hospital each day to see her son. Denise would hold her hand, and didn't mind sitting for hours, until Tyler could get off work, to be there with Megan," Ellie expresses while looking over at Tyler and Megan seated off to the side.

Turning to the final page of her speech, reality begins to set in for Ellie. She will never get to see Denise alive again. What started out as an uneasy assignment and trying to figure how to quickly convey the message, Ellie doesn't want her speech to end. Somehow she feels her words are keeping Denise's spirit alive in the hearts of others.

"Denise knew how to read people and became the person they needed the most. She was so giving, loving, kind, and so special. The most precious gift she gave everyone was her time and unconditional love. She made you feel good about yourself, and if you were in trouble or in the trenches of life, she would be right there with you, regardless of what she had going on in hers. Denise was a spitfire, and God's social butterfly. Anyone who crossed paths with her was fortunate enough to be touched and blessed by her spirit," Ellie finishes.

With only a few lines left, Ellie consoles her family, "Clark, Lisa, and Tina, know that Denise can't make it home on her own. We ask for continued prayers that her location will soon be revealed, so she can be reunited with her family. We truly know God is in control, and everything happens in

His timeframe…not ours. We pray for continued strength, comfort, and peace for her family in their darkest hours."

Lowering her script, Ellie notices a few of Aaron's friends sitting in the back half of the church, and it strikes a few nerves with her. With more confidence, she shares a few more comments with the audience. "We are thankful for God's daily blessings, but how do you move forward when such a huge part of you is missing? How do you keep the hope alive when there are no clues or leads? How do you deal with the emotions, pain, grief, anger, despair, helplessness, loneliness, and sleepless nights? How can some of you in attendance, sit here tonight, who knew Denise and Aaron, and say such terrible things about her online?" Ellie referring to Aaron's friends and family who have tried their best efforts to make Aaron look innocent, while trying to peg Denise as a wandering and irresponsible gypsy. "Do you have no dignity, honor, respect, or common decency? You don't have to like everyone, but to troll the family's page to air grievances about Denise or defend Aaron's innocence is preposterous! Shame on you if you did, and I will say this…" Ellie starts as she fearlessly stares at the select few in the crowd, "if you don't have the courage or guts to say something to a person's face when they are alive, then it tells me everything I need to know about what type of weak, spineless coward you are, trying to kick a person while they're down," Ellie valiantly proclaims, as the small guilted group looks down to avoid eye contact, or their conscience.

"What message is being missed here?" Ellie poses to the remaining members on Denise's behalf. "The value of human life! Once it's taken away, you can never get it back. We live in a time where people deflect and tarnish others from their own personal guilt. People defend and protect those who hurt and harm others. Denise didn't have career accomplishments, win a Nobel Peace prize, or attain a massive fortune, but is this any reason to treat people as diseased lepers, and look down on them, because you're doing better in life? From how I see it, Denise was richer than all of us here today. She didn't care if you were homeless or living in a mansion. If you needed a hand, she treated you as a human being. If you were struggling, she taught you what she knew to help you improve your life. This world lost a priceless and unique treasure when her life was taken from us. Most people value others based on money, social status, level of education, material items, or the color of their skin, but Denise knew this is a shallow and cruel way to treat each other. Whether she even knew it or not, her actions towards others were not much different than how Jesus took in sinners and turned them into apostles. How he preferred the company of the less fortunate and ill, to share his knowledge and abilities, to be a blessing to others, rather than exploiting people for personal gain. Denise, nor Jesus, were rich, but the values they upheld and shared with us all, were wiser than any one man sitting on a mountaintop. They didn't strive to say wise words, or try to gain the approval of others, instead, they just went out there and did what needed to be done. Regardless of what was going on in their lives, they both tried to be a light in the life of others, and to this world," Ellie pauses to wipe the tears from her eyes.

"We are forever grateful to those offering your support. Please continue to share her story, and with your help, Denise will find her way home. Live each day as if it is your last because we never know when that day might be. I'm sure there wouldn't be anything Denise wouldn't give to spend one more day with her boys. To hold and kiss them. To smell their hair, hear their laughter, and tell them once more, 'Mommy loves you!' Denise was a part of us all. She was a daughter, a sister, a cousin, a niece, an aunt, a grandchild, a wife, a mother, a friend, a member of this community, a citizen to our country, and a part of our humanity in this world. We are all connected, and no one is perfect. If you mess up today, then do it better tomorrow. Do the right thing and be good to each other. Value, love, nurture, respect, and protect everyone. No more lies. Tell the truth and stop killing people."

Chapter 20

Our Shattered Looking Glass

Walking over to the sectional sofa in the living room, Jason and Sharon sit on opposite sides facing each other. Taking a sip of water, Sharon recalls everything that's happened so far, "As crazy as it sounds, I hope people realize this is not some fantasy fiction murder mystery and understand this story is based closely on what really happened."

"We shall see. The point of telling the story is to convey this corruption goes far beyond Denise's case, she's not just some isolated incident. This is currently happening, not only in our country, but around the world. I keep seeing Trump trying to make a comeback, but he is running on the same platform, much like Hillary did trying to run for the presidential election in 2008 and 2016. It's the same story. Times have changed, and both keep talking about the past. What about our future? Forget the whole 'Make American Great Again' campaign, we need to 'Make American Proud Again'!"

"Good point!" Sharon compliments.

"We think of greatness as business and financial success while overlooking the means to how it is achieved. As Americans, are we proud of how our officials have turned their backs on us, and billionaires who wouldn't pour his drink on the little guy if he was on fire to save his life? People become successful and then condemn the ones they've

325

stepped on to get there. Then, they have the audacity to treat the ones they've lied to, stolen from, or cheated out of money, as outcasts. As Americans, are we proud of how this country is being run? They claim our school system is number one in the world, yet when tested, our children's scores compare to those kids from third world countries."

"Sherry, from across the street, has been teaching high school English for 15 years, and said the kids today struggle with simple tasks, like calculating averages, or logically figuring out little problems by themselves."

"We've traded logic and common sense for standardized testing. If you ask a high schooler how they plan to overcome getting a divorce in their mid-30's, supporting two kids, a mortgage, and recently fired from their job, what would they say or do?"

"I can guarantee, you would get a blank stare or a dumb look on their face."

"This is exactly what I'm talking about! When it comes to life, kids today don't know what they are doing, or how to even survive on their own...and we call this education? Education has nothing to do with grades and test scores. Education should teach people how to do well in all areas of life, not just a career. Our country encourages people to stop learning when they get out of school. Had I not continued learning on my own, I wouldn't be in a better position, like I am today."

"God didn't intend to have people sad, suffering, miserable, and lonely."

"Here's what I mean by how we culturally think...we see a company dumping toxic waste into our lakes and oceans, so we build another church to pray and hope God comes to clean the mess up. The more problems that arise, the more churches pop up ready to take your money, but does anything change? Do problems magically resolve themselves? Is God there to serve your needs, or are you here to serve God's? Here's a perfect example, let's say you want to lose weight. Where should you go? To church or to the gym? Should you pray or go exercise?"

"Go to the gym!"

"If you want to do well on a test, do you spend hours in a church praying to do well or spend the time studying to prepare yourself?"

"Study!"

"Our country begs and prays for everything to be done for them. Few people pray for the knowledge, wisdom, and guidance to figure things out on their own. They want miracles but won't do the work to get it."

Sharon laughs. "You're preaching to the choir!"

"I don't get what people are waiting on. We are instruments and swords of the Creator, here to do the work. Not to be sideline spectators who constantly complain. If you see something wrong, then do something. Quit waiting and asking for permission. You see legislators and corporate CEO's abusing our Constitution. God didn't create this problem, we did. If you believe in it, then you must defend and preserve our way of life. No one is coming to save the day, except you, but people are too busy talking to the clouds to do anything. Is that how the system works? If so, then why isn't it working? God doesn't take money or play favorites. Whatever messes we allow to be made here, we are responsible for cleaning up."

"God didn't turn this country on its head. It's people not stepping up to stop those who have."

"This has nothing to do with religion. This is just life 101," Jason reminds.

"I know, I was reiterating what you said," Sharon replies.

"That's fine. I just hope people understand a particular religion isn't going to fix the world's problems by itself."

"Neither will throwing money at churches or temples."

"Correct. There is a lot of work which needs to be done and too many people not paying attention or willing to ask the hard questions. Believing problems solve themselves, is like a person wishing to win the lottery to get them free of debt."

"Or thinking it's someone else's responsibility to fix it."

"It doesn't work this way. If you don't pay attention, problems grow and flourish. You must focus on what you are doing. It's like people who text on their phones while driving. They are inviting tragedy into their life because they aren't focused and paying close attention to what they are doing."

Agreeing, Sharon offers, "My mom always taught me, God helps those who help themselves. Which means, if you want a new job, then you need to get out there and hustle to find one. Not just sit around hoping someone will bring a job to you. When you first put forth the effort, then you gain insights, guidance, and assistance to achieve your goal."

"BINGO!"

"Do you know what the saddest part is to learn in all of this, trying to solve Denise's case?"

"What?"

"While there might be outside economic influences involved with Denise's coverup, this all boils down to one man, who is responsible for her disappearance, and those who helped to cover it up."

"You are absolutely correct. Now let me ask you a serious question."

"Ok."

"Are people innately good or bad?"

"Good," Sharon answers.

"If this were true, then why does our world look the way that it does?"

Confused, Sharon asks, "What do you think then?"

"I don't think people are good or bad from birth but are products of their environment and upbringing. People are innately selfish and lazy. When times are tough or they are struggling, what morals or values won't they sell to the highest bidder? What are we witnessing today? A large percentage of selfish people giving in to evil ways, to put themselves ahead of others, regardless of who they hurt to get there. As long as they are comfortable, and their family is taken care of, they easily justify their actions."

"Yeah, but can they sleep at night with a guilt free conscious?"

"The answer to that is no," Jason responds. "They feel shame, regret, and remorse for what they've done, whether they realize this now or later. It grinds at people's souls when they lie, cheat, or steal from others. Yes, people get rich, but at what cost?"

"They see everyone else doing it and figure, why shouldn't they get a slice of the pie as well?"

"Now, is it so hard to believe a small-town law enforcement agency and local politicians are covering up Denise's murder intentionally?" Jason inquires.

"Not after what we have seen."

"Why is this happening? Most people avoid education or being kept up-to-date on current political, economic, and social conditions. They prefer to pay others to do their jobs for them. Take for example, if I make a social media post about how Houston is still ranked as the number one location for human trafficking, I might get one or two replies, but if I post a video about a cute cat falling off the counter or a guy getting kicked in the crotch, it gets a million hits."

"Houston is ranked number one in the nation for human trafficking?"

"It's the perfect hub. These people bring in women captives from other countries, like Korea, Thailand, and China, to be prostitutes for their sex-oriented businesses, like those Thai spas or massage parlors."

"It's unbelievable it is happening right here in our state!"

"Knowing this, doesn't it make you wonder now about the intentions of law enforcement, public officials, and the media? Law enforcement, government agencies, and elected officials know this is happening and the media makes sure to keep it from the headlines."

"While there are major flaws on both sides of the table when it comes to politics, it's not a coincidence, cities being run by Democratic mayors have the highest rates in crime, drugs, and homelessness."

"Don't forget to include the largest concentrations of illegal immigrants. Now, do you see the Texas governor pressing our metropolitan mayors to change their ways?"

"No. We are reaping what we have sown as a country," Sharon comments. "We are now in the beginning stages of getting what has been coming to us."

"What's about to happen to this country and world, is going to be a monumental moment in history and it's not going to be pretty."

"You can say that again!" Sharon replies.

Jason repeats, "What is about to happen to this country and world, is going to be…"

Sharon cuts him off, "I was being facetious, not literal."

Laughing, "I know."

"What can be done? What can we do?"

"Do you know why people have problems in their life?" Jason asks.

"They ignore them or bury their heads in the sand."

"Yes, but why do people do this?"

"I don't know."

"They lack the right education. Knowledge is the key or bridge between a problem and its solution. Knowledge is also the bridge from where you are now to where you want to be. The most common issue today, is when people are faced with a problem. They don't know how to get from Point A to Point B or arrive at a solution. They get stuck. If a rational individual gets stuck, they use their common sense to investigate and learn more about what they are struggling with to solve their problem. Instead, our society teaches people to hope someone will come fix your problems for you. We have many people consciously committing great atrocities against each other because they have problems and can't or won't find humane solutions. People are struggling and make choices to sell drugs or committing crimes because they need money to survive. Some who earn good livings, pay off law enforcement and elected officials to leave their business alone. The business of turning people into drug or pleasure induced zombies are huge market industries," Jason finishes.

"People are getting too drunk from power and money but let me add this little food for thought: It's not that people are lazy. They are in a constant state of distraction. They are too wrapped up in the mundane, day-to-day lifestyles to look up at what's happening around them. People assume law enforcement and elected officials are doing the right thing. You know what happens when you assume anything."

"I agree there are good police officers and civil servants out there, but right now, they are being

331

overwhelmed by this recent trend of corruption happening in broad daylight."

"Yes, but what about some of our judges. Who questions their integrity?" Sharon poses.

"It is when power goes unchecked, that integrity, honesty, and fairness begin to crumble. We are about to experience the worst of both worlds. Not only has our country opened the door to European financial servitude, but we have also allowed communist inspired political leaders to gain a strong foothold in our country's interests. It's a double whammy. This obsession for consumerism has forced people into financial bondage."

"The truth is being distorted and downplayed. The flash, the glam, or seemingly mind-numbing news topics they perpetually run keeps people oblivious from what is really happening behind the scenes. We are all in cycles of some form of incarceration. We have the physical, financial, medical, or mental. It's just to what extent we are locked in some type of prison. "

"How long has it been, since we have progressed as a society?"

"It's been decades."

"What is a key marked quality of a third world country?"

"Extreme stagnation as a population."

"When this happens, violence becomes more prominent in these areas because the people have a child-like mentality, which takes the easy road when faced with difficult issues. Our issues in America aren't because of cultural diversity, because it already exists. What we currently lack is intellectual diversity. That is the real disease of our great nation."

"Getting back to Denise. I know you mentioned this year is going to be the seven-year mark to her disappearance. Are you nervous?"

"About what?"

"I don't know, if they are actually going to follow through and declare her dead, or if someone must put pressure for them to do so."

"If they don't, then pressure needs to be put on them to do it, but more importantly, I already anticipate them delaying this declaration as long as possible."

"Why would they do that?"

Jason explains, "By declaring Denise dead, and her not popping up anywhere else in seven years, Aaron, the Sheriff's Department, and the Texas Rangers are going to have an extremely difficult time convincing the public Denise ever left the area. It would blow a massive hole in their theory. With the release of the book, and getting as much attention on this as possible, they would sink their own ship to not turn this into a criminal investigation. Any more hesitancy or reluctance by law enforcement to pin Aaron as prime suspect number #1 would look very bad on their end. Deputy Ding Dong could figure this case out, and if they can't solve the most blatant and straightforward homicide, should they then be allowed to continue as law enforcement agents?"

"Every last one involved needs to be removed from office, charged with obstruction of justice, perjury to their Oath of Office, and as accomplices to Denise's murder for helping to cover it up."

"We shall see. It's ridiculous seven years has passed since Denise disappeared and the case still remains unsolved. I also found it incredibly difficult to find anyone from her hometown, unrelated to either party, who didn't openly admit they know the husband made her disappear."

"While I know this will never have a happy ending, it's 2022, and I can't imagine how that must feel to not at least have closure."

"Until people learn to rally against law enforcement corruption and political injustice, many cases like hers go unsolved. People must stand up for each other, stand up for Denise, stand up for her kids, demand results, and not back down until it's done."

"It's a shame to those good officers, politicians, news reporters, and government officials who do what's right. It's these bad apples who are giving them a bad name and reputation."

"Which brings me to my final point, let's say we removed every corrupt public official, to include the president, would anything really change? The answer is no. So, what's the problem? Are they the problem or is it the people who let them get away with it?"

Epilogue

Truth is Stranger than Fiction

Highlights From the Real Case File:

This story is based closely on the true events surrounding the disappearance of Danielle Marie Sleeper (Denise Sanders), age 32, which took place in Magnolia, Texas, or Montgomery County.

We have mysteries like the Danielle Sleeper case in Montgomery County because people have struggled to properly identify the true underlying problems in her case. This incident goes beyond just a few people acting unethically or immorally.

As for Danielle Sleeper's case, on March 22, 2015, witnesses testified to seeing Danielle arguing with her husband, Austin Sleeper, before leaving a party at Leaning Oaks Mobile Park at 900 Bowler Road, Waller, Texas, around 1 a.m. The couple left together in Austin's white 1996 Ford F-350, screaming at each other. This was the last time, anyone other than Austin Sleeper, saw Danielle alive.

Eyewitnesses who saw Danielle, Austin, and her youngest son leaving the party on March 22, 2015, have yet to be officially questioned or even interviewed by law enforcement. Even the owners of the wig shop, where Danielle went after Austin chopped her hair off, contacted the Montgomery County Sheriff's Department (MCSO) three times, after she was declared missing. MCSO has never returned any of their calls.

Danielle was 32 years old when she was reported missing from her home in Magnolia, Texas in 2015. To this day, her three boys still do not know what happened to their mother. Danielle's youngest son is still with Austin Sleeper, while her two other boys remain with her ex-husband. Danielle's two older children were removed from her home by Child Protective Services (CPS) after an incident involving Austin and Danielle's two older boys. Austin Sleeper was facing felony criminal charges for injury to a child until Danielle went missing the same week as the trial. The case was dismissed after Danielle failed to appear in court.

The real 42-acre property from the book, where the original MCSO investigator, Detective Thomas Gannucci, was searching before being removed from the case, is located on the southeast corner at the intersection of FM 1488, Bowler and Hegar Road, in Field Store, Texas, in Waller County. Orion and a dog in training detected a dead body on this property.

Joseph Huston, the certified handler for **Orion** (Sirius), a search and rescue (SAR) cadaver dog, has also yet to come forward publicly about the two confirmed hits on this abandoned property. Orion was the dog responsible for finding Naomi Miller on March 5, 2017, in Tom Green County, 12 years after she went missing. The body was found six feet from where Orion pinpointed and 40 inches down.

After Waller County Sheriff's Department elected a new sheriff in 2020, they started the difficult process of cleaning house on their own law enforcement officials. After reaching out to Waller County Sheriff's Department in March of 2022, they confirmed MCSO refuses to share Danielle's case information with them to help to move it forward. In hindsight, with a new sheriff in Waller, at least the people of Waller County can feel assured, serious efforts and measures were taken to clean up the corruption in their jurisdiction. If only Montgomery County residents would demand the same. By voting in a new sheriff and DA for Montgomery County, they too can send a message, that corruption and collusion will not be tolerated from elected officials or law enforcement agents.

The body Orion detected on the search with us, was reported to **Texas Ranger Captain Wende Wakeman,** on April 25, 2018. **NOT ONLY ONE, BUT TWO CADAVER DOGS HIT IN THE EXACT SAME SPOT, ON TWO INDEPENDENT PASSES**. As of March 2022, almost **FOUR YEARS LATER,** the **Texas Rangers have yet to retrieve the body**. **NOT ONCE** have we been followed up with to give the exact location to where the dogs hit or the exact location of where the body was identified. The Texas Rangers, **WAITED EIGHT MONTHS**, to supposedly investigate this area. Did they genuinely search this property in efforts to discover the body?

This was also, NOT THE FIRST TIME, cadaver dogs have been used searching for Danielle that detected human remains. A tip from a local Waller resident, only four miles from the location of the party where Danielle was last seen on 900 Bowler Road, said he noticed a foul decomposing smell coming from the neighbor's property, just days after Danielle was reported missing. A year later, on **May 5, 2016, Klaaskids National Foundation Search Center for Missing Children & Trafficked Children**, conducted a search on his property on 29235 Riley Road, Waller, Texas, 77484. Team 103 of Klasskids, used multiple K-9's on his property and were given trained indications from the dogs pertaining to the same property where the resident said the decomposing smell was coming from a year prior. www.klaaskids.org. Without authorization, the dogs were not allowed search on this private property where the smell had come from. This private property is owned by a former Waller County Sheriff deputy, Bernard Renken II, and he is the father to the best friend of Austin Sleeper.

It has been suspected Danielle's body has been moved to separate locations to deter investigators or to avoid detection. Two searches following the trail or clues looking for Danielle led to two separate properties in close proximity or a few miles from each other. A few questions or major red flags that came up is, after the first search was conducted in **May of 2016,** why weren't there follow-ups to get onto the private property next door? Secondly, why did it take eight months for the Rangers to supposedly go investigate the property we identified using two law enforcement cadaver dogs in **April of 2018**? Are these standard operating protocols or was this intentional obstruction to finding Danielle? **Lastly, why in either search, weren't those closest to Danielle pressing law enforcement to get these properties thoroughly searched and demanding answers?**

Public records will show the sale of a black **Ford F-150, VIN 1FTRX17LXWNC25630** from Danielle, JUST two days before she was reported missing. Strangely enough, when the owner was asked if he knew Danielle, he said they had never met. If they had never met as he claimed when questioned, then this is falsifying or tampering with government records, which penalties for this action can range from a **Misdemeanor** to a **Felony.**

*Under **Texas Penal Code § 37.10- Tampering with Governmental Record***
(a) A person commits an offense if he:
> *(1) knowingly makes a false entry in, or false alteration of, a governmental record;*
> *(2) makes, presents, or uses any record, document, or thing with knowledge of its falsity and with intent that it be taken as a genuine governmental record;*
> *(3) intentionally destroys, conceals, removes, or otherwise impairs the verity, legibility, or availability of a governmental record;*
> *(4) possesses, sells, or offers to sell a governmental record or a blank governmental record form with intent that it be used unlawfully;*
> *(5) makes, presents, or uses a governmental record with knowledge of its falsity;*

*As of March 2022, the owner of this F-150 has yet to be officially questioned by MCSO for denying any knowledge of Danielle Sleeper. On Facebook, the owner was declared dead by his relatives and close friends, but as of March 2022, an official death certificate has yet to be located in any known database.

In March of 2015, immediately after Danielle Sleeper disappeared, MCSO Deputy Steve Degner, was quoted by eyewitnesses to state during the initial search for Danielle, "**Austin killed her and there was blood found in the kitchen. He (Austin) had help, so let's get to work.**" On October 3, 2015, seven months after the initial search, an eyewitness reached out to Steve Degner via text message, asking the status on the Danielle Sleeper case. Degner was also questioned why arrests haven't been made and if this case is classified as a missing persons case, rather than a homicide. Degner responded, "**The case is considered closed. Don't waste any more time or concern yourself any longer with this case**." Steve Degner retired from MSCO in 2018 and is now the President of Montgomery County Police Search and Rescue. MCSO has known from the beginning, that Danielle was a victim of homicide but have gone through incredible means to keep her case deescalated as a missing persons case.

Austin Sleeper has also yet to be officially questioned by MCSO and they still won't officially consider him a suspect in this case. In an informal, unofficial phone interview with the original detective on her case, he stated that Austin's phone had numerous text messages at the time of Danielle's disappearance and other suspicious activity. This was shortly after both Danielle and Austin left the party, from 1 a.m. until 3:12 a.m., the night she disappeared. Also, the original detective confirmed Austin's phone was triangulated in front of this abandoned property, for a long period, during these hours.

After Danielle was declared missing, numerous eyewitnesses came forward to testify against Austin's unusual behavior since the first volunteer search at a Cowboy Ranch church. Witnesses claim Austin, from the beginning, was laughing and making jokes with his friends. They were disturbed by Austin's uninvolved and uninterested attitude from day one. Since then and to this date, Austin has not appeared at another search, refuses to speak to the press, and is unwilling to cooperate with law enforcement in any way. Austin did however, put up several '**No Trespassing**' and '**Beware of Dog**' signs around his property, immediately after Danielle disappeared. Whenever events like Danielle's candlelight service (seven months after Danielle's disappearance) or the annual balloon release held in her honor take place, Austin and his family have never been in attendance. Austin has also failed to keep in contact with Danielle's parents or allowed Danielle's youngest son to see his grandparents.

Both phones seized by MCSO, of Austin Sleeper and his friend, **were destroyed while in their possession.**

SEVEN YEARS has passed since Danielle Sleeper was last seen and she is still considered a missing person. **Danielle Sleeper's Social Security Number was unofficially run through multiple search databases in January of 2022, and she had not resurfaced anywhere. Danielle's personal information had been used by Austin Sleeper in 2020, in connection with another cellphone obtained.**

The original investigator, **Detective Thomas Gannucci,** considered Danielle's case a homicide investigation. After being removed three months into the investigation and replaced by MCSO **Detective (now Lieutenant) Paul Hahs**, the case remains a missing persons case and it has not moved forward.

Texas Ranger Derek Leitner at Texas Department of Public Safety (DPS) in Conroe, Texas, was the Texas Ranger sharing the same building and assisting MCSO Detective Paul Hahs on Danielle Sleeper's case.

Texas Ranger Captain (former Lieutenant) Wende Wakeman agreed to take Danielle Sleeper's case based on MCSO corruption and collusion. Wakeman was informed of a detected dead body by the cadaver dog, Orion**, on April 25, 2018**. Immediately after this meeting, she turned the case back over to **Texas Ranger Derek Leitner**. In a phone conversation, Wakeman claimed she was **too busy** to work the case because she was also attending Sam Houston State University. Wakeman finally graduated from Sam Houston State University in 2020. She was then promoted to **Captain** and is now the highest-ranking female in Texas Ranger history. The location of the **Texas Rangers** office, where the 'anonymous' meeting took place, was held in Huntsville, Texas. The actual building or office remains unlisted. Wakeman's office has also yet to question witnesses or investigate the case, contrary to law enforcement statements. After this initial meeting, multiple email attempts were sent to follow up with Captain Wakeman on the status of her office's investigation. She has only replied to one email.

A **Request for Public Information** was sent to **Montgomery County Sheriff's Department (MSCO)** on **04.19.2018**, three years after Danielle disappeared and still considered a missing persons case, but only two pieces of paper, an **INCIDENT/OFFENSE REPORT** and **INCIDENT/REPORT SUPPLEMENT**, were sent in return. There were multiple discrepancies on the report and the remainder of the case file was not supplied by MCSO.

-**First discrepancy** is based on the report date of **March 22, 2015**. At this time, **Detective (now Lieutenant) Paul Hahs** is listed as the investigator on the Incident/Offense Report and Supplement, **rather than Detective Thomas Gannucci. Detective Paul Hahs** did not take over the case until **THREE MONTHS after this event occurred.**

-**Second discrepancy** is, of the witnesses listed in total on these reports, three names listed were not in attendance at the time this took place. One of the witnesses listed remains unknown to family or friends. Her address was listed at the Lodge Motel & Suites in Conroe, Texas. Danielle's sister was present and listed on the report, but Danielle's father, who was also present, was not listed as a witness.

-**Final discrepancy** is, under **'EVIDENCE'**, MCSO listed **'6 HAIR NETS'**. Danielle's sister confirmed hair nets were never used or collected.

Danielle's sister validated and verified that these are credible discrepancies or inaccuracies.

THESE TWO DOCUMENTS, WHICH CAN BE USED AS LEGAL DOCUMENTS IN THE COURT OF LAW, HAVE BEEN MODIFIED or ALTERED but the original Incident Report was not provided or produced. According to the Texas Penal Code, if the original Incident Report no longer exists, these actions by Detective Paul Hahs could be considered a THIRD-DEGREE FELONY, for AGGRAVATED PERJURY under *Texas Penal Code Title 8, Chapter 37, §37.03 Tampering with Governmental Record.*

> *(a) A person commits an offense if he commits perjury as defined in Section 37.02 (Perjury), and the false statement:*
> > *(1) is made during or in connection with an official proceeding; and*
> > *(2) is material.*
> *(b) An offense under this section is a felony of the third degree.*

THESE DOCUMENTS ARE NOT THE ORIGNALS. Hard copies must be maintained if amendments are made but the original should be kept. Also, any officer or deputy cannot go in and change records without approval from their supervisors. If changed, they must then submit new hard copies to the records division and to the prosecutor's (DA's) office. Did MCSO TAMPER, ALTER, or FALSIFY EVIDENCE from the very beginning?

Changing government documents can affect the course or outcome of an official proceeding and could be considered violations under *Title 8, Chapter 37, §37.04 Perjury and other falsification, §37.09 Tampering with Evidence, and again, §37.10 Tampering with Governmental Record.*

If this is a missing persons case, records not deemed to conflict with "national security" or "private", such as health records, or the case is not part of ongoing litigation, information can be requested under the **Freedom of Information Act (FOIA)**. Any information created by and retained by government actors must be provided upon request under the **Freedom of Information Act.**

> *5 U.S.C. 552- As Amended by the Open Government Act of 2007 and the Open FOIA Act of 2009- Sec. 552. Public information; agency rules, opinions, orders, records, and proceedings.*
>
> **The TEXAS Public Information Act** or Freedom of Information Act (FOIA):

> *TEXAS GOVERNMENT CODE TITLE 5- OPEN GOVERNMENT- ETHICS- SUBTITLE A- OPEN GOVERNMENT- CHAPTER 552. PUBLIC INFORMATION- SUBCHAPTER A- GENERAL PROVISIONS Sec. 552.001. POLICY- CONSTRUCTION (a)*

> *Under the fundamental philosophy of the American constitutional form of representative government that adheres to the principle that government is the servant and not the master of the people, it is the policy of this state that each person is entitled, unless otherwise expressly provided by law, at all times to complete information about the affairs of government and the official acts of public officials and employees.* **The people, in delegating authority, do not give their public servants the right to decide what is good for the people to know and what is not good for them to know. The people insist on remaining informed so that they may retain control over the instruments they have created.** *The provisions of this chapter shall be liberally construed to implement this policy.*

When Danielle's case was considered a **COLD CASE**, a **Public Information Act or FIOA request was sent to the MCSO on April 19, 2018,** at 4:00 pm. After this inquiry was sent, Detective Paul Hahs said the case was reopened and was an active investigation, almost immediately telling us that Danielle had run away or left the area on her own will. Detective Hahs' contradicting statements and lack of investigation efforts are obstructing any efforts to further Danielle's case. As of **March 7, 2022, a SECOND FIOA or Public Information Act request was sent to the MSCO and the Texas Rangers. On March 18, 2022, we received notification that both agencies denied the request** and had to ask for a ruling by the Attorney General's Office. Their reasons for denying the request are, they claim *charges are pending on one or more individuals*. So, which one is it? Is this a missing persons case or an active homicide investigation? If there are charges pending, then why has the case remained in the Cold Case Division for years under Detective Hahs? **AS OF MARCH 22, 2022, DANIELLE'S CASE IS LISTED ON THE MCSO'S COLD CASE WEBPAGE.**

https://cms5.revize.com/revize/mcs/Divisions/Criminal%20Invest igative%20Division/2022.02.10_UNSOLVEDcoldcase.pdf

If this was not contradictory enough, when Detective Hahs was questioned about why he lied about speaking to certain witnesses and why he wasn't searching for more clues to this case, he replied MCSO **COULD NOT ACTIVELY INVESTIGATE** Danielle's case because it was considered a missing persons case. Then when we officially requested to see Danielle's file **TWICE**, they denied our requests because they claimed to be actively investigating potential suspects. Again, which one is it? Did Danielle leave or was she murdered? If all police officers or detectives were perfect and free from fault, then there would not be a need to question their motives, but since we know corruption does exist, how long must the victim's family have to wait before a case is reassigned or removed from their authority? What statute of limitations and assurances do the victim's family have, investigators are proceeding with integrity and ethical behavior or are some cases being left open intentionally so the public cannot request information on their files? Who is policing the police? Had we not been lied to by Detective Hahs questioning and interviewing key witnesses, government documents being altered, evidence being destroyed, the original detective being removed from the case for suspicious reasons, and it is now marking the seventh year since

Danielle went missing, then we would not have any logical need to write this book.

What is **'JUSTICE FOR ALL'** if we continue to harbor partial, arbitrary, or biased legal guidelines to offenders? If we refuse to acknowledge, accept, and change, then the trajectory of this country will continue to create more tragedies, like what happened to Danielle Sleeper. This is senseless and inhumane treatment of human life. Loyalty must have moral and ethical limitations. Otherwise, we are not any better than the liars, thieves, drug dealers, criminals, murderers, and rapists who continue to fill our communities. Saying nothing to protect the guilty, isn't any different then ignoring the corrupt actions of law enforcement agents, government officials, CEOs, and politicians.

Danielle Sleeper and her three young boys need your help! If you are compelled or convicted to get involved, then please do! Her case has remained unsolved because people continue to assume **'somebody'** will do something or the authorities will resolve this. It has been seven years. Without your help, support, and involvement, Danielle's painful injustice will be lost in a file, forever collecting dust.

In all my years, I could not have imagined such blatant disregard by law enforcement agents to uphold their sworn oaths. Here we are yet again, asking to see Danielle's case file, and now they are claiming it is an active, ongoing investigation, but it is officially declared a COLD CASE. Even their request for a ruling by the Texas Attorney General Ken Paxton, is only protocol after denying a request for Public Information. The only problem is, they sent biased and untruthful information to the Attorney General for the purposes to sway a ruling in their favor. **It took SIX YEARS** for MCSO to even contact one of the witnesses. In fact, it was the COLD CASE DIVISION who contacted this witness, not the detective, Paul Hahs, who was assigned to the case. How many years must pass before we can come to the realization, this is intentional obstruction of justice by law enforcement? MCSO is simply checking the box or doing just enough to appear to be working Danielle's case, but as we have seen, they are not actively trying to produce results.

The mere fact Danielle's case is a COLD CASE means, local or state law enforcement officials do not have any further leads existing to investigate. This is when they refer to the case as having "gone cold." Generally speaking, a case goes "cold" once they run out of leads or their investigation has hit a dead end.

We understand that many cases go unsolved, and some have taken decades to close due to lack of evidence. We would have not felt the need to go through the trouble of conducting a personal investigation, interviewing witnesses, searching properties, or even writing a book based on these events, had we been shown the slightest effort or concern by MCSO to get Danielle's case solved. Instead, we caught MCSO in their own lies about who they questioned, the properties they searched, changing official government documents, and preventing public information requests on a 'MISSING PERSONS' CASE FILE. We convinced Texas Ranger Captain Wende Wakeman to investigate MCSO corruption and collusion, but she put Texas Ranger Derek Leitner in charge of investigating his own activity and involvement in this case. How was that not a conflict of interest? This would be the same as contacting Internal Affairs about your boss acting inappropriately at work, and then Internal Affairs leaving it up to your boss to investigate themself concerning your claims. How is this maintaining some form of integrity or check and balance on law enforcement involvement investigating Danielle's disappearance? Whenever there are potential circumstances for any corruption or collusion to have been conducted, it is essential for an outside third party to investigate. Otherwise, the door for an impartial analysis to the claims are slammed shut.

NOTE: Ranger Derek Leitner is also the supervisor who denied the recent Public Information request to the Texas Rangers and one of the law enforcement agents we have been trying to get this case removed from their authority. Detective Paul Hahs directly admitted to us in 2018, he and Ranger Derek

Leitner have been good friends for almost 20 years. Again, is this not a conflict of interest?

Also, it was extremely frustrating to be told by MCSO Detective (now Lieutenant) Paul Hahs, *'When you find her (Danielle) body, then give us a call'*. **This is what they classify as an ACTIVE INVESTIGATION?** We have never asked for the case to be REINVESTIGATED. Instead, we simply requested for the case **TO BE INVESTIGATED**. We need your help, experience, expertise, and advocacy for Danielle Sleeper. For those who have had to endure similar circumstances with law enforcement, we too know how painstakingly frustrating it is to get them to do their job or do the right thing. Please join our cause to start holding accountability on those who are meant to enforce the law in this country. Thank you to all those who wish to help, contribute, get involved, take a stand for integrity, and for Danielle! It's time to make sure this level of injustice in law enforcement agencies is a thing of the past!

I want to personally thank you for taking the time to read this book. Important to note, officials aren't typically held liable for what they do while in office, **it's what THEY DON'T DO**. Please feel free to contact and put pressure on the Houston FBI, Montgomery County Sheriff's Office, Texas Rangers Headquarters, Texas Attorney General's Office, the Texas Governor, news media stations, podcasts, and investigative journalists, as frequently as possible, until Danielle Sleeper's case is solved. Please share her story with everyone you know. It's time to finally set an example and let Danielle and her three boys' voices finally be heard. It's time to start holding officials accountable and stand up for those who don't have the ability to do so. Please follow us on our Facebook page, *Mystery Case Files: Missing in Texas* to share your information, tips, or your stories needing assistance as well.

This book was inspired by and is dedicated to Danielle Sleeper's story. Danielle, you are greatly missed, loved, and may you rest in peace. In continuing our efforts to have Danielle's case brought to justice, we would like you to reach out to us if you want to share information confidentiality. You can also contact us with

any information or send tips on this case at
thepresleyfoundation@gmail.com.

Danielle Marie Sleeper's Case Numbers:

-Texas DPS Case # M1503007
-The MCSO Officers Case # 15A004609

-FBI's Houston Public Corruption Special Division:
* (NEWLY OPENED AND COVERS MONTGOMERY
COUNTY) *
1-800-CALL-FBI
713-693-5000
houstoncorruption@fbi.gov

-The Montgomery County Sheriff's Office (MCSO):
(936) 760-5800.

-Texas Captain Wakeman's office number at the Texas
Rangers location near Sam Houston State University
campus in Huntsville, TX:
(936) 435-0152.
-Texas Rangers (Headquarters - Austin):
(512) 424-2160

-The Montgomery County District Attorney's Office:
(936) 539-7800

-Office of the Attorney General in the State of Texas:
Attorney General - (512) 475-2994
First Assistant Attorney General - (512) 463-2100
Crime Victims - (800) 983-9933
Open Government Hotline - (877) 673-6839

-Office of Texas Governor:
(512) 463-2000

-Crime Stoppers:
1 (800) 392-STOP

Crime Stoppers cash reward is $21,000, for anyone bringing Danielle Sleeper's case to justice.

Final Thoughts

"Any people that would give up liberty for a little temporary safety
deserves neither liberty nor safety."
-Benjamin Franklin

Current Day

Sadly, Danielle Sleeper's case is not unique. In recent years, numerous missing persons crimes remain unsolved. Why? This has become a national and worldwide problem. People aren't recognizing how one action sets off a chain reaction, which can often be felt around the world.

We allow the courts to seal the records of high-profile criminal activity from the public. WHY? What's the point of bringing people to court if justice is allowed to be sealed? This above the law mentality from our elected public officials and the wealthy elite have led our country to this unscrupulous behavior. Politicians are treated like celebrities or professional athletes, but even athletes have been brought to justice. People are smart and they know when they are being lied to. If you know authorities are corrupt and protecting their own interests, then who is going to bring them to justice? What happens when those who you trust, are compromised?

"The very word 'secrecy' is repugnant in a free and open society; and we are as a people inherently and historically opposed to secret societies, to secret oaths and to secret proceedings. We decided long ago that the dangers of

excessive and unwarranted concealment of pertinent facts far outweighed the dangers which are cited to justify it... And it is our obligation to inform and alert the American people—to make certain they possess all the facts they need, and understand them as well—the perils, the prospects, the purposes of our program and the choices that we face."

- John F. Kennedy. "The President and the Press" April 27, 1961

Is criminality instinctual or something that is taught? Are criminals born this way or has their experiences in life and pressures of society nudged them to flip a switch? As a reader, you may or may not agree with everything I pointed out in this book, and this is perfectly acceptable. The objective in writing this, isn't for you to agree on everything presented but expecting you to draw your own conclusions. We earnestly went into this investigation giving the husband, Austin Sleeper, the benefit of the doubt. I honestly believed he was telling the truth and Danielle had suddenly or unexpectedly left. We just wanted whatever clues existed, that would lead us to where Danielle ran off to. Whether she had left for Louisiana or even to Alaska, it didn't matter. We just wanted to know where she was, so we could go find and bring her home. Before spending countless hours investigating Danielle's case, we were quickly met with heavy opposition and confrontation from local law enforcement. Working around these obstacles to get answers on our own, the only evidence we could dig up, had all arrows pointing back to Austin Sleeper. Not only that, but we also realized the investigators on Danielle's case were pigeonholing the public and media's views away from what really took place. To make the situation even more complicated, we found these problems extended beyond the limits of Montgomery County.

In our country, we have seen several cases where law enforcement officials and the legal system wrongfully convict innocent men or women and put them behind bars for crimes they did not commit. In these cases, they convicted the innocent without evidence, or not having any credible witnesses. In some of these cases, the officers or detectives perpetuated false information to get convictions of the wrongfully accused. Important details were distorted, evidence was destroyed, and the legal system became subverted by their actions. The accused became victims to our own legal system. This is not justice. This is corruption. There are those who make honest mistakes and sometimes accidentally overlook pertinent details. It does happen. This is different from those who strive to get convictions rather than solving the crime.

When it comes to the Danielle Sleeper case, we found similar corruption taking place but almost in reverse. This was not a collaborative effort by Montgomery County Sheriff's Office and Texas Rangers manipulating evidence to put a man behind bars. Instead, law enforcement officials have adamantly worked to keep a repeat criminal offender walking free. The neglect from the primary detective in this case, Paul Hahs, and his supervisors, have allowed Austin Sleeper to evade justice being served. His felony CPS case was dismissed and has been able to avoid questioning in the homicide of Danielle Sleeper. Paul Hahs stated Austin Sleeper had retained a good lawyer which prevented them from asking questions of any kind, but even billionaire pedophiles, who retain a team of lawyers, still get brought in for questioning. It isn't their right to not be questioned. Their right is, instead, to have an attorney present or to remain silent during questioning.

Not only did Austin Sleeper retain a lawyer immediately after Danielle Sleeper disappeared, but he also retained this attorney's service to represent their 4-year-old son at that time. To this day, neither the husband nor Danielle's child, has ever been brought in for questioning. The excuse we were given by Detective Paul Hahs (now Lieutenant) for not questioning Austin Sleeper was, Hahs claimed this was a missing persons case, and people must voluntarily bring testimonies and information to them. Based on this, when we asked to see Danielle's case file, he refused. We were then told it is considered an active homicide investigation. So, which one is it? If it's a homicide investigation, then why has the husband not been brought in for questioning? In either scenario, whether it is a missing persons or homicide investigation, the spouse is the prime suspect when the other spouse disappears. The stories and lies continue to change from the Montgomery County Sheriff's Department, to conceal the truth and prevent Danielle's case from seeing justice.

Justice only works when its applied unbiasedly. Where is the justice for Danielle Sleeper? Where is the justice for the bruises left on Danielle's two older boys? Justice often involves addressing the uncomfortable and taboo topics, to discover the truth, rather than continuing to ignore and run from them. As citizens of America, we must remember, children are our future. With our current situation in this country, from corporate and government corruption, collusion, and crime infiltrating every level of our society, what lessons and legacy are we leaving behind for our kids? As citizens of Montgomery County, or as Americans, what point must we reach before putting an end to the abuse of power in positions of authority? Shall we continue to stand by and watch as our government officials and corporate level executives continue to drain our pockets, pillage our resources, and bend the laws to fit their needs? By doing nothing, what are we teaching our children?

What is our country missing right now? We are missing *'Core Values'* and *'Ethics.'* Our towns, cities, states, and country need as many people as possible to fight for excellence, integrity, quality leadership, honesty, loyalty, and respect. We need to remind public officials, once again, that their duty is selfless service to the people. As Americans, are we proud of how this country is being run? Do you think this behavior stems from the actions of a few? Are we not embarrassed by who we call leaders on a local, state, or national level? As the people, we have tolerated officials, who are unable to regulate themselves or even balance a national budget. We have allowed our elected leaders to establish systems of bribery, which they call 'lobbying'. Why must we bribe the same officials we elect to office to do the work they were hired to do?

Each generation has a choice and opportunity to leave their mark on this world. What legacy do we wish to pass on to our future generations? Have we become so afraid to fight against injustice because of not wanting to be inconvenienced or put in uncomfortable situations? If we do not stand up for each other now, who will stand for you when it is your turn?

How can we, as a country, be 'Great Again' or 'Proud,' when a large percentage of Americans have lost faith in our systems of legislation and law enforcement? It's difficult to love a country that doesn't love you in return. As Americans, we must get in the fight, demand results, improvements, and offer humane solutions. Our anguish and pleas fall on the deaf ears of our officials. They take money from the poor to fund the rich. Is this noble, dignified, or humane?

As Americans, should we continue to allow elected officials to dance around doing what is right, or do we stand up and say something? We must quit viewing social dilemmas as left or right and start asking the right questions. We must ask if what we are doing is improving or declining our quality and way of life?

If we treat our entire country as one big home, we wouldn't have streets, shopping centers, and sidewalks full of homeless people and trash. Our country was once considered respectable because many stood for honor, integrity, and bravery. It is up to us to carry the torch once again and reignite this flame in others.

There is nothing wrong with this country. It's a beautiful place to live. It's the bad apples who are working to ruin it for the rest of us. The Constitution doesn't need to be revised or rewritten. It simply needs to be reread and followed. If people have forgotten their rights, duties, and important responsibilities to effectively manage our country and our elected officials, then who will save us from ourselves? How can we hold corrupt law enforcement agents and political officials accountable if people are unaware of their power and their civic duties?

To make errors and mistakes is part of the human experience. It's what people do afterwards that defines them. When our country values honesty and stops covering up, blaming, or silencing others for mistakes, our country will finally free itself from the sinking ship. If we can forgive and learn from our mistakes, then there's still hope for a better and more prosperous future.

Danielle Marie Sleeper
(1982-2015)

About the Authors

Jeff Presley-

Currently studying law at Texas A&M School of Law since 2021. Served five years as a medic in the Army's 82nd Airborne Division. Prior business owner with 10 + years of experience as a retail manager. In 2005, Jeff received a Bachelor's Degree of Science in Kinesiology at Texas State University and was awarded the academic achievement of Dean's List.

Shelley Presley-

Is a 25-year veteran in the mortgage industry. Areas of specialty include Underwriting, Quality Control, and Compliance. Primary focus is on fraud detection and suspicious activity in legal contracts and documentation.

Jeff and Shelley married in 2019. They collectively have four wonderful children and four rambunctious dogs. As newly published authors, they look forward to returning as host to their weekly podcast and striving to assist others in need.

www.ingramcontent.com/pod-product-compliance
Lightning Source LLC
Chambersburg PA
CBHW072313020726
47501CB00002B/500